STINGER

Nancy Kress

A TOM DOHERTY ASSOCIATES BOOK
NEW YORK

STINGER

Copyright © 1998 by Nancy Kress

This book is printed on acid-free paper.

Edited by David G. Hartwell

A Forge Book
Published by Tom Doherty Associates, Inc.
175 Fifth Avenue
New York, NY 10010

Forge® is a registered trademark of Tom Doherty Associates, Inc.

Design by Ann Gold

Library of Congress Cataloging-in-Publication Data

Kress, Nancy.
Stinger / Nancy Kress.—1st ed.
p.   cm.
"A Tom Doherty Associates book."
ISBN 0-312-86536-8 (acid-free paper)
I. Title.
PS3561.R46S7   1998
813'.54—dc21   98-23675
                                                            CIP

First Edition: October 1998

Printed in the United States of America

0 9 8 7 6 5 4 3 2 1

For Charles

New kinds of evil threaten democratic institutions
in these closing days of the twentieth century.
They must be addressed quickly and comprehensively.

—Louis J. Freeh, Director,
Federal Bureau of Investigation, 1996

STINGER

P R O L O G U E

MAY 2

The green Chevy Lumina sped through the darkness. For several miles the two men inside said nothing, until the driver yawned and the other said, "Tired?"

"It's three in the goddamn morning."

"Yeah."

"Well, we're almost to Virginia. Bridge is just a few miles away."

"Pretty heavy woods."

"The ass end of nowhere."

The passenger didn't reply. He stared at the road ahead. The car's headlights carved a narrow lighted path down the highway, itself a gray slash through the black silhouettes of oak, hickory, southern pine. Once the driver reached for the radio, glanced at the other man's face, and drew back his hand. Another car, the first in several minutes, approached in the other lane, and both drivers switched from high beams to low.

The huge buck in full spring antlers dashed from the woods so fast it seemed to materialize directly in front of the Lumina. The driver cried, "Son of a bitch!" and wrenched the wheel to the left, fruitlessly. The Lumina slammed into the buck, flinging its body to the left onto the narrow, grassy median. The Lumina spun ninety degrees while skidding sideways. The rear crashed into a hickory at the edge of the woods. Metal shrieked as the trunk flew open, the rear body crumpled, and the backseat thrust forward, hard. With a final shudder the Lumina came to rest backward against the tree, engine stopped and headlights still shining.

The driver's face was moonlight white. "You okay?"

"Yeah. You? Oh, God—the locals."

The second car had skidded to a stop. A man jumped out and ran toward the crash. In the beam of the Lumina's headlights his deputy sheriff's uniform was clearly visible.

"Anybody hurt? Are you people all right?" His voice was young and excited.

"We're fine," the driver called. He gave his companion a look that said *shit shit shit*. The passenger tried to open his door, but it had been mangled too badly when the rear of the car caved forward. Finally he climbed awkwardly over the gear shift and followed the driver out the left front door.

By that time the driver stood with the deputy at the front of the car, away from the gaping trunk. The passenger walked toward the back and peered inside. The metal cage sat as twisted and crushed as the back end of the car, a cage no longer. Empty.

"Can I see your license and registration?" the deputy said. The passenger walked to the front of the car to join the driver, so both of them could talk to the deputy. Could persuade him of what had really happened here. How the scene had actually gone down.

They had fucking better make it A-one.

May 28

". . . and now, ladies and gentlemen," the local chairwoman finished in her strong Brooklyn accent, "join with me in welcoming the United States senator from Pennsylvania, Malcolm Peter Reading."

Not too bad, Larson thought as he watched the senator mount the steps of the school auditorium. A fairly short introduction, dignified but not starchy, and no *"proud to present to you the next president of the United States"* in that too-insistent, too-confident way that some supporters had. That wouldn't have played well, not in this particular section of Manhattan. Premature. Larson had an ear for these things.

Although maybe, he thought, as he watched Reading launch into his speech, it wouldn't have mattered after all. Damn, but Reading was *good*. The candidate stood on the wooden grade-school stage, under that faded school assembly flag, as if the place were the Oval Office. He had the facts, he had the grasp, he had the vision, and none of that would have mattered if he hadn't also had the touch. Which he did. Able to touch any group—black, white, rich, poor, gay, straight, conservative, liberal, men, women. Furthermore, it was sincere. Larson had watched a lot of politicians over the years. This one meant what he said, and he didn't say what he didn't mean, and he was able to say it in ways that different audiences could actually hear.

Maybe Reading really *could* go all the way.

It was the first time Larson had really let himself believe it. A handler, after all, was paid to manufacture images, not to be seduced by substance. And the skeptic in Larson didn't actually believe the United States was ready for a black president. But listening to Reading in this too-old school with its echoing wooden halls and permanent smell of chalk, Larson suddenly wasn't so sure.

Reading had it all. Intelligent, educated, born in the racial disaster of North Philadelphia but now comfortably upper-middle-class, war hero (only in a "minor" war, although they never were minor to the guys who had to fight them). Solid-gold middle-of-the-road voting record. Faithful husband to the pretty-but-not-too-pretty wife listening to him with her intelligent eyes alight. High-achieving kids, no other women ever, no financial scandals. A capable and decent human being. And Reading had the touch, without which the rest of it wouldn't have mattered for shit.

The audience, mostly left-of-center middle-aged New York types, laughed at something Reading said. Larson could feel them warming. A few more minutes, and Reading would have them eating from his hand. Which was just the right color: clearly black, but not too black. A rich chocolate. Malcolm Peter Reading, he of the racially provocative first name and reassuringly capitalist last one, was a handsome man. On top of everything else.

The audience laughed again. Beside Larson, an elderly white man in preppy khaki trousers nodded thoughtfully. A young black couple in the row ahead—she wore one of those African headscarf things, he had on a Grateful Dead T-shirt—grinned at each other delightedly. Even the cop stationed at the door looked impressed.

Jesus. If Reading could do this equally well in New Hampshire, the primary would be a walk.

Larson's head whirled. In a flash—it felt like that, a brilliant flash of

Technicolor light—he pictured himself at the White House, still advising long after the campaign was over, still necessary . . . to the president of the United States. In the Oval Office, at a press conference in the Rose Garden, on Air Force One . . .

Rein it in, Larson.

He did. From long habit, from innate skepticism. Keep grounded, keep focused. Listen to what the candidate is saying here and now, not at some hypothetical moment in some hypothetically glorious future. More important, listen to the audience. How is the candidate playing *now?*

From his wooden folding chair on the far left side of the auditorium, Larson bent forward, hands on his knees, intent gaze scanning the audience overflowing the small room and craning necks in the hall outside. Thus it was that he missed the beginning of Reading's trouble. He didn't notice it until the audience began to frown, to twitch, to glance at each other in concern. Larson's eyes snapped to the stage.

". . . policies that . . . embrace all of . . . that embrace . . ."

Reading stopped speaking. He seemed dazed, uncertain. Sweat glistened on his forehead. His eyes unfocused, then focused again with what looked to Larson like a supreme act of will.

". . . policies embrace . . . our diversity . . . policies . . ."

Suddenly the left side of Reading's body jerked. His left hand fell from the lectern, dangled helplessly by his side. He swayed and crashed to the floor, thrashing to the left of the lectern and coming to rest at the very edge of the wooden stage.

Anita Reading screamed. People rose to their feet, calling out. A few tried to climb onto the stage. Larson stood immobile. He knew what he was seeing.

"Please let me through, I'm a doctor. Let me through please, I'm a doctor—" A tall woman in jeans, pushing her way determinedly down the center aisle from the back of the room. She leapt onto the stage and bent over Reading.

No. Larson refused to believe it. Malcolm Reading was only forty-nine, healthy as an ox. Never smoked, ate right, exercised. How could he be having a stroke?

Still Larson didn't move forward. The doctor looked up from Reading and said briskly to the people clustered behind her, "Ambulance, please. Tell nine-one-one you need it for a thrombosis—a serious stroke. Go *now.*"

Someone—Larson couldn't see who—went now. Anita Reading had stopped screaming and seemed to be quickly following whatever instructions the doctor was giving her. The crowd changed subtly from startled hysteria to the kind of half-guilty excitement that meant somebody else was the victim. A few people talked excitedly into cell phones. Reporters.

"Bill?" Anita Reading called, her voice high with strain. "Where's *Bill?*"

"Here," Larson said, and finally moved forward. His body felt thick, clumsy, as if he were moving through something sticky and clotted. And he was. Disappointment could be as retarding as mud, slow you down as much as sewage.

Malcolm Peter Reading would never be president of the United States. Bill Larson would never stand in the Rose Garden, advising the president about the world.

June 3

The small Maryland city of La Plata steamed in the humid heat, even at night, even though it was barely June. Over ninety in the day, only marginally below eighty at night. Rain every afternoon, a choking hot drizzle that passed in an hour and left nothing cooler than before.

"Gonna be a wild night," the nurse said, coming back into the Emergency Room from the parking lot. Smoking was forbidden anywhere inside the community hospital, a one-hundred-bed, well-staffed facility that was the pride of two counties. "Lots of violent trauma. I can *smell* it."

The younger nurse smiled nervously. It was her first night ever in Emergency.

"They'll all be outside, escaping the heat. Drinking and fighting and shooting each other. Like they do every hot summer night. You mark my words, Rachel."

Rachel turned away. There was something in the older woman's use of "they" and "them" that the young girl didn't like. Something . . . well, a little racist?

She told herself not to judge too hastily. Manners in the East were just different from the small town in Ohio where she'd grown up and gone to nursing school. People here just talked rougher, didn't consider as much what they said. Just a regional difference. That was probably all it was.

By nine o'clock, two hours after her shift had begun, Rachel still hadn't seen any trauma due to violence. A car accident, minor abrasions only. An infected compound femoral fracture. An elderly phlebitis, a woman in labor, a little kid who had fallen off a fence and needed six stitches. A man brought in falling-down drunk, his speech slurred. An average night.

Just after nine, the ambulance shrieked up. The charge nurse got off the phone. "All right, people, resident's on his way down. Two strokes—not one but two, count 'em—within a few minutes of each other at an AA meeting. Both severe." She talked rapidly, organizing the response duties. The resident rushed in from the corridor.

For the rest of her life, the next half hour remained a blur to Rachel. No matter how hard she tried, she couldn't recall any details. Apparently she did everything she was told to, and did it right, because nobody yelled at her afterward. She must have assisted with the CT scans to determine if the strokes were ischemic or hemorrhagic, must have administered the tPA, must have hooked the patients to acute-care monitors. But she couldn't remember what she had done, or how, or in what order.

She only remembered the patients. A young woman in her twenties, with a ring in her nose and corn-rowed braids. A man in a clerical collar. He died; she slipped into a deep coma. And the falling-down drunk, it turned out later, had no alcohol at all in his blood. They'd just assumed he had, from his behavior and his stinking clothing and the plastic garbage bag full of all his possessions. But he, too, had had a thrombotic stroke. And so had another patient, on toward midnight. A young, active mother of three, her husband said, who had never been sick a day in her life. And then, at 3:17 A.M., a vacationing professor from Howard University, a healthy man in his thirties, who died at 4:30.

The resident frowned constantly, lost in thought. The charge nurse was subdued, not looking directly at anyone. The older nurse said, too loudly, "Coincidence. Bound to happen someplace, sometime. If all the apes in the British museum . . ."

"Shut up," the charge nurse said.

Rachel said nothing. There was a tight mass in her stomach, as if she were constipated in the wrong place. *I'm scared,* she thought clearly. *I don't know why, but I'm scared.*

All five patients had nearly identical thrombotic cerebral strokes. All five were black.

ONE

I do solemnly swear that I will support and defend the Constitution of the United States against all enemies, foreign and domestic . . .
—Swearing-in oath, Federal Bureau of Investigation

Starting over is always more difficult than doing something the first time," Judy Kozinski said from the sofa, where she was knitting something in bright purple wool. "It's the lost innocence. Different expectations."

In his comfortable wing chair across the room, Cavanaugh looked up, alert as a mouse scenting feline. Were they talking now about the FBI or about the marriage thing? Lately, with Judy, he never knew.

He really didn't want to talk tonight again about the marriage thing. Not tonight. Not again.

"I mean, any change of that magnitude—naturally it turns everything in your mind upside down for a while."

No clue there. Cavanaugh made his noncommittal noise, "Ehhrrrmmm."

"I understand how you feel, Robert, even though you think I don't."

Still no clue. He tried a vaguely thoughtful frown.

"Once you get used to the new assignment, you'll probably be as happy there as you were in Organized Crime," Judy said, and Cavanaugh relaxed.

He had been transferred from the Bureau's Organized Crime and Racketeering Section at headquarters to its Resident Agent program only four months ago. No, "transferred" wasn't the word; it had been a goddamn *heist*.

The FBI regs were clear: *"Upon completion of four years in her/her first office of assignment, and until reaching ten years in the same office, a Special Agent can be considered for a nonvoluntary rotational transfer to a second field office depending on the staffing needs of the FBI."* Fair enough. Cavanaugh was able to concede the staffing needs of the FBI. Cavanaugh had been in Washington for over four years—barely—and less than ten. Cavanaugh was willing to learn new roles, new skills, new procedures.

But as a resident agent for southern Maryland?

"You're assistant special agent in charge," Judy said soothingly.

"Out of two people! And Donald Seton is an idiot. I'm the only real, functioning FBI agent in a place where the biggest federal crime is the condition of the roads."

Judy laughed, knitting needles clicking away. The sound irritated Cavanaugh. They'd been living together for over a year now, and only recently had Judy taken up knitting. A freelance science writer, she could work anywhere and had taken the move from D.C. to Rivermount with equanimity. No—with relish. The sight of her hanging curtains and matching fabric swathes and buying scatter rugs for the little house they'd rented—she'd even found the house, falling in love with the view of the Patuxent River—all this made Cavanaugh profoundly nervous. It looked so . . . domestic. And now there was this *knitting*. He had avoided asking what the purple thing was going to be.

Restless, he opened the sliding glass door to the tiny redwood deck and stepped outside. Beyond the air-conditioning, the early June night throbbed hot and fragrant. It smelled of honeysuckle—it seemed to him that all of Maryland smelled of honeysuckle—and of the river marshes below him somewhere at the foot of the bluff. It smelled of intrigue that brought the senses alert and the blood soaring, of mysteries, of surprises . . . The smell was a lie. Nothing surprising was happening in Rivermount, Maryland.

A small town almost straddling the borders of Saint Mary's and Charles Counties, Rivermount was seventeen miles from Cavanaugh's new FBI office in Leonardtown. It really *was* a new office; until now, the

Bureau hadn't had a "Resident Agency," its term for a satellite office, in southern Maryland. "It's part of our expanded community presence," his new supervisor, Jerry Dunbar, had told him. "There's no Bureau presence at all in the southern three counties. And the Patuxent River Naval Air Station needs closer attention, which Don will take care of. You, Robert, will handle the rest of the district. You'll be breaking new ground."

Which was fine for Special Agent in Charge Dunbar, who got to head the Baltimore Field Office. Things happened in Baltimore. Things did not happen in southern Maryland, at least not outside of the naval air station. Not things requiring action by Resident Agent Robert Cavanaugh. The kingpins of serious crime simply didn't frequent salt marshes, state parks, or tobacco farms losing ground to golf courses.

His new and inactive fiefdom was a vast peninsula, surrounded by the Patuxent and Potomac Rivers as they emptied in all their delta wideness into Chesapeake Bay. Every day Cavanaugh drove from Rivermount to Leonardtown, population 1,683, the county seat of Saint Mary's County. Here he sat in his tiny office on the second floor of a remodeled Victorian house and scanned the dailies from D.C., hoping that something was breaking that might involve him. So far, this had not happened. His biggest commitment for the upcoming week was a talk at the local junior high, as part of the Federal Bureau of Investigation Adopt-a-School program.

Cavanaugh stared moodily into his backyard, invisible in the darkness. Probably the grass needed cutting again. He had never before lived in a house; when he'd been married to Marcy, they'd always lived in apartments in D.C. He had never before realized how demanding grass could be. Certainly the lawn demanded more of him than his job did.

"Hunt that crabgrass," he said into the river-smelling darkness. "Indict those chiggers."

His arm stung, and he slapped at a mosquito. Then another. The third one drove him back inside.

"Can't even stand on the deck, the damn bugs are so bad."

"It's all the rain this year," Judy said. "The Benadryl Itch Index is way high. But I'm—"

"The what?" Cavanaugh asked.

She grinned at him. "The Benadryl Itch Index. There really is such a thing."

"I believe it," Cavanaugh said moodily. It fit right in. Saint Mary's County had the most roadkill of any place he'd ever seen; it ranked second in Maryland counties' hog production, and it paid serious attention to an itch index.

"Anyway," Judy persisted, "I'm glad you're back inside because I'd like us to talk." She put down the knitting and looked at him.

Immediately Cavanaugh wanted to be somewhere else. He loved Judy. She was very important to him. She was intelligent, pretty, sexy, warm . . . She also had the acquisitive instincts of a Medici. *"Mad in pursuit, and in possession so . . . "* Cavanaugh had graduated from college as an English major, a fact he tried not to mention at the Bureau.

Looking at Judy curled in one corner of their joint sofa, Cavanaugh wondered yet again where in that tiny body she kept all that steel. Five-two, a hundred twenty pounds tops, her red hair currently in a boyish crop, she looked about twenty-five, not thirty-six. She looked as different from his ex-wife, Marcy, as it was possible for two women to be. Not, of course, that that was a bad thing . . .

"Robert," Judy said, her hazel eyes bolted to his face, "we've been together for two years now—"

"No, only about eighteen months," he said hastily.

"I'm counting from our first date, when you—"

"But those first six months we hardly saw each other at all. You were in Boston and I was in D.C. and—"

"Robert, the exact number of months isn't the point. We've been living together for a year—"

This was incontrovertible. Cavanaugh said nothing.

"—and it's time to think about where we go from here."

"Why do we have to 'go' anywhere?"

"Because I love you. Because I'd like a permanent commitment to, and from, you."

"Judy, sweetheart . . . nothing's permanent." Christ, she of all people ought to know that. Her husband, an eminent microbiologist, had been murdered. Cavanaugh had met her while investigating the case, his first. "We've both been married before, and neither marriage worked all that well, and—"

"But you're not Ben and I'm not Marcy! And I'm getting a little tired of paying for Marcy's sins!"

Cavanaugh walked to the sideboard and poured another vodka and tonic, mostly to give himself time. He plunked ice in it from the filled bucket on the coffee table, which Judy used to replenish her iced tea. He didn't consider that Judy was paying for Marcy's sins. Marcy's sin had been ambition, the slow-growing type that had only gradually realized that her glamorous competence in the corporate world could actually do much better than a fledgling FBI agent four years her junior. Marcy, as far as Robert knew, was now living with her boss, the CEO. Despite the eminence of her first husband, Judy was not ambitious in that way. Judy had her own sins.

"Judy, I've told you before . . . I love you, but I'm happy with the way things are."

"But I'm not!" Judy cried. "Doesn't that count?"

Cavanaugh closed his eyes. He really, really didn't want to have this conversation. Not again. Not tonight. "Judy—"

His official cell phone rang.

Cavanaugh yanked it from his pocket. "Saved by Graham Bell," Judy muttered sourly. He pretended not to hear her.

"Hello! Robert Cavanaugh speaking!"

"Is this . . . Agent Cavanaugh? Of the FBI?" A female voice, young and nervous.

"Yes, this is him."

"I'm sorry to bother you at night, but I called the FBI number in the phone book and a recording gave this number . . ."

"Yes," Cavanaugh said neutrally. The tape recorder was the third and final occupant of his office, unless you counted Seton's daily debris: Dorito bags, soda cans, crumpled printer paper, 302s. It all flourisheth as the grass. "What is your name and how can I help you?"

"My name is Rachel Pafford. I'm a nurse—a new nurse, actually, I just started—at Dellridge Community Hospital in La Plata. I'm calling because I think there's something . . . well, strange going on here that nobody's doing anything about. And I thought the FBI might be the right people to tell. I mean, I told my charge nurse, but she said it wasn't statistically significant. But I think different!" A note of quavering defiance.

Cavanaugh kept his face set in lines of professional concern, even though he'd already decided this was another paranoid call. They came in two varieties: the nuts who called to report UFOs landing in the salt marshes, and the easily frightened conformists who saw conspiracy to overthrow the government in every pierced nose, shaved head, or odd noise on their phone line. A smoke bomb in the high school lavatory made them expect Waco. But Judy sat across the room, purple knitting on her lap and fiery light in her eyes, and Cavanaugh was prepared to listen indefinitely to Nurse Pafford.

"Tell me the events you're concerned about, ma'am. From the beginning, please."

"Well, we kept having stroke victims come into the hospital. I mean, we always do, but not as many as this. I worked the weekend night shift. We had five strokes Saturday night and three Sunday night. And most of them were people who wouldn't ordinarily be in the risk population—young adults, even kids. But the thing is"—her voice dropped—"they're all black."

"Every one? Not even one white patient?"

"Well, no, of course we had that, too. But only *one*. The blacks . . . there are just too many of them to be normal."

"Ehhrrrmmm."

"So I looked up the admission records. The unusual number of strokes started three weeks ago, in the first part of May. I made a graph. The number has just mounted steadily. And all but two are black." The uncertain young voice took on a sudden dignity. "I do know how this sounds, Agent Cavanaugh. But I'm not just being weird."

"No. I'm sure your reasons are of the highest. Look, suppose I come over the hospital and interview you about this. Are you on duty?"

"You mean . . . now? No, I'm at home in Port Tobacco; I didn't want to call from Dellridge . . ."

"Fine, give me your address please," Cavanaugh said briskly. He wrote it down on one of the pen-and-memo pad sets Judy kept all over the house, color-coordinated with the curtains. "I'll be there in twenty minutes."

"Oh, thank you!"

"Gotta go, sweetheart," Cavanaugh said to Judy, "business at last. Up in Charles County." He ducked into the hall that led to the house's two bedrooms, hoping she wouldn't follow. She didn't. He changed from a T-shirt to a button-down, knotted on a tie, and gathered his credentials, a notebook, and his regulation Smith & Wesson. The latter made him feel ridiculous—to talk to a compulsive nurse in Port Tobacco? But he wanted Judy to see this was a legitimate Bureau call, not merely an excuse to avoid their talk.

She sat stonily on the sofa. He kissed the top of her head in passing. "Sorry, sweetheart. I'll try not to be late."

"Right," Judy said. "You wouldn't want to miss all the good sex we've been having lately."

Cavanaugh didn't answer. He was careful not to bang the kitchen door on his way out.

All right, so they hadn't been having much sex lately, Cavanaugh thought, on the drive west. At least, not compared to when he and Judy had first gotten together. Well, that was normal, wasn't it? Sex fell off after awhile together. And Judy had been busy with that big paleontology article for *Science Update,* when she hadn't been creating the Perfect Rustic Dream House. And he'd been busy not being busy. So of course it was natural that they didn't have as much sex. Wasn't it?

Christ, if it wasn't the presence of sex screwing up people's lives, it was the absence of sex. Either way, you couldn't win.

He parked in the large central lot of Rachel Pafford's apartment complex, a well-kept cluster of buildings surrounded by speed bumps, playgrounds, and a duck pond. Kids swarmed all over the place. It was nine-thirty—shouldn't they all be in bed? Wasn't tomorrow a school day? The little kids, Cavanaugh noticed, climbed on the floodlit jungle gym and dug in the sandbox in integrated groups, impartially throwing sand at other black and white cherubs. But the older kids, with their oversized clothing and very cool, nonchalant expressions, kept mostly to their own.

"Ms. Pafford? Special Agent Cavanaugh."

"Oh, *come in,*" she said, sounding as if he was the rescuing cavalry. Cavanaugh wasn't surprised. Anyone who graphed stroke incidence was going to be pretty intense. A thin, wiry brunette with large glasses, she looked fifteen, although common sense told him that she must be at least twenty.

"Would you like a Coke?" He heard the flat vowels of the Midwest.

"Thank you. Now, why don't you show me your graphs."

They were in three colors, each bar drawn with a ruler. Nervously, Rachel Pafford went over the same information she'd given Cavanaugh on the phone, with embellishment. "In a stroke case, you only have about three hours before several million brain cells disintegrate. But before we can do anything, we need to know if the stroke is ischemic, which means it's caused by a blood clot, or hemorraghic, which means a blood vessel burst inside the body. Because if it's a clot, either a thrombus or an embolus, you want to administer medicine to break it up; but if it's a hemorrhage, the same drug will only increase the bleeding."

She stopped and looked at him quizzically; Cavanaugh nodded to show he understood. On his notepad he doodled a large blood clot fleeing from three small bottles of medicine. He always doodled while listening; it helped him concentrate.

"So we did CTs, and that's how I know the clots were all the same: cerebral thromboses. Of the nine patients, seven died. One is in a coma and will probably have severe permanent brain damage, and the last one is in critical condition. Here, I've indicated which is which, with ages, race, and home addresses."

She handed him a chart to match the graph. Christ, Nurse Pafford was more organized than half the agents he'd known.

He said, "Don't I remember reading somewhere that African Americans are more susceptible to stroke than whites?"

"Well, yes. That's true. But not to *this* extent! Anyway, I took all this data to my supervisor. She told me it wasn't important, I was too young and ignorant to know that cases came in unpredictable clumps, and maybe next month it's be a bunch of heart attacks or car crashes."

Rachel Pafford bit her lip. Cavanaugh guessed that the supervisor's disdain had wounded her. But not to the point of giving up.

"I went next to the director of the hospital. She said the same thing, only in nicer words. When my supervisor found out I'd seen her, she was a real bitch to me!"

Cavanaugh was glad he wasn't in the middle of this behind-the-scenes hospital drama. Nurse Pafford, for all her youth and nervousness, looked tenacious. In fact, she suddenly reminded him of Judy.

"So what will *you* do with the information, Agent Cavanaugh?"

"Well," he said, inventing fast, "as you yourself must know, the data sample is small, only nine cases—"

"Yes, of course, we need more. I'll photocopy this week's records when I go in on Friday!"

"I don't—"

"And, of course, if this is happening at Dellridge, it's probably happening at other places in the area, although this is the only real hospital in southern Maryland—but you'll check with private physicians, of course. And the county medical examiner. She'll have to do autopsies on anything suspicious-looking. Then you'll have enough data to run T-tests for significance . . . my training included basic statistics, you know. Will you let me know what you uncover?"

Cavanaugh felt dizzy. She had it all planned out. But "it" was probably just what the supervising nurse had said: a normal variation in the various ways human beings could die. "CIVILIZATION PURSUES NATURE" Cavanaugh scribbled under his racing medicine bottles, closed his notebook, and stood.

"If I uncover anything notable, Ms. Pafford, I'll contact you again. If you don't hear from me, you can assume I found nothing significant."

"But—"

"The Federal Bureau of Investigation thanks you for your patriotic concern as a citizen," Cavanaugh said. This useful formula, the invention of his former supervisor Martin Felders, invariably shut people up. It sounded so final, so official. Rachel Pafford was no exception. She followed him unhappily to the door, but she didn't thrust on him any more graphs or lists.

In his car, Cavanaugh considered. If he drove home, he'd get there by ten-thirty. Judy would still be up. She'd want to continue talking about marriage. He just wasn't up to it.

He drove instead to the main street of Port Tobacco and found a bar. A sign in the gravel parking lot said CUSTOMER PARKING ONLY—NO AUTO REPAIRS. Cavanaugh was lucky. Not only did his car not need repairs, but the bar was actually open. The only other restaurant he'd found open this late in Saint Mary's County was the International House of Pancakes.

Inside, the bar was cool and dim. By nursing two beers and then driving very slowly back across the peninsula, he arrived in Rivermount at fifteen minutes to midnight. The lights were all out in the house on the river bluff.

Before he tiptoed into the house, Cavanaugh used his cell phone to call his office answering machine. Two messages. Nurse Pafford, asking him not to mention her name when he talked to any other medical people, and the principal at the junior high, reminding him that on Thursday, forty-two eighth graders were signed up to hear him talk about all the exciting career opportunities in the FBI.

Two

In medicine, sins of commission are mortal, sins of
omission venial.
—Bulletin of New York Academy of Medicine, 1929

On Wednesday mornings every second week, Cavanaugh reported in to
the field office in Baltimore for a staff meeting. He was the southern
Maryland representative, mostly so Donald Seton, special agent in
charge, didn't have to be bothered.

"Going up to Baltimore?" Seton asked. He was a career agent, close
to retirement, and as far as Cavanaugh could find out, a dead weight on
the Bureau for twenty-three years. Overweight in the way of a once-
handsome man gone to lazy fat, Seton still dressed like a member of J.
Edgar Hoover's FBI: dark suit, narrow dark tie, white shirt now straining
at the buttons. Every morning he puttered around the office. Every
afternoon he either went to the Patuxent River Naval Air Station on un-
explained "investigations" or spent the time in a bar "developing informants." Seton filed more 302s, the form the Bureau used for case
and informant reports, than any agent Cavanaugh had ever seen. He suspected that Seton's informant files were mostly bogus, but so far he
hadn't had the heart to check this out, which he wasn't supposed to do
anyway. Seton was his boss.

Cavanaugh said neutrally, "Staff meeting. Anything to give Dunbar?"

"Of course," Seton smirked. He always had papers to give Dunbar. Informant reports, on-going investigation reports, travel reports, report reports—on paper, Seton looked like the most productive agent on the East Coast. "This folder here."

"A lot going on at Pax River?"

"You know it," Seton said, and winked.

"You must fill me in on all of it soon. In case one of your dangerous suspects tries a hit and I have to finish the investigation."

Seton laughed. He was impervious to sarcasm. "Have a good meeting, Bob."

"Robert," Cavanaugh said automatically, yet again. But Seton had gone back to his computer. Cavanaugh glimpsed graphics of an alien spaceship. Soundlessly it blew up. He left for Baltimore.

Staff meetings were always mixed occasions. Just driving north filled Cavanaugh with intense longing for multilevel cloverleafs, interconnected malls, and Chinese restaurants. The row houses of Baltimore ignited nostalgia. But none of that began to approach the envy of sitting in the meeting itself.

Special Agent in Charge Jerry Dunbar, who supervised over two hundred investigators in Maryland and Delaware, tossed a cigarette-pack-sized object in the middle of the table. Wires dangled from its featureless metal surface. "This thing is our single worst nightmare. And we've made no progress at all on it."

Twenty-four agents stared at the gizmo, which all of them recognized. It was legitimately marketed by mail-order electronics houses. It cost about $1,200. Cabled to a cellular telephone, it allowed criminals to change their cell phone number every three or four minutes with just a few key strokes. It was making wiretaps completely ineffectual.

"If it weren't for that, I'd have had a warrantable transcript on Carlo DiBenedetto," said Alex Vallone, from the Wilmington Office.

"You know what the wiseguys are calling it? 'The magic box,'" said Marie Mooney, from Hyattsville, outside D.C.

"Even the army noncoms have them," said John Stoneham. "I was this close to a warrantable transcript on that weapons-stealing ring at Aberdeen Proving Ground." He held up his thumb and forefinger a quarter inch apart. *"This close."*

"Headquarters says they're working on it," Dunbar said. Sounds of derision around the table. Dunbar stiffened; he didn't have much of a sense of humor.

Cavanaugh reached for his notebook and sketched the telephone device. He gave it horns and a sarcastic leer.

"Robert," Marie said kindly, "have you run into any trouble with these magic boxes from your hate groups?"

"No," Cavanaugh said, trying to keep the envy out of his voice. He hadn't even "run into" any of the hate groups themselves, although southern Maryland was lush with them: home-grown militia, white supremacists, neo-Nazis, religious warriors. In the deep forests and trailer-park dirt roads and tidal swamps, they flourished like kudzu in Georgia. Thanks to Headquarters data, Cavanaugh knew who the hate groups were, and where they were. But lately they had all been quiet or inactive or—for all the opportunity they gave him to *do* anything—completely dead.

He labeled his drawing "THE MAGIC MOCKS."

The conversation moved on: a terrorist investigation in Dover. A kidnapping in Baltimore. RICO statutes, task forces, warrants, informants, subpoenas. Cavanaugh said nothing. He sketched a cat, tightly imprisoned inside a perfect circle, squashed and motionless. Then a second one.

Surveillance, bomb teams, advanced training at Quantico.

A few more lines, and the cats inside circles became the wheels of a police car.

Sabotage, money laundering, bank fraud, problems in coordination with local law enforcement.

This drawing he labeled "UNSTOLEN HUBCATS."

"Well, I think that pretty much wraps it up," Agent Dunbar said. "Anybody need help with anything else? Robert?"

This week I have a housing discrimination in a senior citizen complex and an Adopt-a-School talk to the eighth grade. Want to help? "No," Cavanaugh said. "I'm fine."

He couldn't get out of Baltimore fast enough, and he hated it that he had to leave.

On the way back to Leonardtown, Cavanaugh stopped at Dellridge Community Hospital in La Plata to talk to its director, who turned out to be a woman in her fifties, trim and cool except for her accent, which promised a lush magnolia-scented warmth that her manner did not deliver.

"I have to say that I still don't understand why you're here, Agent Cavanaugh," Dr. Lawrence said, after he had explained for ten minutes why he was there. "Are you asking"—*Ah yew-ah ay-askin'*—"whether or not these deaths by stroke on the dates in question actually occurred? I can, of course, verify that for you." *Vuh-ah-fy.*

"Not exactly," Cavanaugh said. "I'm asking more whether such strokes—such a number of cerebral strokes all in a clump—are normal."

She squinted at him across her desk. "Strokes are completely natural, Agent Cavanaugh, in that the body has a million different ways to malfunction."

"Yes, I know, Doctor. But the unusually high incidence of strokes here at Dellridge last weekend—is that medically notable?"

"Agent Cavanaugh, are you investigating a possible mishandling of medical emergencies at Dellridge? If you are, please tell me outright." *Out-raht.*

"I'm not investigating anything at this point," Cavanaugh said, and saw in her eyes the question, *Then why are you here?* "I'm merely following up on an anomaly. Any insight into the anomaly that you can give me would be very helpful."

"And this anomaly is racial in nature. That's what you mean, isn't it? Let me just put a few facts on the table, if I may. The population of Maryland is twenty-five percent African American, far above the national average. African Americans, for some reasons we understand and some we don't, are twice as likely as whites to suffer a stroke. For African Americans between thirty-five and fifty-five, the rate is four times higher than for middle-aged whites. National studies show that when blacks do suffer strokes, brain damage in survivors is more extensive than in other racial groups. No one knows why. And let me just add that Dellridge Hospital has an unparalleled commitment to providing quality care to *all* our patients. And the unblemished record to back that up. Is that the sort of insight you're looking for, Agent Cavanaugh?"

Cavanaugh said neutrally, "It's very helpful, yes."

"I'm so glad." Dr. Lawrence stood. "If there's anything else I can do to assist you . . ."

"No, I don't think so. You've been very helpful." Clearly expected to stand and leave, he did.

He could feel her eyes on his back all the way down the hospital corridor, through the lobby, and out the door, where the unseasonable heat hit him like a damp shroud.

Here's the lab report you asked for," the young doctor said, laying a sheaf of papers on the desk of the chief of medicine, "on Senator Reading."

Dr. Goldstein skimmed the report. He was a slight, handsome man in his sixties, with a full head of curls the same gunmetal gray as his eyes. As he read, the gray eyes narrowed. "There's some mistake."

"I don't think so, sir. I had the test done twice. Both reports are there."

"Had the senator been traveling overseas? Or even in the Caribbean?"

"Not according to his wife. He's been too busy precampaigning."

Goldstein got up and walked to the window. The view from the third floor was discouraging. Like most New York hospitals, parking was a problem second only to sanitation. Cars jammed the inadequate parking lot, many of them skewed at clearly illegal angles in clearly illegal spaces, blocking Dumpsters and delivery bays and other cars. Among the illegals was a sound truck with CHANNEL SIX NEWS on the side. Goldstein scowled and turned back from the window.

"Rafe, I can't give this out at the press conference. Not unless we're absolutely sure."

The young doctor didn't answer. He had peered through the scanning tunneling microscope himself; he was already sure. He said, "I'm afraid there's something else, sir."

"Something else besides the fact that a United States senator and strong presidential candidate died of a thrombus, but tests show that he also had the beginning stages of malaria when there hasn't been any malaria in the United States since the end of World War II?"

"Yes, sir. The last page of the report."

Still standing, Goldstein shuffled to the last page, past the tests confirming malaria: decreased hemoglobin, hemocrit, platelet count and haptoglobin. Increased levels of lactic dehydrogenase and reticulocytes. Not to mention the *Plasmodium falciparum* parasites viewed under the X-ray microscope. The chief of medicine read the last page once, twice. "No," he said. "Flat out impossible."

The younger doctor said nothing.

Slowly Goldstein shuffled through the pages of lab reports, looking for a way to make sense of the results. He didn't find it.

"Sir, I looked through the microscope myself. The merozoites—"

But Goldstein wasn't in the mood for eyewitness news. He made a sudden decision.

"Rafe, don't mention this to anyone, including the senator's family. Not just yet. And I'm going to leave the malaria out of that damned press conference, too. Meanwhile, package up samples of the senator's blood and copies of all the lab tests, and send them to the CDC in Atlanta, and to the Infectious and Tropical Disease Unit at Walter Reed. Call both places and explain the problem. They're set up for this kind of weirdness. We're not."

"Yes, sir," Rafe said. His eyes met Goldstein's. The two gazes, one gunmetal gray and one bright blue, held briefly. Then both looked away.

Each was intensely conscious of what had not been said aloud. David Goldstein was Jewish; Rafe DuFort was French. Both considered themselves fair-minded men, without prejudice, and politically astute.

"The CDC," Goldstein repeated, "is set up for this. That's what they're there for."

He went off to make his statement to the press on the causes of Senator Malcolm Peter Reading's death.

The package from the New York hospital arrived at the Centers for Disease Control main receiving dock by overnight Federal Express. It was labeled in red magic marker: DANGEROUS. INFECTIOUS SUBSTANCES. DANGEROUS TO HUMANS. The men working at the dock paid no attention. They saw dozens of such packages every week.

The box was routed to Dr. Melanie Anderson, malaria epidemiologist in the Special Pathogens Branch. She read the accompanying letter, studied the lab reports, and removed the tubes containing blood samples from their packing of dry ice, staring incredulously.

Somebody somewhere had fucked up big time. What the letter and reports said just wasn't in the annals of medicine.

Not that Melanie Anderson had any great respect for the annals of medicine. She had graduated third in her class from Yale School of Medicine, had returned to her native Mississippi full of crusading zeal to treat poor up-country folk in areas without a decent doctor, had set up shop in a dirt-poor community—and had then discovered that she hated being a doctor.

She hated it almost as much as she'd always hated her name. What kind of self-respecting black woman, she'd railed at her hapless mother when Melanie had been sixteen, named a black girl after a *Gone With the Wind* magnolias-and-Confederacy belle? Where was her mother's pride, her righteous anger? Patty Anderson, intimidated into helplessness by this verbal and alien daughter, had only shrugged helplessly. She lacked the courage to say that she'd actually told the birth-certificate recorder "Melody," as in "A Pretty Girl Is Like . . ." The white woman had apparently misheard Patty's soft, blurred, childbirth-woozy accent, and the birth certificate came back "Melanie." Patty had settled. Probably Melanie would have thought "A Pretty Girl Is Like a Melody" an even worse insult. It seemed that almost everything Patty said lately somehow was.

At med school Melanie had called herself "Mel." She'd kept to the small number of blacks in her class. It was like that in the midseventies. She'd joined the Black Panthers and worn her hair in an Afro that, since she was light and her hair waved softly, was a pain in the ass to maintain.

Melanie reverted to her full name in her first practice, but within six months she didn't care what she was called as long as she could be called it someplace else. She was bored with treating the same old things over and over, easy nonchallenging things: colicky babies and elderly influenza and summertime rashes. She found—appalled at herself—that she was growing resentful of the obese hypertensives who refused to lose weight, the smokers' coughs who refused to quit smoking, the incipient cirrhoses who refused to give up the bottle. Out of boredom and frustration, she was coming to almost hate the people, her people, that she'd trained herself to help.

Before it reached that point, Melanie Anderson quit private practice and joined the CDC's Epidemic Intelligence Service. If medicine was going to inspire her with hatred, let it be hatred for microbes and not people.

She turned out to have an enormous talent for disease identification and control. Her required field training took place in Africa, during a swine flu outbreak in Senegal. There she discovered that she also had a talent for languages. The natives trusted her, this African American who took the trouble to learn their dialects, and Melanie contributed to the Senegal team a set of outstanding epidemic curves, those all-important graphs that identify the growth and source of an outbreak. She was also a pretty fair lab epidemiologist, at least for anything larger than DNA itself.

Over the next five years, Melanie returned to Africa six times, five of them for malaria. In central Africa, malaria was still the single greatest killer. In some areas, during the most serious outbreaks of the most virulent strain, 40 percent of toddlers died. Melanie was sometimes heartsick by what she saw, but she was always challenged, always useful, never bored. She was happy. The men she dated on two continents, attracted to her silk-and-sass good looks and focused intelligence, eventually learned that she enjoyed their company, but no more. They would always come in second to a good outbreak of *Plasmodium falciparum*.

Now Melanie reread the New York reports, rolled her eyes in private disbelief, and prepared to thaw the blood samples for a battery of tests.

Four hours later, she stood dazed in the middle of her lab. No. No. It simply was not possible. She had made a mistake somewhere.

But she knew she hadn't.

With most Special Pathogens Branch operations, the first, lengthy step was to isolate the unknown pathogen. That meant days—or weeks—of experimenting to find the right medium to grow samples in, the right techniques to manipulate cultures, the right tests and reagents and stains and optimum temperatures and a dozen other factors. This time, none of that applied. The New York lab had known what they were sending her. It just wasn't supposed to exist.

She picked up an in-house phone and called her supervisor, Jim Farlow, head of the Special Pathogens Branch.

Holy Mother of God," Farlow said. "You're sure, Melanie?"

"I'm sure," she said grimly.

"All right, go over it once more. I just want to hear it again."

"The stroke victim, Senator Malcolm Peter Reading, was in the first stages of malaria. Electrophoresis confirms that he was also positive for sickle-cell trait. And that malaria merozoites were *in* the Hb S blood cells."

"That isn't possible," Farlow said.

"I know it isn't possible! Do you think *I* don't know it isn't possible?" Melanie cried. She heard her own anger, but for the moment, at least, she couldn't help herself.

Sickle-cell trait, an inherited blood abnormality, protected against malaria. That had been known for decades. *Plasmodium,* the one-celled parasite that caused malaria, couldn't flourish inside red blood cells with the abnormal form of hemoglobin called Hb S. Those blood cells tended to sickle—that is, to curve into rigid sickle shapes—when they deoxygenated. *Plasmodium* found this uncongenial.

A personal with sickle-cell trait had his own problems, of course, but they were not very serious. Unlike full-blown sickle-cell anemia, which caused frequent pain and sometimes death, the person born with sickle-cell trait carried only one gene for Hb S, not two. This meant that some of his red blood cells would sickle, but most would not. Usually this meant that if he was careful not to exercise way past his limit, or to take long flights in underpressurized airplanes, he might not realize he even had a genetic deficiency. The sickle-cell-trait carrier was slightly more susceptible to blood clots, because the red blood cells that *did* sickle grew sticky and tended to "sludge," clogging small capillaries. This was a constant danger for those with two genes for Hb S, but a fairly minor danger for carriers of only one gene.

In exchange, the sickle-trait carrier was protected against severe malaria, although he might get a mild case of it at first infection—*if* there was malaria to get, which in the United States, for over fifty years, there had not been. The last of it had been wiped out by the end of the World War II. In fact, the CDC had been founded in 1942 as the MCWA: Malarial Control in War Areas.

But now the CDC was looking at evidence that not only said that Senator Malcolm Peter Reading had died of a sickle-cell-crisis thrombosis, but also that the very red blood cells forming the fatal clot had been colonized by *P. falciparum* merozoites, cells with Hb S. Which was flat-out impossible.

Melanie willed herself to calm. "Look for yourself, Jim. There's no mistake. The parasites are *inside* the sickled cells." She pushed him toward the microscope.

Farlow looked. Melanie visualized what he saw: the unmistakable forms of *P. falciparum* like tiny signet rings, stained now to a small ruby nucleus embedded in a wispy blue circlet, *inside* long, banana-shaped, clearly sickled cells.

Farlow gazed a long time, turned away, and rubbed his jaw with the side of his palm. He and Melanie looked at each other.

"Senator Malcolm Peter Reading," Farlow said.

She said clearly, "A black man." And waited to see what he'd say next.

Nearly all carriers of sickle-cell trait were black. The disease's genetic trade-off, hemoglobin S in exchange for protection against malaria, had evolved in Africa. Sickle-cell trait had come to the United States with the slave trade. At present, one in twelve African Americans carried the trait. Almost three million people.

Farlow said slowly, "*P. falciparum* has a high rate of spontaneous mutation. Christ, six percent of its genome is already devoted to antigenic variation. And part of its life cycle is sexual, with more chances for frame shifts. This mutation could have arisen completely spontaneously."

"Or," Melanie said, "it could have been genetically engineered."

"Melanie—"

"In which case we might be looking at an attempt at racial genocide."

Farlow held up a hand. He knew her history: Black Panthers, the arrest for anti-apartheid demonstrations, activism for various black causes, her refusal to date white men, although she accepted them as friends. Melanie had always felt he'd had reservations about her, at the same time that he admired her scientific work. The combination made him uneasy—but that should be *his* problem, not hers.

"Look," Farlow said, "let's take it one step at a time, okay? Without any premature theories. First, I'm going to have somebody else repeat your tests, Melanie, before we even consider vectors. Just as a check. But you're on the epidemiology team for this, of course."

She said grimly, "Just try to keep me off it."

INTERIM

The child lay in her bed, listening to her mother yell at her older sister.

"Don' never gonna get anywhere in this life if you don' go back to school . . . no more sense 'n a baby . . . stuck all the resta her life on some dyin' tobacco farm . . . sixteen years ol' and she think she know everything in God's green world . . ." Bang. Bang. BANG.

The child smiled. The first bang, and the last one, was Mamma clapping around cooking pots, which she always did when she was mad at Rhonda. The middle bang was Rhonda, slamming the screen door as she stamped out of the house. None of this upset Kwansia. It was morning. It was normal.

And it was Saturday.

Soundlessly, Kwansia slipped from her bed. The room was tiny, furnished with only a battered dresser and thin-mattressed bed. The screen on the window bellied inward, worn soft as old cloth, loose at the edges. The child was careful not to tear it any farther as she raised the window and climbed through.

The day was beeee-uuuu-ti-ful! That was the way Kwansia's kindergarten teacher always said it: beeee-uuuu-ti-ful! When school ended in a few weeks, Kwansia would miss Mrs. Calthorne, but not very much. It was too summery out, and summer was too much fun, and right now sunshine made the water on the big farm pond shine like it was gold.

Barefoot, she padded across the back field, keeping out of sight both of her mother's kitchen window and of Rhonda, sulking at the road as she waited for the bus to town. Kwansia wiggled her toes in the grass, which felt so good she started to trot, just to have even more grass stroke her feet. Someone mowed yesterday; the grassy smell was fresh and sweet. Heaven, Kwansia thought, was going to smell exactly like Mr. Thayer's farm just after it done got mowed.

She stopped, out of breath, by the cow barn. Kwansia like cows. She liked the way they looked at her, like they was thinking, chewing their grass gum. She liked the kittens in the hay loft, their eyes just open. She liked—

Something sharp stung her arm. Kwansia jumped, shook herself all over, then looked down. The mosquito was still there. Instead of slapping it again, Kwansia raised her arm until the mosquito was inches from her face. It didn't fly away. She stared at it, fascinated.

Its nose was stuck right in her skin! How did it *do* that? Almost as dark as her arm, the mosquito balanced on six long skinny legs. There were white dots on its wings. It looked so funny, bent over like that, almost standing on its head to eat little bits of her.

"I got lots," the child told the mosquito. "Everything on God's green earth got to eat." Her mother often said that.

"Kwansia, where you at? You outside again without no shoes?"

Guilty, Kwansia yelled, "Here, Mama!"

"You get in here and eat your breakfas'!"

The child brushed the mosquito off her arm and ran toward the house through the glorious spring morning. The mosquito, sated, flew toward the quiet waters of Thayer's pond.

THREE

Fidelity, bravery, integrity.
—FBI motto

Cavanaugh arrived at Rivermount Junior High, a consolidated school district, just as the bell rang to change classes. The central hallway, which moments before had been a peaceful, locker-lined thoroughfare, instantly took on the character of the D.C. beltway during a nuclear evacuation.

Cavanaugh flattened himself against the wall in self-protection. He hadn't set foot in a junior high since he'd *been* in junior high, and surely then it hadn't looked like this? All the boys looked like runts inexplicably dressed in clothes three sizes too big for them. All the girls looked like hookers. Makeup, big hair, short skirts, developed figures—these girls couldn't possibly be the same age as the boys pushing past them. They looked at least five years older and from another culture entirely. Some of them were also dazzlingly pretty.

After the stampede had slowed, Cavanaugh found the principal's office and was escorted to the Large Group Instruction Area, a term he'd never heard before, which turned out to be the cafeteria with a stage built at one end. The eighth grade, eight to a table, awaited him. As he mounted the podium, every male eyed the bulge of his gun, including the teachers. He had no idea what the girls eyed, and didn't want to think about it.

"Hello. My name is Robert Cavanaugh, special agent for the Federal Bureau of Investigation."

Feminine titters from a table off to the right. What was so funny about that?

"I'm here today to talk to you about careers in the FBI. The Bureau needs bright, ambitious young people, and by the time you finish college, it will need even more of them."

Titters from a table to the left. A blonde Madonna-wanna be put her perfectly manicured finger between her bright red lips and made a discreet barfing sound. A teacher stood up and directed "The Teacher Look" at that table. Cavanaugh inwardly cursed the Adopt-a-School Community Outreach Program and whatever underemployed moron had dreamed it up.

But they warmed as he talked, or at least enough of them did so that no other teacher had to stand and give The Look. Cavanaugh covered the standard information: FBI mission, programs, successes, opportunities, employment requirements. Then he threw it open for questions.

An intense-looking black kid in a Dilbert T-shirt stood. "Agent Cavanaugh, how closely do you monitor the Ku Klux Klan activities on the Internet? I don't just mean their Home Page, but the information going by in the chat rooms and stuff like that."

Cavanaugh shifted his weight behind the podium. He had received intelligence about the local chapter of the KKK, of course, but he had no idea they had a Home Page, much less chat rooms. That was the sort of thing monitored by analysts, not agents, who received the information in hard copy as they needed or requested it. And 70 percent of Cavanaugh's civil rights cases, like agents' everywhere, concerned not racial discrimination but alleged police brutality. Although they were often the same thing.

However, looking down into that serious, intense young face, Cavanaugh didn't want to say any of this. For the first time, he realized that the black eighth graders and the whites, with few exceptions, sat at separate tables.

"The Bureau stays on top of Klan developments in every form the information is offered. All agents receive instruction in computer use during initial training at Quantico, and refresher courses afterwards as needed."

The kid nodded and sat down, evidently too young to realize that Cavanaugh had said nothing. A girl stood. "How much money does an FBI agent make? How much do *you* get?"

"Pay scale depends on position and length of service. And you really don't expect me to stand up here and tell you my personal income, do you? The IRS might be listening."

That got a laugh. Other kids asked about weapons training, finger-printing, UFOs (*The X-Files* had a lot to answer for), bombing cases, and if he'd ever met the president. Then a boy stood near the back. Taller than most, he looked as if he had no flesh at all, only skin stretched over bones as sharp as chisels. His hair, skin, and eyes were all the same color, pale as dry sand. He blinked twice and said, "Does the FBI ever hire en-tomologists?"

The whole room exploded into laughter. Cavanaugh couldn't see why, except that it seemed to be provoked by the kid himself, not the question. Catcalls from all over: "Go back under your rock, Insect Boy!" "What a dork!" "Earl, you look like one of your bugs!" Three teachers stood and gave The Look. One also clapped his hands and called out, "People! People!" The students ignored him. Then the bell rang. The eighth grade grabbed its book bags and fled as if from chemical contam-ination. The teachers followed the students.

Only Earl didn't move. He stood rooted, staring at Cavanaugh. In sixty seconds, the room was empty except for Cavanaugh, Earl, and the principal. Cavanaugh addressed this minuscule audience, since clearly Earl was not going to budge until he did.

"The FBI has what it calls Professional Support Personnel positions, who do jobs like computer specialist, lab technician, photographer. I don't know if Professional Support Personnel includes an entomologist, but I would guess not. When we need technical science advice outside of the usual forensic activities, the Bureau often consults with scientists at the National Institute of Health, which is right outside Washington in Bethesda."

Cavanaugh, proud of this answer, waited for Earl to nod and leave. He didn't. Instead he blinked his pale eyes twice and said, "You ought to have an entomologist."

"Well, as I explained—"

Two more blinks. "Insects tell us a lot about everything."

"Thank you, Earl," said the principal. "Now you should go to your next class."

Earl threw the principal a look of utter despair, startling on that bony, washed-out face, and slouched off. The principal climbed the stage steps to Cavanaugh.

"Interesting boy, that. Earl Lester. Absolutely fanatical about insects, and knows everything there is to know about the latest research. But somewhat deficient in social skills, as you saw, which unfortunately evokes a negative reaction from his insecure peers."

Cavanaugh wondered why principals talked like that. The principal walked him to the main entrance, mingling jargon and thanks.

Back in his office in Leonardtown, he sat at his computer, accessed Web Crawler, and typed in KU KLUX KLAN. And there it was: the KKK Home Page, with a history section, frequently asked questions, organization listings (including the chapter on Robert's jurisdiction), and pictures. In fact, it looked depressingly like the FBI Home Page, except that the Klan couldn't spell ("upholding there tradition"). Web Crawler also gave him sites for chat groups about the Klan. He found one billing itself as WHITE PRIDE OF MARYLAND and followed a few of its message linkages through the hateful, pathetic conversation:

I WANT TO BE IN THE KLAN WHEN I'M OLDER. EVERY WHERE I GO ALL THE NIGGERS ARE CUTTING ME DOWN AND I DON'T LIKE IT ANYMORE.

TIM—I WANT TO BE IN THE KLAN TOO. OKAY DO WHAT YOU WANT, AND DON'T LET ANYBODY TRY AND STOP YOU.

BLACK POWER!!! HEY TO ALL OF U INBREEDERS FROM THE KLAN. IM JUST WONDERING WHATS GOING ON IN YOUR LITTLE BRAINS. IM NOT BLACK, BUT ME AND ALMOST THE REST OF THE WORLD LOVE THEM. ON THE OTHER HAND JUST WHERE ARE BLACKS ACCEPTED IN THIS WORLD? ANYONE WANT THEM? HOW ABOUT AFRICA? NO THEY ARE KILLING EACH OTHER BY THE THOUSANDS. BECAUSE BLACK BEHAVE WITHOUT CLASS AND DIGNITY, NO BODY EVER WILL ACCEPT THEM UNTIL THEY TRY AND ACT LIKE THE REST OF US.

HEY DOES ANY BODY KNOW ABOUT THIS BUNCH OF STROKES KILLING NIGGERS IN KING GEORGE VA? MY COUZIN IS A ORDERLY AT MEMORIAL HOSPITAL AND HE SAYS THEY HAVE

WAY TO MANY NIGGERS DYING OF STROKES. GESS WHAT I SAID
BACK?!!

Cavanaugh straightened in his chair. He dragged his cursor to the
SAVE icon on his PC.

The Potomac River Bridge on Highway 301 connected Charles County,
Maryland, to King George County, Virginia. Driving over it, Cavanaugh
noticed the giant waterborne mowing machine cutting channels through
hydrilla, an aquatic weed that had sneaked into the U.S. from someplace
else. The channels ran from launching ramps and marinas to the open
water of the Potomac. Without constant mowing, the hydrilla, which
sprouted as fast as eighth-grade girls, would wrap itself around boat pro-
pellers. The machine whirred along; above the driver's head hummed a
cloud of insects.

Soldiers and Sailors Memorial Hospital in Dahlgren, Virginia, was
about the same size as Dellridge. Cavanaugh talked to the director, who
showed the same paranoid distaste as Dellridge about the idea that
blacks might not receive equal health care to whites. Nor did he believe
Cavanaugh when Cavanaugh said that wasn't his concern. But he gave
Cavanaugh the information he wanted and didn't want:

In the last three weeks, cerebral strokes in black patients had occurred at triple the usual rate. There had been no change in rates for
other ethnic groups, except for Indians from northern India.

"*Indians?*" Cavanaugh said.

"Yes. We have a growing Indian population, many of whom are doctors employed by our numerous pharmaceutical firms. Three Indians
have had similar strokes in the last two-and-a-half weeks, which I have to
admit does seem a little unusual, especially since two were compara-
tively young. And three came from Jamnagar. Does that help?"

"Afraid not," Cavanaugh said, noting that the director had turned
much more cooperative when discussing Indian stroke victims at Memorial Hospital than black stroke victims. Federal civil rights laws did not
extend special protection to Indians. "Were autopsies done on these
stroke patients?"

"I'd have to check, but I imagine they were on at least some of them,
the ones who didn't fit the profile for a stroke—you know, much younger
than average, nonhypertensive, no elevated cholesterol, things like that."

"Would you please fax me copies of those autopsy reports?"

"Certainly," the director said, clearly not happy. "May I ask just what the FBI's concern is here?"

"I'm sorry, I'm not able to say," Cavanaugh said, which was certainly true. He was fishing in the dark. "One more question, Doctor. It's true that an autopsy only finds those things it's looking for, right? I mean, anything large like a gunshot wound would be noticed, but subtle stuff, slight metabolism differences, something like that, that wouldn't show up in a routine autopsy, would it?"

"Such as what?"

Cavanaugh had no idea. "Just . . . differences among brains? Or blood?" He sounded lame even to himself.

The director said neutrally, "It's true that an autopsy includes some tests and not others, since there are literally hundreds of different tests it's possible to perform on a dead body."

"Thank you, Doctor."

"One more thing, Agent Cavanaugh. I just want to add that Soldiers and Sailors Memorial has an outstanding commitment to providing quality care to *all* our patients. And the record to prove it."

They were almost exactly the same words used by the director at Dellridge. Maybe, Cavanaugh thought, hospital administrators had to memorize set speeches, the way law-enforcement officers had to memorize the Miranda Rights. That made sense, when you thought about it. On the whole, Cavanaugh approved. The whole world would be better off if it ran by shared and easily recognizable rules.

The thing is, I don't feel I know the rules here," Judy said. "In our relationship, I mean."

She and Cavanaugh sat on their tiny deck in the red twilight, sipping wine. Judy, who disapproved of pesticides on ecological grounds, had installed a bug lamp on the deck so they could sit there after dark without being nibbled alive by mosquitoes. Every few seconds a hapless insect flew into the lamp's purple light, was fried by an electric field, and dropped to the deck. Small insects made a quiet *zap* as they fried; moths made a loud *ZAP!* that made Cavanaugh's neck crawl. He had read that bug zappers were actually ineffective against mosquitoes; 99 percent of what they fried were some other bugs. However, he didn't mention this to Judy. Things were fragile enough already.

"I've been trying to see this from your point of view, Robert," Judy said in a reasonable voice. "I know you do care for me."

"Yes, I do," Cavanaugh said.

"And I can understand that you're reluctant to risk another marital failure."

"Yes."

"What I can't understand is your belief that *we* would be a failure."

Zap.

"I mean, Robert . . . I'm not Marcy."

"I know you're not."

"Although sometimes I think you wish I were."

Zap!

"No," Cavanaugh said carefully. "I don't wish you were Marcy."

Judy looked out toward the river. Boat lights moved on the dark water. By the purple light of the bug zapper Cavanaugh could see she was trying very hard not to cry, to stay calm and reasonable. This made him feel worse. Judy was not a calm person, she was intense and open, that was one of the things that had attracted him. And now he resented her for it. Was that fair?

Could it be true that he wanted her to be more like Marcy? Cool, controlled Marcy, who never got upset or hurt by anything he did, thereby letting him just be himself . . .

Zap.

Judy said, "Sometimes I think you don't really know what you want."

I want this conversation to end. "Judy, I . . . I'm just not ready."

Her tone shifted. "And when do you think you'll be ready?"

"Don't push me." The second he said it, he knew he shouldn't have. But she surprised him. Instead of getting hurt or angry, she said with genuine contrition, "I'm sorry. I have been pushing, haven't I? That can't feel very good to you. I mean, your point of view is just as valid as mine."

"Oh, Judy," he said helplessly, overwhelmed with love, and guilt, and wariness, and the desire to change the subject. Inspiration suddenly seized him. "Honey, I know I've been distant, but I have a lot on my—there's something at work that I really need your help with!"

"*My* help?"

"Yes! You're the science writer. You know how to really work the Internet, and you have so many contacts in the scientific world. Here's the situation . . ."

He shouldn't do this, he knew. Bureau cases weren't supposed to be discussed outside the Bureau, not even with spouses, which Judy wasn't. But this stroke thing could hardly be called a case as yet—there wasn't a suspicion of any foul play. And Judy really did have solid groundings in the scientific community. And if it would divert her from the idea of marriage . . . Of course, Cavanaugh had also put an analyst on it at Headquarters. Jim Neymeier, Cavanaugh's favorite intelligence analyst, who loved data—especially computerized data—the way moths loved porch lights. Not that Cavanaugh was going to tell Judy about Neymeier.

"Blacks and Indians," Judy said thoughtfully, when he'd finished telling her about Nurse Pafford, Dellridge, and Soldiers and Sailors Memorial. "And you think it's some genetic brain difference, something in the cerebral chemistry—"

"That's only a hypothesis," Cavanaugh said. "But can you check it out for me?"

"Yes," Judy said. She sounded happy again. Almost shyly, she touched his arm in the darkness. "I'm glad you asked me to help, Robert. I like being useful to you."

Her words barely registered. But her touch did. Suddenly, to his own surprise, he had a mammoth erection. He got up from his deck chair, pulled Judy to her feet, and kissed her deeply.

"*Well,*" she said. "And what's all this?" He could feel her grin against her shirt.

"Let's go inside, honey."

"I'm willing," she said huskily, and kissed him again.

So that was all it took! Some affection, some lust . . . sex was the answer then. Or, at least, an interim answer. It distracted her from thinking about marriage. Sex was his best ally.

Pleased with himself, Robert led her inside the house.

ZAP! went the purple light behind him.

Melanie Anderson looked around the table at the other three members of the newly formed CDC team: Gary Pershing, the top laboratory man in malaria; Susan Muscato, experienced veteran of disease outbreaks in the United States—she'd done some good sleuthing with hantavirus; Joe Krovetz, very young, an unknown quantity, whom Jim Farlow was probably giving a chance to do his EPI-AID, Epidemic Assistance Detail, necessary to becoming a full-fledged epidemic intelligence officer. And

Farlow himself, who was supposed to be administrating the CDC Special Pathogens Branch but could never bear to be left out while anything hot was breaking. Melanie took Farlow's inclusion as a sign that the implications of the Senator Reading blood samples were being taken seriously. The team was a good one.

It was also, except for her, all white.

"All right," Farlow summarized, "we have the lab results. We have the stroke data, in rough form, in the weekly morbidity reports for the last month. We have—"

"There's something I don't get," Joe Krovetz said. He was heavyset, with a neck thick and strong as a bulldog's. Everybody at the table, except apparently Joe himself, noted that he didn't hesitate to interrupt Farlow.

"What don't you get?" Farlow said.

"The *Anopheles* is infected, right?" This was a safe assumption; *Anopheles quadrimaculatus* was the only mosquito found east of the Rockies that could carry malaria. "*Anopheles* bites a victim; the parasite enters the bloodstream and goes straight to the liver. All normal so far."

Normal. Young Joe Krovetz had never seen a village devastated by an outbreak of lethal tertiary malaria. Never seen people shivering through bone-shattering chills, followed abruptly by fevers so high that they hallucinated. Never seen mothers too weak and dazed to feed their children, men too sick to reach for the water they craved, while more mosquitoes fed on their burning skin. Never seen a fetal death rate of 50 percent among pregnant women whose bodies could not support both *Plasmodium* parasites and a fetal one. *Normal.*

Joe went on. "The data so far show that the *Plasmodium* parasites leave the liver on schedule, enter the bloodstream, and invade the sickled cells. But when the first batch breaks out of the red blood cells to infect another bunch of cells, the host should start to show signs of malaria, right? Fever, chills, all the rest of it. But Reading didn't, and neither did the others. So that means the sickle cells form a fatal clot almost as soon as *Plasmodium* enters them, before there's even an hour or two for the victim to start feeling sick. Right?"

"Right," Farlow said, smiling faintly. Melanie saw that he knew where Joe was taking this. He was giving the kid a chance to work it out for himself.

"So the victim has a stroke and dies. Most of them, anyway. But that means the parasites die, too—*before* they can be sucked back up into another mosquito and passed on to somebody else. So how is the disease spreading from person to person and mosquito to mosquito?"

Susan Muscato said, "Maybe it's not. Maybe there's only one batch of infected mosquitoes somewhere, and once we get out in the field we'll find that all twenty victims so far were in the same place—a park or something—and got it at the same time. And when they die, the outbreak will die with them."

"Could be," Farlow said.

Joe said stubbornly, "I don't think that's what's happening."

"I don't think so, either," Farlow said. "Joe, what do you think is happening?"

"I think that the new strain doesn't infect only people carrying sickle-cell trait. It infects everyone. But in people with normal hemoglobin, the parasite can't flourish. So those people get a very mild case of malaria—possibly so mild they don't even know they have it. Maybe just a slight fever, headache, little bit of a sore throat. After a few days it's gone, and then they're immune to reinfection. It's the exact reverse of how sickle-cell trait protects against the usual strains of malaria. Except that with *Plasmodium reading*—"

"What did you call it?" Gary Pershing interrupted.

"*Plasmodium reading.* You know, after the senator."

There was a little silence. Usually diseases were named after either the place it first appeared, such as all the Ebola strains, or after the person who discovered it. A National Institute of Health researcher named Don Eyeles had been the source for *Plasmodium eylesi.* But as far as Melanie knew, no malaria had ever before been named after its first identified victim. What a memorial to the man who might have been the next president of the United States.

Farlow said, "Joe's theory about universal infection with *Plasmodium reading* is certainly plausible. We need to check blood samples from victims' family members, neighbors, associates. But there's also another possibility: a second host to sustain the parasite between *Anopheles's* breeding cycles."

"Well, maybe," Susan Muscato said thoughtfully. In her midforties, she still looked like an athlete: strongly built, pared down, not weighted by anything to slow her down. "Transspecies parasite migration has happened before, but only among primates, and never with any variant of *P.*

falciparum. Besides, apes and gibbons are rare in Manhattan, where Reading collapsed."

"It wouldn't have to be gibbons," Joe said—Melanie saw that he was both persistent and humorless: one plus as a team member, one minus—"or any other primate. But I suppose there could be another host."

Gary Pershing, the lab man, said suddenly, "The DNA homology of *P. falciparum* is closer to the malaria parasites of birds than of monkeys."

Farlow said, "Only one way to tell. When we're in Maryland we need to collect blood samples from people without sickle-cell trait who have been in the same locales as the victims. And do interview follow-ups on both."

Gary said, "But if that doesn't play out, we should look at birds. God, Maryland is so species-rich . . ."

Melanie couldn't help herself. She had planned on saying nothing, just listening, until the end of this meeting. But the word just burst out, "*Birds.*"

"No, I don't see how it could use birds as an alternate host," Susan agreed, or thought she did. "Bird malarias use *Culex* mosquitoes as vector, not *Anopheles.* Cattle or pigs or something are more usual."

"Let's not be premature here. About anything," Farlow said, looking directly at Melanie. "One step at a time. Gary, you've had two days with the senator's samples. What can you tell us?"

Pershing shook his head. Melanie could have sworn the gesture was admiration. "It's quite a piece of work. This is just preliminary, of course, but there seem to be three changes from standard *P. falciparum.* First, the merozoites have a surface peptide that attaches itself *only* to a receptor on the surface of a cell with hemoglobin S. I haven't found the peptide or the receptor yet, but I'm almost positive that's what's happening. The surface of sickle cells already differ in so many ways from normal ones: in stickiness, in oxygen acquisition and release rates, all kinds of ways.

"Second, once they're inside the cell, the altered parasites make attaching knobs that prefer the vascular endothelium of cerebral blood vessels rather than any old vessel walls. So the infected blood cells migrate to the brain.

"Third, once they're there, they excrete something, or do something, that makes the blood vessel constrict and the blood clot. My guess is a protein that binds to the nitric oxide that's supposed to act as vasodilator, but I haven't verified that yet. But anyway, the result is a fast, big blood clot in constricted blood vessels in the brain."

"And a fatal stroke," Susan said.

"And a fatal stroke," Gary agreed. "But only in people with sickle cells in their blood. Some Mediterranean peoples, some Indians. But mostly blacks."

There it was, out on the table. Nobody spoke until young Joe Krovetz said, "There's something else I don't get."

"Yes?" Farlow said.

"If only blacks are in danger from this disease, what's Melanie doing on the team? I mean, no offense, Melanie, but you're at risk in a way none of us is."

Melanie saw now the value of Joe Krovetz, despite his inexperience. He would say aloud what everybody else was only thinking.

She said evenly, "No, I'm not at risk. I'm negative for sickle-cell trait."

"And we're all grateful for that," Susan Muscato said, too quickly. They were embarrassed, Melanie knew. Here, in one of the most advanced scientific establishments in the world, in one of the most democratic countries in the world, her colleagues were embarrassed to discuss racial differences. Enlightened America was supposed to be color-blind.

She put both palms flat on the table. "There's something *I* don't get." It came out harsher than she intended, not an echo of young Joe but a sarcastic mockery. Joe didn't react. Chalk up another plus for the kid: he didn't take things personally.

Farlow said, "What's that, Melanie?"

"I don't get why we're not discussing whether this *P. falciparum* strain was deliberately engineered to kill carriers of sickle-cell hemoglobin, which means mostly African Americans."

Farlow said instantly, "Premature. And that's our official stand on this, people. I talked to the director this morning. He's setting up a meeting for early next week. It'll be us, the Public Health Service, the FBI, and a team from the Army Medical Research Institute at Fort Detrick. We'll get in several good days' work on site before the meeting and go in prepared to make recommendations. Until then, the official word is to keep this away from the press until we have more information. If asked, we just say that all theories are premature."

"Which is true," Susan said. "Especially your theory, Melanie.

There's no evidence at all that *P. reading* is any kind of plot against African Americans. It could just be a natural mutation. You know it could."

Everyone looked awkward. Susan was right, Melanie knew. Melanie had no hard evidence that *P. reading* was anything other than a natural mutation. Unless, of course, you counted the statistical chances of three entirely different genetic mechanisms all mutating at exactly the same time, in the same parasite, to produce a disease fatal only to a population subgroup that just incidentally happened to have been oppressed and discriminated against for three hundred years. Yeah, right.

She said, "Right now the official death toll from *P. reading* is one. We may find a lot more once we start field work. My question is, if we don't alert the press, how many more people out there will die who could have been saved by being told about the problem? Radio and TV should carry instructions on using insecticides, using mosquito netting, destroying or staying away from breeding grounds—"

"They will be, Melanie," Farlow said, "they will be. That's on next week's meeting agenda. But first we have to be sure there really *is* a problem. There's no use in causing a panic if it turns out we haven't got an epidemic, just a local pocket of morbidity that disappears with a single batch of mosquitoes. After all, *Anopheles* can't pass on parasites to larvae."

Melanie said, "Jim, tell me we're not going to sit on this very long. Not when lives could be at stake!"

"No, of course not. Not if lives really are at stake. But give it at least a few days of initial field work, Melanie. Don't cry wolf if all we've got is one cub dying from natural causes."

"If you really believe Senator Reading's death was an isolated 'natural cause,' then why is the FBI coming to tomorrow's meeting?"

"I don't know," Farlow said. "Maybe because Reading was a senator and a presidential candidate. We'll find out more tomorrow."

Melanie subsided. She had no choice, really. Yet.

The team began to plan the painstaking interviewing of medical personnel and next-of-kin. That was the first step in finding the patterns of who got infected, where, and how. An indispensable step, Melanie told herself. They needed the data to trace this thing to its source.

But, meanwhile, more people might die. Black people, mostly.

That was the trade-off.

F O U R

Nature does not proceed by leaps.
—Carolus Linnaeus, *Philosopha Botanica*, 1751

Cavanaugh sat in his office, filling out expense forms. This task always made him feel vaguely guilty. On the one hand, it was clearly necessary; agents needed reimbursement for legitimate expenses, and the Bureau needed a record of where and how it was spending its funds. Also, it gave Cavanaugh a sense of satisfaction to complete the neat rows of figures in his small, precise handwriting. On the other hand, this satisfaction was tainted because filling out expense vouchers didn't, after all, lead to the apprehension of any criminals. Every hour spent on paperwork was one hour less spent on real law enforcement.

"Anybody calls, I'll be out till tomorrow," Seton said.

Cavanaugh looked up from his forms. "Anywhere in particular?"

"Out developing informants for the naval complex," Seton said, and winked.

"Those informants sure take a lot of developing," Cavanaugh said evenly. "Why is that, Don?"

"Well, Bob—"

"Robert."

"It's like this. A lot of them aren't too bright. They need to be asked the same questions over and over before they remember the answers. And that takes a lot of time."

"I'll bet."

"Sign me out for six P.M.," Seton said. "That's how long it'll probably take." He winked again and lumbered out the door.

Cavanaugh was just as glad; the very sight of Seton was beginning to make his skin crawl. Seton was a canker sore, a smiling treacherous boil on the ass of law enforcement, a . . . The phone rang.

"Robert? Jerry Dunbar. Listen, I've got something for you."

Cavanaugh's hand tightened on the phone. Oh, God, at last . . . "What, Jerry?"

"Probably not anything real. But it's connected with that report you gave me last week on the high incidence of strokes among African-American patients at Dellridge and at Sailors and Soldiers."

"Connected how? Somebody willing to talk about civil rights infringements? Somebody at one of the hospitals?"

"It's not about civil rights infringements. It's . . . something else."

What else could a difference in the ways blacks and whites received medical care be except a civil rights infringement? Cavanaugh waited.

Dunbar said, "I'm not even sure it *is* connected. But they are. The CDC has formed a task force to investigate the stroke rate."

"The CDC?" Now Cavanaugh was more bewildered. The CDC kept statistics on various health problems, of course. Cavanaugh had even seen copies of its journal of record, the *Morbidity and Mortality Weekly Report,* lying around the house. Judy sometimes used it in writing her science articles. But what did a CDC task force have to do with the FBI?

Dunbar said, "The task force thinks the strokes might not be accidental. Or maybe the USPHS thinks that—you know, the Public Health Service. They made the actual contact with the Bureau. Apparently the USPHS thinks that there's a possibility the strokes could be the result of some sort of selective biological warfare toxin. Something that . . . Robert, are you still there?"

"Yes," Cavanaugh said. He forced himself to relax his grip on the phone. "What sort of toxin? Spread by whom?"

"Unknown. Frankly, I think the whole thing sounds wild-eyed. For one thing, they're dragging in malaria."

"Malaria?"

"Yes. And there's been no malaria in the United States since the end of World War II, except for the odd isolated case coming in from overseas. I looked it up. For another, they've got nothing hard. The CDC guy

I talked to even said that the most likely probability is that malaria mutated by itself. But the USPHS requested we supply FBI presence, and so that's you. Unless Don wants to take it. Is he there?"

"No. He's out with an important informant from Pax River."

"Good. He's doing an excellent job with the naval station. Tell him I said his last report was outstanding. So I guess this one's yours."

"Yes," Cavanaugh said.

"I'll give you Dr. Farlow's number. He and his team are set up at a motel on Route 5, the Weather Vane. Near Hughesville. Apparently they've been there almost a week already, doing whatever they do. They'll meet with you there."

"Okay. Good." Something to do. Something real. Maybe.

Dunbar said, "Nothing they told me sounds concrete or substantial, Robert. The whole thing sounded bogus."

"You never know," Cavanaugh said. "Anyway, I'll check it out."

"Do that. And, Robert—even when it's nothing, anything like this *is* sensitive. Anything racial. It has to stay quiet."

"I understand," Cavanaugh said. Which was the perfect excuse not to tell that moron Seton. At least, not yet. Not while he, Cavanaugh, at least had something to do.

Judy Kozinski was pretty good on the Internet, for someone who didn't understand it at all and didn't particularly want to. She drove the Net the way she drove her Toyota: for purposes of getting to her destination, and without looking under the hood.

She finished with the FTP and Gopher files on her paleontology article. Looking good, looking good. She closed the paleontology files and accessed the medical sites.

Many of these were test files: articles and updates on every medical condition imaginable. Judy read about strokes for an hour, until she was sure she understood enough to know what questions to ask. Everything that she thought Robert might also want to read, she sent to the printer.

Next, she accessed her medical lists. These were closed communications, limited to verified members, most of whom were doctors or medical researchers. Judy had used years of scientific contacts, both her own and those of her late husband, to get on the lists. They provided her with both valuable background and a forum to ask questions. In return, it was understood that she would write about nothing she read on the lists

without express permission from the poster. Much of the discussion concerned research-in-progress, which should not break prematurely to the
public.

Today she posted a short note:

J.K. HERE. ONCE MORE I NEED TO PICK ALL THIS COLLECTIVE
BRAINPOWER. CAN ANYBODY PUT ME ON TRACK OF
INFORMATION ABOUT BRAIN-CHEMISTRY DIFFERENCES,
POSSIBLY GENETIC, SHARED BY ASIAN INDIANS AND BLACKS
BUT NOT WHITES? I DON'T REALLY KNOW WHAT I'M LOOKING
FOR YET—NEUROTRANSMITTERS, FETAL WIRING, SUBMOLEC-
ULAR STRUCTURES—SO ANYTHING MIGHT HELP. IT SHOULD BE
CONNECTED TO ISCHEMIC CEREBRAL STROKES. THANKS. OF
COURSE, NO ATTRIBUTION WITHOUT YOUR WRITTEN
PERMISSION.

OH, ONE THING MORE—THE VENUE IS SOUTHERN MARYLAND,
SO I SUPPOSE ENVIRONMENTAL TRIGGERS FOR GENETIC
DIFFERENCES COULD BE A FACTOR, TOO. THANKS AGAIN.

Hours later, she checked back. Three list members had replied:

JUDY—YOU PROBABLY ALREADY KNOW THIS, AND IT'S
PROBABLY OFF TARGET ANYWAY, BUT YOU DID ASK. ASIAN
INDIANS, ALONG WITH SOME MEDITERRANEAN PEOPLES,
SOME GREEKS, AND MANY AFRICAN AND AFRICAN
DESCENDANTS, CAN CARRY SICKLE-CELL ANEMIA. THAT CAN
CAUSE STROKES IN ACUTE CRISES.—MSJ

TO: J.K.

RE: REQUEST FOR RACIALLY DIFFERENTIATED STROKE
INFORMATION.

NEW RESEARCH HAS EMERGED IN THIS AREA RE MALARIA,
SPECIFICALLY THE SUSCEPTIBILITY OF VARIOUS GENOMES TO
P. VIVAX, P. FALCIPARUM, AND *P. MALARIAE,* ESPECIALLY WITH
REGARD TO CHLOROQUINE AND CYCLOSPORINE RESISTANCE.

SEE MY ARTICLE IN LAST ISSUE OF *MALARIA AND TROPICAL DISEASE WEEKLY.* RICHARD KAPPEL, M.D., NIH

TO JK—YOU MENTIONED SOUTHERN MARYLAND. IS THIS CONNECTED TO THE RUMORS I HEARD ABOUT RACIALLY CONNECTED STROKE RATES AT DELLRIDGE HOSPITAL IN LA PLATA? SUPPOSEDLY, THE CDC IS THERE INVESTIGATING. HAS ANYBODY ELSE HEARD RUMORS? WOULD APPRECIATE FURTHER INFORMATION.

—K. MAHONEY, RICHMOND, VA

Judy frowned. The article in *Malaria and Tropical Disease Weekly* was probably too technical for her to follow; she wasn't an M.D. Still, she could probably get the gist of Kappel's research, and anyway Robert could take the article itself to the NIH for help if it turned out to be really useful. The Bureau used the National Institute of Health, conveniently nearby in Bethesda, for most medical questions.

And what was most important was that she be of help to Robert: to show him how necessary she was to him, how needed, how desirable to have around. Someone, in short, that he'd be a fool not to marry. She cooks, she makes a wonderful home, she's great in bed, she has a flourishing career of her own, *and* she's helpful to his career! What more could anybody want in a wife?

God, she hated herself when she got like this. It was degrading to feel she was constantly auditioning for the part of "wife."

On the other hand, she made herself admit, she *was*.

Judy accessed the Kappel article and began to read carefully.

The Weather Vane Motel was not the sort of place that Cavanaugh would have expected CDC hotshots to stay. Separate bungalows, all with slightly peeling paint, clustered around a pitted parking lot. On one side stood a 7-Eleven, on the other a gas station. But there was no doubt that the CDC was indeed there; behind the motel stood parked a huge trailer, windowless and padlocked, as secure as if it held the FBI's Ten Most Wanted. The trailer was unmarked, but Cavanaugh figured it didn't belong to the vending-machine retailer.

Inside Dr. Farlow's bungalow, however, Cavanaugh could see the Weather Vane's advantages. Evidently the CDC team liked to make itself at home. Pots and dishes littered the kitchen, along with shopping bags from the 7-Eleven. Computers and binders covered every surface. Two of the minuscule "dining tables" from different bungalows had been shoved together to make a meeting area. Coffee and beer were continuously available.

Cavanaugh approved. The setup was an efficient use of taxpayer money. It was also oddly cozy, except for a vague medicinal smell that hung over everything, including the team members.

There were five of them, two women and three men. Only one was black, the younger (and prettier, he couldn't help noticing) woman. Farlow made the introductions. Melanie Anderson smiled at him; the other three did not. So there was an internal split about Bureau presence. Cavanaugh was interested in learning why.

"Let's sit down while we wait for the others," Farlow said. "Coffee, Agent Cavanaugh?"

All the others had some. "Yes, please."

"The Health Service section of this team asked for somebody from the FBI to join us because we wanted to touch all the bases," Farlow said, reminding Cavanaugh of Jerry Dunbar, "even though we're not sure ourselves what's going on yet."

"Some of us are surer than others," Melanie Anderson said, sipping her coffee. Farlow didn't look annoyed. His staff must be used to airing their opinions without reserve. Cavanaugh revised his opinion. Farlow was not another Jerry Dunbar after all.

Farlow continued. "We also asked you here a half hour before the Health Service and USAMRIID—that's the United States Army Medical Research Institute for Infectious Diseases, as you probably know— so we could bring you up to speed. The other groups already have all our data. We've been briefing them right along. Now, Agent Cavanaugh—"

"Robert," Cavanaugh said.

"Fine. Robert, nearly a week ago the CDC received blood and tissue samples from the New York City hospital that treated the late Senator Malcolm Peter Reading. You probably read in the papers about how the senator collapsed with a stroke during a precampaign speech and died."

Senator Reading? New York City? This wasn't what Cavanaugh had expected to hear. Something tingled at the back of his neck.

"The tissue samples showed that the senator had contracted malaria. It also showed that he was positive for sickle-cell trait. Do you know what that is?"

Cavanaugh did, sort of. He nodded. Better to let Farlow talk and than ask questions later. The tingling grew stronger. It said to him, *This matters.* He sipped his coffee.

"The odd thing is that the malaria parasites were inside the blood cells with defective hemoglobin. Usually, those cells can't host *P. falciparum.* But Gary here—he's our lab man; that portable monstrosity outside is his—established the facts without a doubt. This mutant strain of malaria colonizes *only* sickle cells with any real success. It causes them to clot fast and hard near the brain, causing severe stroke. And sickling is a genetic trait, carried mostly by African Americans. That's why we called the FBI in. We thought—"

"*Some* of us thought," Susan Muscato said, not looking at anyone. Farlow plowed on.

"—that since the FBI has jurisdiction over civil rights and discrimination issues, the racial aspect could—"

Cavanaugh asked, "Can Indians from India get this thing, too?"

"Some can. There are segments of the Indian population who carry sickle-cell trait."

Bingo. Cavanaugh's mind raced. The strokes at Dellridge, at Memorial across the river in Virginia . . . but *malaria?* Nobody at the hospitals had mentioned malaria.

He said, "There's been an increased stroke rate right here in Maryland. At Dellridge Community Hospital—"

"Yes, we know," Susan Muscato said. Cavanaugh caught her disdain. "We've spent a week mapping the epidemiology curve. That's what we *do,* Agent Cavanaugh."

Farlow said, "Joe, bring it out."

The youngest CDC guy, Joe Krovetz, opened the door to the bedroom. Immediately the medicinal smell became sickening. Nobody else seemed to notice. Krovetz returned with a rolled up sheet of paper and an ice cube tray. Each of the tray's compartments, which were lined with some sort of paper, held a single dead mosquito.

"See," Krovetz said, unrolling the paper, "the official death count is now forty-six. The epidemiological curves show a recurrent peak, completely consistent with the breeding patterns of *Anopheles* . . ."

"Let me, Joe," Farlow said. "This has to look a little bewildering to someone without our passion for *P. falciparum*. Robert, why don't I start by explaining the life cycle of the mosquito that carries malaria in the eastern United States: *Anopheles quadrimaculatus*."

Cavanaugh blurted, "I thought malaria had been wiped out in the United States."

Susan Muscato said, more forcibly than necessary, "Diseases are reintroduced to geographical areas all the time. And they're virulent because the population has lost all resistance."

Melanie Anderson said, "Or they're virulent because somebody made them that way." The two women glared at each other.

"Made them that way." As in . . . what? Genetic engineering. Suddenly Cavanaugh realized why he had been called. A biological weapon, targeted toward blacks—mostly, anyway—although so far they'd shown him no hard evidence of that.

If this new malaria really was being used as a terrorist weapon, the case would be transferred to Counterintelligence.

No, it would *not*. At least, not until it had to. Until Cavanaugh was sure. From the way Drs. Muscato and Anderson were glaring at each other, not even the CDC team could agree that this malaria was some sort of terrorist bioweapon. Until they did, the case was Cavanaugh's. He shoved away his coffee and picked up his pen.

"Let's start where you suggested, Dr. Farlow. With the mosquito, Anna Follies."

"Anopheles," Susan Muscato corrected, lips tightened.

Farlow said, "Okay. All the anopheline mosquitoes have a rather improbable life cycle. Half of their life is sexual and that occurs inside the mosquito. The other half, the asexual half, occurs inside a vertebrate host, typically a bird or mammal. So starting with a mosquito . . ."

Cavanaugh began sketching.

Ten minutes later, all five members of the CDC team were looking at him doubtfully. Evidently some of his questions had been ridiculous. But it didn't matter. Cavanaugh had a drawing of malaria's life cycle:

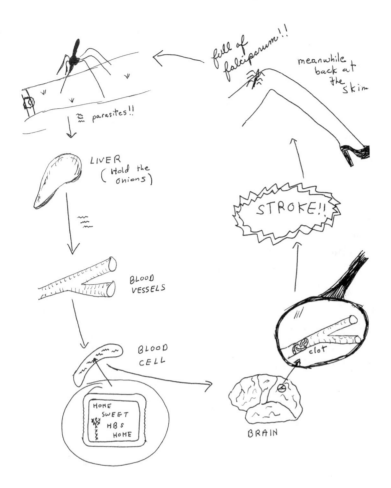

Cavanaugh said, "And you think all this is going on in southern Maryland . . . ?"

"See this graph?" Krovetz said, unrolling another paper. "It plots the stroke rate in the infected three-county area for the last six months. The red line is African Americans, the blue line is whites. You can see that the increase in strokes among blacks starts the second week in May. Now look at this map. From the geographical pattern of the spread, the epidemic seems to have originated *here* and spread out in rough circles. That's consistent with an abrupt introduction of the disease into the area."

Cavanaugh stared at *here.* It was a small circle drawn around nothing in Charles County, a mile or so from the town of Newburg, not too far from the Potomac River.

He said, "You found that out by talking to people . . . to the relatives of the stroke victims . . . But what about Senator Reading? He died in Manhattan, and he was the senator from New Jersey."

"Pennsylvania," Farlow said. "But he had attended a family wedding in the town of Bel Alton just two weeks before his death. The timing is exactly right for *Plasmodium reading* infection. And it was an outdoor wedding, in somebody's garden."

"*Plasmodium reading.*" They had already named the disease, while Cavanaugh still struggled to understand the basics. "So you went to this place near Newburg—"

"The epicenter," Muscato said impatiently.

"—and collected the mosquitoes in that ice cube tray—"

"Among others," Farlow said. "Gary has done nothing but dissect, examine, and run tests on mosquitoes for five days and nights. They're the vector, all right."

Cavanaugh studied his drawing. Something wasn't right, but he couldn't quite put his finger on it. The others looked at him doubtfully, except for Dr. Muscato, who gazed with open disdain.

"Wait," Cavanaugh said. "Wait . . ."

They waited. As the seconds dragged by, Cavanaugh realized that if he couldn't formulate his question, he was going to look like an ass. A bigger ass. Carefully he followed the steps in his drawing: from mosquito to person, who was killed, to . . . He had it.

"If the person dies before the . . . the parasite things can get sucked up into another mosquito, how does the disease spread around in your concentric circles?"

Farlow said, "We asked that question, too. And the answer is: carriers with immunity. We took blood samples from guests at the Reading wedding who do not have sickle-cell trait. Both white and black people. Twenty-one percent were carriers, which is more than enough to reinfect *A. quadrimaculatus* and keep the epidemic going."

Cavanaugh thought of the mosquitoes on his back deck, arrogantly ignoring Judy's bug zapper. He said, "So anybody—like, say, me—could walk around being a carrier for malaria reading without even knowing it."

"Yes," said Gary Pershing, the lab man. "But you're in no personal danger, you know. We found no case of anyone with normal hemoglobin who reported anything more than a very minor flulike illness."

Cavanaugh digested this. "So you know where the epidemic started, and when. And you know how it keeps going, even though it kills its real victims. But you don't know where it came from in the first place."

"It mutated," Susan Muscato said.

"It was introduced by accident via a carrier with natural immunity himself, probably an immigrant or overseas traveler, that we haven't traced yet," Gary Pershing said.

"It was genetically engineered," Melanie Anderson said, glaring at the other two. "The mutations are too extensive and too coincidental to have happened by chance. And if it had been introduced accidentally from somewhere else in the world, the CDC would have heard of it being somewhere else in the world. Which we haven't."

"Yet," Muscato said.

Melanie Anderson exploded. "You just don't want to admit that this thing is a genocide in the making! You told me to be patient, Jim, and I have been. But now we have a week's worth of clear data, and the numbers point to at least a dozen breeding pairs of infected mosquitoes. Not just one mutated female—*a dozen breeding pairs at once.* That doesn't happen by coincidence!"

Farlow said sternly, "The data isn't that unambiguous, Melanie, and you know it. If you up the larval mortality rate by only—"

"There's no reason to up it by anything! Jim, the numbers are there. Why won't you see them? It's the same way all the so-called 'good Germans' wouldn't admit that Auschwitz was going on!"

"I resent that!" Gary Pershing said.

"And I more than resent it," Susan Muscato said. Her face had gone rigid. "My maiden name was Horowitz."

"That's *enough*," Farlow said.

There was a painful silence.

"All right, I'm sorry," Melanie Anderson said. "I overspoke. But it *is* a deliberate biological weapon targeting African Americans. The sooner we admit that, the sooner we can warn people and save lives."

Farlow said reprovingly, "We're all in agreement about that. Even without knowing where this thing originated, we can still create an action plan. That's why the Health Service and USAMRIID will be here in five minutes. And if there *is* criminal intent, the FBI will track it down."

They all looked at Cavanaugh, who now knew why he'd been summoned. Somebody somewhere—Health Service or CDC or the U.S. Army—wanted their ass covered just in case this disease *was* a bioweapon aimed at blacks. The political implications of that were terrifying. Whoever had called in the Bureau wanted to be able to say they'd turned the problem over to the proper law-enforcement authorities early on in the epidemic.

It didn't seem the right moment to say that Jerry Dunbar had a low opinion of "a bunch of paranoid bug hunters." Besides, Cavanaugh agreed with the fiery Melanie Anderson. There was something here. He could smell it.

He said, "How many African Americans have this sickle-cell thing?"

"About one in twelve," Dr. Anderson said. "Over two and a half million."

Two and a half million.

"Yeah," she said, watching his face. "That many."

Cavanaugh looked at the ice cube tray of dead mosquitoes. He saw now that each compartment had a detailed tag stating where and when the insect had been captured. He thought of the cloud of mosquitoes around Judy's bug zapper, above the channel-clearing machine on the Potomac, in the parks where kids played in the hot, heavy twilights . . .

He said, "Suppose for a minute, for the sake of argument, that the parasites are genetically engineered and then put into the mosquitoes. How hard is that to do? What kinds of equipment and talent do you need to do it?"

Farlow said, "A lot of talent. But not much equipment, relatively speaking. That's the thing about a genetic-engineering lab—it's not like producing a terrorist atomic bomb. Everything you need is easily available from any scientific supply house, and any researcher at any private firm can buy samples from blood libraries."

"So we're not looking at a big fancy lab?"

"Hell," Farlow said, "you could put the lab in a good-sized basement."

A good-sized basement. Jesus J. Edgar Hoover Christ.

Farlow said, "How will the FBI handle this, Agent Cavanaugh? On our end, we'll keep mapping the epidemic and searching for the missing alternate host. But what will your people do?"

Good question, Cavanaugh thought. The FBI was a covert investigative operation, and like all covert operations, it valued secrecy. The last thing the Bureau usually did was make public announcements of public problems, especially if it couldn't solve them. *"Confusing the leads,"* it was called. *"Compromising the investigation."* But in this case, a public announcement might be the only thing that would save lives.

"Well?" Melanie Anderson said pointedly. She stared right at him.

"In cases of public danger, the FBI can issue a Terrorist Warning Advisory," Cavanaugh said slowly. "But of course that has to come from Headquarters. And until it does, especially in a situation like this, it's important not to cause a panic, or to encourage false credit claims by various hate groups." Jesus, they'd be crawling out of the woodwork. "So until Headquarters has a chance to work on this a little, I'm going to ask you to discuss it with no one outside the CDC."

Melanie Anderson said, "While more people die! No!"

Farlow said, "You don't understand, Agent Cavanaugh. That part isn't up to us. The CDC has a mandate to control disease. But on this scale, only the army has the actual capability to do it. When USAMRIID arrives, we'll get—here they are now."

Farlow got up to answer the door. But Cavanaugh didn't need him to finish his sentence. Whatever Farlow thought he'd get when the army arrived, Cavanaugh knew what the CDC was really going to get.

A turf war.

They came in like an invasion, five of them, all in full uniform, shoulders straight and back. Next to them the CDC team, all but Farlow in jeans and T-shirts, looked like Sunday picnickers. The scientists rose in a ragged body, nodding at introductions. Cavanaugh took careful note of each name in order to decide if the delegation was, or only looked, impressive. How seriously was the army taking *Plasmodium reading?* By their ranks and titles shall ye know them.

Lt. Col. Matthew Sanchez, M.D., Chief of Disease Assessment for USAMRIID.

Maj. David Seligman, M.D., malariologist.

Capt. Anne Delaney, M.D., genetic microbiologist.

Capt. Neil Hosner, attorney for the United States Army.

Col. Wayne Colborne, M.D., commander of USAMRIID, who explained that he would be briefing both Major General Selby, the head of the Army Medical Research and Development Command, to which

USAMRIID reported, and the commander of Fort Detrick itself, General Campbell.

The army was taking *Plasmodium reading* very seriously.

Trailing behind the brass was a small man with the expression of a nervous rabbit. He was introduced, belatedly, as the representative from the Charles County Department of Health, Dr. Fred Warfield. Cavanaugh thought that never had he seen anyone less suitably named, and resisted the urge to sketch Warfield.

"We've received all your data, Dr. Farlow," said Colonel Sanchez, "and we have some suggestions on how to proceed. The first thing—"

"—is to bring your team up to date," Farlow said smoothly. Cavanaugh heard the opening guns of the turf war. "We have new data since yesterday. Gary?"

Dr. Pershing went into a long technical explanation that Cavanaugh couldn't follow. Colonels Sanchez and Colborne sat, expressionless. But the two noncommanders' eyes gleamed with interest in whatever Pershing was explaining.

Score one for the CDC.

When Pershing had finished, Colonel Sanchez said quickly, "Thank you, Doctor. Now let me clarify our position." He glanced respectfully at Colonel Colborne, who evidently had cast himself as final arbiter, above the interim fray. "USAMRIID's core mission, as you know, is to devise ways to protect American soldiers against infectious diseases and bioweaponry. Your data suggest to the army that *P. reading* may well be one or both of those things. The army has been well aware since 1950 that a biowarfare incident might come disguised as a spontaneous event, and that American troops both here and on foreign soil could be vulnerable to attack in this manner. Therefore, USAMRIID is very grateful to the CDC for bringing *P. reading* to the army's attention."

In other words, *We'll take it from here.* Score one for the army.

Farlow said pleasantly, "We're glad to have your assistance, of course, especially with the manpower needed to protect the public. Which, I'm sure we're agreed, is the first concern at this point, since all the victims thus far have been civilians."

CDC-2, Army-1.

Sanchez nodded. "Yes. In fact, we took the liberty of drawing up a list of priorities. David?"

The army malariologist handed around photocopied sheets. The score was now even. Cavanaugh skimmed the priorities:

1. Safety of the civilian population
2. Containment and destruction of the disease vector, *A. quadrimaculatus*
3. Identification and arrest of person(s) responsible for vector infection, if applicable
4. Advance of scientific and medical knowledge

Farlow said, "Certainly the army is better suited to priority two than we are. I suggest that control of *Anopheles* rest entirely with you, although of course you'll have to work with the EPA on what pesticides they'll allow."

The lawyer looked up sharply from his note taking. Cavanaugh knew that Colonel Sanchez—not to mention Colonel Colborne—wouldn't much like the idea that the U.S. military reported to the Environmental Protection Agency. Farlow continued blandly on.

"We do have some thoughts on containment, however. Melanie?"

Melanie smiled at the army. Well, why not, Cavanaugh thought—they were taking bioweapon theories a lot more seriously than the CDC had. She might as well have been on their side. Had Farlow taken that into account?

"I know that USAMRIID already knows everything I'm going to say," Melanie said graciously, "but please bear with me while I repeat it because I don't think our FBI representative knows this material. Medicine isn't his field. He's responsible for our priority three."

Everyone looked at Cavanaugh, the ignoramus who, single-handedly, was supposed to carry out priority three. Which, now that he thought about it, was priority one from his point of view. He resisted the temptation to doodle on the priority list.

Melanie continued. "Malaria transmission, Robert, is really sensitive to the numbers. Numbers of mosquitoes. Size of the susceptible population. Numbers of gametocytes in the blood of carriers, which determines the number of sporozoites in the mosquito saliva to reinfect people. Even the number of days that the temperature and humidity are favorable for mosquito breeding. There are equations to show how even small changes in the numbers affect the whole course of the epidemic. The equations were developed decades ago, by Dr. George MacDonald.

"We've run the numbers, and I'm sure USAMRIID has, too. In temperate climates it's possible to tip the equation by key containment actions. In the tropics it's not, because both *Anopheles* and *Plasmodium* flourish so well that they just overwhelm any changes you make. Also, of course, places like Africa and the Philippines are too poor to afford the necessary containment resources. But Maryland isn't tropical and the U.S. government isn't poor. Containing this epidemic should be doable—once we actually start *doing* it."

The last was a jab at Farlow. Cavanaugh wondered if he knew he had a mole on his side. Of course he did.

Colonel Sanchez beamed at her. "I'm glad to hear we're in agreement, Dr. Anderson. And, of course, the closeness of Fort Detrick to the pockets of morbidity make USAMRIID the natural choice to direct and carry out the operation."

"Carry out, certainly," Farlow said, the emphasis slight but unmistakable.

Uh-oh, Cavanaugh thought. *Here it comes.* Joe Krovetz, sitting next to Cavanaugh, imperceptibly moved his notepad closer to Cavanaugh. On the bottom Krovetz had written "HISTORY OF FEUD THERE. EBOLA." Cavanaugh nodded, even though it took him a moment to remember that Ebola was another disease that the CDC and USAMRIID had cooperated on containing, in Africa.

Sanchez said stiffly, "The army will direct any operation it carries out."

Farlow said, "And for the civilian population, so will the CDC."

A tense silence fell. Into it the county health official, whom Cavanaugh had forgotten was at the table, said timidly, "Well, then, that's settled."

Everyone stared at him.

"And, of course," he went on in his high, squeaky voice, "the County Department of Health and the U.S. Public Health Service will be happy to help both of you any way we can. If, uh, you need us. Helping with your priority two, Colonel, and your priority four, Dr. Farlow, and, uh, any way you split up the actions for priority one. Or we could take any actions not on either of your priority lists. If, uh, you want us to, of course. If, uh, that."

Warfield cleared his throat. Cavanaugh hid his grin. The little bureaucrat had just settled the turf war by dividing up the turf, and apparently he didn't realize he'd even done it.

"And, uh, one more thing, if you don't think it's, uh, presumptuous. The USPHS is willing—I took the liberty of talking to them—of assigning to their budget center the expense of printing up the flyers. Flyers to give to the public about what to do. If, uh, you want flyers. Won't you? It's up to you, of course, but I, uh, thought they'd be good to supplement the radio and TV public announcements. That, uh, would be our responsibility. With, uh, your consent, of course."

"Assign to their budget center." Cavanaugh didn't know what that meant to the CDC or the army, but he sure the hell knew what it meant to the FBI. It meant that the responsible budget center assumed the blame for screwups. Especially if its name headed anything like public announcements and flyers.

Sanchez and Farlow looked thoughtful. The lawyer, Captain Hosner, pushed a note toward Sanchez. Then Colonel Colborne, the top brass present, spoke for the first time. "Perhaps we should move on to the specifics of this operation." Farlow and Sanchez nodded agreement, and the jurisdiction struggle was suddenly ended. Peace with honor.

Only not quite.

Farlow said, "As part of our priority, the CDC—with the assistance of the Health Service—can assume responsibility for blood testing, both for *P. reading* and for sickle-cell trait. Our thinking is—"

"Excuse me," Melanie Anderson said. "Blood testing for sickle-cell trait?"

Every pair of eyes in the room turned to her, including Cavanaugh's. Until now, no one but the heads had spoken without being invited. From the way that Farlow's eyes narrowed, Cavanaugh was pretty sure the CDC chief wasn't welcoming interruption by one of his own staff.

Melanie wasn't fazed. "Maybe we want to think again about sickle-cell testing—in light of what happened in the seventies." She jerked around to face Cavanaugh, startling him. "Let me give you background here, Robert. In the early 1970's the government funded a screening program to identify all carriers of the sickle-cell gene. The idea was to get help early to people who were at risk for sickle-cell anemia. But no real distinction was made between having sickle-cell trait, which is just one gene, and being at real risk for having a full-blown sickle-cell crisis, which takes two genes."

Cavanaugh nodded. Again she was using him as a pretext to orate about what everyone else in the room already knew. It made him look dumb, although that wasn't her goal. But there wasn't anything he could do about it.

"Because the distinction between one sickle-cell gene and two wasn't made clear, a whole lot of black people who only had the trait thought they had a real disease. You wouldn't believe the things that started happening, Robert. Some insurance companies called sickle-cell trait a 'preexisting condition' and denied health insurance. Some airlines wouldn't hire pilots with the trait. The U.S. Air Force Academy rejected black applicants with the trait. And some scientists actually went on national TV and said that black carriers of the trait should never breed, for the good of public health."

"Melanie," Farlow said tightly, "no one is suggesting—"

"I know, I know," Melanie said, holding up her hands and smiling. Cavanaugh thought she was trying to look conciliatory. It was not a success. "But it did happen. And we wouldn't want it to happen again."

Sanchez said to Farlow, "Are you proposing to leave blood tests for sickle-cell trait out of priority one?"

"No," Farlow said. "But confidentiality issues should be considered as well."

"Certainly," Sanchez said, but he offered no details. Clearly this problem was now Farlow's. Cavanaugh was glad he was not in Melanie's place.

The rest of the meeting went more smoothly. After two hours of discussion, including minor contributions from the lawyer and Warfield, a plan was in place.

The Public Health Service would pass out an antimalarial preventive called mefloquine to every doctor, health clinic, hospital, and nurse practitioner in Maryland and Virginia. They would also collect blood samples for voluntary, confidential screening.

The CDC would create multiple sets of guidelines in easy-to-understand language: What to do if you're positive for sickle-cell trait. What to do if you've been bitten recently by a mosquito. What to do if someone nearby has a stroke. Where to get free head nets and mosquito netting dipped in permethrin, a mosquito repellent harmless to people. Which insecticides were safe to use around your house and children, and which were not.

USAMRIID would create guidelines in simple language about what people should do to discourage mosquitoes from breeding near their houses: Tip out birdbaths. Bury old tires. Fill in tree holes and shallow depressions in the ground. Clean out gutters. Destroy shady vegetation at the edges of ponds. Cover cisterns and water barrels. Drain kids' wading pools every night.

The Public Health Service would print and distribute all guidelines in malls, parking lots, offices, summer schools, public events—everywhere possible. They would also arrange for TV and radio versions.

USAMRIID would use the soldiers based at Fort Detrick, the 110th Battalion, to check that the civilian populations were carrying out domestic guidelines. ("Whoa," Melanie murmured on the other side of Cavanaugh from Krovetz, "police state toehold." But she didn't say it aloud.)

USAMRIID would carry out mosquito-destruction tactics in Saint Mary's, Charles, and King George Counties.

The CDC would continue to research *P. reading,* sharing all data with USAMRIID.

"And with the FBI," Cavanaugh said firmly, his first contribution of the day. "Anything we know about how this parasite might have been created could be a lead to its creator." Everyone nodded except Susan Muscato, who evidently still thought that the creator was the Creator. Well, maybe she was right. Maybe it *was* a spontaneous mutation.

Maybe.

Farlow said, "Dr. Krovetz will be available to you after the meeting, Agent Cavanaugh, to answer any questions you might have."

Their number is legion, Cavanaugh thought. What equipment was necessary for genetic engineering? Where was it usually purchased? What were the regulations? How was equipment tracked? What scientific credentials were required to work on this level? If Cavanaugh were going to convince anyone—including himself—that malaria reading really was a bioweapon, he needed tangible evidence: paper trails, physical objects, photographs.

When the meeting broke up, Cavanaugh asked Joe Krovetz, "Doctor, why aren't you planning to vaccinate people against this thing?"

"No vaccine," Krovetz said. "The disease is too new. And anyway, even normal malaria vaccines haven't been much of a success."

"Oh," Cavanaugh said, trying to make the small syllable sound intelligent. "And what is this new drug that the colonel said Fort Detrick could supply to hospitals and doctors?"

"It's a variation of chloroquine. Do you know what chloroquine is?"

Cavanaugh shook his head. He watched the room empty. The army lawyer was talking steadily to Colonel Sanchez. Dr. Farlow smiled at everyone. And even the rabbity Fred Warfield chatted with Anne Delaney, the microbiologist, without stammering or twitching. Come to think of it, Warfield—

"Do you want to hear this or not?" Krovetz said, with a directness Cavanaugh hadn't expected.

"Yes, I do."

"Well, many strains of malaria around the world have become immune to chloroquine, the standard treatment. So pharmaceutical firms constantly try to come up with new ones. USAMRIID often contracts out to them. One of them, Markham-Jay Labs in Virginia, has apparently just finished beta testing a good one."

"How come you're scowling about that?"

"They didn't offer it to *us*," Krovetz said. "We run malaria teams through Africa and Asia all the time, you know."

Cavanaugh didn't know. But it wasn't relevant to his concerns either. Instead he said, "Look at Dr. Warfield. It's like he's a different person now. Confident. And I don't think he even knows he settled your potential turf war."

Krovetz grinned. "He knows."

"He does?"

"We were at a summer conference together once. Fred knew exactly what he was doing and how to do it."

So Warfield had skillfully directed events, without anyone important realizing it. The man would have made a good FBI agent.

Although nothing Warfield had done—or anyone else at the meeting—had helped Cavanaugh. He now knew a lot about mosquito control, but no more about identifying, finding, or capturing whoever had genetically altered malaria to kill blacks.

If anyone even had. There was no evidence. There were no leads. And, so far at least, there was no public outcry. The public didn't even realize that one segment of the population was dying at anything more than the usual rate. But when they did . . .

The CDC and USAMRIID were right. Everything depended on how the public was told and advised about *P. reading*. With the right handling, you had responsible health agencies doing everything they could to help people survive an inexplicable disease. With the wrong handling, you had a government sitting for two weeks on critical information while citizens died. Farlow was right to restrain Melanie and her explosive pronouncements. Farlow knew what he was doing. That's why he was chief.

Comfortable with this affirmation of the chain of command, Cavanaugh began his grilling of Dr. Krovetz. He took careful notes. When he got back to Leonardtown, he would have to write a report for Dunbar, about a crime that may or may not have been committed by perps who might or might not exist on a public that might or might not believe there was a transgression.

It was going to have to be a hell of a report.

INTERIM

The Saint Mary's County tour bus was always full for the nine o'clock run, the only one that featured dinner at historic Sotterley Plantation, following afternoon drinks at historic inns. Casper Hunt watched the chattering tourists climb aboard his bus. He could already pick out the ones who would be bored. The ones who would ask dumb questions. The ones who would whisper to each other, "Is that man black, Joanie, or isn't he, hard to tell with that light brown color . . ." The ones who would drink too much at the King's Arms, Farthing's Ordinary, and Sotterley.

Not that Casper minded that, or any of it. He'd been driving the tour bus for five years now. Before that he'd spent three decades harvesting oysters off the barrier islands of South Carolina, till the oyster beds were destroyed by the pollution from the Savannah River. The river was supposed to be cleaned up now, Casper had heard. He didn't know for sure, and he wasn't about to find out. Oysters had been a hard life, backbreaking and dangerous and dirt-poor. Driving a tour bus around southern Maryland was about a thousand times easier, and the tips were pretty good. Especially from the drunks.

"Welcome aboard, ladies 'n' gen'lemun," Casper said in his soft North Carolina accent, which he always exaggerated when tour driving. Customers, mostly Yankees, liked that. "Today we're goin' to see beautiful Saint Mary's County, including historic Saint Mary's City, the Civil War prison at Fort Lincoln, and Sotterley Plantation. My name is Casper, and I'm you-all's guide today. I used to harvest shellfish, so I guess I can keep track of you-all."

It always got a laugh. Casper started the bus. A few minutes later he swung out into heavy traffic on Route 235, nimbly dodging the semis and commercial vans.

"Our first stop this mawnin' will be Fort Lincoln, in Point Lookout State Park. The park occupies a one-thousand-thirty-seven-acre site at the come-together of the Potomac River and Chesapeake Bay. The fort was built of raw earth by prisoners of . . ."

Pain shot through his head.

Casper gasped and tried to hold the wheel. The pain came again and suddenly he couldn't see. *Everythin' go dark . . . oh, sweet Jesus Christ, keep me on the river . . .* the bus swung sideways into traffic.

Passengers screamed. Casper heard them, but only dimly. A third bolt of pain screwed through his head, riveting him to darkness. He slumped over onto the steering wheel.

The tour bus slammed into an oncoming 18-wheeler. Both vehicles burst into flame. But by that time, Casper Hunt was already dead.

F I V E

Journalists want blood, death, and screaming people.
—Dr. Pierre Rollin, epidemiologist, 1995

The Web site began with the usual legal disclaimer, this time in bright red capital letters:

STROKEHELP. COM IS DESIGNED FOR EDUCATIONAL PURPOSES
ONLY. THIS INFORMATION IS NOT INTENDED TO SUBSTITUTE
FOR INFORMED MEDICAL ADVICE. YOU SHOULD NOT USE THIS
INFORMATION TO DIAGNOSE OR TREAT A STROKE WITHOUT
CONSULTING WITH A QUALIFIED PHYSICIAN. STROKEHELP
DOES NOT ENDORSE ANY OF THE TREATMENTS, MEDICATIONS,
OR PRODUCTS DISCUSSED HEREIN.

Libby Turner, seated at her desk in the *Baltimore Sun* newsroom, would have snorted if she hadn't been so upset. She'd been with the paper for seventeen years, starting as a lowly police reporter and moving steadily up. Nobody had to tell her the legal limits of the written word, whether paper or electronic.

But she was too upset to feel superior. Her hands, with their short and unpolished nails, trembled on the keyboard. She hated that. She, Libby Turner, never trembled. But, then, she'd never before had a mother with a stroke, either.

Brigit Ryan Turner had collapsed a week ago, alone in her apartment in the Elmcrest Senior Citizens' Home. She hadn't been found for three and a half hours. In that time of oxygen deprivation, her left side had become paralyzed, speech had been severely impaired, and other damage may or may not have occurred. "All we can do is wait and see," said the doctors, which came nowhere near to satisfying Libby Turner. Libby loved her mother, even though they'd fought like pit bulls ever since Libby had been thirteen. More to the point, when Brigit Turner was finally released from the hospital, it was Libby, her only child, who would be responsible for her. Libby wanted as much information as possible on what that might mean.

Only her fucking fingers wouldn't stop trembling!

She mis-hit two more keys, got a URL ERROR, and backtracked. She had to calm down, had to concentrate, had to follow the hyperlinks of information till something proved useful. . . .

"You okay?" her managing editor asked, coming from behind and putting his hands on her shoulders. They were old friends.

"Go away, Alec," Libby said distinctly. "Go away now."

"I will," Alec said. "But meanwhile, here're a few other databases to check. Got them for you from a doctor friend."

Alec went. Libby knew he would get someone else to cover whatever story she couldn't concentrate on today. He was good that way.

Two hours later, her fingers still trembled. But she'd learned a lot about her mother's condition, following the links from one Web site to another. Libby's strength as a reporter had always been thoroughness. She began on the first of the two sites Alec had given her, which seemed to be a private newsgroup for health-care professionals.

J.K. HERE. ONCE MORE I NEED TO PICK ALL THIS COLLECTIVE BRAINPOWER. CAN ANYBODY PUT ME ON TRACK OF INFORMATION ABOUT BRAIN CHEMISTRY DIFFERENCES, POSSIBLY GENETIC, SHARED BY ASIAN INDIANS AND BLACKS BUT NOT WHITES? I DON'T REALLY KNOW WHAT I'M LOOKING FOR YET—NEUROTRANSMITTERS, FETAL WIRING, SUBMOLEC- ULAR STRUCTURES—SO ANYTHING MIGHT HELP. IT SHOULD BE CONNECTED TO ISCHEMIC CEREBRAL STROKES. THANKS. OF COURSE, NO ATTRIBUTION WITHOUT YOUR WRITTEN PERMISSION.

OH, ONE THING MORE—THE VENUE IS SOUTHERN MARYLAND, SO I SUPPOSE ENVIRONMENTAL TRIGGERS FOR GENETIC DIFFERENCES COULD BE A FACTOR, TOO. THANKS AGAIN.

JUDY—YOU PROBABLY ALREADY KNOW THIS, AND IT'S PROBABLY OFF TARGET ANYWAY, BUT YOU DID ASK. ASIAN INDIANS, ALONG WITH SOME MEDITERRANEAN PEOPLES, SOME GREEKS, AND MANY AFRICAN AND AFRICAN DESCENDANTS, CAN CARRY SICKLE-CELL ANEMIA. THAT CAN CAUSE STROKES IN ACUTE CRISES.—MSJ

TO: J.K.

RE: REQUEST FOR RACIALLY DIFFERENTIATED STROKE INFORMATION.

NEW RESEARCH HAS EMERGED IN THIS AREA RE MALARIA, SPECIFICALLY THE SUSCEPTIBILITY OF VARIOUS GENOMES TO *P. VIVAX, P. FALCIPARUM,* AND *P. MALARIAE,* ESPECIALLY WITH REGARD TO CHLOROQUINE AND CYCLOSPORINE RESISTANCE. SEE MY ARTICLE IN LAST ISSUE OF *MALARIA AND TROPICAL DISEASE WEEKLY.* RICHARD KAPPEL, M.D., NIH

TO JK—YOU MENTIONED SOUTHERN MARYLAND. IS THIS CONNECTED TO THE RUMORS I HEARD ABOUT RACIALLY CONNECTED STROKE RATES AT DELLRIDGE HOSPITAL IN LA PLATA? SUPPOSEDLY, THE CDC IS THERE INVESTIGATING. HAS ANYBODY ELSE HEARD RUMORS? WOULD APPRECIATE FURTHER INFORMATION.

—K. MAHONEY, RICHMOND, VA

Libby's fingers stopped trembling.

Not because anything she'd read applied to her mother, a white Irish harridan who did not have sickle-cell trait. Libby's fingers steadied because she was looking at a story.

So that was what she needed. A big story. A flashy dangerous important story: FEDS INVESTIGATE POORER STROKE CARE FOR BLACKS AT MARYLAND HOSPITAL. Work. To steady herself, both for her own sake and her mother's. And this was—or could be—a story about something that already consumed her. She always did her best, most thorough work when she really cared about the topic. It was as if this story was *meant* for her.

Libby Turner strode toward the *Baltimore Sun* elevator that would take her to the parking garage, and southern Maryland.

I'm sorry, Robert. I'm not about to commit manpower to a crime that a bunch of scientists can't even agree is happening. The CDC is on the medical aspects of the malaria, and that's all that actually exists at this point. What would our agents *do?* Question the next-of-kin about where these stroke victims have been that mosquitoes might also have been? The CDC is already doing that. I think we need to wait and see."

Cavanaugh said, "But—"

"Look," Jerry Dunbar said, "we've been discussing this for fifteen minutes. I don't have fifteen more today."

They sat in Dunbar's Baltimore office, Dunbar behind his desk and Cavanaugh in a black, metal-armed chair that looked like a reject from the waiting room. Cavanaugh felt a stab of nostalgia for his previous boss, the toe-tapping, arm-twitching ex-cop, Marty Felders. Felders had been easy to argue with. Felders had flourished on argument, sucking it into his wiry frame like water into a quivering aspen. Dunbar, the Book Man, treated argument as if it were just one step away from insubordination. He made Cavanaugh feel as if there were a bulletproof shield between them.

Nonetheless, he couldn't let it go that easily. "Jerry, if this *is* a sophisticated terrorist weapon, the sooner we start investigating before they know we're doing it, the fresher the leads will be. We don't want to find ourselves in the position of having some subversive group suddenly claim credit for this and we haven't even looked seriously at them. I could—"

"You could do exactly what you're supposed to be doing anyway," Dunbar said harshly, "which is to keep tabs on the hate groups in your jurisdiction. You don't—or shouldn't—need additional manpower to do that."

"No," Cavanaugh said, "not ordinarily. But in this case, I think we should at least inform Headquarters that—"

Dunbar got up and walked out of the room.

Cavanaugh, left sitting there, got a grip on his own temper. All right, he *had* said the same thing over and over—how many times? At least six. Dunbar had heard him out five of those times. But Felders wouldn't have cut short debate like that. Felders would have . . . but Cavanaugh didn't work for Felders any more.

Maybe Dunbar would come back in and let Cavanaugh say it all again.

While he waited, he took out his notepad and doodled. He drew a bunch of upright, hair-on-end people standing close together on a long paddle and labeled it "GODZILLA'S TOOTHBRUSH." He drew a flowering tree with branches connected by sections of L-shaped pipes: "A NORTH AMERICAN PLUMBER PLANT IN BLOOM." Dunbar did not reappear.

Eventually his secretary stuck her head in the door. "Agent Cavanaugh? You have a call on line 3."

Cavanaugh picked up the phone. Who knew he was here? Only Seton. Unless Judy had tracked him down, or Jim Farlow.

"Robert? This is Marcy."

His ex-wife. He hadn't seen her since the final divorce proceeding over a year ago. She'd already been living with her boss, the wunderkind CEO, and had barely glanced at him.

"Robert? Are you there?"

"How did you know where to find me?" he asked, because he had to say something.

"I didn't," she said. He'd forgotten how low-pitched her voice was, a husky contralto. "I called your old office, and they said you'd moved to southern Maryland, and when I called that number your partner said you were here."

"He's not my partner," Robert said.

"Whatever. Robert . . . I'm calling to ask a favor."

That was very Marcy. Leave him, divorce him, have no communication for a year, then call out of the blue to ask for something, without even a "please." Cavanaugh was about to hang up, just as soon as he found the perfect cutting retort.

"Please," Marcy said, in a different tone.

"What is it?"

"I can't tell you on the phone; I have to show you. Could you come over sometime today?"

To the expensive Georgetown townhouse she shared with the successful CEO? Not a chance in hell.

"I've moved," Marcy said quickly. "To a smaller place east of Washington. In Hyattsville. It's on your way home, I think. And I'm in a little trouble."

"All right," Robert said. If she was really in trouble . . . did she know that would be the one thing he wouldn't refuse? Of course she did. "I'll come by about six-thirty. What's the address?"

The apartment might be Marcy's idea of "a smaller place," but it wasn't Robert's. Washington's toniest suburbs lay north of the city. However, Marcy had managed to find the most expensive housing of a nonexpensive area. Marble foyer, carved wooden double doors leading to the living room, a mix of their old Federalist furniture and some new, Oriental-looking stuff. Thick velvet curtains blocked traffic sounds.

"Hello, Marcy."

"Robert. Thank you so much for coming." She gave him her hand.

She looked sensational. She always had, but now there was an additional gloss on it. Slimmer, her hair pulled back into a chignon . . . Robert didn't know how women achieved these things. He only knew she had gone from a beautiful woman to a beautiful woman with a polish that suggested depth. Not unlike the lacquer on the new Chinese furniture.

"Do you want a drink? Vodka and tonic?"

She remembered what he drank. Alarm bells went off in Cavanaugh's head.

"Just coffee."

"I'll just be a minute. Make yourself comfortable."

She disappeared into the vast recesses of her smaller place, and Cavanaugh wandered around the living room, looking for clues to what was going on. He didn't find any.

"Is the coffee okay?"

"The coffee is wonderful," Cavanaugh said, although the truth was that all coffee tasted pretty much the same to him.

So why had he complimented it? He put down the Wedgewood cup.

"Marcy, you said on the phone that you were in trouble."

"Yes, I am. It's Abigail."

"Abigail? Your *dog?*"

"Yes. Since I've moved, she's been a real problem. She howls all day while I'm gone at work, and the neighbors are complaining."

Her dog. She had called him out here to foist her dog off on him.

"Before you say no, just listen, Robert. You always liked dogs. Remember how you used to throw a tennis ball for her for hours at a time? And you're home more than I am—you don't have to travel as much for your job. And you live out in the country; your office gave me your new address and I looked it up on the map."

"No. I can't believe you told me you were in trouble and it's about discarding your dog!"

To his surprise, her eyes filled with tears. Marcy. Who never cried, never lost her glossy poise. . . .

"I don't know where else to turn, Robert. If I take her to the pound, they'll just kill her. She's not a cute little puppy somebody else will adopt. My job does require more and more travel—in fact, I have a nine-thirty flight to Dallas tonight. Abigail mopes and howls at the boarding kennel. And since Hal left me, I'm . . . I'm having trouble holding it all together."

"*Since Hal left me.*" Cavanaugh peered more closely at Marcy. The tears had vanished, a momentary weakness. But even that was more weakness than he'd ever seen from her during the four years of their marriage.

He said, "I'm living with someone, Marcy." If she looked stricken, he was going to leave. None of that rebound-to-a-former-point-of-security danger.

But Marcy only smiled. "Well, does she like dogs?"

Did Judy like dogs? Cavanaugh realized he didn't know, which just proved how little he and Judy really knew each other. How could she want to *marry* him, for Chrissake, when they didn't even know who liked what pets? It was irrational on her part. Premature, presumptuous . . .

He was working this into a mild resentment when Abigail, an aging English setter, trotted into the room. At the threshold she stopped dead, then bounded joyfully toward Cavanaugh, tail wagging. She licked his face, she barked in his ear, she all but clamored onto his lap.

"See, she remembers you," Marcy said.

"Hey, girl. Hey there, old girl. How's the girl . . .?"

Damn. He was already lost. Marcy had won. He was going to take the damn dog.

"Robert, she'd be so much happier with you than with me . . . Oh, don't mind the TV. It's programmed to come on for the seven o'clock news. I usually watch it while I eat dinner."

She said it calmly, but to Robert it sounded sad. Eating alone with the TV. Although, where *was* the TV? He heard a broadcast-type voice. ". . . stories tonight about yet another TWA crash and a sensational . . ." but he didn't see a TV set, not even after he'd pushed Abigail out of his face.

"So, will you take her?" Marcy said tensely.

Cavanaugh finally located the broadcast voice; it was coming from an antique cherry armoire with polished brass knobs. Marcy must figure a TV was too recent for her Federalist-Chinoiserie decor.

". . . just learned that the Centers for Disease Control are investigating in southern Maryland . . ."

"Robert? Will you?"

". . . previously unknown strain of malaria that attacks blood cells that . . ."

Cavanaugh shoved away Abigail, bolted across the room, and flung open the cherry armoire. Tom Brokaw's face lectured him.

". . . urging citizens not to panic. I repeat, these findings are preliminary. Nonetheless, *Baltimore Sun* journalist Libby Turner, who broke the story in this evening's edition of that newspaper, received confirmation from Dellridge Community Hospital in La Plata that . . ."

"Oh, my God," Cavanaugh said. "Shit, shit, shit."

"What is it?" Marcy said. "What's wrong?"

". . . article also raises a sensitive point: Is this new disease, which apparently attacks mostly African Americans, being treated with the same seriousness as if the victims were white? That question is already being debated on the Internet, where rumors first alerted Ms. Dole to . . ."

Rumors on the Internet. Judy? But he had warned her—

"Robert, I asked you what's wrong!"

"It wasn't supposed to happen this way," he said.

"What wasn't?"

"The public was supposed to be told in a reassuring way. Not as a civil rights issue."

". . . further confirmation from La Plata that the FBI has already questioned hospital personnel at . . ."

"Shit," Cavanaugh repeated inanely. His cell phone rang.

". . . speculation that if the new disease is not an act of nature, it could well be a bioweapon disguised as . . ."

"Bob? Listen, it's Felders."

"What—"

Marcy said, "Robert, please tell me what's going on!"

Felders said, "I heard the idiotic news report and realize that if it's in southern Maryland, it's you and Seton."

"Ehhrrrmmm," Cavanaugh said. Could Felders hear Marcy in the background? Would he recognize Marcy's voice after three years? Did Felders think the malaria/stroke outbreak was terrorism? Why *was* Felders calling?

"Listen, I know you don't work for me any more, Bob," Felders said, "but mentoring dies hard, I guess. I just wanted to offer a piece of advice."

Despite himself, Cavanaugh grinned. When Felders mentored, he owned. It drove most agents nuts, but Cavanaugh hadn't really minded. They didn't come any more competent than Felders.

"Like I said, I got Seton in your Resident Agency. What kind of idiot is he, anyway? He shouldn't be in charge of a lemonade stand. He told me he had to get off the phone to 'comment to the press crowd outside.' You should have heard his tone. The pope appearing on his goddamn balcony."

Ah, Felders. Why couldn't Dunbar see through Seton like that?

"Anyway," Felders raced on in his New York rat-a-tat style, "I wanted to tell you to stay away from the press while you're doing this investigation. The whole thing sounds like a nut theory to me, but after Libby Turner and CBS, the Bureau is going to have to investigate it anyway. We'll look like racists if we don't. Anyway, you're going to be talking to local hate groups, right? Those guys only like the press on their own terms. If you're trailed by reporters, you'll never get close to the people you're going to need to talk to. You especially don't want your face on TV. Let that idiot Seton talk for the cameras. You don't go anywhere near your office. Don't go home, either. There're only two agents in southern Maryland, and by now every reporter on the East Coast knows your name and address. They'll be camped on your lawn trying to wring quotes out of you. Tell Judy not to talk to them either."

Cavanaugh suddenly realized that Felders's voice carried beyond the receiver. Marcy was listening intently.

"Got it," Cavanaugh said.

"Good. It's going to be a wild goose chase, but the lower profile you keep, the better you'll come out of it after the insanity stops." He hung up, Felders style, without saying good-bye.

Marcy smoothed her already smooth hair. "Where will you stay while you investigate?"

"A motel, under a Bureau ID."

"You can stay here."

It caught Cavanaugh by surprise, which must have showed on his face. Marcy smiled.

"As I said, I'm leaving on a nine-thirty flight for Dallas. I'll be gone at least a week, more likely two. If you're not going home to . . . to Judy, then you can't take Abigail there. If you stay here, nobody will know where you are, Abigail won't be howling at the kennel, and I'll feel like I've repaid you a little for relieving me of the dog."

The logic was impeccable, the presentation flawless. And yet under the negotiating skill, Cavanaugh sensed something else. Something new in his ex-wife: a desire to be useful. What had her lover the wunderkind CEO done to this self-assured woman to ever make her feel she wasn't?

"Okay, sure," Cavanaugh said. "Thanks."

"Good. Now if you'll excuse me, I need to pack for my business trip."

She left the living room, as graceful and poised as Cavanaugh remembered. He stood still on the Oriental carpet, planning. Call Dunbar, call Judy, call Jim Farlow . . .

Abigail whimpered and rolled over on her belly, waiting for him to scratch her. It brought back a host of memories of his former life. The dog, the picnics at the beach, Marcy . . .

But things were different now.

Before he made the first of the calls to launch his investigation, he knelt and examined Abigail's happily exposed belly, looking for mosquito bites.

We're besieged by calls," Jerry Dunbar said. He ran a hand through his thinning hair. "Half of them are from people 'turning in the terrorist group that caused the disease.' Candidates include space aliens, Republicans, insurance companies, Madonna, the vice president, and the City of New York. Somehow a rumor got started that the big bus crash yesterday happened because the driver was black and had a stroke like Senator Reading's."

"Jesus," an agent said.

"The other half of the phone calls are from Headquarters. They want this thing solved yesterday."

The twelve agents around the table nodded sleepily. It was 7:00 A.M. in Baltimore. The first of the Public Health Service/CDC bulletins had already aired on the radio; Cavanaugh had heard it while driving in. It was sane, balanced, and reasonable. It was also too late. Panic had already flamed, including at the FBI. This was the initial meeting of the hastily assembled—most of the agents had been in bed asleep—team against "the malaria terrorists."

Nobody present was completely convinced it *was* a terrorist attack, not even Cavanaugh. But Libby Turner's follow-up stories had everything: Public danger. Racism. Paranoia. Death. Pictures of malaria-carrying mosquitoes blown up ten times their size, so that they resembled the enormous car-chomping mutated bugs of 1950's B movies. Naturally the journalists loved it. Naturally they wrote about it. To be fair.

Cavanaugh didn't want to be fair. Like most agents, he considered journalists jackals. Howling, braying, preying on the weak, settling for carrion. Interfering with solid, methodical law enforcement.

"Cavanaugh?" Dunbar said, breaking into his train of thought.

"'Let slip the dogs' of the *Baltimore Sun*."

"What?"

"Nothing."

"I *asked* you," Dunbar said, "how much time can you take from your other cases for this special team?"

"All of it."

Dunbar nodded. Apparently he took this as no more than a sign of how conscientiously Cavanaugh took directives from Headquarters. Felders would have known it also meant Cavanaugh had nothing else worth his time.

"I'm case agent on this, on record," Dunbar said, which meant Headquarters needed to show the public that a high-ranking supervisor was in charge. "But you'll do the major field work, Robert. It's your jurisdiction. However, everything to the press goes through me or the Press Office. Everything. That's ironclad."

The twelve agents—the number was another concession to the "terrorism" the public perceived and the Bureau didn't—nodded again. Everyone understood. This one was hot, so they would go through the motions, even if the motions were bullshit. Then Cavanaugh would write a final report, and everybody could forget about the whole thing.

"Okay, let's divide it up. Firchen, Santos, Phaffer, you talk to the hospitals and the next-of-kin. Cavanaugh will brief you. Horne, Mc-Farlane . . ."

Dunbar organized the team, then let Cavanaugh fill everybody in. All the while he was doing so, he kept one ear cocked toward the secure phone at the end of the conference room. The other agents did, too. With a highly publicized terrorist attack—even one with no terrorists except those dreamed up by the press—sometimes a genuinely dangerous group would claim credit. Or more than one group. Headquarters would funnel those claims to this team, and thus provide probable cause for warrants, subpoenas, maybe even grand juries. Very often the result was information useful to other on-going cases. It was like following plastic bread crumbs to real gingerbread houses.

Of course, the claimants might phone the newspapers instead of the FBI. But in that case, the *Post* or *Sun* or *Times* would phone Head-quarters.

However, by the end of the meeting, no one had as yet taken responsibility for malaria reading. The secure phone stayed silent.

Melanie Anderson gulped the last mouthful of hot coffee in the kitch-enette of her Weather Vane Motel room. Late, late. It was already 7:00 A.M. and she and Krovetz were supposed to leave at 7:10 for the field. Melanie wore only a white, one-pocket T-shirt and panties, her thick, shoulder-length hair half-combed. And Krovetz, that hotshot, would knock on her door early, she just knew it. He was that eager.

Well, so was she. She and Krovetz were going to take a break from interviewing next-of-kin for the epidemiological curves. Instead, they would leave the rest of the team issuing more guidelines for protecting the populace, and they would visit the epidemiological center: twenty-five square miles of small towns, woods, fields, and marshland. A lot of space—but Melanie had a theory to narrow it farther. To test it, she and Joe would gather specimens.

Thank God things were finally getting done.

No, actually, thank that reporter, Libby Turner. Although thinking about Libby Turner's article in the *Sun* made her think about Robert Cavanaugh, which made her so furious she slammed her empty coffee mug into the sink.

He had actually called her last night to suggest that *she* had leaked the *P. reading* terrorism theory to the press! After she'd given Farlow her word of honor that she wouldn't! Melanie had blistered the phone receiver with her reply, then hung up. Arrogant honky cop!

She yanked on socks and jeans, dragged a comb through the other half of her hair and pushed it into a ponytail, smeared on insect repellent. She was lacing up her field boots when the phone rang. Krovetz. No, he'd just show up. Cavanaugh? If he dared accuse her again . . .

"Is this the CDC nigger bitch?"

A heavy male voice. Melanie went still.

"Yeah, I know where you are. I see you every day, running around with those white men scientists. What're you, their off-duty recreation? Well, not for long. Get out of our state, bitch, or else you might be next to get bitten by some rabid mosquito." Forced heavy laughter.

Quietly she hung up the phone.

Call Cavanaugh? Tell Farlow? No. Whoever made that hate call wasn't responsible for genetically engineering a parasitic variant. An organization that could do that owned brains, and this was just a stupid racist pig. Another in the sty.

She found she was standing with her arms wrapped around her body, protective. Impatiently, she bent to finish lacing her boots, then looked for her cap. But she jumped when the knock on the door came, and she kept the chain on until she saw it was Joe Krovetz.

"Mel? Ready to go? Car's loaded."

"I'm ready. Did you remember the dry ice?"

"Of course." He grinned at her, so eager to get started that Melanie grinned back. They weren't all like that caller.

Crossing the parking lot, she eyed the teenagers lounging around the gas station, the motel employee hosing down a sidewalk, the customer pulling away from a unit on the far end of the motel, people going in and out of the 7-Eleven. Did you call me? You? You?

Why do you hate us so fucking much?

❖　　　❖　　　❖

They drove southeast toward the river. A mile or so short of the Potomac River Bridge, Melanie pulled the car off the highway and onto a side road, and they entered a different decade.

Away from the highways, she'd found, much of southern Maryland looked just like this. Dirt roads cut through dense woods of mixed hardwoods and pine. Whenever the land lifted, small hidden farms appeared: fields of corn or carrots or tobacco. The scattered homes were either farmhouses or trailers, their small yards splashed either with flower beds and statues to Saint Mary, or with abandoned tires and rolls of chicken wire. One sign, sometimes hand lettered, appeared over and over: DOGS TRAINED FOR AGGRESSION.

Between the isolated farms or trailers, the land was still wild: steep ravines, fallen trees, the constant drone of insects. A deer flashed across the road, melting into the woods.

"Okay, here," Melanie said. "You take that side of the road and I'll take this."

"Gotcha." Joe stopped the car and climbed out. To the left the woods weren't quite as thick as in other places, patterned with sunlit dells and fallen logs. In the distance, barely visible above the trees, rose a dilapidated barn roof. To the right the ground fell away sharply in a muddy bank, then leveled off into swampy ground covered with reeds, stagnant pools of water, and the drowned remains of small trees. Both left and right were good breeding grounds for *A. quadrimaculatus.*

Joe said, "I'm still not sure we're going to find anything new, Mel."

"You got a better idea?"

"Nope," Joe said, unoffended.

Melanie liked that. The kid was easy to work with. He was always cheerful, he was willing to think out of the box, and never once had he shown the slightest awareness that she was female. That made things much easier. Melanie didn't date white men, and it was tiresome having to explain why not.

Joe loaded himself with light traps, plus the subliming dry ice that mosquitoes mistook for human breath. He vanished into the trees. Melanie slid down the steep bank toward the swamp.

This wasn't a part of epidemiology that Melanie usually engaged in. But this was her theory, and so far she was the only one who believed in it. She'd begun with the fact that the center of this attempt at genocide was centered in a rural subsection of Maryland rather than, say, in D.C. That suggested two possibilities, neither of which precluded the other. The first was that whoever had done this horrendous thing had deliberately released the altered and infected *Anopheles* in an out-of-the-way location, where the epidemic would have a chance to take firm hold before the small rural hospitals even realized it existed. And that's exactly what would have happened if a United States senator hadn't been bitten and then died at a sophisticated New York hospital that ran obscure tests to find out why. If Senator Reading hadn't been an inadvertent meal for a diseased mosquito, God knows how many more poor blacks would have died before anybody realized what their strokes actually were.

As it was, the official death toll had reached fifty-six: fifty-three blacks, one Greek, two India Indians. Many of the dead were kids. Kids liked to be outdoors in the summer.

The second possibility was that the release of the diseased mosquitoes had been accidental. Premature. Somebody had been transporting the vectors from wherever they had been created to wherever they were supposed to be used. And some had escaped. That's why Melanie and Joe were out in tall, wet grass, looking for clues. Route 301 ran right through the epidemiological center, and it contained the bridge to connect this God-forsaken backwater with Virginia and the deep South.

The ground was wet. Mud rose almost to the top of Melanie's field boots. She squished halfway across the open ground and bent over a ditch. *Anopheles quadrimaculatus* deposited its eggs on the surface of standing fresh water, usually water surrounded by heavy vegetation, with some shady areas. That described most of southern Maryland, where the water table was so high that inland swamps were as common as salt marshes. *Anopheles* larvae, called wigglers, liked to feed in the sun, rest in the shade. Sure enough, the ditch held a floating mass of eggs. Melanie scooped them up carefully and put them in a collector. Gary would examine some, hatch some. It was a numbers game. Were there pockets of third-or-fourth generation breeding that could indicate a single-point release of initial vectors? The only way to find out was to carefully sample the undisturbed breeding grounds.

"Hey! You! Look this way!"

Her head jerked up. Two men splashed across the wet ground toward her. Fear iced her spine—until she saw the logo on their truck, parked behind Joe's car: CHANNEL SIX NEWS.

"Damn!" one of the men said. He raised his leg and tried to shake the mud off his polished leather shoe and bottom four inches of pants leg. "Hey, Dr. Anderson! Look this way!" The other man raised a mini-cam.

Melanie pulled the brim of her baseball cap down and turned her back. She waded away from the men, across even swampier ground. The newsmen weren't dressed for that. But the two splashed after her, the cameraman filming, the reporter cursing the mud and muck. "Dr. Anderson! Don't go! Could you please show us which mosquitoes are the ones carrying the malaria? Do you have one in a jar we can shoot?"

She turned back. "Look, gentlemen, this is a scientific task, not medical theater. The CDC has a vital job to do here. If you could just contact the CDC Press Office for the information you need."

The reporter didn't even deign to answer that. The cameraman kept shooting. The reporter looked around hopefully for mosquitoes. Back at the roadside, a second sound truck screeched to a halt beside the first one. It said UPI.

"Oh, my God. Look, guys, if you go stomping through the environment you're just going to—"

Three people jumped out of the second truck and waded into the field.

Melanie hurried toward them, her boots sticking in mud at every step then pulling out with a little sucking noise. "You! Don't come in here. Do you even know if you're positive for sickle-cell trait?"

The black man stared at her. Instantly she disliked him. One of the brothers who thought black women existed to serve their needs. She knew the type. "Look, unless you know for sure that you're negative for sickle-cell trait, this isn't a safe place for you."

"I've got a story to file," he said. "Who are you?"

"Dr. Melanie Anderson, CDC!"

"Oh, yeah. Well, stand over there and give us about sixty seconds. Not too technical."

She said coldly, "Forget you."

Before he could answer, two white kids appeared from a copse of trees on the far edge of the swamp. The sloshed toward her. "This the epidemic center? We're graduate students from the university on a collecting expedition. Who's in charge here, please?"

"How did you—"

"Come one, come all," said the UPI man sourly. Mud caked his pants legs. "They followed us, obviously."

One of the grad students said, "There're some other researchers down the road, but they didn't speak English. I think they're from the Institute of Tropical Medicine at Antwerp. My French isn't so good."

"It wasn't French, you dork," his companion said. "It was Dutch. Hey, look—CNN!"

Another car approached from Route 301, slowed, and stopped. Then another truck.

Melanie took a long deep breath and put her face in her hands.

S I X

**Americans have every reason to expect a nuclear,
biological, or chemical attack before the decade is over.**
                              —Senator Richard Lugar, 1995

The fax in Judy's office beeped and began to whir. She swiveled her
chair away from her computer and stared at it. *Let it be a cartoon from
Robert.*

He had courted her—if you could call it "courtship" when it didn't
lead to actual marriage—by sending her his whimsical drawings. By fax,
by letter, by e-mail. Judy loved them. She loved the side of Robert that
the cartoons revealed: not the dogged, persistent FBI agent, but the
skewed humor, the zany tenderness. Her favorites were pinned to the
corkboard above her desk, which at the moment she could barely see because the only light in the room came from the computer screen. She
didn't want to let the reporters camped outside even know which room
she was in. That was irrational, yes, but there it was.

The curtains, tightly drawn across the window, blocked out the
trucks rutting the lawn; the discarded Styrofoam coffee cups blew down
the slope into the river. When Judy went outside to get the mail, they
shouted questions at her. Yesterday night there had been a lot of them;
today there were fewer, since presumably they had found other connections to what the press was now calling "malaria reading." Apparently
"Plasmodium reading" didn't sound scary enough.

The worst of it was, Judy couldn't blame Libby Turner. Turner was a journalist, doing just what Judy herself did when she was researching a science story. In fact, it was what Robert did in tracking down *his* cases. But that didn't make him any happier with her.

"I told you to keep this all confidential!" he'd said last night on the phone. "'Confidential' does not include letting in the six million people on the Internet!"

"I'm sorry, Robert, I didn't think—"

"That's evident," he'd said, and hung up. That wasn't like him, but, on reflection, Judy was glad he had. It put him in the wrong. That shifted the balance of power to her. Now *he* would have to apologize, or at least make it up to her, and that would probably have to include forgiving her for the Internet gaffe. Being Robert, he would most likely apologize through a cartoon.

So she waited for a cartoon.

The fax stopped whirring. Judy crossed her study, tore off the transmission, and took it back to read by the glowing terminal. It was printed in his small block letters:

JUDY—I WON'T BE HOME FOR A WHILE BECAUSE I NEED TO
STAY UNBROADCAST. YOU CAN REACH ME AT 301-5555. *DON'T*
TALK TO THE PRESS.—ROBERT

No apology. And how long was "a while?" And what did he mean "need to stay unbroadcast"? He wasn't an undercover agent for God's sake! The undercovers were an entirely different breed—edgy, thrill-seeking loners, who were all a little nuts. Judy had heard Robert say so dozens of times, with the mix of admiration and disconnection all agents seem to have for the undercovers. So what was going on here?

Judy chewed on her thumb, staring at the number on the fax. Not his cell phone. Well, that wasn't surprising; the cell phone belonged to the Bureau and was supposed to be reserved for official business. And "301-5555" was a suburban number, not D.C. She pressed it.

A woman's voice on the answering machine: "You have reached 301-5555. Please leave a message and I'll get back to you as soon as I can."

Who was she?

Judy punched in another number. Science writers met a diverse lot of people. A year ago, she'd interviewed a female state trooper who had located what she thought was the skeleton of a murder victim under her rented vacation house. The skeleton had turned out to belong to a five-hundred-year-old Cherokee. This had made the skeleton an embarrassment to the law, which had already opened a murder-case file, but a boon to science. The trooper was rueful and funny about her mistake, and she and Judy had become close friends.

"Maryland State Police."

"Officer Tess Muratore, please," Judy said.

"Just a moment."

No cartoon. Not even a 'Love, Robert.' Why not?

"Muratore."

"Tess, this is Judy Kozinski. Listen, I have to ask an enormous favor."

Tess's voice lost its wary cop formality. "Hi, Jude. As long as the favor's not illegal."

"Only a little illegal."

Tess said nothing.

"I just need a name and address to go with a phone number."

"You know I can't—"

"It's personal, Tess. About Robert. Who's still being a dum-dum about marrying me. And I give you my word your name will never come up."

Tess had her own man troubles, as Judy well knew. Tess's husband, another cop, was a skirt chaser, like Judy's late husband, Ben. Judy and Tess commiserated with each other, listened to each other, supported each other in that highly verbal sisterhood of emotional anxiety that no man really understood.

Tess said, "All right. Give me the number. I'll call you back." Fifteen minutes later, she did. "The phone is listed to an M. Gordon in Hyattsville. The address is—Judy? You there?"

"Yes," Judy said numbly.

"You okay?"

"Yes. No."

"Well, write down the address and phone because I have to go now. But if you want to talk, I'll be home tonight."

"Thanks," Judy said. It was hard to get the word past the constriction in her throat.

Marcy Gordon. Robert's ex-wife. And he was staying there for an indefinite "while."

Judy sat down carefully and stared at this week's screen saver, maniacally leaping dinosaurs. It was important not to jump to conclusions. Robert might have a perfectly good reason for staying with Marcy.

Oh, yeah? Like what?

Trust was important. She had to at least give Robert a chance to explain.

And how was she going to do that if she didn't see him? Over the phone? And how was *she* going to explain to *him* how she knew whose apartment he was inhabiting? She'd overstepped the information limits once already with the Internet leak.

No, she had to trust him. She *did* trust him. Robert wasn't like Ben. Robert was a fundamentally decent, honest man. And faithful.

So why hadn't he told her outright he was with his ex-wife?

Judy put her hands over her face. All those nights Ben hadn't come home, all the other women, the scientific colleagues and star-struck lab techs and academic-conference hotel clerks. Perfume on the lapels of his suits. Hang-up calls when the caller heard a woman answer. Master Card bills for flowers she never got, jewelry she never saw . . . She couldn't go through it again with Robert. She just couldn't.

And she wasn't going to.

She peered through the curtains. The last of the reporters had left for more promising prey.

Here it is," Agent Chuck Romano said when the secure phone from Headquarters rang. "I'm offering bets of three whole dollars."

"No takers," said an agent by the coffee machine.

Since the initial meeting of the malaria reading FBI team, things had changed. The media had changed them. Malaria reading was now firmly established in the public mind as a terrorist disease, and so it had become a terrorist case. Too many citizens were dead, too instantly, too dramatically. Therefore, someone must be to blame. Therefore, the FBI must locate that someone. So far, the FBI had failed to do this. Therefore, the press was entitled to headlines like "OVER 100 DEAD—BUT FBI HAS ZERO" and "IS FBI CHIEF BROYLIN A RACIST?"

Therefore, Dunbar had set up a "secret" command center in a South Maryland motel, away from the Leonardtown resident agency. The room's twin beds had been pushed against the wall. Phones, fax, computer, and coffee machine—the four indispensable mechanical devices of law enforcement—covered desk and dresser and table. Extra chairs had materialized. The blinds were drawn, and empty Coke cans from the machine outside already grew in a precarious pyramid on the windowsill.

Romano held the phone to his ear, saying little until the call was over. The agents waited.

"Okay, here's what we've got. Credit is being claimed by a group called Caucasian Caucus. Robert?"

"Yeah. There's a chapter in Saint Mary's County. White suprema- cists. But it's got about fifteen members, and we have them tagged as dummkopfs." This, in the classification system Cavanaugh had borrowed from Felders, meant the Caucasian Caucus talked and published white supremacy but had never committed any actions in support of it, not even legal ones like marches. "They're empty windbags."

"Well, we expected false claims," another agent said. His mouth twisted. "Getting in on the glory."

Romano said, "The claimant sent a manifesto, mailed it U.S. post to the Bureau and the White House and the *Washington Post*. At least it's short—five paragraphs. Headquarters is e-mailing us a text."

"Coming through now," said Agent Walter West at the computer. He printed multiple copies. Cavanaugh studied his and found, to his sur- prise, this group was actually literate:

GIVEN THAT THE CAUCASIAN CAUCUS EXISTS FOR THE
PURPOSE OF RECOGNIZING THAT THE CAUCASIAN RACE HAS
BEEN RESPONSIBLE FOR THE MAJOR ADVANCES IN SCIENCE,
POLITICS, AND THE ARTS, AS WELL AS FOR THE FOUNDING AND
ECONOMIC DEVELOPMENT OF THE GLORIOUS UNITED STATES
OF AMERICA; AND

GIVEN THAT THE NEGROID RACES HAVE DAMAGED AND
ATTEMPTED TO DESTROY THESE GLORIOUS ACHIEVEMENTS
THROUGH THEIR GHETTO VIOLENCE, WELFARE DEMANDS,
DRUG USE, AND GENERAL SOCIAL UGLINESS IN RAISING THEIR
OWN KIDS; AND

GIVEN THAT MISGUIDED CAUCASIAN LEADERS HAVE ACTUALLY
FAVORED THE DESTRUCTIVE NEGROID RACES OVER

CAUCASIANS THROUGH SUCH UNJUST PROGRAMS AS
AFFIRMATIVE ACTION AND ELECTING NEGROIDS TO
INFLUENTIAL OFFICE;

THEN ANY TRULY PATRIOTIC GROUP IS LEFT WITH NO CHOICE
BUT TO FIGHT FOR ITS COUNTRY'S INTEGRITY WITH EVERY
WEAPON AT ITS DISPOSAL. ANYTHING LESS WOULD BE TO
BETRAY THE TRUE SPIRIT OF THE UNITED STATES, AND TO
UNDERESTIMATE THE POWER OF THE ENEMY AT WAR WITH
THE WHITE RACE; AND

THUS THE CAUCASIAN CAUCUS IS PROUD TO CLAIM CREDIT
FOR THE RELEASE OF A BIOLOGICAL WEAPON DESIGNED TO
RIGHT THE PROPER BALANCE OF POWER, IN THE FORM OF THE
ALTERED *ANOPHELES* MOSQUITO TO DEMONSTRATE WHO
OWNS THIS GREAT COUNTRY AND ITS SCIENCE. HEED THE
DEMONSTRATION.

"Charming," West said. "How seriously do we have to take it?"

"Not very," Cavanaugh said, "unless Headquarters knows something about other chapters of these guys that isn't true in Saint Mary's. They're hollow megaphones. All right—I'll take this group. Walt, you and Danny—" The phone rang again. Another transmission from Headquarters flashed on the computer screen.

Cavanaugh made sure he had his copy of the notes from the CDC team on the particulars of the epidemic transmission. The Bureau was going to have to separate a lot of chaff from the rotten wheat. Assuming the wheat was actually there at all.

Willis Hartman, information minister of the Saint Mary's chapter of the Caucasian Caucus, both was and was not typical of the hate-group members Cavanaugh had found in southern Maryland.

Hartman's home was typical. He lived in a small, isolated house on a narrow spit of rocky land—"upground," the locals called it—at the edge of a salt marsh. Here the Potomac River had almost, but not quite, become Chesapeake Bay. On the front of the house, a roofed porch furnished with chairs faced the water. A quarter mile farther inland the coast lifted into thick woods turned gold by the setting sun. Somewhere in the woods, Cavanaugh knew, the Caucasians would have hidden caches of weapons, radios, and paramilitary gear. With any luck, they would only use it for the internal "readiness drills" that made them feel heroic.

Hartman's education, however, was not typical. FBI files showed he had a B.S. in engineering from Georgia Tech. He had worked for Florida Power and Light until dismissed for "failure to carry out duties as specified," and then had worked at successively more unskilled jobs until he'd landed in Maryland, working at a crab-canning factory. A misfit. His file said he was forty-one, never married, no police record. He was licensed to own a nine millimeter.

Hartman's house had no sidewalk from the road, just a semisoggy path among the marsh plants. Cavanaugh picked his way. A fresh breeze blew from the Potomac, cooling his face. To his right a heron took sudden flight, graceful against the darkening sky. Not for the first time, Cavanaugh wondered why some of the least worthwhile people on the planet should live in some of its most beautiful locations.

Hartman met him on the porch. He was tall, thin, balding, dressed in jeans and a gray cotton work shirt. "Who are you?"

"Mr. Hartman? FBI, Special Agent Robert Cavanaugh. I'd like to ask you a few questions."

"Of course you would," Hartman said. He smiled slightly. "Sit down."

Cavanaugh sat. A cat, striped gray and white, regarded him impassively from the porch railing.

"I'm here to check some facts," Cavanaugh said. "Are you a member of Caucasian Caucus?"

"I'm the information minister for southern Maryland," Hartman said. He seemed amused.

"The FBI, the White House, and the *Washington Post* all received the following communication." Cavanaugh handed him a copy. "Have you seen this before?"

Hartman didn't glance at the paper. "No."

"How do you know you haven't seen it if you don't look at what it is?"

"I saw it this morning in the *Post*. I can read, Agent Cavanaugh." Hartman's smile broadened slightly, a fraction of an inch. Cavanaugh saw that he was doling out the smile, making it last, using it to comment on this pointless exchange.

"Did this communication originate from you?"

"Obviously not, if I never saw it before."

"What are your duties as 'information minister,' Mr. Hartman? I'd like to remind you that it's a federal offense to lie to an FBI agent."

"I issue all communications originating in the southern Maryland chapter of Caucasian Caucus. Also, I act as liaison to pass on, as appropriate, all communications coming from National."

"Yet you never saw this particular communication."

"No." Another fractional inch of smile.

"Isn't that a contradiction?"

"It would seem to be."

Cavanaugh leaned forward. "All right, Hartman. Let's not waste both our time. This thing is signed 'Caucasian Caucus,' and in southern Maryland that's you. Are you claiming credit for the outbreak of stroke-inducing malaria among sickle-cell carriers?"

"I thought only God could take credit for malaria."

Cavanaugh stood and looked down at the man: intelligent, well-groomed, smiling faintly; a piece of slime. He said, knowing what the answer would be, "May I look around inside?"

"Not without a warrant."

"Then one more question. Is there anything you'd like to tell the Bureau?"

"Yes," Hartman said, surprising Cavanaugh. The question was pro forma. "Tell Director Broylin to fire all the nigger agents before they subvert the entire government."

Hartman wanted him to react. With an effort of will, Cavanaugh didn't. He turned and walked calmly down the steps.

"Mind the mosquitoes," Hartman called after him. "In today's corrupt world, you never know who's got some nigger blood."

Cavanaugh continued along the path through the salt marsh. Green-flies buzzed in a cloud around his head, and a bird lifted off from the reeds, calling raucously in a language he could not understand.

FBI SLOW TO INVESTIGATE MALARIA READING

The *Washington Post* has learned that the Federal Bureau of Investigation had been informed of the increased stroke rate among African Americans two weeks before any full investigation was launched. This means that over three weeks elapsed before the public was alerted. A nurse at Dellridge Community Hospital in La Plata, Maryland, told the *Post* that she had spoken with an unidentified FBI agent on June 4, informing him of the increased stroke rate for African-American patients. The nurse, who did not want her name used, said that although the agent wrote down the information, "I never heard from him again."

Malaria reading, as it is now being called, attacks mostly African Americans carrying the sickle-cell trait, usually resulting in fatal cerebral stroke. Sickle-cell trait itself is not the cause of the disease, which . . .

CDC/USPHS GUIDELINES CALLED IMPRACTICAL BY ACTIVIST GROUPS

New York—The Coalition of African-American Activist Groups (CAAAG) today issued a strong condemnation of the guidelines issued jointly by the Centers for Disease Control and the United States Public Health Service. The guidelines are designed to protect African Americans against infection by malaria reading. " 'Stay indoors from dusk on, drain all pools of standing water, wear insect repellent and body-covering clothing'—those rules don't make sense for real people," said CAAAG Jesse Lawrence Arnold. "There's a heat wave in Washington. If poor people stay indoors, they're going to suffocate. Many can't afford insect repellent, and how do you get kids to wear 'body-covering clothing' in a torrid summer? Not to mention the impossibility of 'draining' urban ditches, rain gutters, and roof puddles. Get real, CDC."

"WHO COULD DO SUCH A THING?" ASKS BEREAVED MOM

La Plata, Maryland—The mother of six-year-old Thomas "Junior" Carter, who died yesterday of malaria reading, is fighting mad. "Somebody done this terrible thing to us," said a tearful LaWanda Carter, interviewed yesterday at her home. "Who could do such a thing to a child? I ain't going to rest till I find out who killed my baby."

Many other people would also like the answer to that question. The FBI Office of Public Affairs says the list of possible suspects is long. Although the FBI has been reluctant to give out much information—"It might hamper the investigation"—they are reportedly investigating foreign governments' espionage organizations, biotech companies in the area, animal research firms, and various "hate groups," including the Ku Klux Klan. The white supremacist Caucasian Caucus, which yesterday claimed credit in an anonymous communication to the FBI and the *Washington Post . . .*

I'm Special Agent Robert Cavanaugh, Federal Bureau of Investigation. I'd like to ask you a few questions, ma'am."

"Go ahead," Catherine Clarke said. To Cavanaugh, she didn't look like the head of an important scientific supply house. About forty, no wedding ring, dumpy and round-shouldered, she wore a baggy brown suit that even Cavanaugh could see was a disaster. Had he passed her on the Baltimore street outside this building, he wouldn't have noticed her. If he *had* noticed her, he would have assumed she was a low-level government clerk. So much for first impressions.

"You sell, among other things, live insects for agricultural research, is that correct?"

"Yes, it is. Would you like a catalogue?"

"Thank you," Cavanaugh said. He leafed through it quickly, to show interest, although he couldn't imagine himself ordering a shipment of milkweed bugs ("Ideal for physiological studies or demonstrations") or fig wasps ("Hardy pollinators for your Smyrna figs").

"Do you sell any species of mosquitoes?"

"Oh, yes," Ms. Clarke said. She pulled at her suit jacket, which had somehow rucked itself up on one side. "We offer both adults and larvae in seven different species. Although, of course, *Culex* is our big seller."

"Of course," Cavanaugh said.

"After fruit flies, I mean. Everybody wants fruit flies."

"Who wouldn't?" he said, and she didn't even blink. "Is one of your seven species *Anopheles quadrimaculatus?*"

"No, it's not. There's very little call for any of the anophelines."

On his notepad Cavanaugh wrote "no an." "Do you know of any other supply houses that offer *Anopheles?*"

"Let me check." She swiveled toward a computer and began to pull up files. Cavanaugh doodled. He turned the "o" and the "a" in "no an" into eyes, and both "n's" into ears.

"The only place on the East Coast that offers *A. quadrimaculatus,* both eggs and larvae, is Stanton Supply in Atlanta. Would you like the address?"

"Yes," Cavanaugh said. She gave it to him. He wrote it on his pad, then sketched a grinning face around the eyes and ears.

"This must be about malaria reading," Catherine Clarke said. Suddenly she straightened her hunched shoulders. "You're the one who first noticed the case, aren't you! If there's anything I can do to help, anything at all . . ."

Cavanaugh had run into law-enforcement groupies before. They were an odd breed. Thrilled by what they imagined the job to include: danger, high action, split-second decisions. He said, "Thank you, ma'am. You've been very hel—"

"I could furnish you with other breeds of mosquitoes, if you're trying to see what kind of cross-engineering produced these mutants. Free of charge, of course."

Cavanaugh pictured Jerry Dunbar's office full of buzzing mosquitoes. They'd compete with the buzzing faxes and computers. "Thank you, but—"

"We have lots of *Toxorhynchites rutilus.* Used in biological control of other species, you know, plus using the larvae as fodder. Very versatile. We can produce up to a million a day in our lab."

"The Bureau doesn't—"

"Or maybe some *Aëdes taeniorhynchus?* The salt marsh mosquito. Maybe the bad guys cross-engineered from those! The female is a notable blood sucker!"

I'll bet, Cavanaugh thought, but didn't say aloud. Catherine Clarke had inched her chair closer to his. She put a hand on his arm.

"I've always been a tremendous admirer of the FBI, although this is my first chance to become personally involved. Which I'm very eager to do."

"In that case, I'll pass your name on to Dr. Melanie Anderson of the CDC, who's coordinating the scientific end of the investigation. I'm sure she'll welcome your kind donations of insect supplies. She's an amazing woman."

Catherine Clarke removed her hand. She said colorlessly, "We already have an established contract with the CDC."

"I'm glad to hear it," Cavanaugh said. To cover the sudden chilly silence, he finished his drawing: a body and wings around the grinning face. And then lipstick. The mosquito was female.

"Best of luck in Atlanta then," Catherine Clarke said, standing. She didn't offer her hand.

"Thank you," Cavanaugh said. No more information here. He'd clearly turned off his informant. Too bad he didn't have Seton's touch.

"Ms. Clarke—"

"Please have Dr. Anderson contact me directly. My secretary will show you out." She turned her back.

It was always sex that screwed everything up. You could count on it.

INTERIM

Hey, Charlotte! You want to go to the movies Friday night? To see Brad Pitt?"

The girl looked up from stowing books inside her school locker. "Who's going?"

"Everybody. Cam and Sue and DeShaun and Tomiko and Bob and Carol Ann."

"Well . . . I don't know." She became very absorbed in finding the exact right place for her advanced physics textbook.

The boy moved closer. He was tow-headed, thin and freckled, with the kind of intense awkwardness that would not seem attractive for another ten years. But Charlotte liked him. He was the smartest boy she'd ever met, in a magnet school designed for smart kids. And unlike some of them, he was kind.

"Is there something wrong, Charlotte? You don't seem like yourself lately."

"I'm all right," she said, which was a lie.

He touched her arm, and her belly shivered. *Not a good idea,* some of her neighborhood friends said. *Let like keep to like.* But if people all did that, how would the world ever change? And wasn't change what a school like this was for?

He withdrew his hand and his freckled skin mottled. "I'm sorry. If you don't want to go with me . . . with us . . . if you . . . I'm sorry." He turned to go.

"Bill, wait." Now her hand was impulsively on his arm, chocolate on cream. "Don't think that. It isn't that I don't want to go out with you. I mean . . . it isn't you." God, she sounded stupid! But at least she didn't blush. "It's just . . ."

"Just what?"

They stared at each other. The bell rang for class, but neither moved. His eyes were so beautiful . . . something in their depths let Charlotte blurt, "I'm afraid. To go out at night."

He understood instantly. "The mosquitoes."

"I'm probably being dumb."

"You could never be dumb. Then how about if I come over to your house tomorrow night, and we can study for the calculus exam? Inside?"

"That'd be great. Oh, God, I'm late for French!"

"*A demain,*" he said, and she couldn't stop grinning as she flew down the deserted corridor to class.

S EVEN

Law enforcement's mission is really very simple—to
protect the people we serve.
            —Louis J. Freeh, Director, FBI, 1996

When Cavanaugh woke, he didn't know where he was. He sat up in the
darkened room, groping for his Smith & Wesson on the bedside table,
which wasn't there either. Then the smell hit him, and he remembered.

Marcy's perfume. Overlaid with the pungent doggy odor of Abigail.
He was on the living room sofa in Marcy's apartment, Abigail asleep at
his feet. It had been two in the morning when he'd arrived back from Atlanta, where he'd fruitlessly interviewed people at Stanton Supply. Yes,
they sold *Anopheles* among their standard insect stock. Yes, all their customers were reputable scientific establishments or universities. Yes, of
course they could furnish Agent Cavanaugh with a list. Stanton Supply
had been courteous and eager to help. The list had been completely useless.

Cavanaugh had spent the next ten hours interviewing other re-
spectable scientific establishments in Atlanta, and the three hours after
that sitting in the airport while his flight was delayed, announced, delayed again, and finally rescheduled. He spent the time reading newspapers:

FBI ACCUSED OF POINTLESS ACTIVITY
IN MALARIA READING

"Bureau should have time limit to show that somebody violated something," says Congressman

Washington—James L. Winstead, House majority leader, told reporters today that the FBI investigation was "a joke. People are dying of disease, not felonies. The CDC is the appropriate agency to deal with this crisis, not the FBI. By generating public panic over unsubstantiated terrorism, the Bureau has only made it harder for health agencies to do their jobs."

Citing interviews with respected scientists stating that the malaria reading parasite is most likely a "natural mutation," Winstead attacked the FBI for "trying to obtain evidence against Natural Tragedy." His remarks came in response to a statement by FBI director Peter Broylin that more agents were being committed to . . .

RIOT OUTSIDE WHITE HOUSE OVER MALARIA READING

FOUR HURT, TEN ARRESTED

Rioters outside the White House this morning protested government handling of the malaria reading crisis. "The death toll is over 200, and all but four are African Americans," said one protestor. "The damn government don't care."

The riot, which did not appear to be an organized or sponsored activity, allegedly began when a transient hurled a racial insult at a tourist. Abusive exchanges concerning malaria reading escalated into thrown punches. By the time police arrived, at least thirty people were involved, some of them hurling rocks or soda cans. Ten people were taken into custody on various charges from assault to resisting arrest.

"This is just the beginning," said patrolman Carl L. Brand of the D.C. police. "People are getting mad. We're gearing up for a lot of civil unrest. It's going to get a lot worse."

The White House declined to comment, even though the altercation was clearly visible from . . .

When Cavanaugh ran out of Atlanta newspapers, he read the late editions of the *Post* and the *Times.* More of the same. The FBI wasn't doing enough, the FBI was doing too much, the FBI didn't know what it was doing, the FBI had damn well better *do* something. People were angry, people were dying, people were rioting, people wanted someone to blame and the Bureau was it. Nobody knew who or where the monsters were (if there were monsters), but everybody knew where the FBI was. Devil you know.

When he finally reached Marcy's apartment, bone-weary, Abigail greeted him frantically. She wanted a walk, needed a walk! Now! Now!

"Hey, girl, good girl, not tonight, how about we wait till morning . . ." Abigail barked harder. Robert looked at Marcy's carpets—white, naturally. How did you get dog pee stains off carpet? He didn't know. He walked Abigail.

By the time he returned, it was almost 3:00 A.M. There were three messages from Judy asking him to call her, each message more icily polite than the one before. Cavanaugh would have groaned, but he was too exhausted.

Because of Judy, he slept on Marcy's sofa, not in her bed. Somehow he owed Judy that; somehow that made it better. At some level he knew this made no sense. He fell asleep to Abigail's happy snufflings beside the sofa, and awoke to the sound of the phone.

"Cavanaugh," Dunbar said, "where the hell are you?"

"I'm . . . here," Cavanaugh said, idiotically.

"Yes," Dunbar said, with his special-agent-in-charge neutrality. "But you need to be *here*. Meeting this morning, remember?"

Christ. What time was it? The room was pitch black. "Sorry, my plane was delayed in Atlanta, and then . . ." Cavanaugh trailed off. Dunbar didn't want excuses. Nor should he.

"We'll start without you," Dunbar said crisply. "But do come in as fast as possible. It's not a routine meeting. They're giving malaria reading to Division Five."

"Shit," Cavanaugh said.

"Yeah. Well, those are the rules."

This fatalism didn't fool Cavanaugh. Dunbar, the rule man, nonetheless minded. Division Five was the National Security Division, sent in for cases bumped up from "criminal activity" to "international or domestic terrorism." Theoretically, the Division Five agents would be working with the field office, but in actuality the Division Five guys would be the big cheeses, and the case as a whole would be micromanaged from Washington. It was no longer Dunbar's case.

Or Cavanaugh's.

"Oh, and another thing," Dunbar said, "we've already taken two messages this morning from Judy Kozinski. She's looking for you. Says it's important."

"Okay," Cavanaugh said.

"The office has better things to do than track your personal life," Dunbar said, and even though Cavanaugh knew it was just irritation at the world in general, Dunbar's words stung.

"Right," Cavanaugh said. "I'll take care of it. And I'll be there as soon as I can." What time *was* it?

It was nine o'clock. The room was still pitch black because of Marcy's thick velvet draperies, so unlike the rough-weave burlap that Judy had hung in their perfect rustic house on the Patuxent. Oh, Christ, *Judy.* Two messages already today. And Division Five—they'd just steamroll over the local agents. This was the media's fault, all the hype for the Bureau to do something, do something, do something . . . and Headquarters had caved in. Maybe Dunbar even had something to do with it. After all, Special Agents in Charge were rated partly on how well their offices handled the press.

He rushed around Marcy's apartment. Within five minutes he'd brushed his teeth, changed his shirt, and was running for the car, leaving Abigail barking sadly after him. He'd listen to the radio news on the way in, see what fresh horrors had broken overnight, call Judy during the first meeting break . . . Division Five. Shit shit shit. He wouldn't get to do anything now except what he was told to do. When Division Five moved in, they took over. Whatever they wanted, they got. Two agents on every tiny lead, priority lab work, planes, subpoenas and warrants in ten minutes at 4:00 A.M. . . . For a high-profile national-security terrorist case, the rest of the FBI just *stopped.* Malaria reading would definitely be taken seriously now. Which was, of course, the main thing Cavanaugh had wanted anyway.

Wasn't it?

At least, don't let there be one of those supercilious behavior profilists from Quantico, who thought they could solve crimes without so much as knocking on one lousy door themselves.

The meeting had just reached the behavioral profilist from Quantico when Cavanaugh rushed in. Introductions were made, and Dr. Arnold Gissing resumed handing out his packets.

"This is the probable profile," Gissing said, as everyone except Cavanaugh started to read. Cavanaugh was still catching his breath, dazed from both the sprint from the parking lot and the size of the meeting. No more reluctant, part-time agents in a motel room. The conference room was jammed. Chairs jostled each other around the large oval table, with a second ring of chairs against the walls. Agents. Specialists. Dr. Farlow from the CDC, today in a suit and tie. The Baltimore Field Office media representative. Liaisons from federal agencies whose names Cavanaugh hadn't caught. The two Division Five newcomers, Agents John Meath and Bruce Maloney, both sitting quietly and giving nothing away. And Dr. Gissing, whom Cavanaugh disliked even more for sounding reasonable and unpushy.

"The individual we're looking for belongs to the category 'organized killer.' He—and it *is* a male—is intelligent, plans very carefully, and understands exactly what he's doing. He's a Caucasian in his mid-to-late forties. He's trained in microbiology, obviously. He—"

"Excuse me," Cavanaugh said, "but are we assuming here that we've got a lone perp and not an organization? Why?"

"We covered that before you arrived, Robert," Dunbar said, pointedly. Cavanaugh nodded. He'd have to get the scoop on that afterward . . . but it sounded nuts to him. A lone perp? For genetic-engineering terrorism? That didn't make sense. Maybe there was some explanation in the papers stacked at his place on the conference table. Maybe the sheets would also explain the massive increase in manpower since yesterday. Nothing on the radio had.

As unobtrusively as possible, he started to shuffle paper while everybody else concentrated on the profile report.

"He did well in college," Dr. Gissing continued, "possibly even brilliantly, but did not complete his Ph.D. Since then, his career has not lived up to everyone's early expectations, including his own. This is most

likely due to conflicts with superiors, or to a certain rigidity in procedures that he will not adapt to accommodate team projects. He may or
may not still be working in a scientific field."

There was nothing among the papers that explained why the Bureau
had decided to focus on an individual perp. But there was an airtel—an
urgent internal memo—from Director Broylin himself. Routing info
showed that it had been sent to all 25,000 FBI employees. It announced
that this case was now the Bureau's number-one priority.

Since two days ago? Why?

Cavanaugh found the answer by peering at a note the agent on his
left had scribbled at the top of his pile of papers. The note said, "Lena
Penniston 12 **12 12** years old!!!!" Leonard Penniston headed the Criminal Investigative Division; he was the highest-ranking black in the FBI.

Any war only hit home when it came home.

Gissing was still talking. " . . . heterosexual and has a stable home
life. He lives with or is married to a woman his pronounced intellectual
inferior. No children. Probably estranged from his birth family, or at
least not close to them."

All 25,000 Bureau employees. That meant secretaries, lab techni-
cians, janitors, analysts, and the clerical staff that handled expense
vouchers. That sort of mobilization was more than a reaction to young
Lena Penniston's death. It was also a press maneuver. *Look how much
we're horrified at the mounting deaths of our black citizens. All 25,000 of
us will throw ourselves at this, even people who can't possibly influence
the outcome at all.*

" . . . not openly affiliated with any hate group, although he may follow their activities with paternalistic approval from a distance . . ."

Another sheet of paper announced that the FBI was offering a
$500,000 reward for information leading directly to the apprehension of
the terrorist.

" . . . is following events of the case closely in the media, although too
smart to collect clippings or—"

"Excuse me," Cavanaugh interrupted again. Dunbar looked at him
wearily.

"Have we discussed the fact that a reward offer like this is going to
produce even more leads about alleged individual terrorists? A huge
amount of manpower is going to be diverted from looking at groups,
both domestic groups and international."

Now the two agents from Division Five, Maloney and Meath, were scrutinizing him as carefully as Dunbar was, although more quietly. Dunbar said, "We're not neglecting possible group involvement, Robert. Domestic hate groups will continue to be checked out whenever they meet the three guideline criteria—you do remember what they are, don't you?"

Cavanaugh nodded. Of course he knew: *"A threat or advocacy of force; apparent ability to carry out the claimed act; potential violation of federal law."* Dunbar wasn't happy with him.

"And Agents Graham and DiPreta"—Dunbar nodded his head to the two people on his right, one of them a woman—"are legats. As we discussed *before* you arrived."

"Legats" were legal attachés, agents posted to foreign offices to co-ordinate work with local law-enforcement officials in those countries. They worked openly, unlike the CIA, who were probably also at work on the foreign terrorist angle. Of course they were, Cavanaugh realized, but one wasn't supposed to mention it. The two legats studied him expressionlessly.

"If I may finish," Dr. Gissing said coldly.

"Please," Dunbar said. His neck was flushed, just above the collar.

"Thank you. The key to this individual's character is his sense of superiority. He imagines himself a powerful behind-the-scenes figure, manipulating entire bureaucracies—such as the FBI—into doing his bidding. Because of this, he has told no one what he's doing, not even his wife or live-in woman. The lab where he has created the malaria parasite and infected mosquitoes is thus not in his home. No one but him knows about it. No one else is worthy to appreciate his achievement.

"And to him it *is* an achievement. His delusions of grandeur are so deeply rooted that he may be one of those rare individuals who can beat a polygraph test. He sees himself as cleansing society for its own good, which few people beside himself are perceptive enough to comprehend. His belief in this is total."

Dr. Gissing paused and consulted his notes. Cavanaugh had been too busy rifling papers to count how many of the agents in the room were black. He counted now. About 6 percent, the same proportion as the FBI as a whole. Somebody was being very careful.

He thought of Melanie Anderson, and hoped all these black agents were negative for sickle-cell trait.

"Finally," Dr. Gissing said, "because this individual considers himself a natural aristocrat, he will pride himself on his superior taste in at least one consumer area. It might be his car, or his clothing, or his choice of wines. We can't predict which, and he does not have the income to do all of them. Most likely he earns between forty and sixty thousand, which he manages very shrewdly. But in some area of aristocratic taste he will buy the best and will be supercilious about anything less.

"Do we have any questions?"

Everyone glanced at Cavanaugh, Dunbar very steadily. Cavanaugh spoke anyway.

"Yes, Doctor. I know that behavioral profiles—"

"'Criminal investigative analyses,'" Dr. Gissing corrected.

"Yes. Right. I know that they're compiled from profiles of other perps who have committed the same kind of crime in the same way. But nobody has ever committed this crime before in any way. So how did your unit put the analysis together?"

Gissing smiled. Clearly he relished setting Cavanaugh straight. "You are wrong, I'm afraid. Terrorists may differ by individual act, and killers may differ by behavior pattern. But by putting them together, we obtain a profile of great probable accuracy. And we have considerable information about individual killers. In seventy-seven percent of cases later solved, the investigators say the profile was of great use in focusing the investigation."

"Yes," Cavanaugh said, obscurely pleased that Gissing himself had called it a "profile," "I know. But that means your entire analysis is based on the idea that it is an individual acting alone. I mean, profiles can only reflect the initial assumptions about the crime. If this is a group—"

"I think we covered that already," Dunbar said stiffly. "Any other questions?"

The meeting moved on. Cavanaugh sat deep in thought. After a while he noted that the two Division Five agents, Maloney and Meath, were both studying him. When he caught their eyes, neither smiled. *Stick to looking for individuals,* the looks said. **We're now covering the possibility of terrorist groups.**

Turf wars. Felders never permitted his agents to conduct them. Cavanaugh missed Felders. He missed their fierce, unstifled arguments about how to proceed on everything. He missed being key to a case, rather than just another legman. He reached for his notepad.

As he listened to the people who would get to be key, Cavanaugh sketched the Division Five agents. He gave Maloney, who had a long, thin face, a head that was a sausage. He gave Meath, in his fifties, a head like an ancient goblet, spilling out drops of wisdom. He labeled the drawing "LAW FOOD: BOLONEY AND MEAD." He didn't ask any more questions.

He called Judy at noon, while caterers from a local deli distributed the sandwiches and other goodies apparently ordered before Cavanaugh's belated appearance. Dunbar had ordered him something; he didn't know what. There wasn't enough room for everyone to eat in the conference room; and since it was raining outside, agents spilled into nearby offices and lobbies, munching ham-on-rye, dropping crumbs. Cavanaugh found a public phone on another floor.

She answered on the first ring.

"Robert?"

"Yes, it's me." She'd been sitting by the phone. He was in deep shit.

"Look, Judy, I'm sorry I didn't get back to you before now. I was in Atlanta yesterday and didn't get back until—"

"Don't lie to me, Robert. Please."

Anger flared in him. "I am not lying. I was in Atlanta until very late."

"Oh, I believe that," Judy said. "That isn't the lie. The lie is that being in Atlanta is the reason you didn't call me. Are you telling me there are no phones in Atlanta?"

He visualized the banks of phones in the airport. Phones at Ticketing, phones at gates, phones by newstands, phones along corridors. Defensiveness sprouted on top of the anger. "Yes, there are phones in Atlanta. I could have called, I suppose. But I really had a lot on my mind—"

"Not me, obviously."

"Damn it, Judy, why do you always have to run everything to earth like some sort of bloodhound?"

"Oh, don't say that to me!" she cried, and he realized that it must have been something her rotten dead husband had said, something that he had used to counterattack for his infidelities. Well, Cavanaugh wasn't Ben! Why the hell couldn't she realize that? To anger and defensiveness were now added a feeling of injustice. She was unfair. She was impossible.

He said evenly, "Maybe I say it because it's true. Can't you just ever let me be? You insist on running me to earth over every little thing—"

"Moving in with your ex-wife without even telling me is not a little thing."

It knocked the breath out of him. After a moment he said quietly, "How do you know that?"

"The point is not how I—"

"You checked up on the phone number. Through that cop friend of yours. Tess what's-her-name."

"Don't try to—"

"You put me *under surveillance*."

"No, I—"

"I don't like this, Judy. We've talked about how important it is to trust each other. I'm staying at Marcy's to avoid the press so I can work on this case with some minor anonymity"—not that that would matter anymore, now he was only a bit player in a cast of thousands—"and Marcy, for your information, isn't in her apartment. She's in Dallas. I'm dog-sitting. And I don't like being checked up on."

"But you didn't tell me, so I—"

"I don't have to tell you everything! Stop hounding me!"

His voice had risen, a good measure of his anger. But was the anger at her or at himself? He knew he was being unfair. But, perversely, that only made him angrier. She had forced him into this position. She was always *at* him!

"I'm sorry," she whispered, and now he heard that she was scared: scared she'd driven him away from her, scared he'd leave her, scared he'd romance sleek, glamorous Marcy, just as Ben had always romanced sleek, glamorous women. But he wasn't Ben! His anger grew, in exact proportion to his remorse over awakening all her old fears. He'd sworn to himself he'd never do that, that she'd be able to rely on him as she never had been able to on Ben.

Oh, fuck, fuck, fuck.

"Robert," she whispered, "when do you think you'll be coming back home?"

And if he just said, "Tonight, sweetheart," it would have been all right. The fighting over. But he couldn't say it. She would just be controlling him again, this time through her weakness. She was always trying to control him, to become surer of him, safer, until he couldn't breathe. It wasn't fair.

He said coldly, "I'll be home when I come home. Not before."

"I see," she said, not whispering anymore, and the phone clicked in his ear.

A disaster. A complete disaster. It would be better if he'd never called. He hung up the receiver, turned, and saw one of the secretaries standing there. Her young face said that she'd been listening, and that he was a shit.

"Mr. Dunbar sent me to tell you the meeting is about to resume," she said, very clearly. Without waiting for an answer, she turned her back and walked away.

Thank you for rejoining us," Dunbar said coldly. Once again everyone at the table looked at Cavanaugh. He reached for his notepad.

Apparently Maloney had been talking. He resumed. "As I was just saying, Agent Cavanaugh, Washington has decided to issue a Terrorist Warning Advisory to the public. The director has called a press conference for three o'clock."

Cavanaugh nodded and kept his eyes on his "notes." What could he say? He was minor, he was late, and he didn't believe in the entire idea of a lone terrorist. It was wishful thinking, to avoid the racial and political implications of an organized antiblack group, possibly based in another country. Oh, the Bureau would investigate that possibility thoroughly, Cavanaugh knew, behind the scenes. So would the CIA. But for public consumption, they'd downplay it. Too panic-inducing. Too riot-inducing, like the riot in front of the White House. Nobody liked riots.

Better to let the public believe there might be a single nut out there, a nut the Bureau would catch just as they'd caught the Unabomber. Better to issue bullshit all-bureau memos and Terrorist Advisory Warnings, which made it look like the FBI knew more than it actually did. There was no need for a Terrorist Warning Advisory; there was nobody left in America who didn't know what was happening with malaria reading. Not unless they didn't have a TV, a radio, a newspaper, or any neighbors for five miles around. And if they lived in Maryland and Virginia, even that wouldn't help, because the CDC, USPHS, or army would show up on their isolated doorstep to ask questions, tell them to empty their bird-bath, or urge them to have their blood tested.

The meeting proceeded. Teams were organized for scientific-equipment tracing, suspect identification, surveillance, background checks, CDC liaison, international investigation. Cavanaugh doodled on his notepad.

He drew a huge Venus flytrap, swallowing an FBI agent. All that was left were the agent's gun and badge. The Venus flytrap keeled over woozily. A neighboring daisy said disapprovingly, "I TOLD HER NOT TO EAT THAT THING!"

He drew a stone. Eight panels, and in every one of them the stone looked exactly the same. He labeled it "ADVENTURES OF ROCKY."

He drew a man and a woman talking on a sofa. "NEAR HUMAN DIALOGUE," he called this one. The man was saying, "What's for dinner?" The woman answered, "Yes, but should I wear a penguin?"

Cavanaugh realized the couple looked like him and Judy.

He turned the notepad facedown and paid attention to the meeting. It was no surprise that the Southern Maryland Resident Agency, which was him and Seton, was assigned to continue investigation of the local hate groups. Nobody believed the local hate groups had the capacity to create a genetically engineered strain of malaria. "We need to make sure we cover all possible bases," Dunbar said. *We need to keep you sidelined and unvocal*, he didn't say. Cavanaugh heard it anyway.

Only midafternoon, and he'd managed to piss off his girlfriend, his boss, and, apparently, the gods of law enforcement. Probably a personal record.

There was just no end to his talents.

INTERIM

The truck pulled up to the shacks just before dawn. Inside, the workers were already up, eating fried bacon, nursing babies, trudging to the privies and the rough, wooden shower house. The shacks had no indoor plumbing.

The truck beeped its horn twice. Men and women, shadowy in the gray dawn, walked toward it and climbed into the back.

"I count sixteen," the driver said. "Christ, that ain't enough."

The man beside him said nothing.

"Well, it *ain't.* Berenger'll have my balls I bring him just sixteen. We're weeding today, for Chrissake." He rolled down the window and waved his arm outside. "Hey! Time to go! Hey!"

The arm waving outside the truck window looked ghostly gray in the predawn. But the migrant workers didn't have to see its color. They knew from the voice.

"They're scared," the second man in the truck cab said abruptly. He was black. "Can't blame 'em. Mosquitoes all over this year."

"I don't blame 'em. But I still gotta make my crew." He waved his arm again. "Hey! Hey!"

"Can't yell 'em into goin'."

The driver pulled in his arm and snapped on the radio. "Rioting again today in Washington, where protestors and looters alike—"

"Turn it off," the black man said.

The driver did. In the east, the very beginnings of sunrise stained the sky. Bugs swarmed in the truck's headlights.

"And close the window," the black man said.

"Sorry," the driver said. He rolled up the window. Neither man looked at each other. One more figure emerged from the closest shack, a woman, making her reluctant way to the open back of the truck through the wing-buzzing darkness.

E I G H T

The value of biological warfare will be a debatable
question until it has been clearly proven or disproven
by experience. . . . There is but one logical course to
pursue, namely, to study the possibilities of such warfare
from every angle, to make every preparation for
reducing its effectiveness, and thereby reduce the
likelihood of its use.

—Henry Stimson, Secretary of War,
in a letter to Dr. Frank B. Jewett,
President of the National Academy of Sciences, 1942

Six weeks into the epidemic, Melanie Anderson thought as she fried herself an omelet in her Weather Vane Motel kitchen, *and they still had shit.*

No, not exactly shit. They had the most complete epidemic curves in disease-control history. People graphs detailing precisely who'd gotten the disease, when and where they'd gotten it, how it had run its course, and how often it had turned fatal. Vector graphs, showing everything about *Anopheles* except when the little suckers got horny. Time graphs coordinating the spread of malaria reading with *Anopheles* reproduction rates.

They also had several thousand infected mosquitoes, dead and alive. They had a complete understanding of the altered genetic mechanisms that let the malaria parasites colonize sickled blood cells, where no malaria parasites had ever been able to boldly go before. They had photographs and computer simulations and tagged exhibits and duplicate files. Finally, they had every epidemiologist specializing in malaria crawling over Maryland and Virginia. You couldn't walk around without tripping over an epidemiologist from places like the Antwerp Institute of Tropical Medicine, the Microbiology Research Establishment at Porton Down in England, the World Health Organization. The woods around Newburg sounded like the Tower of Babel. Joe Krovetz had found a Brazilian coin and a Danish candy wrapper.

So many of the CDC's own malaria people were involved, either here or in Atlanta, that the CDC hadn't even been able to respond to a call for help from one of their established clients. The Democratic Republic of the Congo was having another outbreak of malaria, but, then, Congo was always having an outbreak of malaria. The CDC couldn't spare a team. It wasn't like it was Ebola, after all. Africa was used to malaria. The United States was not.

Melanie flipped her omelet so viciously it landed half-in, half-out of the frying pan. She scraped it back in and dumped chopped vegetables on top. She didn't feel like eating with the team again tonight. She was sick of all of them, except young Joe Krovetz. He was the only one who agreed with her that this was an attempt at genocide. Except for the entire FBI, who might or might not believe malaria reading was criminal, but at least they were acting as if they did. The rest of her own team, in contrast, held out for a spontaneous mutation, an accidental introduction from another country ("possibly in larval form in agricultural produce," Susan Muscato had said, the head-in-the-sand bitch) or—for all Melanie knew—an insectoid immaculate conception. Fools.

She dumped the omelet onto a plate. The underside, which was now the top side, looked scarred and patchy from her inept flipping. Green vegetables stuck through the half-cooked patches like mold under viscous gauze. Well, hot sauce would help. She searched through the cupboard. She was out of hot sauce.

Figured. Just one more thing she didn't have, along with belief from her colleagues. Along with an end to the epidemic. USAMRIID's mosquito-eradication program was working well, but in this unseasonably hot and wet summer, *A. quadrimaculatus* still flourished. The epidemic curves projected that they were still weeks away from ending the epidemic.

She slashed at her omelet. The door opened and Joe Krovetz walked in. He didn't knock any more; if she didn't want company, she kept the chain on. Except that this evening she'd forgotten.

"Brought you an ice cream cone," he said. "We stopped on the way back from McDonald's. Good God, what's that thing?"

"My dinner," Melanie said shortly. "It's an omelet. You know, healthy egg dish with healthy vegetables?"

"What'd you do to it?"

"I *cooked* it. And I don't like ice cream."

"You don't even know what flavor it is yet," Joe said affably. You couldn't offend him. It was one reason Melanie found him restful. *"You're snapping at everyone,"* Farlow had told her. *"Act like a professional, damn it."*

It wasn't Farlow's brothers and sisters that somebody was killing off.

"Okay, Joe, what flavor is the ice cream?"

"Chocolate swirl."

"I don't like chocolate swirl."

"Okay," Joe said, and dumped the cone into her garbage can. He sat opposite her at the tiny table. "You hear what happened today? Big news."

Melanie stopped eating. "What happened?"

"The FBI declared a Terrorist Warning Advisory and got all twenty-five-thousand Bureau people involved. It was on the six o'clock news."

Melanie laid down her fork. "Really? What does that mean?"

"What do you mean what does it mean?"

"Well, are they going to do something different? Whatever they've been doing so far hasn't led anyplace."

"I don't know," Joe said. "The news didn't go into details."

"Of course not. It's *TV.* And probably the FBI is just bullshitting anyway. I'll believe they're doing something when they actually arrest somebody."

For the first time since she'd known him, Joe looked troubled. His downy eyebrows drew together, making an artificial wrinkle across his young skin. "Mel . . . you're not saying you believe the FBI is in on this? That our own government is collaborating with killing off blacks . . . you're not saying that, are you?"

"Do I look that paranoid to you, Krovetz? No, I'm not saying that. The government doesn't have to be collaborating. All they have to be doing is look like they're investigating when they're actually doing shit. After all, it's no secret that our government doesn't much like blacks."

"Mel . . . you don't believe that."

"Don't tell me what I believe!" Actually, she didn't believe the government was condoning genocide. But they weren't making any progress toward arresting anybody, either, and it made her furious that Joe wouldn't see that . . . Joe, the one white person she thought really grasped the full monstrosity of what was happening. Melanie had told him about the Tuskegee Institute experiments on syphilis, where four hundred black men had deliberately been left untreated so the government could study the progress of the disease. She'd told Joe about the deliberate infection of prisoners in the Atlanta Federal Prison with malaria in order to test experimental drugs, a program legitimized by an act of Congress. Supposedly the prisoners were all volunteers and no deals were cut (yeah, right). She'd told Joe . . . Oh, she was sick of it. Not even the best of them could really see how pervasive and destructive the prejudice was. Especially not the best of them.

"Mel," Joe said gently, "you're losing it."

"Thank you so much, Dr. Krovetz."

"No, I mean it. You have to—" The phone shrilled.

Immediately Melanie cried, "Don't answer it!"

"I wasn't going to. But why not?"

She didn't respond. Two rings, and the answering machine came on. She picked up her knife, without knowing she did it, and clutched the handle.

"Hello, Melanie," the same deep voice said. "Go back to Atlanta, black bitch. You aren't safe here. If the mosquitoes don't get you, the white citizens of Maryland will. Clear out while you can." Click.

Melanie was abruptly calm. She walked to the machine, pulled out the tape, and recorded the date and time on its label. She dropped it in a drawer will all the others. Then she slipped a fresh tape into the machine.

Joe was staring at her. "Fucking shit, Melanie. How often does this happen?"

She said crisply, "I have sixteen tapes. That's number seventeen."

"Have you told Farlow?"

"No. And you're not going to either."

"Why not?"

"Because I want to stay on this project." She sat down again and leaned toward him. Her mood changed yet again, and suddenly she wanted to make Joe Krovetz understand. "Don't you see? Farlow would like to replace me here. Preferably with another black who's negative for sickle-cell trait. Farlow agrees with you that I'm 'losing it,' only he says it more forcibly and more often. But I'm staying on this epidemic. I have to, Joe. I *have* to. So don't you dare tell him about these calls. I mean it. Do I have your word?"

Krovetz sat thinking. After a minute he said reluctantly, "Okay."

"Good. Now let's go get some ice cream."

"I just had ice cream. And you said you don't like it."

"So I lied," Melanie said. All at once she wanted to get out of the motel room. The ugly sounds of the hate call seemed to hang in the air, dirtying it. She could hardly breathe in here. And she'd be damned if that telephonic slime-monger was going to make her a prisoner in this room. She'd slogged through infested African jungles, looking for dangerous disease vectors or their victims; she wasn't going to be intimidated by some pathetic maggot-souled small-brained skinhead.

"Well, I suppose you need to eat something besides that," Joe said, pointing at her omelet. "Not that you're eating it anyway."

"No, because you're right. It's disgusting. I want a hamburger."

"Okay. Lock your room. And keep it locked, Mel. It wasn't when I came in."

Melanie locked her door. Walking across the street to the diner, she kept a good distance away from Joe. They'd spent a lot of time together lately. She didn't want to start any rumors.

Still, although she hated to admit it, she was glad his solid masculine bulk walked beside her.

Judy had told the boy no. He'd phoned her right after the call from Robert, and she'd still been numb. Robert, whom she'd hoped to marry. Staying with his ex-wife, telling her he'd be home when he damn well felt like it, treating her just as Ben had. Robert, who'd been her chance to start over, to love again, to this time oh-please-God-get-it-*right*. Robert.

After she'd hung up on Robert, she'd sat staring at the phone as if it were alive. At some level, she couldn't believe everything was over. Was it over? Did Robert still want her? Did . . . When the phone rang again, she'd seized it, so grateful she was afraid she'd cry. "Robert?"

"No, ma'am." A strange voice, slow and southern. "This is Earl Lester, ma'am. Can I have words with Agent Cavanaugh?" On the last sentence his voice abruptly cracked, and Judy had realized it was a young teen.

"He's . . . not here," she said, her own voice breaking in a way she hated. Would Robert ever be here again? Was he moving out for good? What was happening?

"Then can y'all tell me where to find him?"

"No, I'm sorry. I'm . . . sorry." She hung up.

For ten minutes she didn't move at all. Then she tried to pull herself together, act normally, do some work. That was it, work. Wasn't that what feminist movies were always saying? Men came and went, but you always had your work.

She stared at the computer screen, with the first draft of an article on left-handed molecules for *Science Today*. Five minutes later, she changed a word. Five minutes after that, another one. The doorbell rang.

"I'm Earl Lester, ma'am. To talk to Agent Cavanaugh."

"I told you he wasn't here."

"Yes, ma'am. But I figured I'd jest wait for him." The boy blinked twice. He was tall, skeletal, and a uniform pale, washed-out color, like dirty cream: skin, hair, T-shirt. Even his eyes were pale, somewhere between blue and gray. When he blinked like that, he looked like a rabbit.

Judy said, too harshly—she was talking to a child, for God's sake— "There's no point in waiting, Earl. Agent Cavanaugh's not returning."

Two more blinks. "He done left you?"

"I don't really think that's any of your business!"

"No, ma'am. Just being conversational. My daddy done left my mama four or five times. Always comes back though. Sooner or later."

The boy was trying to comfort her. This inept, weird-looking kid . . . It was touching. All of a sudden Judy felt much better. Fuck Robert. He'd either come back, or he wouldn't. She'd be damned if she'd let either one destroy her.

"Thank you, Earl. I can give you Agent Cavanaugh's current number if you'd like."

"'Preciate it."

She gave him not only Marcy's number but also Marcy's address. With any luck, the kid would interrupt Robert and Marcy at some critical moment.

"Thank you, ma'am." Earl walked unhurriedly—Judy had the impression it was his only mode—down the front path and disappeared behind a clump of trees. There was no bicycle or car. He must have walked.

She shrugged and went back to her computer. For the rest of the afternoon, she made herself concentrate on left-handed molecules. In the evening she cleaned house, weeded the garden, ironed a skirt, moved some furniture—anything to tire herself out so that she might have a chance of falling quickly asleep. So she wouldn't have to lie awake alone, wondering where he was and what he was doing. Anything but that.

UNDERGROUND SOVIET HARDLINERS CREATED MALARIA
READING, SAYS VET GROUP

PATRIOTS GROUPS USING MALARIA READING TO
UNDERMINE GOVERNMENT AUTHORITY,
SAYS WHITE HOUSE AIDE

WHITE SUPREMACISTS CREATED MALARIA READING,
SAYS NAACP

MALARIA READING ESCAPED FROM BIOTECH LABS—
PROOF AVAILABLE, SAYS CITIZEN COALITION

SAME PEOPLE MADE MALARIA READING WHO MADE AIDS,
SAYS GAY SPOKESPERSON

IRAN CREATED MALARIA READING TO GET EVEN FOR
GULF WAR, SAYS RETIRED COLONEL

GOD SENT MALARIA READING AS PUNISHMENT FOR FAILING
FAITH, SAYS BLACK MINISTER

PHARMACEUTICAL FIRMS GUILTY OF CREATING MALARIA
READING TO BOOST SALES, CLAIMS CONSUMER
WATCHDOG ORG.

MALARIA READING RESULT OF ALIEN LANDING—
CLEAR REVENGE FOR ROSWELL

SHOCKING SECRET DOCUMENTS TRACE MALARIA
READING TO IRS!!

The trouble with investigating an epidemic, Cavanaugh discovered, was that the pace wasn't set by the investigators. It wasn't even set by the criminals. It was set by the mosquitoes.

The breeding cycle of *Anopheles*, Melanie explained to him, was about eighteen days. That was how long it took for each new generation of mosquitoes to appear—and each new infected area had its own new victims. Fresh information about the epidemic was unlikely to become available until a new generation of victims did.

So for the next two weeks, Cavanaugh gave his attention to southern Maryland hate groups and their neighbors, which was what Dunbar had assigned him to anyway. None of the groups, in Cavanaugh's opinion, had the capacity to engineer a one-cell battery, let alone new genes. All of them, in Cavanaugh's opinion, were nuts. The neighbors ranged from disgusted to admiring.

"When I received the flyer about a tax-protest meeting, I went," said one attractive, fortyish white woman in shorts and a tie-dyed T-shirt, whom Cavanaugh approached while she was weeding flowers in her front yard. "But then it turned out to be this separatist group. 'Arcadia,' they call themselves, and the leader says he's the 'ambassador from Arcadia to the United States.' They consider that they've already seceded, and the taxes being 'forced' from them are a form of illegal tribute. Like 'the Roman Empire levied on Atlantis.'" She hummed the *Twilight Zone* theme, waving her trowel to the beat.

"Were there any black people at the meeting?"

"Oh, yes. The group made a big point of not being discriminatory. It's just the government they hate, not individuals."

"Thank you for your help," Cavanaugh said.

"Any time." She went back to her azaleas.

The next interviewee was not so cooperative. He lived in a cabin on a dirt road. "You got a warrant?" the man asked, glaring at Cavanaugh through an amazingly worn and battered screen door.

"Sir, you're not a suspect. I just want to ask you about a group allegedly headquartered at the place next to yours, the Christian Crusade."

"I don't know nothing about them." He slammed his inner door.

Cavanaugh got into his car and drove the quarter mile to the next cabin down. A skinny, elderly black woman dressed in jeans and a faded cotton blouse came to the door. "Yes?"

"FBI, ma'am. I'm Special Agent Robert Cavanaugh. I'd like to ask you a few questions."

"I'm Mrs. Hattie Brown," she said, from behind a screen door worn as soft and pliable as cheesecloth.

"About the Christian Crusade group allegedly headquartered at number 487 on this road."

Her face changed. She came out from behind her screen door and peered up at him. She was tiny, no more than five-one, maybe a hundred pounds. But Cavanaugh recognized the type. She had lived too long, and too hard, to fear much of anything anymore.

"You gonna bust their ass?"

He smiled. "I don't know yet."

"You should. They ain't no good. They hate black folk, Jew folk, Spanish folk, Catholic folk. Calls 'em 'seeds of Satan' and says they ain't even human and got no right to no respect. One of 'em came right into my church and had the gall to stand up durin' speakin' and gush out that shit. Most unchristian thing I ever done heard. Right in my church."

Cavanaugh took out his notepad. "Go on."

"Ain't no 'on.' I stood up and hollered for him to get his ass out of there, and Sister Walters, she joined in. That made some of the men finally move, and the scum left."

"Have there been any retaliatory actions?"

"'Scuse me?"

"Has that guy, or anybody else from Christian Crusade, tried to get even with you or Sister Walters? Or even threatened to get even?"

"Nah," she said scornfully. "They ain't that kind. Stand up to 'em and they back down. All talk."

"Well, that's good, isn't it?" Cavanaugh said. It was an unprofessional remark, but he was liking the old woman immensely. A tough cookie.

She threw back her head and laughed. "Sure is. Talk don't get nobody's ass killed."

"One more question, ma'am. Have you ever been aware of any scientific activity at Christian Crusade? Seen any science-looking equipment go in and out, or heard any talk about mosquitoes or genes or diseases?"

Her smile vanished. "You investigatin' *that*? Lord, son, Christian Crusade ain't made this plague. They way too stupid. Most of 'em never finished their schoolin', and all of them think science is 'most as evil as popery."

"Thank you, ma'am. You've been very helpful."

"No, I ain't, but I wish I could be. My grandniece was one of 'em that died of this new plague. Twenty-six years old." Her old eyes turned inward, to private pain. Suddenly she said fiercely, "You catch 'em, son, you hear? You catch 'em good!"

"We're trying, ma'am."

She nodded vigorously. "They gotta be stopped. But you know what, son? People like Christian Crusade ain't the ones making this plague. They too stupid. So why you wasting FBI time out here asking about 'em?"

"Because my boss told me to."

She nodded again. "I see. FBI covering its ass?"

"That's about it. The FBI's covering its ass." It was a relief to say it out loud and have someone understand, even if it was someone with no authority except that of years of survival. He liked this old bird.

"Ain't it always the way." She sighed, and again the sunken eyes turned inward. "Be a whole lot of time saved in this world if people warn't made to waste it covering their ass."

"I couldn't agree more," Cavanaugh said. It was the first time he'd felt cheerful all week.

Aryan Nation had the motivation and the wealth to have created *Plasmodium reading*, but their bent wasn't scientific and their money went for paramilitary equipment.

White Maryland were a nasty bunch. They'd throw rocks through the window of a six year old displaying a menorah on his windowsill, through the window of a black candidate for the state legislature, through the window of a white public health nurse who visited black homes. They stuffed hate pamphlets in mailboxes, scrawled graffiti on public buildings, harassed a pair of high school kids who were dating interracially. Key members had arrest sheets as varied as their spewings were monotonous. Harassment, assault, theft, fraud, DWI, disturbing the peace, striking a law officer, carrying an illegal weapon, narcotics violation, parole violation, even rape. But nowhere could Cavanaugh find any trace of genetic engineering or any capacity to do so.

Not that he'd expected to. These weren't the kinds of groups he'd meant when he'd told Dunbar the lone terrorist theory was ridiculous. And Dunbar knew these weren't the kinds of groups Cavanaugh meant. Dunbar was just "being thorough," both because he was a book man and because of the press. The groups Cavanaugh had meant were, presumably, being investigated through Washington: Russian hard-liners, Iranian warmongers, German neo-Nazis, South African white supremacists resenting the end of apartheid, South Americans with a grudge against the United States. Plus the homegrown insect research and genetic-engineering companies. The good stuff, which Cavanaugh only got to hear about, enviously, at meetings in Baltimore.

"Talked to another reporter today." Seton swaggered into their tiny shared Leonardtown office. "That gal from the *Sun*. The one who broke the story."

"Libby Turner," Cavanaugh said automatically. "I thought all press communication was supposed to go through the media representatives in Baltimore or Washington."

"Yeah, well, I didn't say anything they'd disapprove of. Gotta keep the old schnozz in front of the public, though. I retire next year, and good publicity can't hurt a second career."

"And what second career might that be?" Cavanaugh didn't really care, but he was tracking his hate groups' bulletin boards on the Internet, and the postings were even more depressing and monotonous than Seton.

"Haven't decided yet." Seton unwrapped another Snickers and dropped the wrapper into the four inches between their desks. He was such a slob. Every night Cavanaugh picked up empty Doritos bags, Coke cans, used tissues.

"Could you please put that in the garbage can?"

"Oh, sure," Seton said, but he didn't. "You finding anything worth following up on the Net?"

Cavanaugh stopped scrolling and looked at Seton. "Why, you interested in helping?"

"Can't. Got too much to do with my informants about Pax River. Althoooooo . . ." He drew the syllable out and looked expectantly at Cavanaugh.

"Although what, Seton?"

"Although you'd be surprised how cases intertwine. And what you can learn from informants who don't know what they're giving away."

Cavanaugh sat very still. "You got something on malaria reading, Seton? Give it to me."

"Not a chance. This is *my* lead. And I'm the boss, remember? Oh, by the way, how come Judy hasn't been calling here with her usual messages about picking up milk on the way home or meeting her someplace for a cozy drink? Your little domestic paradise gone bust?"

"Fuck you, Seton," which was something Cavanaugh usually never said, but Seton could provoke him to it. Pointedly he swiveled his seat back to face his computer. Seton only laughed and went back to filling out 302s, the forms that recorded information that might eventually be used in court. Seton filed more goddamn 302s than anyone Cavanaugh had ever seen. Dunbar had commended Seton more than once on the completeness of his records.

No leads. No talk with Judy. No progress. And when Cavanaugh dragged himself back to Marcy's apartment, after yet another futile day, Marcy was there.

Had it been two weeks since she'd left for Dallas? Yes. It seemed like two years.

"Hello, Robert," Marcy said. "There was some kid here looking for you."

"What kid?" She sat curled in a corner of her black sofa, watching some ballet program and sipping a Scotch. She wore jeans and a scoop-necked blue leotard, and her blonde hair was pinned casually on top of her head, with strands falling down the sides and over one eye. She looked sensational.

"Some little cracker. Blinked a lot. He wrote his name and number on the phone pad, but said he couldn't come back 'cause it was 'too fur a piece to hike.'"

Earl Lester. And he had hiked in? From . . . ? Just the thought of it tired Robert. Although maybe the kid meant he'd hitchhiked.

"Have a drink, Robert," Marcy said. "You look like you need it."

He poured himself a double vodka and tonic. Marcy watched two ballet dancers wave their arms and mince across a stage, her eyes intent on the screen. Robert suddenly liked that she wasn't waiting on him.

Judy would have jumped up, all solicitous service, which always made him feel he had to be ardent and communicative in return. He didn't want to talk. He didn't feel ardent. He wanted to be left alone, to brood undisturbed.

Marcy watched the rest of the ballet program, while Robert had another double vodka. When the show was over, she rose and stretched. "I'm hungry. Want something to eat before you go?"

"You're going to *cook*?" In all the years of their marriage, Marcy had cooked about six times, never with memorable results. She preferred catering, restaurants, takeout, or yogurt. She could eat or not eat with impunity, and it never seemed to affect either her energy or her figure.

She laughed. "Well, no. I was going to send out for a pizza."

"Sounds good to me," Cavanaugh said. "Pepperoni and olives."

He finished his drink while she ordered a large pizza with pepperoni, olives, onions, green and red peppers. Robert hated peppers, but she'd probably forgotten that. He was pleased that she hadn't asked, hadn't been all anxious to know his dislikes so she could make a show of avoiding them. Marcy looked out for herself. Cavanaugh suddenly found that restful.

He sipped a third drink while Marcy found an emery board and filed her nails, humming to herself. Abigail, who'd been asleep on the hearth rug, woke up, trotted over to Cavanaugh, and licked his hand. Lazily—or maybe it was starting to be drunkenly—he scratched her ears, and her tail thumped on the floor in a comfortable rhythm.

When the pizza came, Cavanaugh let Marcy pay for it. He fetched plates, napkins, and cutlery from the kitchen. It felt good to be doing something for himself again. They ate from the coffee table. Cavanaugh sipped his vodka between bites, and Marcy—unlike Judy—didn't mention his liver.

"Damn, I smeared it," Marcy said. A slice of sauce-wet pepperoni had fallen on the front of her blue leotard. She picked off the pepperoni and scrubbed at the stain, which only made it worse. Under the stretchy material, her beautiful breasts bounced gently. She leaned forward for another napkin, and the front of her leotard gaped slightly.

Robert felt dizzy. Lust hit him like . . . like what? Desire interfered with finding a metaphor. Wordlessly, he watched Marcy rub water on the tight cloth over her breasts. Watched the stain grow lighter and wider. Watched the thin material grow transparent.

"There, I think that's . . . Robert?"

He staggered when he stood up, but he didn't let it stop him. Navigating the treacherous straits around the coffee table, he inched toward her.

Her blue eyes darkened slightly with amusement. It was his last clear sight before his eyes closed and his arms went around her.

She tasted of pepperoni, of promise, of yesterdays. Her lips smiled under his; he didn't care. His right hand cupped her breast.

"Upstairs," she whispered, and took his hand. He lurched after her, watching her hips and ass move under the tight jeans, the ache in his groin so powerful he thought he would burst before they even reached the bedroom.

Fortunately, he didn't. Marcy pushed him gently onto the bed. She undid his belt and zipper, and eased him out of pants and briefs. He watched her undress: parts of her toned, full-breasted body coming into view one by one: Legs, as she pulled down her jeans. Waist and shoulders, as she slid the leotard over her head. Breasts, as she unhooked her bra. Robert closed his eyes, dizzy. When he opened them again, she was climbing onto him, loose strands of her blonde hair falling across her face, her breathing already quickening.

"Marcy . . . Marcy . . ."

He didn't last very long. She didn't seem to mind, continuing to move above him until her head jerked back and she made the same little cry she always had. How had he forgotten that little cry? Or the soft ritual stroke of her palm against his cheek immediately afterward?

How had he forgotten any of it?

"I never stopped wanting you," he murmured, but Marcy probably hadn't heard him, since his words slurred so much . . . or maybe she had . . . or maybe he hadn't actually said it aloud . . . or maybe . . . By the time she nestled naked by his side, he was already asleep.

When he woke in the morning, there was a note from Marcy on the nightstand beside the clock. The clock said 6:25. This was good; plenty of time for him to get to work and for Marcy to work out at her gym, which is where he presumed she'd gone. The note said only *Yum*.

Cavanaugh's heart swelled with affection. She was being sweet; there was no way his brief and drunken performance could have been *yum* for her. But the next one would be. Tonight he would make it up to her. After all, unless she'd changed drastically in three years, he knew everything she liked best. Tonight.

That was when he remembered Judy. Immediately his hangover kicked in. Cavanaugh staggered to the bathroom and found ibuprofen in Marcy's medicine cabinet. He swallowed four pills and shook his head from side to side. This was a mistake. But at least it showed he wasn't poisoned enough to vomit.

The best thing to do with a hangover, he'd decided years ago, was to ignore it. Just carry on with one's usual routine, from both defiance and self-punishment. He showered, shaved, put on coffee. Then he unlocked the front door, hoping Marcy had left the newspaper for him. She had. It was the *Sun,* not the *Post,* since Marcy had never trusted the *Post*'s liberal bent.

FBI PUTS POSSIBLE PLAGUE SUSPECT
UNDER HEAVY SURVEILLANCE

BY LIBBY TURNER

The Baltimore Sun learned today that the FBI has singled out a suspect in the creation of malaria reading. Although the FBI press office will neither confirm nor deny that Dr. Michael Sean Donohue is a suspect, *Sun* reporters observed for themselves the unusually heavy surveillance of the forty-eight-year-old microbiologist. The surveillance apparently began only two days ago, but since then at least four agents have been assigned to continuously follow Donohue, including a stakeout at his College Park apartment.

Donohue holds an M.D. from Yale Medical School, plus a Ph.D. in genetic research from the same institution. Until six months ago, he was employed by Genemod, Inc., a small and struggling Virginia start-up company in the booming field of genetically engineered pharmaceuticals. Dr. Chris Allenwood, the CEO of Genemod, declined to answer questions about the reasons for Donohue's dismissal.

The FBI surveillance of Donohue comes at a time when a large percentage of Bureau resources are being poured into the malaria reading investigation. This strongly suggests that

Donohue may be a suspect in that extremely prominent case.
A few weeks ago FBI director Peter Broylin issued a memo to
all 25,000 Bureau employees emphasizing that . . .

Son-of-a-bitch. Broylin needed a suspect, so he'd found one. And
the Turner woman had put tails on the tails to find out who the Bureau
was watching.

Cavanaugh read the first two paragraphs again. "Forty-eight-year-
old microbiologist . . . M.D., from Yale Medical School, plus a Ph.D. . . .
employed by Genemod, Inc., a small and struggling Virginia start-up
company . . ." *Fired from his job.* They were using the profile put together at Quantico. Plus whatever else they thought they had.

It was possible someone at the Bureau had even leaked the surveillance information to Libby Turner to make sure the public knew the Bureau was on the road to success. This was not an unknown tactic. On the
other hand, the skimpy information on Donohue suggested that the *Sun*
had come across the story just the way it said it had, and had wanted to
release it with skimpy details rather than wait to be scooped by the *Post*
or even the *Times*.

Cavanaugh turned off the water for coffee and headed for the Baltimore Field Office. On the way he called in, but it was hardly necessary.
He knew Dunbar would call a meeting of the investigative team. What
he didn't know was how much the Bureau knew that the press didn't.

Yet.

INTERIM

When the old woman wheeled her chair into the living room on Sunday morning, Cindy was already watching cartoons. Cindy's braids stuck out at all angles; it had been at least a week since the child's mother took her down to LaWanda's to get them done. When the old woman had been a girl, folks did their own children's braids. But that was a long, long time ago.

She rubbed her hands together before pushing again at the high, round wheels. It got harder every day, like everything else. Her granddaughter kept wanting to get her a motorized chair, but the old woman wasn't having that. Motors were for machines, not to be people's legs. "The Good Lord don't intend me to walk no more," she told her granddaughter, who just pursed her lips and shook her head.

"Cindy," she said softly. "Chile."

Her great-granddaughter looked around and smiled, only one tooth left in the front. Even so, someday the girl was going to be too pretty for her own good.

"Hi, Gramama."

"Hi yourself, chile. Come wheel me outside."

Cindy glanced reluctantly back at the TV, where some white doll-toys in boots and capes were shooting guns at something. But she was a well-brought-up little girl.

"Sure, Gramama. But it's still dark out."

"It's light enough. I want to smell the Good Lord's mornin' grass."

The little girl grabbed the handlebars of the wheelchair and pushed it effortlessly out the kitchen door and down the ramp into the backyard.

"Park it over there, behind them trees. That's good. Now you go back on inside."

"I wanta stay and smell the Good Lord's mornin' grass too."

"No, you don't. Your favorite TV show is on. Git." She watched Cindy bound back inside, on the way turning a somersault, just because she could.

The old woman's stomach rumbled. She couldn't eat much anymore, not without terrible pain in her belly and gut. And whatever she ate took days to pass through her, until she felt like she might burst from the gas. Her arms and neck and hands ached from the arthritis, and lately it seemed like she was losing what little taste she had left in her toothless mouth. But the worst was the diapers. Her granddaughter called them something else, but they were diapers all right. Nowadays, before she ever knew it, her water gushed out right on the bed or the chair or, once, before the diapers, on her granddaughter's brand-new sofa.

She sniffed the air. Smell mostly gone, too. But not sight, not completely, not yet. She could make out the toys scattered over the grass and the birds still singing their hearts out in the trees, it was so early. She could see the morning glories still closed up tight and the pearly gray in the eastern sky just starting to turn pink.

She couldn't quite see the mosquitoes. But they were there.

They swarmed in the evening and the early morning. It had been that way when she was a little girl, and it was that way now that she was old and past her time. The Good Lord, she often told the doctor, had overlooked her in His gatherin' in. But the Lord helps those who help themselves.

Shrugging her shawl off her shoulders, the old woman waited, thinking of what a different doctor had told her years and years ago when she got hit by that car and had to have a blood transfusion in the hospital. Didn't think she'd ever need that information again. Funny what came in handy, wait you long enough.

She felt the first sting and peered down at the mosquito. It was almost standing on its head on the inside of the arm she'd exposed by painfully inching up the sleeves of her nightdress. The mosquito had white patches on its dark wings. After a moment, another one landed on her exposed thigh.

"It's time, Lord," she said aloud. "The folks inside, they won't wake up for hours, but it's time now. Please, Lord. Do it now.

"Call me on home."

N I N E

We're all mutants. Everybody is genetically defective.
—Geneticist Michael M. Kaback, University
of San Diego, quoted in *Scientific American*, 1994

Mel," Joe Krovetz said on the phone, "unlock your door; I'm coming over."

Melanie glanced sleepily at her watch. "Christ, Krovetz, it's six-fifteen!"

"I know. Get up." The phone went dead.

Melanie groped for her robe and then stumbled toward the door. What the hell did Krovetz have for her at six-fifteen in the goddamn morning? It had better be good or his young ass was dead meat. It had better be at least some genetic clue that *Plasmodium reading* had been deliberately engineered after all. . . . Suddenly she felt more awake. On her way from the bedroom, she turned on the burner under her teakettle.

When she slipped the chain off the motel door and unshot the bolt, Krovetz was already there, carrying a newspaper. He marched word-lessly to the kitchen, checked the water kettle, and then held her firmly by both shoulders.

"Listen to me, Mel. The FBI has a suspect. I'm telling you now so you don't go off the deep end when Farlow makes his announcement at the meeting this morning."

She shook her shoulders free. "Why would I go off the deep end? That's pretty insulting, Krovetz. Unless you think the suspect is just a cover-up, a phony fingering to hide the—"

"How would I know that? I'm not in law enforcement, thank God. But I was with Farlow, just shooting the breeze, when they called him late last night. Maybe you'd better read the story first."

Melanie read the front page he thrust at her. The headlines were nearly two inches high.

FBI PUTS POSSIBLE PLAGUE SUSPECT UNDER HEAVY SURVEILLANCE

Libby Turner had written the article, which was short. Like Joe, Melanie couldn't tell if the suspect was genuine or a sop to the public. Nor could she tell why Joe looked at her as if she were a bomb about to go off.

"So? They've got somebody. That's good, isn't it? And it doesn't mean they'll stop investigating other suspects until this one is at least charged with something."

"No. Yes. I mean, there's something more." He ran a hand through his rumpled straight hair.

Melanie had never seen Joe nervous. She would have said it wasn't possible. Her throat tightened.

"What is it, Joe? Spit it out. You said you were with Farlow when 'they' called late last night. Who're 'they'? The FBI?"

"No. The *Baltimore Sun.*"

"Who said what? What's Farlow going to announce at the meeting?"

"A reporter called to ask if the CDC had any comment on the surveillance, which Farlow didn't because that was the first he'd heard of it. But, you know, the CDC maintains a hiring file, with both résumés and interview reports. On a hunch, Farlow accessed the CDC computer to see if this Donohue had applied for a job after he terminated at Genemod in Virginia. And he had." Again the gesture with the hair.

"Go on."

"Someone in Personnel did the preliminary interview. His—or her—report said that Donohue seemed both defensive and superior. He justified having been terminated by three different corporations since college on the grounds of bosses, quote, out to make trouble for me, unquote. When the interviewer asked why they'd want to do that, Donohue said it was because even though he doesn't look it, he's of racially mixed background. His father's people were Irish, but on his mother's side one of his grandparents was black."

Melanie couldn't breathe. "Black?"

"Yeah. The FBI must know that, but this reporter, Libby Turner, probably hasn't had time yet to—"

"*Black?* You're saying a black man is committing genocide against his own people?"

"*I'm* not saying anything. But Donohue himself says—"

"Are you crazy? Or just corrupted?"

Krovetz drew a deep breath.

"Do you even realize what you're spouting? Do you? You—or Farlow, or the FBI, or the press, I don't give a goddamn *who*—are trying to blame this evil on *us!* Killing off our own! So it's just a civil war, nothing to threaten the white folks, just those crazy niggers killing themselves again. What's a little more black-on-black murder, hey, hey—"

"Stop it, Mel."

"Stop it? Don't you dare tell me what to do! You stand there and repeat to me the most evil lie in the world like you believe it's true and I'm not supposed to—"

"It's not the most evil lie in the world."

"How the hell would you know? How would *you* know anything? How would you know what it feels like to . . . to . . ." She couldn't go on. This was Joe, one of the most decent human beings she'd ever known. She was wrong to blame Joe, wrong wrong wrong . . . and yet she wasn't. Something coalesced inside her, crystallized, something so old it wasn't even hers. . . . She'd inherited it from her parents, and they'd gotten it from their parents and so on back to the lash, the auction block, the slave ship, the casual tossing away of lives just because those lives were black. . . . The crystallized something pierced her, sharp and hot as burning brands, and she gasped.

"All right, Mel," Joe said. "All right."

"It's not true. It's not true."

"Maybe not."

"'Maybe?' For you to say—for them to say . . . to say . . ."

The teakettle whistled. Joe walked into the kitchenette and made instant coffee. When he handed her a cup, she gulped it black, not even feeling the burn in her mouth. Krovetz waited.

"I'm sorry, Joe," she whispered, when she could talk. "I just . . ." Just what? Just can't take much more of this.

"That's why I wanted to tell you first, alone. So you could get over the initial shock. Because, Mel, if you act like this at the meeting, Farlow's going to remove you from the project. You know he is. He doesn't like researchers who he thinks can't be objective. And if you're removed, you can't help anybody at all."

It was true. Melanie grasped onto this like a lifeline: If she so much as looked distraught or dysfunctional, Farlow would remove her from the project. And then she couldn't help anybody at all. Joe was right.

She took a sip of the coffee.

"That's better," Joe said quietly. "You'd better get dressed. Farlow's going to phone about the meeting any minute now, before anybody leaves for the field or goes on-line."

"Okay." After a moment she was able to add, "Thanks."

"We need you, Mel," Krovetz said. "Be sure to lock the door tight behind me."

The meeting at the Baltimore Field Office contained three surprises. To Cavanaugh, all three were shockers.

First, Dunbar stated clearly that no one in the FBI had leaked news of the surveillance to Libby Turner at the *Sun*. "We've checked this out already this morning. Turner learned about the surveillance just the way she said she had, by staking out the FBI agents on the stakeout. Unfortunate, but there it is."

No surprise there. Dunbar the Book Man was peeved but not angry. Reporters were reporters.

"Also, I wan to make perfectly plain that Bureau surveillance of Michael Donohue in no way means a slacking off on all other aspects of the investigation. International, national security, hate groups, genetic-engineering companies—all the angles are still going to be covered just as thoroughly. Everybody clear on this?"

Apparently everybody was; nobody protested. And nobody looked surprised. The men and women around the conference table hunched blearily over their coffee. Some team members were missing. Investigating, Cavanaugh presumed, except for the media representatives, who were probably frantically trying to keep up with calls from press, radio, and TV.

"Third—and this comes straight from the director—nobody talks about this case to anyone outside the Bureau. Nobody, about anything. Not even about how committed the Bureau is to solving it. The only permitted comment is 'No comment.' The director has personally asked me to remind you all that under the new guidelines issued last year, unauthorized disclosure is grounds for censure, suspension, or dismissal from the FBI."

Hardball. But not surprising. Libby Turner was only the tip of the media combat about to be staged outside the Hoover Building. Let the games begin.

Then came the first of the lions.

"The document I'm passing out now," Dunbar said, "is what we know at this point about Michael Sean Donohue. Everything in the Turner article was true. But in addition, there are two other major facts the press doesn't have so far. One, we have a file on Donohue in connection with the Irish Republican Army going back to 1984, when Donohue worked in Boston. The evidence is scanty and no charges were ever brought, but at the time the SACs in Boston deemed there to be enough to open a file."

The agents around the table lost their bleary looks and sat up straighter, including Cavanaugh. *The IRA.* But that made no sense. The Irish had never had a strong quarrel with blacks, American or otherwise. If they had somehow developed, or gotten hold of, something like an engineered parasite for a mosquito, half of London would now be down with sleeping sickness. Or dengue fever. Or whatever else they could make the dank British climate support.

Only the Division Five agents looked unsurprised; they apparently already had counterintelligence on the connection. A young female agent Cavanaugh didn't recognize blurted, "But why would the IRA want to—"

"We don't know that they *did*," Dunbar snapped, the first break in his aloof formality. "Please remember, Agent McDougal, that what you're holding is a preliminary information sheet on a suspect, not a final investigative report."

Agent McDougal reddened and raised her coffee. Cavanaugh wondered how many meetings would go by until she said anything again. Dunbar didn't really like rookies on his cases, although he must know they had to learn someplace. Felders had welcomed rookies, for their fresh perspectives. Cavanaugh missed Felders all over again.

"Finally," Dunbar said, "if you'll turn to the last page of the document, you'll see another key point about the suspect. This one is potentially very explosive. Michael Sean Donohue's blood heritage is three-quarters Irish, one-eighth German, and one-eighth African American."

Cavanaugh drew in his breath. There it was, on the last page: maternal great-grandmother Fleur D'Orsay, born 1874 of freed slaves, married in 1903 to Hans Pfeiffer in New Orleans, Louisiana, after ten years of common-law cohabitation.

"How available is this information to the press?" Agent McDougal asked, showing to Cavanaugh that he'd underestimated her. It just proved how little he knew about women.

Women. Marcy. Judy.

Dunbar said, "The family background is in the public records, so they might have it as early as the six o'clock news. The IRA connection, to the best of our data, is known only to the FBI and the CIA. Probably the—Agent Cavanaugh, do you have something to add?"

"No," Cavanaugh said, trying to wipe his face clean of whatever expression had prompted Dunbar's notice—*Marcy, Judy*—"no, I . . . no."

"Well, that's too bad, because I'm moving you from South Maryland hate groups to surveillance of Michael Donohue."

That was the second surprise. And not only to Cavanaugh. Glances were exchanged among agents, all of whom quickly returned to studying the profile of Donohue. Then Cavanaugh got it.

Dunbar wanted him someplace where he wouldn't stir up questions nobody wanted to hash out openly. What better place than on the surveillance team? Cavanaugh would be continually in the company of one-track, unimaginative agents with high testosterone and low doubt factors, which was what surveillance agents tended to be like. They would surround Cavanaugh, neutralize him. And since the press would be tailing the tails, the gag order on talking to them would be uppermost in everyone's mind, thereby keeping Cavanaugh from pretty much asking anything inflammatory of anybody. Plus, he would be the junior agent on surveillance. He wouldn't be writing any official reports. He'd just be along for the ride.

"I think maybe—"

"That's it, people," Dunbar said crisply, and the scraping of chairs and murmuring of voices drowned out whatever Cavanaugh was going to say.

Not that he knew what that would have been. A challenge to Dunbar the Book Man was equivalent to a challenge to the cosmic order. Nonetheless, Cavanaugh tried.

"Jerry, I appreciate you moving me closer to the center of the case. What with it having started in my jurisdiction and—"

"Seton's jurisdiction," Dunbar said, pointedly.

"Yes. Of course. But even though I do appreciate it, there are a few more leads I'd really like to follow through on, so if the surveillance assignment—"

"Turn the leads over to McDougal. They haven't turned up anything remotely useful yet, according to your own reports, so it'll be a good place for her to learn technique."

"But—"

"They *haven't* turned up anything, have they?" Dunbar asked. His gray eyes fixed on Cavanaugh like a tractor beam. "And you yourself were the one who said the domestic hate groups were just red herrings anyway."

Hoist with his own petard.

"Didn't you say that, Agent Cavanaugh?"

"Yes," Cavanaugh said resignedly.

"Well, then, there it is. Report to Pilozzi in Surveillance, ASAP."

Cavanaugh didn't answer. No point. He was assigned to Surveillance.

On his way to Pilozzi's office, he called Marcy at work. Her secretary said she was in a meeting. He couldn't face the call to Judy just yet. It was going to be awful. Judy would cry, and he would apologize, and if he weren't such a worm, he'd go see her in person instead of making a lousy phone call. But when he thought of Marcy, of another unstrained, easy dinner on the coffee table and another sweet reunion romp in bed, he knew he just couldn't do a personal scene with Judy. No matter how much she deserved her say. He just wouldn't be able to stand there and meet her eyes.

Thus conscience doth make cowards of us all.

He went downstairs to Pilozzi's office.

❀　　❀　　❀

The reporter caught Melanie as she left the house of an interviewee, mother of a six year old who'd died of malaria reading the day before. "I'm Shakita Franklin, Dr. Anderson, from radio station KQLN."

Melanie stopped resignedly, sweating in the black dress and stockings she always wore to survivor interviews. Mourning clothes. It was little enough to do to show respect.

"I know this is a hard time for me to be asking you questions, but KQLN would appreciate a comment from one of us who's close to the investigation."

"One of us." The young corn-rowed sister didn't say it as if to claim privilege, but merely as fact. Melanie said, "Go ahead."

"Thank you, Dr. Anderson. May I record?"

"Go ahead."

"You've heard, of course, that the *Baltimore Sun* has identified a suspect in malaria reading and has him under heavy surveillance."

"The whole world's heard that by now."

Shakita watched her closely. "Yes. And you know that the suspect is part black."

Melanie didn't ask how the girl knew this even before it had appeared on the six o'clock news. The world of reporters had just as many weblike bonds of favors, family, markers, and friendship as any other. Undoubtedly Shakita had some sort of deal that said she couldn't run her interview until after the six o'clock news. But being young and ambitious, she was out here digging.

"You don't look surprised, Dr. Anderson. Did the CDC already know that?"

"I can't speak for the CDC, Ms. Franklin. You'd need to ask Dr. James Farlow, head of the epidemiology team."

"I understand. Can you tell us, please, what effect this new information will have on the CDC investigation?"

"None. A Special Pathogens Branch investigation is concerned with identifying an epidemic, tracking it, and devising ways to end it."

"And is it ending?"

"It's too soon to tell," Melanie said. Sweat trickled down her neck and between her breasts. "The death rate, as you undoubtedly know, is falling. But the drop coordinates with the breeding cycle of *A. quadri-*

maculatus, so it could just mean that there's a temporary lull while the next generation of larvae mature and hatch."

"I see. The press has included much speculation about whether malaria reading could have evolved naturally, without human engineering. The CDC must be investigating that possibility—from a scientific point of view, I mean. How is that search going?"

"Again, you'd have to speak with Dr. Farlow for the most current information. I can tell you only that we've identified a list of amino-acid-level differences between *P. falciparum* and *P. reading.* The list implies heavy genetic linkages among at least three major mutations, possibly more."

"That's a lot of mutating to happen by coincidence all at once."

You know it, girl. But all Melanie said aloud was, "Yes, it is."

"Thank you, Dr. Anderson. This is Shakita Franklin of Radio KQLN in Washington."

SUBJ: OUTRAGE

FROM: MX87@AOL.COM

TO: MALAR-R@WORLDNET.NET

SO THE FBI HAS DECIDED THAT A BLACK MAN CREATED MALARIA READING. THIS IS A <BALD-FACED LIE.> WAKE UP, AMERICA? DON'T YOU SEE WHAT'S HAPPENING HERE? THE GOVERNMENT WOULD JUST LIKE THE PROBLEM TO GO AWAY, SO THEY CONVENIENTLY CHOOSE TO SHOVE IT ONTO US. I CAN'T IMAGINE A MORE DESPICABLE, COWARDLY, OUTRAGEOUS LIE. WE MUST <DO SOMETHING.> ANYTHING AT ALL WILL HELP—PICKET, RIOT, WRITE YOUR CONGRESSMAN, MAIL LEAFLETS. IF YOU HAVE TO GET ILLEGAL, DO IT—<THEY> ARE! WE MUST MUST MUST SHOW THEM JUST HOW DEEP THIS BETRAYAL GOES, AND THAT WE AREN'T GOING TO TAKE IT ANYMORE!

SUBJ: DONOHUE

FROM: REMAILER@WORLDNET.NET

TO: MALAR-R@WORLDNET.NET

LET THE SPEARCHUCKERS ALL KILL EACH OTHER OFF.
PROSECUTING DONOHUE IS JUST A WASTE OF TAXPAYERS
MONEY. GIVE HIM A LAB TO MAKE SOMETHING THAT WILL GET
THE OTHER 90% OF NIGGERS. GO, ANNIE QUAD!!!!

Judy rubbed her eyes. She'd been sitting for hours at her computer in the Rivermount house, surfing the Net. The medical lists, the government bulletin boards, the news channels, and now the chat rooms on malaria reading. Why? She didn't know exactly. Because it was important. Because it threw into sharp focus the mess simmering—now erupting—just below the surface of American life. Because she might want to write an article about it, if she could find the right angle.

Because somewhere out there, Robert was investigating it.

He was going to call her today. He hadn't called for two weeks, but he was going to call today. She'd woken up this morning knowing that, and hadn't been able to work since. Noon, and she was still in her nightgown. Noon, and she hadn't eaten anything. Noon, and she was surfing the Net on one phone line while her eyes strayed to the phone on the other line. She was acting like a clinging brain-dead dependent stereotype, and she knew it, and she couldn't seem to do anything else.

SUBJECT: (NO SUBJECT ENTERED)

FROM: MELORIAD@RPI.EDU

TO: MALAR-R@WORLDNET.NET

THE POSTINGS TODAY SICKEN ME. WE NEED TO PULL
TOGETHER HERE, NOT GET CAUGHT UP IN BLAME OR
GLOATING OR PARTISANSHIP. DON'T YOU SEE THAT IF
SOMEONE COULD DO THIS TO ONE ETHNIC GROUP, SOMEONE
COULD DO IT TO ANY OTHER? EVERY HERITAGE HAS SOME
GENETIC ANOMALIES THAT COULD BE EXPLOITED. <NO ONE>
IS SAFE!

Judy nodded. This MeloriaD was right. And that might make a hook for an article, if Judy could find out enough about the specific genetic anomalies of other ethnic groups. The Irish, say—until the last few hundred years they'd been isolated for centuries; maybe that was long

enough for viable genetic mutations to occur and be dispersed throughout a population. Maybe the Chinese? No, some group better rep-
resented in the United States would make a stronger article. Not the
Italians; everybody in the Mediterranean world had tromped through
Italy. Not enough genetic isolation. The Swedes?

The phone rang.

Judy closed her eyes, listening to it ring. Then she reached for the
receiver. "Hello?"

"Judy. It's Robert."

"Hello, Robert." She was a little surprised how calm she sounded.

"I'm sorry I haven't called you sooner. It's been . . . well, you've seen
the papers. On malaria reading."

The old masculine excuse: press of work. But she could hear the nervousness in his voice.

"Only now . . . well, something's come up. I think . . . are you still
there, Judy?"

"Yes," Judy said.

"I couldn't hear you breathing or anything. Jude, I think we both
know this relationship hasn't been going very well for quite a while now."

"Do we?"

"Yes. I do. *We* do. You're a wonderful person, but we just want different things, and that isn't going to change. I mean it when I say you're
a wonderful person, but I don't think we have a real future together; and
somewhere down deep I think we both know that."

Judy listened to this bullshit, thinking *I thought he was more original than that.* She said nothing.

"So what I'm saying, what I mean, is that I think I should move out.
I'll come for my stuff, or send somebody for it, on Saturday. I'll . . . Judy,
are you *there?*"

"Yes."

"I'm sorry about this. I know it isn't what you hoped for, but I think
we're both old enough to know that sometimes these things don't—"

She said, "Are you back with Marcy?"

On the other end of the line, Robert drew a sharp breath. She could
picture him, his eyes widened, his hand holding the receiver. No rings.
He never wore rings. Nails cut short, neat and square. Palm square, too,
and callused from the odd way he held his drawing pencils. He would
answer her question, Judy knew. He was a total screwup with women,

but he was honest. Judy had loved that about him, especially after Ben, who'd lied as easily as he dropped his pants.

"Yes," he said, very low. "I am. Judy, I'm so sorry. I never intended this to happen."

"It's all right."

Long pause. "It *is?*"

"Yes," she said, clearly. "If you haven't got the sense to appreciate me, then you don't deserve me."

He was silent. Stunned, Judy hoped. Well, she was pretty stunned, too. That was why she sounded so calm; she was stunned, like an animal just hit between the eyes with a two-by-four. From experience with herself, she knew this calm wouldn't last.

"Well," Robert said cautiously, "you're probably right. You deserve better than me."

"Good-bye, Robert. I'll mail you the papers to cancel the lease on the house." She hung up.

For a long time she sat staring at her screen saver. Then she went into the living room, found the purple sweater she'd been knitting for Robert, and calmly pulled it apart, unraveled strand by unraveled strand.

INTERIM

The USS *Bryant* cut through the water of the Potomac River just before dawn. The executive officer, who was the only one on the bridge who knew what the mission was, gave the helmsman the order to steady up. Then for the next few minutes the orders flew thick. The ship came to a stop and dropped anchor.

Light fog swirled over the river. Through it the exec could just make out the facilities of the Naval Surface Weapons Center on the Virginia shore. He stepped outside the glass-enclosed bridge onto the metal deck and raised his binoculars.

"Mr. Horton, summon the ordnance officer and crew."

"Yes, sir," said Ensign Horton, junior officer of the deck, who was on his first sea duty after Annapolis. He saluted smartly, executed a perfect ninety-degree turn, and marched away. The exec, who had been in the navy for seventeen years, smiled to himself.

In five minutes Mr. Horton was back. "Sir . . . there's a . . . problem."

"A 'problem'?"

"Yes, sir. One of the ordnance crew. Stanners. He won't come on deck."

"Do you mean 'can't,' Mr. Horton? Is Stanners ill?"

"No, sir. 'Won't.'"

"Are you telling me that a crewman of this ship has chosen to disobey a direct order?"

"Y-yes, sir."

"Why?"

"He says it's because of malaria reading, sir. Stanners says this is near where it started. He says he won't risk the open air in the early morning hours when mosquitoes feed. Sir."

The two officers stared at each other. The exec was white; the ensign black. As was Stanners. The exec did not know the sickle-cell-trait status of every sailor on the *Bryant.* A complicated emotion filled him: irritation, distaste, guilt, reluctance to deal with the situation. He ignored all of these.

"Mr. Horton, tell Stanners that he will be on deck in three minutes or face a court-martial. This is the United States Navy, and he is a sailor in that navy."

Something shifted behind Horton's dark eyes. His thumb moved up under his palm to stroke the Annapolis ring. "Yes, sir."

Horton returned to belowdecks. The exec rested one hand on the bridge railing and renewed his scan of the Naval Surface Weapons Center. He had seen action in the Persian Gulf, where sailors had died. He firmly believed that every military man owed his life to his country. And he had read in the newspaper that the death rate from this so-called "malaria" was falling anyway. It was half of what it had been a month ago. And perhaps mosquitoes didn't even venture offshore, even when the shore was this close. Stanners was a weak sister, all too typical of the kids who signed up now, wanting the GI Bill and the structure and the health benefits and the regular pay, but not wanting to take any risks in between. As bad as the reserves. Cowards.

And against all that, a sudden image of Stanners keeling over with a cerebral stroke, in what only the exec and the captain knew was a very minor naval test exercise. Dead at nineteen. At *his* order.

The exec watched the rest of the ordnance crew assemble crisply in the cool dawn and waited to see if Stanners showed.

TEN

For extreme illnesses, extreme treatments are most fitting.
—Hippocrates, *Aphorisms*, fourth century B.C.

Cavanaugh had never seen anything like it.

Dr. Michael Sean Donohue lived in a modest, slightly peeling town house in College Park, six miles from D.C. The townhouse was an end unit, two stories high, with a one-car garage underneath. In the front a short walk led from the door to a large, curving, asphalt parking lot for the apartments opposite the townhouse that did not have garages. On the east side, Donohue's garage opened to an equally short driveway connecting to the parking lot. In back, sliding glass doors opened to a shared lawn. Scattered over the weedy grass were a few dilapidated picnic benches and many toys. It was suburbia writ small.

Sound trucks jammed the parking lot, their booms jutting over the horde of reporters waiting patiently on lawn chairs and camp stools and cars, AC running with the doors open. Pizza trucks came and went. Two enterprising teenagers sold coffee and Gatorade. Every once in a while a neighbor, or even a dog, would emerge and everyone would leap up and start frenziedly snapping pictures or rolling film. Reporters interviewed anyone who emerged from any door within a hundred yards. Between frenzies, everyone lapsed again into sweating torpor. Styrofoam cups and pizza boxes littered the ground, smelling strongly in the hot sun. A camera was permanently trained on the garage door.

As the sun moved, the entire ménage shifted around the curving parking lot, following the shade.

Even in this throng, the FBI surveillance team stood out, or at least part of it did. Two agents sat on the picnic bench in back, the only ones authorized to trespass past the parking lot. Another agent watched the front door, the bulge of his gun unmistakable under his light summer suit. Somewhere three additional unmarked FBI vehicles—"Bucars"—waited. Cavanaugh, in one of them, said to his surveillance partner, "Jesus J. Edgar Christ. Does Donohue go out at all?"

"Oh, he goes out," Arnett said. Slow-moving and laconic, he had the sleepy-eyed, dim look that Cavanaugh had once thought meant hidden strengths. Now he just thought that such men were laconic and dim. "Wait."

"'They also serve who . . .'"

"What?"

"Nothing."

Arnett gave him a doubtful look.

The trouble with waiting—*a* trouble with waiting—was that it let him dwell on the conversation with Judy. He'd gotten off very easy, he knew. No scene, no tears. She'd sounded pretty laconic herself, except for that one perceptive question about Marcy. Well, he'd hadn't lied to her. And he hadn't wanted to hurt Judy, although he knew he had. But he couldn't help it. She—

The crowd suddenly erupted. A white Mercedes sailed down the driveway toward Donohue's garage.

"Mr. Erickson! Mr. Erickson!" reporters screamed. Photographers leapt into position. The garage door slid up, the Mercedes entered, and the door slid down again.

"Who's Erickson?" Cavanaugh asked, since Arnett apparently wasn't going to volunteer any information. He was the kind who liked to be asked.

"Donohue's lawyer." Arnett turned the ignition key. The Bucar, which had been idling so the air-conditioning would work, came to life.

"Where are we going?"

"Tailing."

Cavanaugh didn't point out that Donohue and his lawyer were clos-
eted in the town house, or that it was difficult to "tail" inside 1,235
square feet (plus garage). Cavanaugh was the new kid on the block. He
waited.

After a few minutes the garage door slid up again. The white Mercedes backed out. Erickson drove. Beside him Donohue smiled faintly,
dressed in a pale gray suit. He never glanced at the reporters shouting
and snapping and pounding on the car window, begging for a quote. Erickson clutched the wheel, but Donohue kept his faint smile, cool and
unruffled.

Cavanaugh said, "Is he always that cool?"

"Yes."

Arnett was a better driver than conversationalist. His was the first
car behind the Mercedes, and he kept the position effortlessly. The
other Bucars would trail unseen. Behind Arnett most of the sound trucks
and press cars boiled along, the messy tail of the comet. Cavanaugh
watched the back of Donohue's head. It told him nothing.

They drove west into D.C., finally slowing at a nondescript building
on Georgia Avenue. Erickson parked in a commercial lot and the entire
entourage jammed in after him. The attendant, a middle-aged black
man, evidently didn't recognize Donohue; he looked perplexed and
alarmed at the haphazard circus being made of his tidy rows of parked
cars.

"You go in with him," Arnett said, startling Cavanaugh with his lo-
quaciousness. "Stay close. Take notes. I stay with the car and watch the
front entrances."

"Okay," Cavanaugh said. Somehow they had switched verbal roles.

Erickson and Donohue got out of the Mercedes. Erickson handed
the keys to the attendant. Donohue strolled casually toward the building. Reporters shouted questions at him.

"Dr. Donohue! What do you think of the heavy FBI surveillance that
led the press to you?"

"Dr. Donohue! What comment do you have on malaria reading?"

"Hey! Mike! Did you kill all those people just for the fun of it?"

Not even the last question made Donohue lose his faint, contemp-
tuous smile, although the parking attendant's eyes went wide. Donohue
strolled into the building and waited for the elevator, still acting as if he
were entirely alone. And yet Cavanaugh saw that he was very aware of

the attention he generated. Phrases from the Quantico profile rose in his mind: "*. . . imagines himself a powerful behind-the-scenes figure, manipulating entire bureaucracies—such as the FBI—into doing his bidding . . .*"

Twenty-two people crowded into the elevator. A sign inside said CA-PACITY: SIXTEEN PERSONS. The reporters continued their fruitless yammering as the elevator groaned its way to the fifth floor, which the floor posting identified as:

SELENE FASHIONS, EXECUTIVE OFFICE

CATHAY AUCTION HOUSE

JENSEN & JENSEN, ATTORNEYS AT LAW

Cavanaugh assumed Donohue was adding to his legal team, but he was wrong. The noisy cavalcade was stopped by a polite doorman outside Cathay Auction House.

"Do you have a bidding number, sir? Ma'am?" No one had a bidding number, which, it turned out, required advance reservation, but Cavanaugh had his FBI credentials. He was the only one allowed to follow Donohue inside.

Cavanaugh had never been to an auction. He read the catalogue of Chinese and Tibetan antiques, one eye on Donohue, who sat two rows ahead with his arm stretched negligently along the back of an empty chair. Only a dozen people sat on the velvet chairs. It was very quiet.

From the Sung period, a crane carved in jade, showing the characteristic . . .

"Welcome to Cathay Auction House," a dazzlingly groomed woman announced from the podium. "Please remember that smoking is forbidden." She then went through the bidding rules and introduced the auctioneer, who appeared to be her male clone.

Ceramic bowl from the T'ang period, 6¼ inches in diameter. The thick-walled, single-color porcelain illustrates well the superb . . .

Donohue didn't bid on anything until Lot 39. Cavanaugh read in the catalogue that this was a small, early-Ming painted vase, seven inches high, decorated with the elegance that had recently replaced simplicity in landscape painting. He paid close attention to the bidding. Donohue got the vase, for two thousand.

"*. . . because this individual considers himself a natural aristocrat,*

*he will pride himself on his superior taste in at least one consumer
area . . . earns between forty and sixty thousand . . . in some area of aristocratic taste he will buy the best and will be supercilious about anything
less . . ."*

But did Donohue fit the profile so well because the profilists knew
their stuff? Or did he fit the profile so well because the Bureau had
looked for a suspect who fit the profile, thereby justifying its existence in
the first place? Criminal profiles were usually developed from evidence
at the crime scene. But in this case, the crime scene was all of southern
Maryland and part of Virginia, and the only "evidence" was several million insects doing the things insects naturally did: Breed. Feed. Bleed.

So far Cavanaugh had seen nothing, been told nothing, read nothing
about Michael Sean Donohue that convinced him this man had killed
597 people by means of an unelegant, untasteful, unaristocratic mosquito.

The rest of the day produced nothing. Donohue went home, still acting
as if two dozen reporters, eight tails, and a score of heckling citizens did
not fall within his notice. Curtains stayed drawn at the College Park town
house. An elaborate flower arrangement, roses and sweetpeas, arrived
from a local florist. "Who's sending him flowers?" Cavanaugh asked
Arnett.

"Networks."

Courting, of course. An exclusive interview with Michael Sean
Donohue! A heavyset woman in a faded dress opened the door a slit and
refused the flowers.

"Donohue's wife?" Cavanaugh asked. Arnett nodded, having used
up the hour's allotment of words.

A sack of mail as large as a boulder and apparently as heavy was
dropped on Donohue's doorstep and ignored. Reporters salivated at it,
but apparently weren't quite up to violating federal postal statutes by
opening the sack. Eventually the heavyset woman dragged it inside.

A representative from the *National Inquirer* knocked on the door,
probably to offer a story contract. Nobody answered. The media all took
pictures of the guy knocking.

By the time Cavanaugh's shift ended, at 7:00 P.M., he was exhausted.
How could he be so tired when he hadn't done anything except sit? But
he was.

However, he perked up on the drive south, even though the Beltway was the usual mess. Marcy would be there. The Marcy of last night, scrubbing pizza off her low-cut leotard, straddling him in bed . . . the Marcy of the early years of their marriage, laughing at dinner, cuddling on the sofa to watch the news, telling him about her day in the corporate wars. Marcy.

He stopped at a florist near her building and bought her a dozen yellow roses. She had always liked yellow roses.

"Why, Robert, how lovely of you!" She'd been passing through the foyer when he turned his key in her lock. Abigail bounded up, tail wagging frantically. Home.

Marcy hadn't changed her clothes after work. She wore a dark blue suit and white silk blouse, her blonde hair twisted high in a French roll. She looked so delectable that Robert immediately laid the flowers on the hall table and put his arms around her.

She stiffened.

Over her shoulder, he suddenly saw that the living room was full of packing boxes.

"Robert, please don't," Marcy said, disentangling from his embrace. "I mean, last night was lovely, and I'm glad I could thank you like that, but . . . please don't."

On top of the packing boxes sat his computer monitor and squash racket.

He got out, "Thank me? For what?"

"For watching Abigail for me, of course." She looked at him blankly. "For watching Abigail."

"Yes. Oh, God, Robert, not even *you* could have thought that I . . . that you . . ."

"No, of course not," Robert said. His chest felt as if it had just been smacked with a sledgehammer.

"Well, thank God for *that,* anyway."

"Yes. Thank. God."

"I've packed your things, since I knew you'd probably have put in a long day on your case," she said, all crisp efficiency. "The boxes will all fit into your car on one trip, won't they?"

"Yes."

"Then I guess that's that." She smiled brilliantly. "I'd stay and have a drink with you, but I have a date. But of course you can help yourself to drink or dinner or whatever. Just lock the door behind you and slip the key under the door."

"Yes."

"Well, then, I guess that's it. Unless you want to walk Abigail one last time."

"Walk. Abigail."

"Oh, don't look so put-upon, Robert. You don't have to walk her. Richard and I will do it when we get back. And thanks again for taking care of her for me."

She gave him a brief peck on the cheek, waggled her fingers at him, and was gone.

Cavanaugh walked into the living room. He sat down on one of the packing boxes. He had a strong urge to laugh, or cry, or something. Maybe just call himself names.

Idiot, sucker, moron, sentimentalist . . .

And where was he supposed to go with his neatly packed boxes? Judy's? Unthinkable. He'd jerked her around enough for one day. A motel? Probably. Until he could find another apartment.

Stupid fool, icky romantic, easy mark, dummkopf . . .

Abigail trotted over and licked his hand. Groaning happily, she curled herself at his feet. As far as Cavanaugh could see, she was the only female he'd succeeded in pleasing all day.

Laughter won. At the tone of Cavanaugh's laughing, Abigail stirred uneasily and peered up at him.

Sex. It would get you every damn time.

But he took Abigail with him. Out of chagrin, or anger, or maybe just pity that she should stay behind with someone who didn't care if a dog spent its night bewildered and alone.

DONOHUE MAY HAVE TAKEN PRIVATE POLYGRAPH TEST

BY LIBBY TURNER

College Park, Maryland—Last night at 8:14 EST reporters staking out Michael Sean Donohue's town house in College Park observed two men being admitted inside. The *Sun* has discovered that the car is registered to Stanley J. Osborne of Washington, D.C. Osborne, formerly employed at the office of Virginia attorney general Lionel Davis, recently set up a private polygraph firm. Also present was Donohue's lawyer, Stuart Erickson.

Speculation runs high that Donohue is preparing for a possible arrest by arming himself with his own polygraph results. Although neither Erickson, Donohue, nor Davis has as yet issued a statement on . . .

DONOHUE SUBSCRIBED TO INTERNET MAILING LISTS ON MALARIA, GENETIC ENGINEERING

BY JONATHAN KRAMER

New York—The *Times* learned last night that Dr. Michael Sean Donohue, the prime suspect in the creation of the allegedly genetically engineered malaria reading, subscribes to Internet mailing lists on both malaria and genetics. The mailing lists are closed, with scientific updates sent only to subscribers. Clearly qualified to receive the lists, Donohue, who has a Ph.D. from Yale in microbiology, was unable to be reached for comment.

"These lists are one way scientists keep up with the latest developments in their fields," said Dr. Anna Weinstein, professor of microbiology at the State University of New York at Stony Brook. "They are a major Internet service."

Although the FBI Media Office cautioned that merely belonging to a specialized-topic list in no way constitutes evidence of having abused that knowledge, nonetheless . . .

ELEVEN

Extremist groups worldwide are increasingly learning how to manufacture chemical and biological agents, and the potential for additional chemical and biological attacks by such groups continues to grow.
—Gordon Oehler, Director of CIA Nonproliferation Center, Report of the Executive Committee on Special Material Smuggling, 1996

I just want to see him," Melanie said, "Just once."

"Why?" Krovetz said, biting into his Big Mac. Special sauce ran down his chin. Nobody in McDonald's was eyeing them, the interracial couple. Melanie always knew.

Krovetz swallowed. "What would you gain, Mel? Donohue's not going to lay eyes on you and suddenly blurt out, 'Yes, I did it. I engineered malaria reading. In your presence, I must confess.'"

"I know that. Give me some credit; I'm not moronic."

"No. But the wish to see him is." He took another bite.

Just watching him made Melanie queasy. She couldn't eat much anymore. She played with the straw to her orange juice. "I don't expect him to *confess*. But I can't help it. I just want to see him."

"You don't even think Donohue did it."

"No, I don't." She pushed the orange juice away and leaned forward.

"Joe, did you ever read any of the books or articles about the WHO theory of HIV?"

Krovetz looked at her in disbelief. "Oh, God, Mel, not that garbage. Not from *you*."

"I'm not saying I believe it exactly."

"Then what exactly? A nut theory that the World Health Organization had AIDS created in an American laboratory—"

"Not just any lab. Bethesda or Fort Detrick."

"—as a biological weapon and then deliberately spread it around black Africans and gay Americans through contaminated vaccines in the 1970s—"

"Not necessarily 'deliberately,'" Melanie said. "It might have been accidentally. Through culture contamination, or experimentally."

"Well, at least you're not a total conspiracy loonie. You've only let your imagination break into a gallop."

"Joe, the Department of Defense *did* approve a twenty-three-million-dollar appropriation for bioweapons in 1969! You know that!"

"Sure. Cold War stuff. But then they discontinued the program and—"

"Do you believe that?"

"Do *you* believe WHO was into genocide as a means of population control?"

"Well, no," she said, and heard that she sounded reluctant. "I think the AIDS virus did come out of the rain forest. But malaria reading is different, Joe. This plague *is* deliberate."

"I agree. And more and more, so does everybody else. You're just too impatient, you know that? People are coming to agree that *P. reading* was engineered. But that doesn't mean WHO created it, for God's sake. They're the good guys, remember?"

Melanie didn't answer. Joe munched on French fries; the smell of the food made her stomach lurch. After a moment he said, with an all too obvious attempt to change the subject, "Speaking of WHO, have you heard the rumors about Farlow? No, of course you haven't. You haven't been near your own team, except for me, in three days."

"I've been in the field," Melanie protested. "In fact, after we finish this disgusting lunch, I have to change and go on another call. What about Farlow?"

"Promotion. To second-in-command at WHO."

"In Switzerland? Do you think he'll take it?"

"Wouldn't you?"

"I don't know," she said slowly. "It's a coup, of course. But given everything, all the unresolved issues about AIDS and even Ebola . . ."

"Oh, god, not Ebola, too. Mel, Ebola is *not a manufactured disease.* Outbreaks have been recorded since the plague of Athens and—"

"You can't tell from ancient records what those diseases actually were, and you know it. They didn't *know* anything! A hundred years ago most doctors still believed that malaria was caused by 'bad air,' for God's sake!"

Her voice had risen. People at the next table turned to stare. More than stare—purse their fat redneck lips and look from her to Joe and harden their pasty jawlines. Ignorant honkies. She glared back.

"Melanie," Joe said quietly, "you're losing self-control."

"Thank you very much, Dr. Krovetz."

"I mean it, Mel. You've got to chill out or something will happen."

"Yeah? Like what? A brush with actual truth? Excuse me, I've got work to do." Suddenly she couldn't stand McDonald's a second longer. "Bad air." She had to get out of there to breathe. Standing up so abruptly that her chair fell over, she marched across the street and put on her mourning dress and hat for her next objectively scientific epidemiological interview.

She walked back to her car after the interview in Faulkner, Charles County. It had clouded over; the humidity must be close to 100 percent. Inside the car, she turned on the AC, hiked up her dress, and peeled off her panty hose. She threw her high heels in the backseat and slipped on sandals. Her head felt as if a vise squeezed her brain.

It was always worse when it was a child. An impish, grinning little boy. The mother had insisted on showing her an entire photo album of pictures, as if that could somehow bring her son back. Dead at four years old.

And yet she'd seen dead four year olds before, hundreds of them, in her trips to Africa on epidemic teams. Four year olds dead of malaria, of typhus, of dengue fever, of all the horrible things that went on tormenting Africa no matter what anybody did. She'd grieved for those four year olds, but not like this. Why not? Was it no more than the crudest kind of nationalism?

No. It was because despite what she'd said to Joe at lunch, she believed the African epidemics were natural. Heart-breaking, enraging, worsened by callous political stupidity—but still natural. Not engineered by human evil, as this was. So that even with the death rate dropping—this was her first case this week, and it was already Wednesday—the death of a four year old by malarial cerebral stroke was murder, with all the gut-twisting horror of child killing.

Suddenly, she had to get a look at Michael Sean Donohue. Even though he didn't do it. She just had to look at him. There was a team meeting in an hour, but she'd blow it off. Probably just the announcement of Farlow's move to Switzerland, now that the epidemic was waning and the FBI had the cause safely in custody, where he could do no more harm to middle America. Yeah, right.

Melanie headed the car north. The decision finally made to see Donohue, she was suddenly ravenous. When had she last eaten? Not today, barely yesterday. Her stomach howled for food. She drove into a plaza somewhere in Prince George's county and spied a Burger King. Well, okay—this hungry, even fast food would do.

It was evidently a black area: sisters and brothers thronged both in front and behind the counter, the lines sliced and resliced by children running amok in their Burger King crowns. Melanie got in line behind two teenage boys with partially shaved heads and baggy clothes, and watched two tiny girls in pink sunsuits chase each other between the tables. They were having a wonderful time. The vise in her head eased a bit.

"A Whopper," the boy ahead of her said to the counter clerk, "and . . . and . . . oh, fuck . . ." He clutched his head and collapsed on the floor.

A woman screamed. The boy's friend dropped beside him, shouting "Cal! Cal!" The two little girls stopped running by, petrified. One of them started to cry. People crowded around the fallen boy.

No, no, no. Not again. Not another kid, not here—She couldn't move.

"Call nine-one-one!" somebody yelled, and there was a stampede to the phone. The kid on the floor lay still. His friend started to sob.

"Let me through," Melanie said, although she didn't know if any sound actually emerged from her vocal chords. "Let me through; I'm a doctor—"

The crowd parted. The sobbing boy abruptly stopped sobbing and stared up at Melanie. His expression changed. Before she could register what that meant, the fallen kid leapt up from the floor and both of them started laughing and dancing around. "Got you! Got you all, suckers!"

Melanie stopped cold. The entire scene froze for her, as if she—or it—were encased in ice.

"Got you!"

Abruptly, the ice cracked.

She tore forward and grabbed the boy by the front of his T-shirt. "How dare you! How *dare* you, you lousy little motherfucker! How dare you!" She punched him in the face: once, twice, three times. Even though he was three inches taller than she, he didn't hit her back. He stared, stupefied.

"How dare you! How dare you . . ." She was sobbing now, her voice jagged, her final punch missing his face and landing on his right ear. But her other punches had connected. The boy's nose bled, gushing blood over his chin, his shirt, her hand.

"Hey!" the boy's friend finally yelled, and he grabbed her from behind. He pinned her arms to her side. Melanie kicked him.

"That ain't no doctor," somebody said.

"Kid deserved it. Doing us like that!"

"Here come a cop . . ."

"How dare you!" Melanie screamed one last time. "With your own people dying for real—you stupid-ass motherfucker! You imbecile!"

A commotion behind her, and a babble of voices. Melanie couldn't distinguish anything; the ice field was back, only this time it was freezing everything, killing off all decency, all good, all compassion. . . .

The second boy's hands released her, and handcuffs clamped her wrists behind her back.

"That's enough," the cop said. He was stern, and disgusted, and white. "What happened here?"

Immediately six people tried to tell him. He listened to the babble, studying Melanie's face. Suddenly he said, "I know you. You're that woman on TV, on the malaria reading task force from Atlanta. Dr. . . . Anderson."

The crowd fell quiet, looking at her.

"Did you attack this boy?"

Melanie said nothing. The cop looked at the kid. His nose still bled, and he was going to have a purple-and-blue shiner. Her ring had torn open the skin on his cheek, a raw, jagged laceration.

"She done it," the boy's friend said sullenly. "Bitch just went for him like a cat!"

The cop looked at the crowd. Some turned away. A few nodded. The cop's partner came into the Burger King from the patrol car and took out a notepad. The first cop turned back to Melanie.

"Ma'am, you're under arrest for assault. You have the right to remain silent. Anything you say can and may be used against you . . ."

She called the Weather Vane Motel from the police station. The cops booked her, fingerprinted her, took her statement. Across the room the two teenage boys looked at her with hatred, a particular punishment in itself. The cops put her in a cell by herself, where she sat huddled and numb for two hours until Farlow, accompanied by a lawyer, came to pay her bail and get her out.

The lawyer left in his own car. Farlow said nothing to her until they sat in his. Then he turned to her. "Where were you going that you ended up in that Burger King?"

"To College Park." She was surprised at the sound of her own voice, low and thin. She sounded exhausted.

She *was* exhausted.

Farlow said, "To get a look at Michael Donohue."

"Yes."

"Jesus, Melanie." He gripped the wheel, silent, thinking. Melanie saw the minute he made his decision.

"I'm taking you off the team and sending you back to Atlanta. For a vacation first, then for reassignment."

"No, Jim . . . no."

"Yes. You're lucky there was no press at that Burger King, although they'll have a field day when they get to that kid. Besides, Melanie, you can't do anything else here anyway. The epidemic is under control. US-AMRIID disrupted the lines of transmission, and all that's left is the mop-up stuff."

"Not quite," Melanie said. An epidemic wasn't officially over until a period of twice the disease's maximum incubation period elapsed from the date of the last known case, without any new cases reported in the interim. They weren't there yet. People were still dying.

"It's mostly over," Farlow insisted. "But with the political situation so hot . . . God, what came over you? Never mind. I know."

"No. You don't."

"Your arraignment is Monday. You can stay at the Weather Vane until then, at CDC expense, or you can go home and fly back up. I'd recommend going home." He let go of the steering wheel and turned to face her. "This has been coming on with you for a long time. We've all seen it. I should have sent you back before this. It's my fault."

Something was wrong with his tone, but she was too exhausted and whipped to figure out what it was. He looked at her, started to say something more, stopped. Instead he stared out the front windshield, and his mouth trembled.

"Let's go," Melanie finally said aloud. They did.

They drove in silence through the ugly suburban sprawl. Melanie watched black children playing on the steaming sidewalks, the ragged lawns, the streets. Women sat on sagging steps watching the children, as women did everywhere in the world, caretaking and chatting. But here the caretaking would have an extra desperate edge, and the chatter would not be light.

I'm not leaving Maryland for very long, Jim. Not till it's completely over. But that she did not say out loud.

Cavanaugh rode in the second car, with Dunbar and two members of the evidence-protection team. In the car ahead were Pilozzi and Arnett, an FBI medic, and one of the Division Five agents, Bruce Maloney. Two more cars followed with the scientific team, the physical evidence team, a media representative, and God-knew-who else. Twenty unsmiling agents in four dark cars. If they turned on their lights, they'd look like a funeral.

Dunbar, officially the case agent, carried the search warrant. "Can I see it?" Cavanaugh asked. Dunbar gave him a hard look that meant, *Don't start anything, Robert.* Cavanaugh knew by now that Dunbar disliked him. Cavanaugh minded, but at least it made Dunbar, with his J. Edgar Hoover sense of Bureau solidarity, bend over backwards to be "fair" to Cavanaugh. He handed over the warrant.

It was thick, at least thirty pages, A copy had been delivered to Donohue's lawyer earlier this morning. Cavanaugh skipped past the legal formalities and the object-of-search section, which he had already seen. It listed sixty-four categories of items that could be seized from Donohue's town house. These included "materials used for scientific experiments;" "paraphernalia associated with genetic engineering, blood drawing, storage, or use;" "correspondence, books, or magazines connected to genetic engineering, malaria, or mosquitoes;" "hate literature;" and "equipment, specimens, or instruments, or tools associated with the breeding, altering, collecting, control, or breeding of mosquitoes, especially but not limited to *Anopheles quadrimaculatus.*" Oh, great. "*Tools associated with the . . . control . . . of mosquitoes.*" What if Donohue owned a fly swatter?

Cavanaugh turned to the section on probable cause.

He expected, given Maloney's presence, to see an evocation of national security. The Supreme Court had declined to comment on whether the Fourth Amendment, which guaranteed "the right of the people to be secure in their persons, houses, papers, and effects," applied in cases of national security. However, the Court had said that whatever powers the president had to dump the Fourth Amendment in order to preserve national security should be used very, very cautiously. In fact, they should be limited to "instances of immediate and grave peril" to the nation. Also, the search warrant should be authorized directly by either the president or the attorney general. Given the high profile of malaria reading, Cavanaugh expected to see that this search was in response to "immediate and grave peril" to 25 percent of the population of the state of Maryland. He expected to see the attorney general's signature.

None of it was there.

The warrant had been issued by a federal judge. And although there was a nod toward a "serious health emergency," probable cause rested mostly on the Hobbs Act and on information from informants. Just like a routine drug bust.

"The *Hobbs Act?*" Cavanaugh said out loud. Immediately he regretted it. Dunbar looked even stonier than usual, if that was possible. Cavanaugh returned to reading.

The Hobbs Act was certainly a safer, less controversial choice on which to base a search warrant than was national security. In fact, the

Hobbs Act was the FBI's best friend. It prohibited the use of interstate facilities, such as mail or phone, to advance illegal activities, such as murder. The Hobbs Act kept so many investigators off unemployment that Cavanaugh had once referred to it in a Bureau meeting as the Jobs Act. This had amused no one.

According to the warrant, the FBI had probable cause to believe that Michael Sean Donohue had used both mail and telephone to advance the genetic engineering of *Anopheles* into a killer of at least 917 people in at least three states.

"Reliable informants" had stated that Donohue had received packages from both scientific and insect-supply houses. The supply house itself, in Los Angeles, confirmed his order for six thousand *Anopheles* mosquitoes.

Donohue had opened a PO box in Bel Alton, Charles County, Maryland, forty miles from his home, and very near the epicenter identified by the CDC. The mosquitoes from California had been sent to this PO box.

Two security guards had seen him illegally remove a gene sequencer from his former place of employment, Genemod, Inc. One of the guards had also seen him carry out late at night "other scientific equipment."

Citizen informants, deemed by the court to be more reliable than criminal informants, stated that on at least three occasions Donohue had expressed "murderous contempt" for African Americans.

Finally, and most damning, was a statement from an informant named Curtis P. McGraw, of 658 Crestview Avenue, Chevy Chase, Maryland, and 841 Beach Road, Town Creek, Maryland. McGraw, personally known to and deemed reliable by an FBI agent, told the agent that Donohue had shown him a "small cardboard box with holes covered with cheesecloth." In the box, visible through the cheesecloth, buzzed live mosquitoes. McGraw said that Donohue said, "These are instruments of death like the world has never seen. And like nobody else is smart enough to make."

Attachments to the warrant included signed and sworn affidavits, invoices, bills of lading, PO documents, correspondence. Cavanaugh went back and read through the "probable cause" section again. It was not illegal to order mosquitoes through the mail. It was not illegal to order scientific equipment through the mail. It was not illegal to open a post office box in another city. It was not illegal to sit around a bar and air your prejudices.

It *was* illegal to steal equipment from your employer, but it was a state crime, not a federal one.

A magistrate who issued a search warrant was supposed to take into account the "totality of circumstance." Still, most of this search warrant depended on the affidavit of one informant, as vouched for by one FBI agent. The whole thing puzzled Cavanaugh.

"All right," Dunbar said, "let's go."

At the sight of four more Bucars, added to the four surveillance vehicles already present, the waiting media went crazy. They photographed, they filmed, they climbed on top of vehicles for wide-angle shots, they shouted. "Hey, Agent Dunbar, you making an arrest?" "You doing a search?" "Just one comment! Look this way, please!" Dunbar ignored them all, and everybody else followed Dunbar. *A twenty-faced Mount Rushmore,* Cavanaugh thought. *Only not as cheerful.*

Erickson, the lawyer, answered the door. The FBI filed in past him. Donohue sat in his living room, reading a magazine. He barely looked up as Dunbar ran through the formalities.

Cavanaugh studied the town house. On this level were a living/dining area, tiny kitchen, half bath, another room with closed door that might be a den or a small bedroom. Stairs led to the upper level. Donohue's furniture was clean-lined but a little shabby, his pictures all prints or posters. The only expensive item was a glassed and lighted display case filled with Oriental bowls, vases, and small statues. Some were painted, some lacquered, some made of jade or stone. Even Cavanaugh, who had studied art in college but barely knew what he liked, could see that these were beautiful.

The agents began their methodical work. "One issue of *Cell Biology,* June 1998," an agent announced, putting it into a bag.

"Noted," said a second agent, recording the item, labeling the bag, and starting a stack of seized objects.

"One large scientific beaker being used as a planter for . . . um . . . plants."

Bird's nest fern, Cavanaugh thought but didn't say aloud. He was technically still assigned to Surveillance. Silently, he surveilled.

"Noted."

"One book, paperback, titled *Field Guide to Insects,* by John G. Barnaby, with handwritten comments in the margins."

"Noted."

"One book, hardcover, titled *Short Protocols in Molecular Biology.* Lots of drawings and stuff, but I don't see any handwriting."

"Noted."

Cavanaugh watched as the agent leafed through the book. He caught words like "oligonucleotide" and chapter titles like "Construction of Hybrid DNA Molecules." A full-color drawing looked like a lava lamp in progress, but probably wasn't. Donohue, whatever else he might be, was a bona fide scientist. They should all remember that.

"Dr. Donohue," Dunbar said, the medic beside him, "the warrant specifies two vials of your blood. Will you come into the kitchen, please?"

Donohue looked at his lawyer, who nodded. Cavanaugh followed. In the kitchen, agents pulled cupboards apart, stacking skillets and dishes and candles, granola and ketchup and chutney on the counter. While the medic drew his blood, Donohue gazed at nothing, smiling faintly.

"Now a voice exemplar, please," Dunbar said. "Just speak clearly into this microphone."

"And what am I supposed to say?"

"Anything you wish."

The lawyer said quickly, "Mike, just recite . . . oh, 'Twinkle, Twinkle, Little Star.'"

Donohue said, clearly and without hesitation, "The Federal Bureau of Investigation is at present dismantling my house. They are most thorough, most intrusive, and most mistaken. Twinkle, twinkle, agents blind, I wonder what you think you'll find. Up above the real so high, truth escapes your misled eye. Twinkle, twinkle, agents blind."

Dunbar said tightly, "I advise you to be careful with your name calling, Dr. Donohue. The FBI already has evidence tying you closely to a white supremacist hate group."

Cavanaugh hid his surprise. It wasn't illegal to lie in order to get a statement out of a suspect, but it was unlike Dunbar. And Donohue wasn't the kind of suspect to crumble under accusations; Dunbar must know that. The case agent stood stiffly, arms rigid at his side, obviously controlling some emotion.

All Donohue said, one eyebrow raised, was, "Oh? How interesting."

A sudden commotion upstairs. Two agents clattered down the stairs, one carrying a cardboard box. Inside were two insect carriers like the ones Cavanaugh had seen in the insect-supply-house catalogues. The agent flipped open the lids and tilted the box toward Dunbar. Cavanaugh knew what he was looking at. The bottoms of both cages were piled with the dark brown, patchy-winged corpses of *Anopheles quadrimaculatus*. Some of the tiny dead bodies were tagged, just like the ones Melanie Anderson had shown him at the CDC temporary lab.

The lawyer groaned. Donohue gazed blankly ahead, faintly smiling.

Cavanaugh drove south from College Park to the Weather Vane Motel, where his peripatetic belongings now sat in Marcy's neat packing boxes. It seemed as good a place as any to park himself temporarily. Abigail hadn't seemed to mind the move, although Cavanaugh had already had one complaint that she howled when he was away all day.

As he drove, Cavanaugh went over it all again and again. Dunbar's strange, unidentified emotion. Dunbar's lying to Donohue. Most of all, the discrepancy between what Donohue had said and the informant had said he'd said. Not a discrepancy of content.

Of style.

"These are instruments of death like the world has never seen. And like nobody else is smart enough to make." That was one.

"The Federal Bureau of Investigation is at present dismantling my house. They are most thorough, most intrusive, and most mistaken." That was the other, followed by the "Twinkle, Twinkle Little Star" parody, without preparation, right off the top of Donohue's head.

Both the informant's hearsay and Donohue's mocking description of the search used parallel structure, true. But the hearsay statement just didn't sound like Donohue's balanced sentences. And "like" was a preposition, not a conjunction. And the awkward verb. Wouldn't Donohue have said something like, "These are instruments of death such as the world has never seen, and such as no one else is intelligent enough to create"? The word "create" would fit with Donohue's demeanor; he'd sat among the scurrying, bustling agents like a god among mortals.

Or maybe he, Cavanaugh, was just reading too much into diction and sentence structure. After all, the informant, this Curtis P. McGraw, might have simply paraphrased what he'd heard, in words that *he* would have used. Especially if McGraw were uneducated, or flighty, or on drugs. Or maybe he had a tin ear for the cadence of English prose. Many people did.

Nonetheless, Cavanaugh worried the problem for another ten miles. Then he pulled over and phoned Dunbar at his home. Special Agent Dunbar, his wife said in a voice as tight-assed as Dunbar's own, had not yet arrived home. She would turn on the machine so that Special Agent Cavanaugh could leave a detailed message.

He did, explaining about the parallel structure and incorrect preposition, feeling every second like more of a fool. He ended, lamely, "So there it is."

Pause.

"For you to consider."

Pause. Then, lamest of all, "I was an English major."

He drove on to the Weather Vane Motel and his howling dog.

INTERIM

The woman took her jacket and skirt and hung them carefully in the narrow locker. Jil Sander. Who would have thought that she could ever afford Jil Sander? Actually, she couldn't. But the raise that accompanied her promotion would come through next paycheck, and anyway she deserved this suit. She'd bought it in a haze of euphoria just yesterday when the CEO himself had told her about the promotion. "Outstanding qualities of leadership," he'd said. If that didn't justify Jil Sander, what did?

The noontime buzz in the locker room rose, but the woman didn't join in. She preferred to keep to herself. She was going higher than all the rest of these women and in the not-too-distant-future. It wasn't a good idea to form friendships that could prove awkward later.

Her euphoria lasted throughout the aerobics class—fueled her, strengthened her. She had a great workout. Afterwards, stripping off her sweaty workout clothes in the shower booth, she couldn't stop grinning. Damn, but she felt good. She had to restrain the impulse to sing.

Soaping her arms under the stinging spray, angling herself to keep her hair dry, she noticed a small red patch high on her left shoulder.

No. No. It wasn't.

But it was. She calculated rapidly. She'd worn a white silk tank top to Wolf Trap two nights ago, and they'd sat outdoors. Had she applied the insect repellent high enough on the shoulder? She thought she had. But here it was, a mosquito bite, and she'd never even felt the goddamn little thing get her. . . .

Calm down, she told herself. *Calm down. You can handle it.* Yes, she was sickle-trait positive, her blood test early during the epidemic had confirmed that. But the bite was only two days old. The *Plasmodium* parasites took seven to ten days inside the liver before they were released into the bloodstream. That's what the CDC bulletins said: on TV, on posters, on the flyer in her briefcase. She was still okay, as long as she went to the clinic immediately. They'd had months of experience with this thing; they'd learned what to do. Her next move was simply to get herself to one of the epidemic clinics, and they'd advise her from there.

Quickly she dried herself, pulled on fresh underwear, and ran back to her locker to put on the new Jil Sander.

TWELVE

Healing is a matter of time, but it is sometimes also a matter of opportunity.
—Hippocrates, *Precepts*, fourth century B.C.

Melanie sat numbly in front of the TV, its flickering grays the only light in her motel living room. It was six forty-five. The others had gone out to dinner. They, or maybe just Joe Krovetz, had knocked on her door, probably to ask her to join them. She'd kept the curtains closed and the lights off, and eventually they'd gone away.

She was no longer a member of the malaria reading team.

It could have been worse, of course. Farlow could have fired her. Instead she got a paid vacation, no official reprimand, the chance to work on other epidemics. It could have been much worse. All she'd failed at was this one epidemic.

Except that she, Melanie Patricia Anderson, didn't fail. Ever. She'd been *summa cum laude* at Berkeley. She'd graduated fourth in her class at Yale School of Medicine. She'd earned glowing recommendations and universal trust during her epidemiological work in Africa. Even when she was doctoring in Mississippi, hating it, she'd been a good doctor. Melanie Anderson did not encounter situations she couldn't master.

Except, of course, she had. And though she'd tried and tried to shame herself into recognizing that, next to the brothers and sisters who were dying, her own setback was pathetically minor—she somehow couldn't do it. All she could do was sit numbly and stare at a newsman with carefully moussed hair, grinning about the "favorable developments" in malaria reading.

"Only two deaths this week—a significant drop from just last week, which was, in turn, a drop from the week before. In a press statement this morning, Dr. James Farlow, head of the epidemiological team from the CDC, had this to say."

A picture of Jim flashed onto the screen behind the anchorman's left shoulder, then enlarged and started talking. Farlow looked solemn. "The CDC is convinced we've pinned down the major components of this disease. The public-health measures undertaken by Maryland and Virginia, plus our new understanding of the biology involved, make us feel pretty sure that the public-health crisis is essentially over. The Health Service and the army will remain in southern Maryland, but the CDC team is ready to return to Atlanta and continue our research there."

Back to the anchorman. "But for at least one person, the crisis is not over. In fact, it may be just beginning. Today FBI agents obtained a search warrant for the town house of Dr. Michael Sean Donohue. Twenty special agents combed every inch—"

"Melanie," a male voice called, to vigorous knocking on the door. "Melanie, you there?"

Cavanaugh. Melanie watched a tiny version of him on the TV screen, one of twenty men filing into Donohue's home, while the anchorman did a voice-over and a larger Cavanaugh banged on her door. Well, in a few minutes he would go away.

"—carrying boxes of items to the FBI labs in Washington for thorough analysis—"

"Melanie? Melanie Anderson?"

Why didn't he go away? She didn't want to see anybody or talk to anybody, and if she did, it wouldn't be him.

"—case agent Gerald L. Dunbar had this one pithy comment—" Dunbar, in a dark suit beside a dark car. He looked even more solemn than Farlow. He said stiffly, "I'm convinced we have the man we're looking for."

"Melanie! Open up!"

She walked to the door, unlocked and unchained it, opened it. "*What?* Don't you realize that when someone doesn't come to the door maybe it's because they don't *want* to come to the door?"

"Yes," Cavanaugh said, unembarrassed. For some reason, a dog trailed him. He held out a sheet of paper. "This was in my E-mail just now when I got home from work. It's an internal memo for the CDC team, copied to USAMRIID and the Health Service and the Bureau. What's it all about, Melanie?" He handed her the paper.

THE CENTERS FOR DISEASE CONTROL REGRETS TO
ANNOUNCE THAT DR. MELANIE ANDERSON WILL BE LEAVING
THE MALARIA READING TEAM IN SOUTHERN MARYLAND DUE
TO PRESSING FAMILY CIRCUMSTANCES. HER WORK ON THIS
EPIDEMIC HAS BEEN INVALUABLE, AND THE CDC WISHES TO
COMMEND HER FOR HER MANY IMPORTANT CONTRIBUTIONS.
DR. ANDERSON WILL BE RETURNING TO WORK AT THE SPECIAL
PATHOGENS BRANCH OF THE CDC IN ATLANTA SOMETIME
NEXT MONTH.

She held the paper, saying nothing, staring bleakly at the heading. The E-mail transmission time was 2:14 P.M. Farlow must have prepared the press statement even before he bailed her out of the police station.

"Melanie, are you all right?"

She said tonelessly, "Oh, yes, of course I'm all right. I assaulted a teenage kid. I got fired off the most important project of my career. Your precious Bureau is doing a cover-up of attempted genocide. But of course I'm all right."

"Assault?" Cavanaugh said. "Fired?"

"Please leave." She tried to shut the door on him. He shoved past her into the room. The dog followed, wagging its tail.

"Melanie, just tell me what happened. Please."

"Why should I? It has nothing to do with you. You guys 'got the man we're looking for.' And none—"

"No, we don't," Cavanaugh said, but she was trying to finish her own sentence.

"—of you care that what's going on here isn't the result of one hate-filled nut. There's a group behind it, and their goal is no less than African-American genocide."

He said, "It's not really genocide."

"What?"

He explained to her. "This isn't really 'genocide.' That word means killing total populations. Only twelve percent of African Americans carry sickle-cell trait, so even in a worst-case scenario, only twelve percent could be killed. That doesn't qualify as actual 'genocide,' even in intent."

Melanie stared at him. "Not genocide? I suppose you think Dachau and Auschwitz weren't genocide either, because some Jews escaped them?"

"No," he said patiently. "You don't understand. That was different because—"

"It's you who don't understand! Not a fucking thing!" Suddenly her numbness shattered. All her rage, her hurt, her frustration rose in her throat and vomited itself out on this one person who was challenging all of it. "No, you sure the hell don't understand. And you know why you don't understand a fucking thing? 'Cause you're white!

"You don't understand what it's like to visit a house for an epidemiological interview where a healthy four-year-old child has just died. Four years old, beloved of his grandma and his mother and his sobbing older sister . . . and murdered! That's genocide—of a whole family's future, all the black children that murdered black child might have had. And *their* children.

"But we don't even need to take it to that level, Agent Cavanaugh. No, we don't. You don't understand a fucking thing at a much more daily level. You don't understand how a black woman gets tailed by a security guard the minute she walks into a pricey store because the assumption is that *of course* she's a shoplifter. You don't understand how a black man crossing a street, minding his own business, *of course* causes all the car door locks to click for half a block in either direction. You don't understand that black people riding in a Lincoln Continental get stopped by the cops twice every mile because the cops *just naturally* think they're drug dealers. It doesn't matter if they're dressed for church on a Sunday with their kids in the backseat; they get stopped anyway. You ever get stopped because you were riding in a Lincoln Continental, Agent Cavanaugh? I don't think so."

She moved so close to him that her spittle landed on his tie. He tried to move away, but she went right with him. "You don't understand why a black woman with a medical degree from Yale has to wear a suit just to check into a hotel because otherwise they'll assume she's either a hooker or one of the maids. You don't understand how that same black woman, even in her suit, is looked at and talked to in the hotel bar by all the nice out-of-town white businessmen with a little too much to drink. 'Hey, brown sugar.' 'Nice ass, baby.' 'How much for one hour, sweetheart?' You don't understand how that same woman feels knowing that everyone in the seminar she's teaching is coolly appraising her and thinking, 'Did she really get here on merit, or is it all affirmative action?' You can't understand anything, Cavanaugh! And on top of what you don't understand 'cause you're white are all the things you don't understand 'cause you're a goddamn FBI agent!"

"Calm down, Melanie."

"Don't tell me what to do! Do you know what your J. Edgar Hoover did to African Americans? He targeted them in the sixties for special surveillance, smear campaigns, harassment of leaders like Martin Luther King. He used agents to deliberately set civil rights groups against each other, until even a Senate investigating committee concluded that the FBI—and I quote—was 'fomenting violence and unrest'!"

"Hoover's dead," Cavanaugh said. "He died in 1970, remember? The Bureau's different now. The—"

"Oh, right! That's why in the nineties your black agents had to band together and threaten lawsuit before the FBI would agree to promote some of them to supervisor positions! Or didn't they teach you about that at Quantico? No, they fucking sure didn't! How you can stand there and say . . . and say . . ."

She was crying now, which was worse than yelling. She hated it. She put her hands over her face to hide the tears from him, but she couldn't stop sobbing, couldn't get words past her throat to tell him to get the hell out, couldn't go on being a member of the CDC team. . . .

He was patting her shoulder, fumbling in his pocket for a tissue. She took it and swiped at her eyes, but more stupid fucking tears came to replace the ones she'd wiped away. She couldn't stop crying and now the tissue was soaked through.

His arms went around her.

Instantly she froze. And he must have been encouraged by her sudden quiet, because he lifted her chin and kissed her.

She tore herself free. "You bastard. Get out."

He looked bewildered. "I only—"

"I know what you only." She barely recognized her own voice, thick and quiet and deadly. "You only thought your simple ass saw a way in, right? She's crying, she's vulnerable, pat her a little, kiss her a little, and you're halfway to the bedroom and a little black nookie to brag about to the other agents, right? You make me sick. Get out."

"No, I—"

"Get out. Before I scream rape and report you to your tight-assed supervisor, Special Agent Got-Our-Man Dunbar. And if you ever dare touch me again . . . I don't do white men, you got that, cop? I wouldn't let one of you hold my hand!"

"I—"

"GET OUT!"

He went. The dog, whom Melanie had completely forgotten, trotted out with him. Melanie bolted and chained the door and then stood leaning against it, panting as if she'd just had a fistfight. Stupid bastard, opportunistic pussy-chaser, fucking white *cop*.

You're losing it, girl.

Slowly she slid to the floor, suddenly seeing the whole awful scene with Cavanaugh from the outside, as if she were watching it on TV, one more newscast in the malaria reading plague. Her tears stopped. For a long time she just sat there, motionless, trying to understand what was happening to her, trying to get a grip.

A long time.

Eventually she pulled herself up off the floor and reached for the phone.

"Mama? It's Melanie. How are you? That's good. Uh, Mama, I have a few days off, and I was just wondering . . . could I come home for the weekend? Just to sort of wander around the old places and just sort of . . . see you. And . . . everything. Would that be okay? Mama?"

Cavanaugh made his way to his own room at the Weather Vane Motel, Abigail at his heels. And a lot of good Abigail had been while Melanie berated him. If she had thrown a frying pan at him, Abigail would probably just have tried to fetch it.

He sat on the edge of the bed, shaking his head.

He'd only been trying to comfort her.

Really? Then why had he kissed her?

Male instinct. Testosterone. Distraction from the afternoon's misguided warrant search. Sexual deprivation. General cluelessness about women.

Judy. Marcy. Melanie. Strike three and you're way, way out. *It's not the heat, it's the stupidity.*

The red light on his answering machine was blinking. Not the Bureau; they'd call him on his cell phone. Unless somebody wanted to talk to him without having to actually talk to him. Answering machines were good for that.

"Robert, this is Special Agent in Charge Dunbar, returning your call."

Such formal wording—not a good sign. Well, so what. Dunbar the Human Metronome always sounded both formal and stiff. But all day today, it seemed to Cavanaugh, there'd also been something more.

"I'd like to see you in my office tomorrow at seven-thirty A.M." Pause. "That's all."

Cavanaugh was left staring at the answering machine light, now unblinking, an insectlike red dot on the machine's trim black case.

He didn't sleep much. At 7:22 he walked into the Baltimore Field Office. Down the hall from Dunbar's office stood a knot of agents, including Maloney from Division Five and Borelli from Headquarters. They all wore television-ready suits and carefully knotted ties, and Maloney carried a sheaf of paper.

They were going to arrest Michael Sean Donohue, and Dunbar hadn't included Cavanaugh.

The agents stood carefully out of earshot of Dunbar's office. Only one looked directly at Cavanaugh, and that one, even as he nodded, seemed embarrassed.

So it was like that. Cavanaugh knew now what was coming. He just didn't know why, or what he was going to do about it.

"Sit down, Agent Cavanaugh," Dunbar said. "We have something important to discuss. Did you, on or about June 21, interview a Mrs. Hattie Brown of Loveville, Saint Mary's County, during the course of your duties on the malaria reading case?"

Mrs. Hattie Brown. As soon as he heard the name, Cavanaugh saw her. A skinny, elderly black woman dressed in jeans and a faded cotton blouse, standing on her front porch in rural Maryland. A tough, likable old bird.

"Yes. I interviewed Mrs. Brown about the Christian Crusade hate group."

"And did you reveal to her any information about the case that you were not authorized to disclose?"

"I don't remember discussing anything unauthorized."

"She does." Dunbar opened the *Baltimore Sun* to page 3.

FBI ADMITS MUCH OF ITS WORK ON MALARIA READING DONE FOR POLITICAL REASONS

BY LIBBY TURNER

As long as well over a month ago, some segments of the FBI had doubts that the Bureau's investigation of malaria reading was directed merely by law-enforcement or humanitarian objectives. A citizen interviewed by Special Agent Robert Cavanaugh, whose Resident Agency in Saint Mary's City was the first to launch legal investigation of the epidemic, told the *Sun* that Cavanaugh had talked about much different motives. "They covering their ass," was the way Mrs. Hattie Brown of Loveville reported the conversation to this reporter. However, Mrs. Brown insists that this colorful wording is not hers, but a direct quote from the agent himself.

Mrs. Brown, along with several of her neighbors, was contacted about the Christian Crusade, a religious group that . . .

"But you know what, son? People like Christian Crusade ain't the ones making this plague. They too stupid. So why you wasting FBI time out here asking about 'em?"

"Because my boss told me to."

She nodded again. "I see. FBI covering its ass?"

"That's about it."

"Ain't it always the way. Be a whole lot of time saved in this world if people warn't made to waste it covering their ass."

"I couldn't agree more."

"Agent Cavanaugh?" Dunbar prompted.

"Yes."

"Yes what?"

"Yes, I said that to Mrs. Brown. But you have to understand the context. We—"

"No, I don't have to understand the context." Dunbar rose behind his desk. "There's nothing to understand. The revised Bureau regulations that all agents received a copy of, including you, are very clear on this. 'Disclosure of unauthorized information is considered a serious exhibition of faulty judgment, which calls into question an agent's ability and commitment. Such disclosures are grounds for investigation and disciplinary action.'"

Cavanaugh's stomach lurched. Dunbar had taken time before this meeting to memorize the exact wording. "Disciplinary action" at the FBI could range from a letter of reprimand all the way to dismissal, with a number of unpleasant options in between. Probation, transfer, demotion, suspension, request to resign . . .

"In view of the serious circumstances surrounding the entire case, and the many explicit requests for confidentiality to all agents from the director himself," Dunbar said, still standing behind his desk, "I am requesting the Office of Professional Responsibility to begin an investigation of your conduct. In the meantime, you are removed from the malaria reading case, and you are suspended without pay for a period of one month."

Suspended. Not dismissed, not even forced into a loss-of-effectiveness transfer. Suspended. That was bad enough, and so was the OPR investigation, but at least he was still an agent. For now.

"Agent Cavanaugh, do you have anything to add?"

"No, sir."

"Then if you'll excuse me . . ." Dunbar came around his desk and walked past Cavanaugh. His gait was stiff, even for Dunbar.

Cavanaugh waited until Dunbar and the arrest team had enough time to leave the building. He had no wish to see them pretend he didn't exist. Nonetheless, he was more relieved than upset. Much more relieved. He was still an agent.

Thank you, J. Edgar Hoover Christ.

❖   ❖   ❖

Neither gratitude nor relief lasted through the drive south from Baltimore.

About twelve hundred agents were investigated every year by the OPR. Offenses ranged from misuse of Bureau cars for personal purposes (the most common offense) to espionage against the United States. Offenses also included lying to a grand jury, sex with informants, taking a cut of drug sales, and murder. And what had Cavanaugh done? Shared a small joke with a likable old woman. Not exactly treason.

Of cases the OPR investigated, most resulted in some disciplinary action. But he was getting disciplinary action *before* the investigation. That was allowed, but not usual for offenses like casual unauthorized disclosure. Agents crabbed all the time about the Bureau's ass-covering, although you weren't supposed to indulge in that with a citizen informant. Still . . . it wasn't major.

And another thing: OPR investigations averaged seven months from beginning to final administrative decision. It could take as much as a year. During all that time an agent was under suspicion within the Bureau itself. The outside world wouldn't know, but other case agents would regard Cavanaugh as less than effective, working under a cloud.

Plus, after this month of suspension—"beach time"—the malaria reading case would probably be over. The death rate had already dropped to almost nothing. The evidence against Donohue would have gone to a grand jury, and thus have been turned over by the FBI to the Department of Justice for prosecution. Out of his reach.

A suspicion began to form in Cavanaugh's mind.

To give the suspicion a better growth medium, he pulled off the highway and parked in a mall. Turning off the engine, he sat and thought it through.

He had been removed from the case for a minor offense. *But,* it was a very public offense, thanks to Libby Turner of the *Sun,* on a very public case.

For the last week, Dunbar, the Human Metronome, had been acting uncharacteristically. Like a man under terrible strain. *But,* this case *was* a terrible strain. Look what it had done to CDC superepidemiologist Melanie Anderson. Dunbar wasn't black, but he was the case agent for an enormity that had led to deaths, riots, vituperation, countervituperation, and relentless public pressure to *get this thing solved.*

Dr. James Farlow, head of the CDC field team, was suddenly being promoted to Switzerland, well away from Washington. *But,* people got promoted all the time. Farlow had done a good job, and from what Cavanaugh had gathered, the World Health Organization post that Farlow was accepting was a plum.

Dr. Melanie Anderson, the most outspoken of the CDC people, calling malaria reading "genocide," had also been removed from the field team. *But,* Melanie had assaulted a kid in a Burger King. The assault had been all over the morning news, which Cavanaugh had listened to on his car radio. Assault was not the right public image for a CDC disease fighter. Even though the kid allegedly had a long history of causing trouble and pissing people off, assault was still illegal.

None of it really added up to anything.

Cavanaugh sat and thought longer. Then he pulled out his drawing pad. Doodling helped him concentrate. He drew a teddy bear sitting on a shelf, then added a tin soldier, a doll, a beach ball, and a Frisbee. He gave the teddy bear a thought balloon saying, "I wish I were a *real* avocado." By the time he labeled the drawing "STUPID TEDDY BEAR DEPRESSION," he knew what he was going to do next.

Seton wasn't in their Leonardtown office, although he'd left behind plenty of spoor: Pepsi cans, Dorito bags, Snickers wrappers. Probably Seton was in a bar near the Pax River naval base "developing informants." By now, Seton should have everybody in Patuxent turning each other in for federal crimes. Or at least have the navy well on the road to sharing Seton's alcoholism.

Seton was a terrible agent. But he was clever enough to have hoodwinked Dunbar, who hardly ever saw Seton, and who was overly impressed by the avalanche of correctly prepared paperwork that rolled into Baltimore every month. Moreover, Seton had a family, and he was very close to retirement. Those agents in the field office who did know how terrible he was would nonetheless protect him. Even Director Broylin had admitted that marginal agents were still tolerated more than they should be, although usually they were stuck someplace doing background checks on job applicants. Too bad Seton was so good at churning out 302s.

Cavanaugh wanted a look at those 302s.

He didn't have the password to Seton's computer. But he did have a key to the locked hard-copy cabinets. Most agents didn't keep hard copies once the reports were turned in. Too much bother. But Seton, so careful to impress his superiors, probably had neatly filed hard copies of everything, just in case he ever had to impress Dunbar the Book Man in person. Cavanaugh started on the last cabinet.

Not only filed, but cross-filed. It took Cavanaugh all of ninety seconds to find the duplicate 302.

On Tuesday, August 4, I met with informant Curtis P. McGraw, of 658 Crestview Avenue, Chevy Chase, Maryland, and 841 Beach Road, Town Creek, Maryland. Mr. McGraw is the owner and CEO of McGraw Contracting. Currently this company builds condominiums and apartment houses along the eastern shore.

Mr. McGraw told me that four months earlier, on April 2, he had met Dr. Michael Sean Donohue, of College Park, Maryland. They met at an evening seminar held by Tuchings, James, & Costain of Bethesda, Maryland, a private investment firm. (See attached seminar enrollment statement from Tuchings et al.) This seminar was held at the investment firm offices in Bethesda. Mr. McGraw and Dr. Donohue sat next to each other during the seminar and chatted during the coffee break. At the conclusion of the seminar they agreed to have a drink together at a nearby bar, Ramona's.

According to Mr. McGraw, the discussion that evening was about Chinese art. Both men collect it. Mr. McGraw told me, "I thought his collection sounded interesting, although not as good as mine. I had the impression he wasn't particularly well off. But he was very knowledgeable, and his taste sounded good."

Cavanaugh looked up from the 302. Donohue buying the little painted vase for two thousand dollars at Cathay House. The lighted display cabinet in his townhouse, filled with exquisite things.

The following week, on April 7, Dr. Donohue visited Mr. McGraw at his residence during the evening, Mr. McGraw stated. No one else was present. On April 13, Mr. McGraw briefly visited Dr. Donohue at Dr. Donohue's residence sometime during the afternoon. Business required Mr. McGraw to be in the area. Again no one else was present. Dr. Donohue showed Mr. McGraw his collection of Oriental art, which Mr. McGraw said consisted mostly of vases, bowls, and statues.

According to Mr. McGraw, Mr. Donohue's collection was "disappointing" and not as good as Mr. McGraw had expected. He expressed disappointment to Dr. Donohue. Mr. McGraw now says he can't remember his exact words.

But he does remember Dr. Donohue's reply. Dr. Donohue allegedly said, "I have something that will impress you, Curt. Wait here." Dr. Donohue then left the room. When he returned, he was carrying a small cardboard box with holes covered with cheesecloth. Inside, visible through the cheesecloth, were live mosquitoes, buzzing and flying. McGraw said that Donohue said, "These are instruments of death like the world has never seen. And like nobody else is smart enough to make."

There was the wording that had bothered Cavanaugh in the search warrant. And Seton had been the unnamed FBI agent responsible for supplying it.

Mr. McGraw does not remember his reply to Dr. Donohue. He says he left shortly afterward and did not contact Dr. Donohue again. "I decided he was a nut," Mr. McGraw said to me. Dr. Donohue didn't call Mr. McGraw again either.

When the suspicion of Dr. Donohue was made public on television, Mr. McGraw came to me with his information. Mr. McGraw is personally known to me as a citizen informant. At one time I was investigating him for illegal activities involving buildings constructed by his firm at the Patuxent River Naval Air Station (see Southern Maryland Resident Agency, 302 Report Nos. 896, 899, and 905). Since then, however, further investigation has cleared Mr. McGraw and established that reports of the alleged illegalities were engineered by a rival firm in the highly competitive contracting business (see Southern Maryland Resident Agency, 302 Report Nos. 1146 and 1147).

Mr. McGraw is thus a citizen informant of good standing. His statement should be thoroughly investigated by the appropriate case agents.

Special Agent Donald R. Seton
Southern Maryland Resident Agency

How long had it taken Seton to put this thing together? Because it *was* put together. Concocted. Assembled from bits of plausible fact into something that had never happened.

Why was Cavanaugh so sure of that? He didn't know. But it wasn't just because he didn't trust Seton, or just because Cavanaugh had been removed from the case. No. His former boss Marty Felders had taught his agents to always follow up on what Felders called "those old heebie-jeebies." A hunch, a suspicion, an epiphany. Felders was the best agent Cavanaugh had ever seen, and before he was an outstanding agent he'd been an outstanding cop in New York. Felders was worth listening to. Seton's report gave Cavanaugh a major dose of heebie-jeebies.

Something was going on.

This Curtis P. McGraw was being let off the hook for federal construction fraud in return for supplying "evidence" against Michael Donohue. McGraw even came off looking like a patriotic hero. Not hard to figure his motives. They went back to Brutus.

Nor were Seton's reasons obscure. Retire with a triumphant bang. Make up for all those "informant reports" that seldom led to any concrete action.

But Dunbar had bought this charade. So had Bruce Maloney, from National Security Division. So, for all Cavanaugh knew, had Director Broylin himself. The search warrant for Donohue's town house had been based mostly on Seton's report. Although, Cavanaugh now remembered, it had been issued by an ordinary federal judge, not the attorney general. And the warrant had not claimed any special intervention due to national security.

Besides, the whole scam somehow was just too grandiose for Seton. Seton stuck to the inconsequential lie, the small cover-up, the petty fraud. He was a petty man.

This was not petty.

So what was going on? Was the whole thing merely a ruse to get in to search Donohue's apartment in hope that once the FBI got that far more leads would present themselves? Such things had certainly been known to happen in the Bureau. But not on this scale, this publicly. And was it just coincidence that Dr. Farlow was moving to Switzerland, *and* Melanie Anderson was off the malaria reading case, *and* ditto for Cavanaugh himself, *and* Dunbar was acting as if he bore the weight of civilization on his Hoover-uniformed, soldier-rigid soldiers?

If not coincidence, then who was covering up what? And why?

Cavanaugh had no answers. But his heebie-jeebies clamored loud and strong.

He copied Seton's report, returned the original to the filing cabinet, and pulled out Seton's numerous 302s on Seton's interactions with Curtis P. McGraw. He started to read.

T H I R T E E N

**The FBI is a cruel organization in that it is highly
bureaucratic, rule-oriented, rule bound. It's cruel in the
sense that it doesn't treat its people very well sometimes.
—Lee Colwell, former Associate Director
of the FBI, 1992**

I see on *Sixty Minutes* that there's doubt about whether Donohue's arrest will hold up legally," Tess Muratore said to Judy Kozinski over lunch at a coffee shop. The two women sat in a booth at the back, surrounded by a comfortable lunchtime bustle. Tess, who only had an hour off duty, was in her state trooper uniform. "The show said Donohue's lawyer is going to challenge on probable cause. Although, of course, *Sixty Minutes* always goes for the hysteria."

"I didn't see the show," Judy said airily.

"Really," Tess said.

"No. I've been so busy with my new apartment. Curtains, some new furniture . . . I want you to come see it soon."

"Sure," Tess said. "Has Robert called you?"

"You know, this salad is really pretty good. Especially for a coffee shop. I think the dressing's fresh."

"Stop trying to change the subject, Judy."

"The salad *is* the subject."

"No, *you're* the subject," Tess said. "Do you think I'd give up a chance for a pepperoni sub in the patrol car with my Neanderthal partner if I wasn't concerned about how you're doing?"

"I'm doing fine." She speared an olive.

"Okay, you're fine. What about Robert? How's he? Has he called?"

"No. And I don't expect him to." Judy ate the olive, which stuck in her throat. Tess watched her as she forced it down with an entire glass of water.

"Uh, huh," Tess said. "Did you see him on TV at the warranted search of Donohue's premises?"

"Yes, it just so happened that I caught it. 'Warranted search of Donohue's premises.' You sound like a cop, Tessie."

"I am a cop."

"Well, stop investigating *me*."

"I thought we were talking about Robert," Tess said innocently. "He didn't look good on TV. Sort of pasty. And now this new allegation that he disclosed unauthorized information to an outsider. Did you just so happen to catch that news, too?"

"Hard not to," Judy said lightly. "The papers are full of it."

"It's bullshit. Robert was just working the woman, getting her with him so'd she talk. If all law-enforcement personnel who did that were charged with misconduct, there'd be no cops left on the streets. You see Arnfeld's column about it in the *Post*?"

"Yes."

"You see where Robert's boss, Dunbar, is going to the International Law Enforcement Academy in Budapest? He's been named to head of the FBI detail that's there to train international police."

"Yes."

"Pretty nice. You see that announcement by Donohue's lawyer that Donohue had a private polygraph test and it came out 'no deception'? That's the highest rating. And now he's agreed to let the FBI give him a polygraph of their own. You know about that?"

"I know about it."

"Ah," Tess said. "But you aren't paying any attention to Robert's case. Oh, no."

"It's not just 'Robert's case'; it's public news involving a genuine tragedy!" Judy flared. "And whose side are you on, anyway—mine or Robert's?"

"I'm on your side. Always will be. But you aren't handling this as well as you think, Jude. Look at you. You're losing too much weight, you hardly touched that salad you raved about, you cram your days with busywork, you look terrible."

"Thanks a bunch!"

Tess pushed away her sandwich and leaned forward. She dropped her voice, which meant that to hear her in the noisy lunch-hour rush of dropped forks and human babble, Judy had to lean forward, too.

"You can't run away from pain, Judy. It took me two marriages to learn that. You gotta go *through* it. It won't help, in the long run, for you to pretend Robert's leaving doesn't matter to you and you don't still love him. It does, and you do."

Judy said nothing. She gazed down at her uneaten salad. Then, very low, "I feel like he reached into my chest and tore my heart out."

"I know. I know you do. Just let yourself feel that, just face it, and you'll get through it. And maybe he'll call."

"No," Judy said clearly. "I don't want him to call. I'm not clinging to somebody who treats me like that. I clung and clung to Ben, and it only meant I ended up putting up with shit nobody should put up with."

"All right," Tess said, "then let's hope he doesn't call. I don't care about him anyway—*you're* my friend. Oh, shit, look at the time. I gotta go."

"Take care, Tessie. And thanks."

"*You* take care, buddy. I'll call you later in the week."

Judy watched Tess swing down the aisle and out the door. The olives in Judy's salad still glistened, but she couldn't eat any more. Still, she'd do what Tess said: face the fact that she missed Robert terribly. Although she couldn't let herself think too much about him. About him reading the newspaper and telling her how everybody should have done everything differently. About his quotations of nineteenth-century poetry and his quirky drawings. About his dogged, graceless persistence in any task he decided he was absolutely going to do. About him in bed, doing . . .

But she especially wouldn't let herself think about that. If she thought about sweet and hot lovemaking with Robert, it would paralyze her for the whole rest of the day, she'd miss him so much.

Sex. It always did women in, one way or another. Always.

✴   ✴   ✴

As soon as Cavanaugh finished reading Seton's 302s, he left their office. He didn't want to see Seton. He went back to the Weather Vane Motel, packed up his things, and moved them to another motel, registering under one of the FBI alternate identities so no reporters could locate him. This motel, called for no visible reason "The Pines," was worse than the Weather Vane. Much worse: sagging bed and torn shower curtain and cigarette-scarred dresser. Also, the floor tilted at a definite angle. But, then, the FBI wasn't paying for this motel, and he was suspended without pay. Besides, the place allowed dogs.

Abigail took this move with the same equanimity she'd taken the last one. She sniffed the decrepit furniture, lapped from the toilet, and settled with a happy groan across the doorway to the bathroom. Evidently, Abigail didn't care where she lived as long as Cavanaugh was there. She was happy.

Cavanaugh, on the other hand, was getting tired of living out of suitcases. Whatever he needed was always in a different packing box in the car, even if he thought he'd lugged it inside. With repeated rummaging, Marcy's neat boxes were becoming a slovenly mess. And he missed his furniture, which was in storage. He'd half hoped to see Judy the Saturday he'd had it moved from the Rivermount house, but she hadn't been there. Eventually he'd have to rent another apartment, probably in Leonardtown, near his office. *If* he got to stay on as an agent after the OPR made its final report.

He dumped his suitcases in this new temporary home, grabbed a bowl of stew (or so it called itself) at the motel restaurant, and spent the rest of the day on-line, the radio going at the same time. At 6:30, when the work day of the unsuspended was over, he could finally make the phone call to Felders at Felders's home. Which, of course, unlike Cavanaugh, he had one of.

"Marty? Robert Cavanaugh."

He heard Felders draw a sharp breath. "Bob."

Despite everything, Cavanaugh smiled. Felders was the only person allowed to call him "Bob." This liberty, which Felders had taken without asking, suddenly seemed a good thing. *Someone* felt comfortable with him.

"Bob, what the fuck did you screw up?"

Ah, Felders. Straight to the point. "I talked to an interviewee. Joked, really. About the FBI covering its ass."

"That's it? There's not more to it than the news said?"

"No. Yes. I mean, there's a lot more, but it's not about me."

"Then what's it about?"

Cavanaugh explained. He told Felders all of it: Seton's 302s about Curtis McGraw. The so-called "probable cause" in the search warrant. Donohue's diction patterns, habitual versus as reported in the 302, and the search warrant. Dunbar's tense behavior. Melanie Anderson's stubborn insistence that genocide was occurring, and her removal from the malaria reading team. His own suspension. Farlow's promotion to Switzerland. And now Dunbar's promotion to Budapest, which he'd just heard about on the radio news. Cavanaugh was scrupulous; he also explained the evidence for each of these events happening independently.

When he finally finished, Felders said, "Pretty thin."

"I know."

"If you know, why are you calling me?"

Cavanaugh said, "Heebie-jeebies."

Felders laughed. To Cavanaugh it sounded like the most unwilling laugh he'd ever heard. But, still, it was a laugh, and Cavanaugh took advantage of its presumed good will, however tenuous.

"Marty, I need you to do something for me."

"Oh? And what's that?" Felders's voice prickled with wariness.

"I need you to find out everything you can about Fort Detrick."

"Fort Detrick? You mean because USAMRIID was the CDC's partner in the epidemic squashing."

"No. That's not why."

Cavanaugh waited. It took Felders a minute to put it together. When he did, he said, "My God, Bob."

"I'm not saying I believe it. It's just a hunch. But everybody knows that Fort Detrick has a shady past."

"Which is *in* the past. Yeah, at one time the fort was used for developing biological warfare. It was *supposed* to develop them—FDR himself gave them the mission. And they did it. But that was forty years ago!"

"Closer to sixty. And, yes, Nixon ordered the entire stock of bioweapons destroyed in 1970. But when a Select Committee of Congress looked into that, in 1975, the CIA director testified that, yes, well, whatdaya know, bioweapons are still present at Fort Detrick. Sorry about that. Along with some germ-warfare microbes that had been moved to commercial drug firms but were still accessible to a very few—very few—top CIA types, who were the only ones who knew about them."

Felders said, "And after *that* congressional hearing, the stuff was destroyed."

"Really? Given the CIA's overall record, do we know that for sure?"

Felders, however much he hated it, was fair in arguments. "No, we don't. So maybe—just maybe—some of that old anthrax or whatever is still on ice somewhere. Hoarding old bioweapons is still a long way from developing new ones against direct executive order."

"Granted. But—"

"You're blowing smoke, Bob."

"Maybe. Maybe not. But I'm asking you to get together anything you can about Fort Detrick. Anything covert, I mean. I have all the unclassified stuff. Use whatever channels you have."

A long silence. And then Felders said, "No."

"No?"

"No."

Cavanaugh closed his eyes. Felders was not an ass-coverer. Not a misty-eyed Bureau worshipper. Not a one-track thinker. And, above all, not a coward. If Felders said no, it wasn't because Cavanaugh's request was dangerous, disloyal, or divisive. It was because Cavanaugh's request was ridiculous.

"Give it up, Bob," Felders said. "It's so far in left field it's not even on this planet. I mean it."

"Your metaphors are mixed, Marty."

"Damn my metaphors! Listen, the FBI invested thirty thousand dollars in training you. You're a good agent, no matter what the assholes in OPR eventually decide. And in ten years you'll be even better. Don't blow it for some paranoid nut theory you've got no solid evidence for. Zilch. Nada. Snake eyes. Don't do it, Bob."

"You're right. I haven't got solid evidence." He paused. "Yet."

"Goddamn it, Bob—"

"Bye, Marty," Cavanaugh said, and hung up before he damaged the only semigood relationship he had left with someone who didn't drink from a toilet.

✿   ✿   ✿

After Melanie had spent three days back in Arlo, Mississippi, which she remembered as one of the most beautiful places on earth, she couldn't stand it any longer.

Arlo was still beautiful. Distant from the great river, and from everything else, there were no large industries, highways, or suburban sprawl to spoil the rural beauty. Trilliums grew in thick shade in the oak-and-pine woods. Columbine, scarlet and yellow, grew thickly up its own tough stalks. The hot air smelled of thunder and rain and pine needles and the thick, sweet, antebellum fragrance of magnolia. Under the persimmon trees, the sad, cool call of the mockingbird lingered in the stillness, just as Melanie remembered.

The people, too, were just the same. Melanie's grandmother, her old body fined down and twisted but still strong, reading the Bible every morning and going to church twice a week in a flowered hat and white gloves. Her mother, who waitressed at the Live Oak Inn, still pretty and still able to dance till 3:00 A.M. at the one tiny black "nightclub," gyrations from the sixties that showed off her trim figure. Her brother, successful and expansive at the town's one small factory, importantly overseeing the manufacture of glass bottles. Her best friend, who was the only one who'd changed. Coreen was pregnant with her fourth child, whose father had disappeared. She was defeated and bitter and poor, and she refused to admit any of these things, which made Melanie alternate between admiration and despair.

Except for Coreen, nothing in Arlo had altered. But Melanie had.

Still, she took long walks through the woods, well slathered with insect repellent, and conscientiously tried to manufacture the peace of mind that Farlow had told her she needed to acquire. She ate the sweet, sun-warm blackberries that tasted of her childhood. She fished for bluegill. She picked masses of bloodroot and arranged vases of them around the house, until her brother claimed they aggravated his allergies. She dutifully tried to dance with her mother, flinging herself around the living room in something improbably called the Mashed Potato.

She didn't tell her mother that her mother's consciousness as a black woman was in a sub-subbasement of a deep mine. She didn't tell her grandmother that Melanie didn't believe in God. She didn't tell her brother that the way he treated his women was sleazy and immature. She didn't tell Coreen that wallowing in anger and self-delusion got you nowhere. Of all people, Melanie realized, she herself had the least right to deliver that message to anybody.

And every day, every minute, she longed for Atlanta. For Africa. Even for the Weather Vane Motel.

She had told her family no details of her "vacation," merely saying that she'd been working too hard. If they knew more from the papers, they didn't say. What they did do was give her advice.

From her mother: "You gotta get out more, baby. Have yourself a little fun. Life too hard not to laugh when you can."

From her brother: "Your problem, girl, is you ain't getting it. Find yourself a man and get you some."

From her grandmother: "Turn to the Lord, child. He always there when you need Him."

From Coreen: "You ain't gonna get shit from your CDC, Mel. Or from nobody else. They gonna get you in the end anyways. But dragging your ass around this sorry place when you got someplace else to go—that be the worst. Get out while you still can."

So was she taking Coreen's advice when she called back East? Or was she just hitting bottom in Arlo, like some cheap wino finally ready for AA? God, she hated that thought.

It wasn't true, anyway. She called Robert Cavanaugh because she owed him an apology. When he'd kissed her, he'd only been trying to comfort her (maybe). And she'd charged him with all the crimes of J. Edgar Hoover, all the crimes of every white man who believed black women were all easy nymphomaniacs, all the crimes of contemporary white America. Which was hardly fair. She'd only missed charging him with slavery because, in her distraught state, she hadn't thought of it.

Melanie waited until the house was empty. She billed the call to her phone card. "Robert? This is Melanie Anderson."

"Melanie." His tone told her nothing.

"Yes. I'm calling to apologize. When I shouted at you last week, I wasn't . . . I wasn't myself. I said some harsh things, I know, and blamed you for some things that weren't your fault. I just want to say I'm sorry."

"Where are you?" he said, which wasn't what she'd expected. Was he just going to brush aside her apology? Did he—God, no—mistake an apology for a come-on?

But then he said, "Are you at the CDC?"

"No. In Mississippi."

"Oh. Well, then, you need to come back. Listen to this, Melanie. I think you were right about Donohue's being innocent, and also about a far more dangerous thing for black people." And then he proceeded to talk for ten minutes straight about his partner Seton, the FBI, Farlow and Dunbar, USAMRIID, Fort Detrick, the CDC, Donohue, the search warrant, and the CIA.

When he finally finished, she was stunned. "The *CIA?*"

"You're going to tell me you don't believe the government is targeting its own black citizens."

"No, I don't. A cover-up, yes, I could easily believe that. Foot-dragging because after all it's only blacks—I could believe that, too. But not that the United States government is deliberately killing black citizens . . . Robert, that's major paranoid. Somebody is targeting us, but it isn't the United States government. Even *I'm* not that paranoid!"

"Well, that's where the evidence points at the moment. Although maybe there's more to it. Come back to Maryland to help me get to the bottom of this, Melanie."

"Help you? What do you need my help for? The medical aspects are solved, the epidemic is over, and you have the entire FBI to 'help you.'"

"No, I don't. I got removed from the case and suspended from the Bureau. Don't you read the papers?"

She hadn't, since she'd arrived in Arlo. Not conducive to Farlow's dictate to seek "peace of mind."

"What'd you get suspended for?"

"Doesn't matter. Something minor. They wanted me off this case, and that's significant, too. But I'm not giving up. This is too important."

"Are you sure you aren't just trying to prove the FBI wrong for having the gall to suspend Robert Cavanaugh?"

"Don't you want to prove the CDC wrong for daring to suspend Melanie Anderson?"

She felt punched in the solar plexus. Damn, he wasn't somebody you should mess with. She said coldly, "I was *not* suspended. I'm here visiting my family."

"Visit them some other time. This is important, Melanie. I don't have to tell you that. And I think we can crack it. One thing about the military—if it *is* the military—they do things by the book. There'll be a trail someplace."

"The CIA doesn't do things by the book. That's why they're the CIA." Listen to herself—she was actually getting sucked into this paranoid delusion.

"We'll see. Has anyone contacted you in Mississippi?"

"What sort of 'anyone'?"

"I don't know. That's why I'm asking."

She said, "Not in Mississippi. And not about malaria reading."

"Where then? About what?"

God, he was persistent. She told him about the hate tapes. Why? Because she hadn't been able to tell anyone else, except Joe Krovetz, whose calls she'd been refusing since she arrived. Robert listened, then said, "Bring the tapes with you."

"There is no 'with me.' I don't believe your wild tale, and I don't think it's worth the time and effort to look into."

And then he said the one thing that could move her. How did he know?

"All right, Melanie, don't come. But what else better have you got to do with your two weeks' nonsuspension?"

Melanie closed her eyes. This house, her family, the town closing in around her, suffocating her. And then, when her "vacation" was finally done, the sideways looks and too-hearty sympathy at the CDC.

"Okay, Robert. I'll come. What's your address now?"

He told her. She said good-bye and hung up. Her brother stood there, grinning.

"How long have you been eavesdropping on a private conversation?" Melanie demanded.

"I'll just bet it's private," he said. "You goin' to him? Good for you, girl. You finally gonna get some."

She thought of correcting him, or slapping him, or lecturing him. All of it would be wasted effort. She turned on her laptop to go on-line and book the earliest possible flight to Washington.

Cavanaugh wasted a whole day trying to track down Earl Lester, the Insect Boy of Rivermount Junior High. The scrap of paper with Earl's address, which Marcy had written down from Judy's answering-machine message, had been lost somewhere during Cavanaugh's residential musical chairs. He couldn't call Judy. Or Marcy, who wouldn't remember it anyway. The secretary at the junior high school said it was against school policy to give out students' addresses. From her tone, she suspected that Cavanaugh was probably a child molester. The principal was on vacation in the Greek islands. The Lesters had no phone.

He was finally reduced to driving to Rivermount and accosting groups of junior-high-looking kids to ask if they knew where Earl Lester lived. Cavanaugh stuck to large groups of kids, so that the secretary's fears would not be duplicated. Despite the blazing sun, high humidity, and temperature over ninety, the kids all seemed to be outside: on basketball courts, down by the river, strolling Main Street. No one, however, gave him any useful information. Either they didn't know where Earl Lester lived, or they didn't want to say.

He got back to The Pines motel at 4:00 P.M., sweaty and hot. The OPR investigators were waiting for him.

"Agent Cavanaugh? We represent the Office of Professional Responsibility," the older agent said formally.

"Hi, Miguel."

Miguel Sierra nodded and looked briefly at the ground. Cavanaugh didn't know him well, but he'd seen him around the Baltimore Field Office. Except for high-ranking officials charged with "allegations of misconduct," the OPR used local agents to conduct internal-affairs investigations. An OPR agent at Headquarters would assign specific interviews and write the final report, but Cavanaugh's peers would do the legwork. Which meant Miguel Sierra and the woman with him, whom Cavanaugh didn't recognize.

"This is Agent Eileen Morgan."

Cavanaugh nodded at Eileen, a small, unsmiling woman with the look favored by female trainees at Quantico: short hair, no makeup, no jewelry, conservative dark pants suit. They needed to strike the old-boy-network as serious individuals, not fluffy dating partners, and they knew it. "Come in, Miguel, Eileen."

Abigail bounded to meet him, and Sierra unbent enough to tousle her fur and run through the inanities people reserved for large dogs: "Hey, Abigail. What a dog. Yessir, she's a dog all right, she is!" Eileen Morgan looked as if she'd like to do the same thing but found the cost in dignity too high. Instead she eyed Cavanaugh's motel room, which looked even worse than yesterday. Housekeeping either had overlooked him or didn't exist. The bed stood in all its unmade squalor, the paint still peeled, the curtain still sagged. Eileen Morgan pursed her pale lips. Cavanaugh was only glad his laptop hadn't been stolen. His gun and FBI credentials were locked in his car, since he wasn't allowed to use them while on suspension. The laptop, however, wouldn't do well in the 140 degrees of a locked car standing in the Maryland sun.

"We have some questions to ask you," Miguel said, unnecessarily.

Cavanaugh went through the incident with Mrs. Hattie Brown yet again, sticking to the bare facts. Miguel and Eileen asked a few questions. Everybody already knew everything said, so the interview didn't last long. Cavanaugh was glad.

When they left, Eileen with a last disapproving glance at the unmade bed, Cavanaugh felt depressed. He didn't like living this way either. Basically, he was an orderly man. "Methodical" was the word he preferred, although Marcy had been known to use "compulsive." He liked having a home, with cheerful fuzzy rugs underfoot and designated drawers for different kinds of silverware and shared meals and stuff stuck around the place. Female stuff: flowers and pitchers of ice water and throw pillows that matched the curtains. Even purple knitted things that no one could tell what they were.

Everything, in fact, that had irritated him when he and Judy actually had it.

He pressed Judy's new number. He'd gotten it over a week ago from the phone company.

"Judy? This is Robert."

Pause. Then, neutrally, "Hello, Robert."

"How are you?" God, that sounded feeble. And suddenly his heart was not behaving: beating too fast and arhythmically.

"I'm fine. And you?"

"Fine." They sounded like they were at a tea party. Before he said something like *Pass the scones, would you?* which would really piss her off, he plunged into cold, deep water.

"Judy, I'm calling to say I miss you. I know I acted like a lunatic. I was wrong. Really, really wrong, and I'm sorry. Marcy doesn't mean anything to me, I know that now—" Was that true? He didn't slow down to investigate "—but *you* do. You mean a lot. I want more than anything to see you. To be with you. Will you let me?"

She said, "Are you asking me to marry you?"

His breath imploded. *Marry* her? What was with these women? They gave no quarter, took no prisoners, showed no mercy. Melanie telling him he was only following up on malaria reading to help his OPR case. Marcy telling him he was more expendable than Abigail, although not a bad lay. Judy telling him to propose or disappear. Every single damn one of them would have made a good torturer.

"Judy, I don't think we're . . . I mean . . ."

"'Bye, Robert."

He listened to the click of the phone, and heard it in a door bolt sliding decisively shut.

His depression deepened. He wasn't hungry. It was too early to sleep—only 6:00 P.M. He couldn't imagine himself going to a movie. He poured himself a beer from his cooler. The ice had melted and the bottles sloshed like so many desperate-message carriers from an island castaway. Cavanaugh turned on the motel TV. It didn't work.

He listened instead to the radio, and learned that Michael Sean Donohue had, according to the press conference held by his lawyer, passed two separate FBI polygraph tests, both with the most truthful rating possible.

The next day Cavanaugh drove back to Rivermount. He'd been walking down Main Street for five minutes when he saw Earl Lester.

No, it wasn't Earl. This kid was too small to be Earl. But he looked just like him: hair, skin, and eyes all the same color, a faded dun. Skin stretched over sharp bones, and none too clean. The child blinked twice as he stared back at Cavanaugh.

Another miniature Earl Lester, female this time, came out of Wal-Mart. Then another, a tall young woman holding a tiny, skinny, faded-dun Earl in diapers and Baltimore Orioles T-shirt. Cavanaugh stepped forward.

"Excuse me, miss, but are you Earl Lester's . . . ah . . . sister?"

She blinked twice at him. "Yeah. So?"

"Is he here with you? My name is Robert Cavanaugh. I gave a lecture at Earl's school in June, and he asked some questions I finally have answers to. Could I talk to him, please?"

She said nothing, studying him, until she pushed past him on the sidewalk and walked on. The three small children followed.

"Please, Miss Lester. It's important." She kept on walking. Cavanaugh was reluctant to identify himself as FBI because she might ask to see his credentials. Cavanaugh was not allowed to carry them, or his gun, while he was on suspension. He was not supposed to be investigating this case, or anything else. He was supposed to be repenting in sackcloth and ashes, which was what Miss Lester appeared to be wearing.

He said to her retreating back, "I was hoping to hire Earl to do some work for me. Work with insects. At seven dollars an hour."

She stopped, turned around, and blinked twice. "Seven?"

"Yes."

"You come along."

Around the corner was parked a pickup with several more Lesters of various ages in the truck's bed. They all looked alike, and they all blinked twice at Cavanaugh.

Miss Lester said to the truck generally, "Earl, you know this guy?"

"Sure," Earl said, without expression. "Agent Cavanaugh. FBI."

She considered this information. "Then I guess he ain't no pervert. Okay, Earl, get out. He's got work for you killin' bugs. Seven dollars an hour. You take my watch."

She juggled the baby, unstrapped an $8.99 Timex off her wrist, and handed it to Earl. All the Lesters except Earl climbed on or remained in the truck, Miss Lester and the baby in the cab. She drove off. Earl and Cavanaugh were left staring at each other on the hot sidewalk. Earl waited, blinking.

Cavanaugh said, "The work isn't killing bugs. It's about bugs, but it's not easy to explain because I don't understand myself what I need you to do until I ask you a lot of questions. Why did you call me a few weeks ago and show up at my house?"

"Wanted t'offer help on the malaria case," Earl said. "Like I told you once before, insects tell us a lot about everything. But you din't get ahold of me."

Cavanaugh sensed a grudge. He said, "Well, I'm ahold of you now. And I need your insect expertise. Malaria reading—"

"You said you got the whole NIH for insect expertise," Earl said, still expressionless. "Din't need me, you said. And anyways, the epidemic's over."

Cavanaugh saw he wasn't going to get off easily. On the other hand, he didn't really feel like explaining his misconduct, suspension, and OPR investigation to an accusing eighth grader. He said testily, "Well, I need you now. Are you interested or not?"

Earl still waited. Cavanaugh started to repeat the tactic that had moved his sister: *seven dollars an hour.* Some instinct told him not to. Instead he said, "This job will need insect equipment I don't have. But you tell me what you need, and I'll buy it. Afterward, you can keep it."

For the first and last time, Cavanaugh saw Earl Lester's eyes blaze. Without blinking. It was like looking at a steady pale nova. The boy started around the corner to Cavanaugh's car.

Cavanaugh faced his investigative team around a table in Melanie's motel room, which was considerably nicer than his own motel room. After one look at The Pines, she'd demanded a room for herself someplace else. They'd found a nice bed-and-breakfast two miles away. The room had a working TV, Victorian escritoire, and Jacuzzi bathtub. How much did CDC scientists earn? Never mind; it wasn't important.

"What's important here is to go back to the site of the start of the epidemic and develop physical evidence that's been overlooked so far," he said.

His team stared back at him: Melanie incredulous and Earl Lester expressionless, except, of course for blinking twice. His surrogate FBI. Hadn't there once been a Children's Crusade? He knew better than to say this aloud.

She said, "You've got to be kidding. Do you know how thoroughly the *Anopheles* breeding sites have been gone over? By us, by USAMRIID, by infectious-disease researchers around the world, by the media, by gawkers—Robert, there *is* no 'physical evidence that's been overlooked so far.'"

"There's got to be something," Cavanaugh said stubbornly.

"Like what?"

"I don't know. But something at the crime scene."

"The *crime scene?*" Melanie's tone could have boiled him alive. "The 'crime scene' is southern Maryland and eastern Virginia! How do you expect to search an area that size?"

"Not the whole thing. The epicenter."

"The epicenter is exactly what's been combed by every infectious disease agency on three continents. I myself ran into epidemiologists from Antwerp, Brasilia, Porton Down, Geneva, and Walter Reed. And I don't even work on the vector end of an epidemic."

"All right, then," Cavanaugh said, "*not* the epicenter. Somewhere out on the edges, where something might have been overlooked." He sounded lame, even to himself. But something had to be out there, somewhere. Something.

"It isn't done that way, Robert. And anyway, we don't have access to labs to analyze anything we do happen to find. You need a scanning probe microscope to identify small changes to malaria parasites. They're *small*. And if we did use commercial labs, and your conspiracy theory is right, we'd just tip our hand to these hypothetical government criminals who left this hypothetical biological evidence at your hypothetical crime scene."

Cavanaugh started doodling. She sounded logical. Nonetheless, the other evidence—none of which had convinced her, either, nor even convinced Felders—said to him that something was going on here. He was going to find out what. And he couldn't think of any other place to start to which he had actual access, except with the mosquitoes, where everything else had once started. Once more, from the top. This time with feeling.

Yes, he was hanging on to this case with one slipping finger, but he was still hanging on. Despite Melanie Anderson's logic.

"Robert, you have to see—"

"No, you have to be willing to explore—"

"Not to explore totally silly—"

"It's only silly if it doesn't yield—"

"Don't you see you're completely dismissing—"

This was getting them nowhere. To divert the discussion, Cavanaugh cut her off in midsentence and turned to Earl Lester, who had said nothing.

"Earl, you're the field expert on mosquitoes here. What do you have to say?"

Earl said, "When do we go buy the collecting equipment?"

INTERIM

The family lugged the picnic from the car and plunked it down on a weathered wooden table set under a grove of trees. Tupperware boxes of crab sandwiches, potato salad, fruit, brownies, lemonade. An ice chest with Tequila Sunrises in a tall thermos. And for the grandfather, who would drink nothing else, cold beer.

"Can we go down to the water, Mommy? Can we? Can we?"

"I'll go with them," the mother said to her husband.

The three set off for the sandy shore, the children running and shouting, the woman walking sedately behind. The two men settled in at the picnic bench, drinking in companionable silence.

Suddenly the old man quavered, "Mosquito!" He flapped one thin arm at the air.

"It's all right, Dad. The epidemic's over."

"Eh?"

The man raised his voice. His father was going deaf. "I SAID THE DISEASE IS ALL GONE NOW."

"Maybe is, maybe isn't." His eyes filled with the easy tears of the very old. "Why we here, Clarence? Why we takin' a chance?"

"BECAUSE IT ISN'T A CHANCE. WE WERE TESTED. REMEMBER THE ARMY GUY WHO DREW EVERYBODY'S BLOOD AT THE MALL? AND WE'RE ALL SICKLE-CELL NEGATIVE."

"Why we here? We belong at home!"

"THAT ISN'T EVEN AN *ANOPHELES* MOSQUITO, DAD. I CAN SEE ITS WING MARKINGS CLEARLY. AND THE PLAGUE IS ALL OVER."

"When we goin' home? It ain't safe in this here park!"

The man stopped himself from shrugging. He had told Lorraine this would happen, but she'd insisted on the picnic. They hadn't done anything as a family in a long while, the kids wanted to swim, Papa would forget about the epidemic like he forgot about so much else lately. It would be fun. She'd promised everybody it would be fun.

But not if his father kept this up all afternoon. They'd have to take him home before he became too upset, maybe even before they got to eat. The man fished out another beer from the ice chest and opened it.

"HAVE ANOTHER, DAD."

The grandfather sucked appreciatively at the brown bottle. The muscles of his gaunt face relaxed. His son smiled out at the blue water, the blue sky, the blue bathing suit on his wife's shapely figure. Lorraine could really wear the hell out of a bathing suit.

"Sometimes things you think be over, ain't over at all," the old man said, with sudden calm, and took another swig of his beer.

FOURTEEN

Every particle of an insect carries with it the impress of its Maker, and can—if duly considered—read us lectures of ethics or divinity.
— Sir Thomas Pope Blount, *A Natural History*, 1693

In the end they chose three sites. A patch of low, scrub-wooded, fresh-water marsh in Virginia, at the far eastern edge of what had been the epidemic area. A similar locale in northwestern southern Maryland, on the border of Charles and Prince Georges Counties at the western edge. And, over Melanie's protests, the epicenter near Newburg, which did indeed look as if it had been trampled by a retreating army. Tire ruts crossed the fields. Ecologically correct synthetic powder, designed to kill *Anopheles* larvae but little else, floated on pools of standing water. Litter dotted the ground: soggy film boxes, soda cans, a pair of green plaid boxer shorts.

"Bet there's a hell of a story there," Cavanaugh said, trying to lighten Melanie's mood, but she didn't even answer. Cavanaugh would have shrugged, but he was loaded down with the first set of bug paraphernalia, all of which was awkwardly shaped, large, heavy, or poisonous. Melanie and Earl both wore sturdy boots, but Cavanaugh's sneakers squished with every step through the muddy marsh. *They also serve who only slosh and stagger.*

Earl Lester was actually smiling. At least, it might have been a smile.

The bottom half of his pale, bony face lifted a little at the sides, slightly pulling his mouth upwards. He unfolded the first of the three Malaise traps, which Cavanaugh had bought and paid for. Along with everything else.

This was an automatic collecting device for daytime use. Green netting made a tall pyramid over a tripod whose legs pushed deep into the mud. On two sides of the pyramid, the netting touched the ground. On the other two, it ended three feet above ground. At the top of the tripod was a large, elaborately mazed box impregnated on the inside with potassium cyanide.

Setting this up, Earl suddenly became talkative, an event as startling as if he'd suddenly flown into the Malaise trap himself.

"See, insects, they tend to fly upward when they encounter a barrier," the boy said, sounding as if he'd memorized some book. "So they'll fly right up into the killing jar on top. There are eight hundred thousand species of the class Insecta, which is about eighty percent of all the animal species on this here planet. We're after phylum Arthropoda, class Insecta, order Diptera, family Culicidae, genus and species *Anopheles quadrimaculatus.*"

Melanie finally smiled. Cavanaugh hadn't been able to soften her, but the boy did. Well, as long as something did.

"See that there?" Earl pointed. "That itty bitty orange bug on that leaf? That's a *Metrior hynchromiris dislocatus.* They eat plants, includin' crops. The Miridae are the biggest family of true bugs. Bring along that light trap to the patch of dry up-ground yonder, Agent Cavanaugh."

Cavanaugh obeyed. The light trap hung suspended from a pole, which Cavanaugh hammered into the ground under Earl's direction. The insects, attracted by the circular light, would hit an upright baffle and drop into a pail of alcohol below.

"We gonna get a lot of moths and beetles in this," Earl said. "Can't be helped none. But we want a good cross-section of whatever's flying here by night, as well as by day. But we'll get us some mosquitoes. You know what a female potter wasp does? *Eumenes megaera.* She constructs a little pot out of clay on some branch to put her eggs in. Then she fills the pot with a mess of paralyzed caterpillars and seals it up. If you cut the bottom off the pot, she'll still put them caterpillars in it, even though they're all just fallin' out the bottom. Instinct. But she only puts in so many, and then stops. Some other species that do egg pots, they go on puttin' in caterpillars and puttin' 'em in and puttin' 'em in until they die of exhaustion. *E. megaera* is right smart."

"Unlike some people," Melanie murmured, "who just go putting evidence in leaky vessels until death by exhaustion."

Cavanaugh ignored her. By now his socks were completely sodden. Earl finished setting up the light trap and turned to Cavanaugh.

"Now for the fun part. You take that net, Agent Cavanaugh, and you take this killing jar, Miss Melanie."

Cavanaugh waited for her to say coldly, "Dr. Anderson, please," but she didn't. She must really like the kid.

"Don't you go breathing in that killing jar, now. Potassium cyanide is serious poison."

"I know," Melanie said, still smiling. She must *really* like him.

"I'm gonna take the water net and get us some aquatic specimens," Earl said. "Agent Cavanaugh, Miss Melanie'll show you what to do. Looky there—a *Papilio glaucus*. Only one other butterfly, swallowtail butterfly, got as much yellow at the base of the front wing, excepting *P. rutulus*. Did you know that if anything bothers them two butterflies, they attack with a foul-smelling scent off'n their heads?"

For the next half hour Cavanaugh tramped around after Melanie, helping to free bugs from her net and dropping them into a succession of killing jars. When that was done, the three of them beat vegetation for a while, making insects drop onto white drop cloths and then sucking them up with aspirators before the bugs could recover. When that was done, they set up pitfall traps and Berlese funnels. Cavanaugh learned earwigs never actually crawled into campers' ears, that damselflies had been seen settling on ships far out at sea, and that brown-banded cockroaches liked to hang around electrical appliances. Also that the male scorpion fly brought a present of a captured insect to the female he was courting.

"Sensible," Melanie said, who seemed more relaxed dropping bugs into a killing jar than Cavanaugh had ever seen her before. "I personally would have a lot of trouble resisting a man who brought me a nice juicy insect for a present." She grinned at Earl, who blinked twice and blushed.

Each time more equipment was needed, Cavanaugh trudged back to Melanie's rental car. His own car was still jammed with everything he owned that wasn't in storage. By the third trip his wet socks itched, his insect repellent had failed, and he felt as if a foul-smelling scent was attacking off'n his head.

When they finished at the epicenter, they repeated the whole thing over again. Twice.

It was late afternoon before they stopped at a Wendy's for hamburgers, then took the insects gathered so far to Cavanaugh's motel. At Melanie's trim place, several thousand extra bugs would be noticed, whereas at The Pines they would blend right in. Melanie and Earl immediately spread out a batch of dead specimens on a white sheet on the floor and began counting and analyzing. Abigail watched with interest.

This left Cavanaugh the car, where he played over the tapes of the hate calls to Melanie. He didn't want Earl to hear. Or any other kid within earshot.

The tapes were nasty, especially cumulatively. He began to sense the kind of tension Melanie had lived under. When he'd played every tape, he started over again, this time listening for any unusual background sounds. However, his small tape recorder couldn't distinguish among the many indistinct sounds.

Finally Cavanaugh picked four tapes and slipped them into a padded mailer. He wrote the note to Felders by hand:

> Marty—
> I know you said you wanted nothing to do with my requests on this case. But this does not involve any other governmental agencies, although I don't have the authority to order it myself. I'd really appreciate a psycholinguistic analysis of the enclosed tapes by Dr. Pritchard at Syracuse. The tapes are hate calls made to a young woman while she was in my jurisdiction. There are twenty-seven tapes, but these four have clear, inflected speaking and some background noise.
> Please.
>
> —Robert Cavanaugh

Cavanaugh studied the note. A letter, rather than a phone call, would give Felders more room to decide if he was willing to help. This letter seemed specific enough for Felders to comply—or not comply—but general enough so that if anyone else read it, Felders would not be implicated in anything. Cavanaugh couldn't think of any way to improve the note. It would have to do.

The FBI had worked with the Psycholinguistics Center at Syracuse University since 1974, and with Dr. Jonathan Pritchard since 1991. Pritchard was astounding. He listened to a tape of a kidnapper, a terrorist, or a bank robber, and then told law-enforcement agencies the perp's social class, home state, state of mind, motivation, and probable fate. He paid attention to the way phrases were constructed, pronounced, stressed, and a half a dozen other things. From the background noise, Pritchard suggested locations and time of day where the call might have been made. And if he didn't know these things, he was modest enough (unlike the profilers at Quantico, Cavanaugh thought) to not guess.

From phone-call tapes, Pritchard had successfully predicted two callers' suicides, three escapes, and a score of surrenders. He'd identified innumerable locales from which perps had made their calls. No other linguist came close to matching his record.

Cavanaugh mailed the package and strolled back to the motel. It was full dark; he had to get Earl back home.

"You tie up that dog now, Agent Cavanaugh. Otherwise she's goin' to get into our bug piles and mess 'em up good. Might even eat a few specimens."

"I'll tie her in the bathroom," Cavanaugh said. Abigail would hate that.

"She lay on them piles, all our work's wasted."

"I understand."

"She so much as poke her nose at even one pile and—"

"Earl, I'll tie up the dog. Now come on, your family's going to wonder what's happened to you."

At Rivermont, Earl's sister was outside before the car came to a complete stop. "Eleven hours and thirty-seven minutes. You got the money, Earl?"

"Not yet."

"Mister, you pay him. We done made a bargain."

Cavanaugh forked over eighty-four dollars. He offered it to Earl, but the sister's hand snaked out and slurped it from midair. Earl blinked twice, and Cavanaugh said hastily, "We aren't finished yet, Earl. Tomorrow at eight in the morning?" The boy nodded, his face relaxing slightly. Cavanaugh was starting to understand nonspoken Lester.

Back at the motel, he sent Melanie home, tied Abigail in the bathroom, and fell into bed, surrounded by a white-sheeted sea of dead insects.

Something's weird here," Melanie said on the fifth day. Three days of trap emptying, bug collecting, and sheet spreading had been followed by two days of counting and graphing. Cavanaugh had helped with this, doing what he was told to do, until Melanie and Earl said he was missing too many anomalies and sentenced him to the sagging armchair they'd moved into the bathroom, which he shared with Abigail. Except for very narrow walking aisles, the entire floor was covered with piles of decaying bugs on white sheets, as were the dresser, table, and, during the day, the bed. Housekeeping had never so much as knocked at the door. This was undoubtedly a good thing.

Cavanaugh put down the book Earl had loaned him: *The Astonishing Ant.* "What kind of something is weird? About *Anopheles?*"

"No," Earl said. "'Bout *Toxorhynchites rutilus.*"

"Oh," Cavanaugh said, trying to look intelligent.

Melanie smiled at him, a first.

"Elephant mosquito, Robert. Here, look at this graph. It's a projection backward of the elephant mosquito breeding patterns. We took how many we counted at the Virginia site. From that, plus their known breeding and survival and area-specific die-back rates, we figured out how many elephant mosquitoes hatched over the last four months at the Virginia site. That's the blue line."

Cavanaugh studied her graph. "What's the green line?"

"The numbers of elephant mosquitoes at the other viable site, at the eastern edge of the epidemic area. See, the blue and green lines start out nearly identical."

"And the red line?" Cavanaugh said, just to be sure.

"That's the epicenter site, near Newburg. But it's useless—the environment is too compromised. Look at the blue and green lines. We know from the mortality rate that the epidemic mostly spread west. The blue-line site is west, the green-line site is east."

Cavanaugh studied the graph. The two lines stayed nearly identical until June 3—the day before the day he'd interviewed Nurse Pafford about the stroke rate at Dellridge Community Hospital, Cavanaugh remembered. Then the number of elephant mosquitoes at the Virginia site abruptly and dramatically shot upward. It stayed higher than the eastern site for the rest of the graph.

Cavanaugh waited for somebody to tell him the significance of this. Surely it didn't have anything to do with elephants, which were scarce in southern Maryland.

"This here's a elephant mosquito," Earl said, picking a dead bug from one of the hundreds of piles on white sheets and dumping it on Cavanaugh's palm. Evidently to Earl the concrete fact of the bug's existence was what mattered, not its significance. Cavanaugh inspected the mosquito. It had shiny metallic blue scales and a long, curved nose. No, not nose—proboscis.

Melanie took pity on him. "Elephant mosquito larvae are predaceous. They feed on aquatic arthropods, especially the larvae of other mosquitoes. The adults feed on plant juices and nectar, never blood. They're easy to breed and raise in large numbers in supply houses."

Cavanaugh still didn't get it. "So? What does it mean?"

"It means that there have been experiments done, some successful, to use elephant mosquitoes to control other, more dangerous species by releasing huge numbers of elephant mosquitoes in epidemic areas. So they will eat the larvae of more dangerous species. The graph means somebody was trying to do that in Virginia to stop the epidemic, *before* it even went public."

"Din't work," Earl said. "*T. rutilus*'ll breed this far north, 'specially if it's real hot, but they don't like it much. They're happier in South Carolina and Georgia and Florida."

Cavanaugh looked at the unhappy dead insect on his palm. "You said they grow them in supply houses?"

"Yes," Melanie said.

"Which supply house?"

"Undoubtedly more than one. The biggest one in the east—"

"I know. Stanton Supply, in Atlanta."

"Yes, but they don't offer *T. rutilus*. I know that because I know their insect catalogue practically by heart. The CDC has an account with them. They don't find *T. rutilus* profitable enough. The biological-control experiments are still very new, and it's easy to rear *T. rutilus* for ourselves when we want a few. They thrive in Georgia."

South Carolina, Georgia, and Florida. That's what Earl had said. But not necessarily Maryland. "So where would somebody who was trying to control malaria reading go to buy elephant mosquitoes?"

"I told you, it could be anywhere," Melanie said. Her eyes kept straying back to the piles of bugs and graphs, which Earl had already returned to. Clearly she was itching to get back to work. But first she said to Cavanaugh, "Who do you think tried to surreptitiously control the epidemic that early?"

"I don't know yet," he said. This seemed obvious.

"Well, to find the source for the vector, try Baltimore. Fielding's offers them."

Fielding's. The moment Melanie said the name, Cavanaugh remembered his previous trip to the insect supply house. Catherine Clarke, the dumpy amorous director who was a cop groupie. "*We have lots of* Toxorhynchites rutilus. *Used in biological control of other species, you know, plus using the larvae as fodder. Very versatile. We can produce up to a million a day in our lab. . . . Or maybe some* Aëdes taeniorhynchus?"

He handed the dead mosquito to Earl, and a piece of paper to Melanie. "Write down the scientific name of the elephant mosquito."

"You going to Baltimore? You don't look very happy about it."

Catherine Clarke's hand on his arm. "I'm not. Just write it down anyway." After a moment he added, "And a phonetic spelling, too, so I can pronounce it right."

"Tox-uh-rine-kite-eez roo-till-us," Earl said from the floor. He turned his bony, washed-out face up to Cavanaugh's. "Ev'rybody knows *that.*"

"*Somewhat deficient in social skills . . . which unfortunately evokes a negative reaction from his insecure peers,*" the school principal had said of Earl. Cavanaugh bit back the negative reaction on the tip of his tongue. He didn't want to look any more insecure than he already felt.

Catherine Clarke was icy. Clearly, she too remembered their former meeting, and his romantic rejection. Her flirtatious manner had disappeared. She sat in her cluttered office, dressed in what appeared to be the same rumpled brown suit as before, and said formally, "And what does the FBI need to know now, Agent Cavanaugh?"

"I need to know more about mosquitoes, Catherine." He smiled, carefully leaving the Bureau out of it. Catherine Clarke reacted to neither the smile nor his use of her first name. Clearly he was going to have to work harder. "Perhaps I could ask you some questions over lunch?"

"Lunch," she said.

"Yes. Are you hungry? I know I am." He smiled again, letting his eyes linger on her.

She repeated, "Lunch."

"Or dinner. Dinner would be even better. Is there some place you especially like, someplace nice with good wine and—"

"Agent Cavanaugh," she said. Her tone could freeze glaciers. "Fielding's Scientific Supply is always happy to cooperate with law-enforcement agencies. Even when, as in this case, the agent is temporarily suspended but still pursuing the case, and the agent's tactics are a disgrace to his position. You do not need to pretend to a romantic interest you do not feel. I want to see these terrorists brought to justice as much as you do. Ask me what you wish, but without the insincere and unnecessary personal overtures."

Cavanaugh shriveled. She had kept her dignity, displayed her intelligence, offered her disinterested cooperation. Her quiet composure made him look like a maggot, like slime, like an indiscriminate predator. Not unlike the larvae of *T. rutilus*.

Averting his gaze from her, he handed over the slip of paper. "Do you offer these for sale?"

"*Toxorhynchites rutilus*. Elephant mosquito. Yes, of course. For a while there was a flurry of interest in using *T. rutilus* to control nuisance mosquitoes, *culex* and so forth. But the problem, of course, was that you had to keep seeding the area with *rutilus* larvae over and over, because as soon as *rutilus* succeeds in controlling the other mosquitoes, they run out of food and die off themselves. The whole process is just too much trouble and expense."

"Who has bought a supply of *rutilus* from you in the last four months? Especially buyers who don't usually order that mosquito?"

"I'll need to pull the records." She turned to her computer, brought up several screens, and frowned at them. Next she walked over to a locked file cabinet, unlocked it, and rifled through folders for several minutes. Cavanaugh watched her. In profile, she was much prettier. And her legs were lovely. Or maybe it wasn't that—maybe it was her calm pride that was lovely, her valuing of herself enough not to chase a man who wasn't interested, but not to punish him either. In fact, she was a very classy lady. Now that he'd made it impossible, he wished he *were* having dinner with her.

She came back to her desk and sat behind it. "We've had only eight orders for *T. rutilus* in the last five months. Seven were standing orders from universities; they use them in their graduate lab courses. The eighth order was from a buyer with whom we have a standing account, but who has never ordered *T. rutilus* before."

She hesitated. Cavanaugh waited.

"It's a complex account, with one facility housing a number of different organizations. Thirty-seven, to be exact. Usually the order is billable to a specific tenant organization, but this order was billed to another entity at the same place, identified only as 'Birthday Project.'"

Again she hesitated. Again he waited.

"The account is for Fort Detrick, Maryland."

He drove back to Maryland, drove Earl home, forked over another sixty-three dollars, and drove back to The Pines to tell Melanie what he'd learned.

"Well, Robert, that's good, but it doesn't really prove anything."

"I know it doesn't prove anything," he said, irritated. "That's not how it works. It's just one more piece. Collect enough of them, and you have a case."

"Sort of like beer bottles," Melanie said. But her face was thoughtful. "Did you listen to the news on your drive back?"

"No." He'd been too busy evaluating possibilities, looking for connections, planning next moves.

"The grand jury met. They didn't find enough evidence to indict Michael Donohue. Now the FBI is standing there with egg on its face."

"It's not the first time," Cavanaugh said. Christ, she could irritate him. "We're not gods, you know. And don't say that we think we are, either."

"Okay, I won't say it," Melanie answered. "Aloud. So tell me this instead: What is '*Bevins v. Six Unknown Agents*'? Donohue's lawyer said in his press conference that America should keep it in mind."

Cavanaugh drew a deep breath and calculated rapidly. *Bevins v. Six Unknown Agents* was the legal precedent for a citizen to sue the Federal Bureau of Investigation. Or, rather, not the FBI as an entity, but individual agents who had violated a suspect's civil rights. Cavanaugh had been part of the surveillance team on Michael Donohue and had also been along on the warrant search. . . . No, it wasn't enough. If Donohue actually sued anyone, it would probably be only Dunbar and Pilozzi. Plus, maybe, the FBI medic who'd drawn Donohue's blood. That would make the strongest case.

"I'll tell you at dinner," he said. "I'm famished."

"Did you eat today?"

"No. Did you?"

"Of course I did, and I fed Earl. *We* take care of ourselves. Let me just get my purse."

While she tiptoed through piles of bugs, the phone rang. After a moment Cavanaugh remembered that it was his room, not the insects', and he picked up the receiver.

"Bob, Marty Felders. Do you have a fax?"

"Yes," Cavanaugh said, although it was in the car. There hadn't been either use or room for it amid the piles of graphs and bugs. "Give me three minutes."

"Okay," Felders said, and hung up. He never wasted words when he had something.

Did that mean Felders had something?

Cavanaugh dashed out to the car and rummaged in the trunk, flinging books and shoes and boxes onto the parking lot until he found the fax machine. He galloped back inside and got it hooked to the phone line just seconds before it began to beep.

"What is it?" Melanie said on a high, rising note, but Cavanaugh was too busy reading the incoming fax, line by line, to answer.

FROM: SYRACUSE UNIVERSITY, PSYCHOLINGUISTICS CENTER

TO: MARTIN FELDERS

178 SYCAMORE LANE

HYATTSVILLE, MD.

(301) 555-6745

Marty had had the report sent to his home, not the Bureau. Good.

RE: VOICE TAPE ANALYSIS

FOUR TAPES WERE RECEIVED VIA U.S. MAIL ON AUGUST 9. ANALYSIS WAS CONDUCTED USING HIGH-RESOLUTION EQUIPMENT, INCLUDING PHRASING, DICTION, PRONUN-CIATION, STRESS, INFLECTION, SPEED, CONTENT, AND BACKGROUND NOISE. ANALYSIS FOLLOWS:

THE SAME SPEAKER TALKS ON ALL FOUR TAPES.

THE SPEAKER IS A CAUCASIAN MALE BETWEEN THE AGES OF THIRTY-FIVE AND FORTY-FIVE. HE HOLDS AT LEAST A B.S. DEGREE (PROBABLY NOT A B.A.), BUT NOT A GRADUATE DEGREE. HE IS FROM GEORGIA ORIGINALLY, BUT HAS SPENT SIGNIFICANT TIME IN NEW ENGLAND WITHIN THE LAST FIVE YEARS. HE IS EXCITED BY WHAT HE IS SAYING, BOTH EMOTIONALLY AND SEXUALLY. HE IS PROBABLY NEITHER MARRIED NOR LIVING WITH A WOMAN. THE SPEAKER IDENTIFIES WITH TRADITION AND STRUCTURE, THE MORE STRUCTURED THE BETTER, AS A DEFENSE AGAINST A VERY CHAOTIC INNER SELF. HE FEARS ANYTHING THAT SEEMS TO HIM TO THREATEN THAT TRADITION AND STRUCTURE. BECAUSE HE FEARS BEING ALONE, HE MOST LIKELY SPENDS TIME AWAY FROM HIS JOB SURROUNDED BY LIKE-MINDED INDIVIDUALS. HE MAY PARTY A LOT.

ANALYSIS OF BACKGROUND NOISE:

TAPE #1: NONE DECIPHERABLE. PROBABLY INDOORS.

TAPE #2: INDOORS. AMPLIFICATION REVEALS A VIDEO GAME, PINBALL MACHINE, CLINKING GLASSES, AND A GREAT MANY INDISTINGUISHABLE CONVERSATIONS. SETTING IS EITHER A BAR OR A LARGE PRIVATE PARTY.

TAPE #3: PROBABLY SAME SETTING AS TAPE #2, BUT WITH FEWER PEOPLE PRESENT.

TAPE #4: INDOORS. ONE DISTINGUISHABLE BACKGROUND NOISE: MUSIC IN THE DISTANT BACKGROUND, MUFFLED IN A WAY CONSISTENT WITH FILTERING THROUGH CLOSED WINDOW GLASS. INSTRUMENT IS A SINGLE BUGLE, PROBABLY

RECORDED. MELODY IMPOSSIBLE TO DISCERN WITH
COMPLETE ACCURACY, BUT NOTES THAT CAN BE IDENTIFIED
ARE CONSISTENT WITH "RETREAT."

CONCLUSION: THERE IS HIGH PROBABILITY THAT THE
SPEAKER SERVES IN THE UNITED STATES MILITARY.

JONATHAN PRITCHARD, PH.D.
SYRACUSE UNIVERSITY

"Good Lord," Melanie said, reading over his shoulder. "The military. And the CIA has long and deep ties with Fort Detrick. God, Robert, maybe you *are* right about who created malaria reading!"

"We don't know that yet," Cavanaugh said. She was so emotional—as quick to conclude as she had been to deny. That wasn't the way it was done. The way it was done was with persistent doggedness, accumulating evidence drop by hard-squeezed drop. He didn't say this aloud. He'd heard the fear and dread in Melanie's voice.

Felders phoned a second time. "Bob, listen. One more thing." Felders sounded as unhappy as Cavanaugh had ever heard him, and he hesitated before going on.

"I don't like telling you this, and if anybody ever asks me if I did tell you, I will deny it. Do you understand?"

"Yes."

"I called in every marker I was owed in Washington, New York, and Virginia. Probably left a talk trail that'll set the OPR after *me* eventually. Fort Detrick has the CIA, as you know, and the CIA has a secret dirty-tricks unit stationed at the fort. They don't report to the commanding general, except as a hidden part of the CIA. It's possible he doesn't even know the unit is there, although not likely. I couldn't get names, duties, or even the size of the unit. Probably small. But they're there, and I'm told they've pulled some nasties, although nobody can give me specifics. Or won't. And I didn't tell you any of this."

"Yes. No. Can you find out what 'the Birthday Project' is? I know it's something to do with Fort—"

Felders hung up on him.

"What?" Melanie said in a high, strained voice. "What was that about?"

He told her. She listened, expressionless, then turned away.

"Melanie, it's not conclusive. It's just one more lead. One piece. As I told you—"

"I know what you told me. Now let me tell you something. I've been reworking that *T. rutilus* data all afternoon. And I've got some thoughts about it."

"Go ahead," Cavanaugh said.

"Somebody tried to use *T. rutilus* to stop the infected *Anopheles* even before the CDC was called in or the epidemic became public knowledge. That suggests to me that whoever started the plague tried to stop it before it got out of hand."

This wasn't consistent with her usual genocide theories. Obviously she had put professional objectivity in the forefront. Finally. Cavanaugh listened more closely.

"Now, by mid-June every infectious-disease unit in the Western world was crawling over the epicenter in Newburg. Most of them were only here briefly, to get specimen samples and victims' blood samples to take back home. But a few stayed at least a week—people from WHO and from Antwerp, to name just two. They combed the place. Even concentrating on *A. quadrimaculatus*, there's no way everybody could have missed the unusually high numbers of *T. rutilus*, or not known what those numbers implied."

"Go on. So?"

Suddenly she put her purse down, straight onto a pile of salt marsh mosquitoes. She didn't seem to notice. "So I don't know yet. I want to check something. Meet me at my bed-and-breakfast after you go to dinner. I'm not hungry."

"Neither am I. I'll stay with you."

"Robert, your stomach is grumbling. I can hear it from over *here*, for God's sake. Go eat and come back after. I'll be there."

He left her at the bed-and-breakfast, raced to a McDonald's, and ate a Big Mac in the car on the way back. A pickle spilled across his tie. The trip took him sixteen minutes and forty-two seconds.

Apparently it was enough time. Melanie's computer was turned off. She sat quietly at her desk, her eyes blank, her mind someplace else.

"Melanie . . . Melanie?"

Slowly she focused on him. "Robert."

"What were you checking? What did you find?"

"I was checking the weekly World Health Organization report to the CDC. It's just bald data, a summary of what's happening around the world. Health-wise."

Melanie never used nonwords like "health-wise." She continued to gaze at nothing. Robert stepped closer. "And what did the weekly report show? For what week?"

"I scanned six months' worth of reports, by key word. We have the software to do that. I looked for malaria outbreaks. Of course, there were dozens. Did you know that nearly three million people die every year of malaria worldwide?"

"No. Did you find any . . . anomalies?"

"Yes. A set of data that graphs to an anomalous epidemiological curve. In Africa. The Democratic Republic of the Congo, that used to be Zaire. That's what they're calling it now. There was a revolution, you know."

"I know," Cavanaugh said. She was rambling. "Go on."

"The anomalous epidemiological curve shows a much smaller number of infectees than usual. And it just breaks off abruptly, as if it were brought under sharp control very quickly. In a little over a month."

"Maybe the public health service in Congo got right on it. Like we did."

"There *is* no public health service in Congo, except in name. There was one once, but it collapsed during the corruption before the last revolution. And nobody brings a malaria epidemic under sharp immediate control in Africa. They don't have the resources. We only did it so fast here because the army mobilized, with money and expertise and manpower and supplies. The United States isn't Africa."

"Okay," Cavanaugh said. "Then what did cause their malaria outbreak to end so fast? And was it malaria reading or a normal kind?"

"There's no way to tell from the data. Or from here. You'd have to go to Congo."

Cavanaugh stared at her. Through his head whirled a number of little pictures, like icons on a demented screen saver: Visas. Vaccines. Languages. What languages did they speak in Congo? He didn't even know. Money. He'd been spending too much lately, what with moving house every fifteen minutes, and he was suspended without pay. And the Bureau had forbidden him to work on this case. A visa to Congo was trace-able . . . and what about Fort Detrick. He needed to go there, follow up on the voice analysis . . .

"Melanie," he said, "I can't go to Congo to investigate."

For the first time since he'd come in, he had her full attention. She swept him a look of utter scorn.

"Not you—what good would *you* be in Africa?" she said. "Not you.

"Me."

FIFTEEN

**The climate of Zaire is especially conducive to germs,
fungi, and carriers of numerous pests and diseases.**
—Compton's Encyclopedia

Africa could break your heart.

Melanie stepped off the plane at N'Djili Airport in Kinshasa and
walked toward the cinder-block terminal. The heat was no worse than
summer in Mississippi, but the quality was different. She couldn't put it
into words: it was a combination of smell, vibration, some ineffable sense
of portent. It was different. It was Africa.

As soon as she walked through the terminal door, the "officials" de-
scended. They clamored in French and broken English that she give
them her tickets, her luggage, her passport. Later they would demand
"fees" for the return of all these items. Behind them came the fixers,
with promises to guide a foreigner through this maze of "travel fees"—
for, of course, a fee for themselves. Melanie waved the whole crowd
away, gripped her two carry-ons, and backed herself into a corner to
study the situation.

Congo was between wars. The airport held foreigners she judged to
be businessmen, refugees, even a few tourists. Or maybe they were min-
ing financiers. At its lowest points, Congo lost its international financiers,
its sole means to foreign trade in copper, diamonds, cobalt, and man-

ganese. Like robins in an American spring, returning financiers were a good sign.

A television set high near the ceiling was actually working, although only audio, which was in French. The screen showed a fixed title: "Communiqués et Messages." A few shops inside the terminal displayed perfume, Belgian chocolates, and jewelry. This was encouraging. The last time Melanie had come through N'Djili Airport, with a CDC team, the only things in the terminal were bayonet-carrying soldiers and wrecked furniture.

Kinshasa itself was less encouraging. After expertly negotiating the upturned palms at N'Djili, she took a taxi to Mama Yemo Hospital. The taxi inched slowly and painfully over streets with broken pavement and deep potholes full of fetid water. Several times the taxi had to detour. Through the cab's open windows—it had no air-conditioning—Melanie surveyed the capital she had seen four times before, in various states of functioning under various regimes in various degrees of civil strife.

Women filled the main market, selling cassava, bananas, sugarcane. Business looked brisk.

The zoo was still a charred rubble, the buildings burned and the animals dead.

The Intercontinental Hotel gleamed amid its fountains and gardens, guarded by army soldiers, a luxurious haven for the rich. A uniformed valet parked Jaguars and Mercedes.

At Lovanium University, students climbed briskly up and down neatly whitewashed steps.

Beggars thronged the edge of La Cité, Kinshasa's vast slum. Many looked sick or deformed. But they didn't all move with the terrible shuffling dullness of misery and malnutrition that Melanie had observed on her last trip.

And even the beggars wore plastic shower thongs. Mostly.

The fishermen living in tin-roofed shanties by the great river now possessed nets.

Best of all, Melanie saw a woman in a bright cotton dress on her knees, weeding a dozen stalks of corn growing beside her hut. If corn could grow that tall in Kinshasa, without being stolen or vandalized, Congo had come a long way since the last war.

Mama Yemo Hospital, however, reminded her that compared to the rest of the world, Congo's "long way" was measured in inches.

There were still more patients than beds. Sick people lay on flaking white metal beds, on sheetless gurneys, on straw pallets, on the floor. Some she could diagnose with one glance: that's malaria, that's malnutrition, that's gangrene, that's dysentery. She clutched her two valises and kept on walking. The only medicines she had with her were ones that any knowledgeable American could be expected to carry for personal use: a few antibiotics, first-aid supplies, the antimalarial prophylaxis mefloquine, some Lomotil for diarrhea, which she hoped to hell she wouldn't get because Lomotil cross-reacted with mefloquine.

"M'sieu le docteur Ekombe Kifoto?" she called loudly. No one paid any attention.

She wasn't here as a CDC representative or even as a private doctor, which would have required notifying half a dozen different agencies in and out of Congo. She was here as an anonymous tourist. She couldn't help the suffering people jammed into the stinking corridors. She kept on walking.

"M'sieu le docteur Ekombe Kifoto?"

Finally a Congolese nurse directed her to the ward where Kifoto was administering chloroquine to malaria patients. The minute he spotted Melanie, he rushed over to her. *"Melanie! Vous êtes ici!"*

"But where is 'here'?" she answered in French. "Hell?" An old joke from a previous epidemic, a previous joint CDC-WHO-Zaire Health Ministry campaign. During an epidemic, Ekombe Kifoto was among the best.

He led her to a tiny, vacant break room with chairs and a small refrigerator, but no table. They drank Primus beer while they caught up on old friends, new epidemic. In Congo, you drank bottled water or beer. You even brushed your teeth with beer. Or with the equally ubiquitous Coke, which somehow appeared everywhere on Earth even during violent wars. If WHO were as efficient as Coca-Cola, Melanie figured, antibiotics would turn up in the deepest rain forest.

"Ekombe, I need a favor," she said, when the social chat was finished.

"Yes?" He watched her carefully.

"I need to go into the rain forest. To a village called Yamdongi, in Kinsangani Zone."

"Ah. Where the last malaria epidemic was. I hear it was mercifully brief. But why come to me? The CDC—"

"I'm not here on behalf of the CDC. I'm unofficial and alone. But I need a medical visa to get through to Yamdongi without delay. And I need you to radio both the Catholic mission in Lubundu and whatever medical facilities remain in Yamdongi from the epidemic."

"There remains a tent hospital and a physician from Doctors Without Borders. Mopping up." During his work with the Americans, Kifoto had delighted in translating American slang into French, Bantu, and Tutsi. "But why, Melanie? The epidemic is over."

"I know. Did you see the curves?"

Kifoto shrugged. "You know how it is. So much work here, always."

"I know. Please do this for me, Ekombe. Without questions."

"I will. You know I will. Melanie—" He eyed her valises. "Do you have medicines with you? We are so short. No, of course you don't. Not if you arrived in Congo without official notice."

"I'm sorry," she choked out. "I couldn't—"

"I know. Do not concern yourself about it."

As if, surrounded by malarial and worm-ridden children, that were at all possible.

Armed with the papers from Kifoto, including a medical travel pass that he'd gotten signed by the new minister of health (now *there* was a hopeless job), Melanie's identity changed again. She was no longer an anonymous tourist. Now she was a doctor. The medical pass was the only thing that allowed her to travel into the rain forest unaccompanied by an "escort" of army officers asking questions and demanding bribes and intimidating villagers. A medical pass allowed you to go anywhere, although not necessarily safely.

She took another cab to N'Dolo, Kinshasa's smaller airport, and then took a very old, much-painted prop plane to a small airfield in Kinsangani, seventy miles from Yamdongi. She was met by Sister Marie-Stephanie, a Catholic missionary who had been in Congo for thirty-five years, teaching three generations of Bantu girls to sew, boil drinking water, and stumble through the writings of Saint Theresa, the Little Flower. Nothing could surprise Sister Marie-Stephanie. She had witnessed epidemics, revolutions, paramilitary bandits, crop failures, floods, famines, and witch doctors. Her sun-creased face under its traditional white coif sized up Melanie in thirty seconds and kept the results to herself.

After a night at the mission, Melanie was driven by Land Rover to

Yamdongi, which took eight hours. The driver was the most cheerful person she'd ever met. He whistled for the entire eight hours, alternating atonal native tunes with outdated American and British rock. Melanie thought she recognized "Can't Get No Satisfaction," but over the motor of the Land Rover it was hard to be sure. Between songs, the driver kept his vocal chords moist by sipping beer as he bounced and bumped along rutted paths through the lush rain forest.

Maps in Congo were always a hopeful fiction. Indicated roads did not exist, and never had. "Highways" turned out to be rutted dirt that flooded after each explosive rain. Bridges had been washed away, or burned, or dismantled for the metal.

Throughout the trip, Melanie watched for monkeys in the trees. Monkeys were a key economic indicator. In good times, they swung and chattered. In bad times, they'd all been eaten. This time, Melanie saw monkeys.

Eventually, just before her teeth felt about to be rattled out of her gums, they reached Yamdongi. "Hello! Dr. Spencer?"

He came out of the tent hospital, smiling. "Dr. Anderson?"

"Yes." Shakily she climbed down from the Land Rover. The driver looked at her expectantly, optimism undimmed. She gave him five American dollars—a fortune—and watched his face light up. He tossed down her bags and drove off, singing.

Brian Spencer said, "Dr. Kifoto radioed that you were coming. But the epidemic is quite over, you know." His accent said the north of England.

"Yes, I know. I just have some follow-up questions."

"Fine, fine. Glad to be of help. Possibly you'd like to eat."

"Yes, thank you," she said. He was very young—twenty-six? Twenty-eight? Brisk, idealistic, talkative. Over stew and beer he told her what he could about the epidemic.

"The usual thing, you know, except that the victims died unusually quickly. Much tertiary cerebral stroke, I rather suspect, although of course we haven't the resources for autopsies. Time, mostly. And also, the epidemic ended quite abruptly. Odd, that, but we were all grateful. At the zenith we were giving three hundred shots of chloroquine a day. No time to do more than that. They were coming from as far away as Bienge. Fortunately I had top-drawer Congolese nurses. Only one left here now, Sebo Masemo. She and I return to Kinsangani next week. I've put you up in one of the other nurse's rooms. Not luxurious, I'm afraid, but tolerable."

"Thank you. Dr. Spencer, while the epidemic was on, and especially just before it ended, did you notice any unusual movements in the village or the forest?"

"Movements? Of what?"

"Soldiers. Or resources for *Anopheles* control that aren't usually available here."

He lit a French cigarette. Melanie wasn't surprised. In Africa, even for doctors, future emphysema looked better than present insects. The smoke wreathed his head.

"Dr. Anderson, there are no resources for *Anopheles* control available here. Not for the last epidemic, nor the one before that, nor the next one to come." Suddenly he looked much older.

Melanie didn't tell him that she'd joined her first epidemiological team before he entered med school. The less she gave away, the better.

He said, "I expect you'd like to have a look at the hospital."

"Please."

A small wooden sign outside the gray tent said MÉDECINS SANS FRONTIÈRES. Inside were the usual: wooden bedframes with palm-leaf mattresses, an electric generator saved for times of real need, autoclave and refrigerator, locked meds cabinet. A "lab" with cultures and reagents to find out what microbe you were dealing with, but no electron microscope to really find out what you were dealing with. Melanie didn't see automatic rifles, but they were probably here.

This close to the equator, night fell at six o'clock. Brian Spencer lit a kerosene lamp and walked Melanie through the wards, of which there were two, men and women. Children were in with the women. The hospital was down to fewer than a dozen people in each ward; there were beds for all.

"*Ça va, Mbuzu?*" Spencer said to a woman, who smiled at him weakly. To Melanie he said in English, "Malaria. One of the last cases to fall ill."

Melanie smiled at the patient, who let her do a quick examination. Enlarged and stiffened spleen; hard, hot belly; face and neck emaciated. The same symptoms Hippocrates had described accurately two and a half thousand years ago. Still here.

At the next bed, Spencer said, "Dysentery."

"Malnutrition."

"Malaria."

"Miscarriage."

"Malaria. Doing very well now."

"Broken arm."

"Dysentery."

"Malaria."

Spencer stopped at the last bed. A woman lay motionless, both her arms chopped off just below the elbows. The stumps were freshly bandaged, and the woman looked sedated, although not so much that the anguish had faded from her eyes.

"I don't know what happened here," Spencer said. "She staggered into the hospital alone, although I think someone must have helped her get this far. She speaks no French, and my nurse doesn't know this dialect."

Melanie knelt beside the woman's bed and tried each of the languages she sketchily knew. Finally the woman murmured back.

Melanie stood. "She said soldiers did it. Because they wanted diamonds and she had no diamonds."

"Probably paramilitary bandits," Spencer said. "A few groups are still in the bush, although the army is doing pretty well at finding them. You speak several dialects, Dr. Anderson."

"Badly," she said. The woman on the bed had finally closed her eyes, as though the simple act of telling someone what had happened to her could bring sleep. Melanie watched, gut churning. Every time she came to Africa, she was overwhelmed by guilt. For not doing more for these people, for living in America, for carrying around in her own well-cared-for veins a dozen vaccinations against diseases that killed Africans by the millions. Every time she came to Africa, Africa pierced her heart, and she couldn't wait to leave so she could yearn to come back again. Every time.

"Even badly, speaking several African languages is an achievement," Spencer said. And then, "Maybe you *can* do this job after all. Whatever it is."

Melanie said nothing. She'd been thinking just the opposite.

❖   ❖   ❖

At sunrise she started, walking the short distance to the village, which looked serene in the delicate light. About four hundred people, Melanie estimated. Maybe four-fifty. Goats grazed outside the huts, which were a mix of timber and mud-and-wattle, with thatched roofs. Gardens held sweet potatoes, corn, cassavas. The women had already kindled the morning fires in the communal cooking area. Children fetched wood or water from a small river. They stopped cold to stare at a black woman in khakis, boots, and sun hat from Macy's.

"Hello," she said in Bantu, which made them all giggle. "Where is the house of"—she consulted Spencer's list of village family heads—"Kambidi Mabalo?"

More giggling, mouths hiding behind small black hands. God, they were adorable. She wondered how many were positive for sickle-cell trait.

"Please, Kambidi Mabalo?"

Finally one of the little boys said boldly, "He's at his second wife's house."

"And where is that?"

He pointed to one of the largest structures and then suddenly they all fled, water sloshing from their buckets, giggling as they ran. Within two minutes, the entire village would know that a foreign woman was seeking Kambidi Mabalo.

The second wife let her in, listened silently to Melanie's speech about being a colleague of Dr. Spencer's, and inspected the gift Melanie had brought. This was an electric flashlight, purchased from Spencer. Melanie hadn't been able to carry many goods into the country, but she had carried her checkbook. Spencer was leaving Yamdongi in a week; money was easier to transport than goods and always in short supply at Doctors Without Borders. Melanie had purchased a few of everything: flashlights, disposable razors, kitchen knives, dishes, clothing, even empty water bottles useful for carrying whatever liquids the villagers wanted carried. She was well prepared with guest gifts.

Kambidi's second wife nodded and indicated Kambidi, who sat close nearby and had heard the entire exchange. Nonetheless, Melanie repeated it, from the necessary respect. Then came the ritual drinking of "tea," after which she could finally get to work. Her Bantu was strong enough for this, but if she had to, she would switch to French.

"Elder Kambidi, have you ever had malaria?"

"Did your father ever have malaria? Was he very sick? Did he die? How about your father's oldest sister? What is her name? Was it a very severe case? Now your father's second-oldest sister . . ."

She was constructing a genetic chart. The method was crude, but blood tests were not practical here. Anyway, Mendel's laws held as well here as anywhere else. With painstaking questioning, and then cross-questioning of the people named (if they were still alive), she would end up with a complete kinship chart for, she hoped, several generations. Bantu remembered their ancestors.

Sickle-cell trait was inherited. It protected against malaria, at least enough to mitigate its severity. By drawing the gene map of who had experienced a severe case of malaria, who a light case, and who none at all, even when an epidemic raged, Melanie hoped to determine who carried the sickle-cell trait.

Then she would graph that onto the list of people who had died of this last brief epidemic of malaria. *"Much tertiary cerebral stroke, I rather suspect."* No kidding. If the epidemic that had *"ended quite abruptly. . . . Odd, that . . ."* had indeed been malaria reading, then the *only* mortalities would be to people carrying the sickle-cell trait.

"Now your mother, Elder Kambidi. Did she ever have malaria? Are you sure it was not the black sickness? What about her mother?"

Melanie talked to Kambidi Mabalo for two hours, and then to his second wife for another hour. People appeared at the door to gaze at her silently before vanishing again. The life of the household went on around her. She was taking a lot of these people's time; she hoped the magic of Dr. Spencer's name would keep everyone cooperative until she finished.

Certainly, Third World villagers had valid reasons not to cooperate with foreigners who said they were there to control malaria. Too often, the foreigners just didn't have time to grasp the entire situation. When WHO had sprayed the houses of Malayan villages with DDT to eliminate *Anopheles*, it had worked. But it had also eliminated wasps that lived in the palm-frond roofs and ate caterpillars. The wasps died, the palm-frond-eating caterpillars flourished, and the roofs all fell down. WHO retreated hastily, helped along by roofless and angry Malayans.

Now, at this moment, Yamdongi was grateful to Médecins Sans Frontières. But gratitude could wither quickly under the strong hot relentless sun.

❖   ❖   ❖

Gratitude held. After a week of so much questioning that Melanie grew hoarse, she had her answers.

She also had mosquito samples. She'd paid the village boys one makuta for each live *Anopheles,* giving them homemade killing jars furnished with carbon tetrachloride from Spencer's stores. She'd also paid them for live larvae, which she'd killed by the simple method of letting the aquatic creatures dry out. The boys took to this with wild enthusiasm. When she had two huge piles of specimens, she'd finally had to call in her hunters, who were dejected that the great adventure was over.

Melanie picked through the insects, choosing the best preserved. That was all she could do in Congo. The African malaria carrier was *Anopheles gambiae,* not the American *A. quadrimaculatus,* but the *Plasmodium falciparum* parasite was the same. No way to tell if these particular mosquitoes carried malaria until the samples were analyzed in Atlanta.

But the specimens were secondary, the genealogy charts were what mattered.

There were seven hundred highly inbred people on Melanie's chart, some living and some dead. From their personal histories of illness, an estimated 17 percent carried the sickle-cell trait, but not the double gene that resulted in full-blown sickle-cell anemia. In this harsh environment, the latter seldom survived long enough to reproduce. Of the people who had died in the latest malaria epidemic, plus the few who had survived it, *every single one stood in a position on the chart to have inherited sickle-cell trait from their parents.* Without blood tests on the dead, of course, there was no way to be sure that they had inherited sickle-cell trait. But they certainly could have. And most of the people untouched by the recent plague stood in a position where they could not have inherited sickle-cell trait.

It had been here. In Yamdongi. Malaria reading had been here, and it had vanished with the same abruptness that the U.S. Army had brought to Maryland through the most efficient disease-control methods in the world.

But there had been no efficient disease-control methods in Yamdongi. She had questioned everyone closely about this, especially the children. Congolese children, like children everywhere, explored everything. They ran through the forest, poked into strange objects, talked to strangers even when warned not to. The children Melanie talked to, sweetening her questions with various small gifts, had all said the same thing. No strangers in Yamdongi during the sickness, except hospital people. No soldiers spraying in the forest (she'd illustrated "spraying" with an old disinfectant bottle filled with water). No powder floating on the waters. Nothing new given to the villagers to put in their houses.

The malaria mini-epidemic in Yamdongi had not been stopped by conventional disease-control measures. So how had it been stopped?

By whom?

And why?

Melanie lay awake most of her last night in Yamdongi, worrying the data. Maybe there was another way to explain it. She looked at alternate scenarios, finally forced to reject each one because of some major misfit with the facts. No, there was only one explanation that fit the data.

Whoever had loosed malaria reading in Maryland had also loosed it here. And then had stopped it abruptly.

A double test—control and variable? But both outbreaks of malaria contained the same variable: *this* malarial parasite colonized cells with sickled hemoglobin. The diseases were identical, at least as far as she knew now. Maybe the CDC analysis would show differences.

A double test to see if one epidemic could be ended, while the other ran its course? But someone had ended both epidemics, with the same abruptness.

A laboratory escape? Mosquitoes, after all, could fly out easily, and you'd only need a few escapees. Under the right conditions, the disease would spread quickly. But two identical lab escapes on two continents six thousand miles apart? Not likely.

So what? A practice run at genocide on two different populations, African and American—the two largest Negroid populations in the world.

By whom?

For what terrible purpose?

She tossed on the hard bed, under her mosquito netting, until after dawn. Then she got dressed, finished packing, and said good-bye to Brian Spencer and Sebo Masemo. Things had turned cool between her and the young British doctor. Professional courtesy demanded that she share the results of her work with him. But she couldn't. Not this. Not yet.

"Got what you wanted, then, Dr. Anderson?"

"Yes. And thank you again for your hospitality."

"No need to mention it," he said stiffly. "Good journey."

She climbed onto the Catholic mission's Land Rover, which was driven by the same Bantu singing the same dated rock for eight bone-jarring hours. After one night at the mission, she flew back to Kinsangani and then Kinshasa. In N'Djili Airport, before her flight to Washington, customs officials tore apart her valises, her handbag, her money belt. It didn't matter. The genealogy charts were just so much foreign gobbledygook. And the intent, corrupt officials were looking for something to tax or confiscate or exact a bribe for. They never suspected that between the double layers of Melanie's long, loose, bright-cotton dress were sewn, each in a separate tiny cloth bag, a hundred dead *Anopheles gambiae,* plus a few dead larvae. The specimens would stay there until she'd passed through customs in the United States.

She hadn't seen a newspaper in ten days. The plane had yesterday's *Washington Post.* For the first time all summer, malaria reading was not on the front page, which brimmed with yet another sex scandal of yet another congressman. It wasn't until page four that she found even a related story, and then it was only poll results. The confidence of the American people in the FBI, the poll said, had dropped drastically due to both the mistaken arrest of Michael Sean Donohue and the unfruitful failure to arrest anybody else for causing the epidemic.

Melanie put the newspaper on the empty seat beside her. She was exhausted. But she didn't dare sleep; she might crush the layer of insects that justified her, haunted her, swathed her like an invisible shroud.

INTERIM

The adjunct professor stopped by the faculty room to pick up his mail. Colleagues sitting at the broad center table nodded and went on with their discussion. Beyond the window, the incoming freshmen, who were here for a four-day summer orientation to the strange rigors of college, trailed nervously after an upperclassman, who waved at buildings with giddy confidence.

The mail was the usual. Notice of a faculty meeting. A required paper three months late, accompanied by a desperate plea from the student author citing dire stress and enormous regret. Flyers about a book sale, a blood drive, and a library display. And a small envelope from the professor's insurance company.

He ripped it open. As an adjunct, a gypsy scholar who taught a few courses at a great many places, he carried his own health insurance. It cost him a few thousand a year in exchange for assurance that he would not end up dying in his sister's crowded apartment untended by anyone who could dispense pain-easing medication.

> Dear Dr. Marlin Scott:
> We regret to inform you that your health insurance policy with this company (Policy ___#4873___) is canceled as of ___August 31___ due to a previously undisclosed preexisting condition: namely, ___sickle-cell trait___. You will recall that your original policy required complete disclosure of all preexisting conditions.
>
> If you have any questions, don't hesitate to call your policy representative, ___Sandra Scott___, at the number below.

The professor read the form letter twice. A form letter—that meant the bastards were sending them out in batches. Dumping whoever they wanted, including blacks too poor and too unschooled to know the maneuver was illegal.

The professor's eyes gleamed. He loved a good fight. With proper research, this one could be a doozie. Class-action material.

Carefully he folded the letter and put it in his briefcase.

S IXTEEN

CIA association with Fort Detrick involved the Special
Operations Division of that facility. This division was
responsible for developing special applications for
biological warfare agents and toxins. . . . Only two or
three Agency officers at any time were cleared for access
to Fort Detrick activities.

—William Colby, CIA Director,
testifying before Congress, 1975

Cavanaugh liked bars, but not bars like this one.

A good bar should have a selection of drinks, both basic and exotic.
A TV tuned to sports, but a discreet TV, over the bar, not too loud. Local
people of different ages, including some pretty women. Maybe a pool
table. Quick service, light sandwiches, a clean men's room, and a bartender who observed things and was articulate enough to report them
accurately to interested inquirers, such as, for instance, FBI agents. That
was what made a good bar.

The Bull Shift was nothing like that. Behind the bar a huge TV
screen blasted baseball and car racing at the decibel level of a jackham-
mer. Any air space left was filled with bells from the pinball machine and
waves of whiny country and western. The menu consisted of greasy
chicken wings and greasier French fries. The men, all between twenty
and forty, wore identical jeans and cowboy boots. The women looked

like whores look everywhere. The bartender, who said "Huh?" when he asked for a vodka and tonic, was a busty redhead almost wearing a turquoise blouse and tangerine shorts. Cavanaugh suspected that if she'd ever overheard anything of interest, it had been dissolved by the fumes from her hairspray. He didn't even want to think about the men's room.

There was also a mechanical bull ride.

Studying the room from his stool at the far end of the bar, Cavanaugh spotted three possibles. A group of five men at a table, two men talking to two women by the far wall, and two more men playing pool. All had the short hair, clean fingernails, and ineffable wariness-plus-cockiness that went with a certain kind of low-ranking member of secret organizations. Not that that meant they were necessarily with a CIA dirty-tricks unit. In the last week, Cavanaugh had checked out a lot of men in a lot of bars surrounding Fort Detrick. He was getting sick of devoting his nights to semidrunks and his days to scouring southern Maryland for a cheap apartment that would allow a dog and that in no way reminded him of Judy.

Cavanaugh finished his beer and strolled casually toward the jukebox. He figured he better start with the two men chatting up the two women before all four struck their deal and disappeared.

He studied the music selection, which appeared to have been chosen forty years ago: Hank Williams, Johnny Cash, Patsy Cline, Jim Reeves, Loretta Lynn. Ninety seconds into eavesdropping, one of the hookers said pointedly, "Let's move on, boys, away from the *cop*." She was pretty good, Cavanaugh thought. Sharp. She'd make a better agent than, say, Seton.

And anyway he'd heard enough. Both men had spoken. Neither had matched the voice on Melanie's tapes, which Cavanaugh had listened to over and over. That was the other thing he did with his days. Memorize a racist voice and a psycholinguistic profile:

THE SPEAKER IS A CAUCASIAN MALE BETWEEN THE AGES OF
THIRTY-FIVE AND FORTY-FIVE. HE HOLDS AT LEAST A B.S.
DEGREE (PROBABLY NOT A B.A.), BUT NOT A GRADUATE
DEGREE. HE IS FROM GEORGIA ORIGINALLY, BUT HAS SPENT
SIGNIFICANT TIME IN NEW ENGLAND WITHIN THE LAST FIVE
YEARS. HE IS EXCITED BY WHAT HE IS SAYING, BOTH

EMOTIONALLY AND SEXUALLY. HE IS PROBABLY NEITHER
MARRIED NOR LIVING WITH A WOMAN. THE SPEAKER
IDENTIFIES WITH TRADITION AND STRUCTURE, THE MORE
STRUCTURED THE BETTER, AS A DEFENSE AGAINST A VERY
CHAOTIC INNER SELF. HE FEARS ANYTHING THAT SEEMS TO
HIM TO THREATEN THAT TRADITION AND STRUCTURE.
BECAUSE HE FEARS BEING ALONE, HE MOST LIKELY SPENDS
TIME AWAY FROM HIS JOB SURROUNDED BY LIKE-MINDED
INDIVIDUALS. HE MAY PARTY A LOT. . . . TAPE #2: INDOORS.
AMPLIFICATION REVEALS A VIDEO GAME, PINBALL MACHINE,
CLINKING GLASSES, AND A GREAT MANY INDISTINGUISHABLE
CONVERSATIONS. SETTING IS EITHER A BAR OR A LARGE
PRIVATE PARTY.

TAPE #3: PROBABLY SAME SETTING AS TAPE #2, BUT WITH
FEWER PEOPLE PRESENT.

Cavanaugh moved on to the next group of forty-year-old Caucasian
males partying hard with like-minded individuals in their traditional
place with clinking glasses and a pinball machine. This was the group of
five men at one table. Only three were talking; the other two concentrated on drinking. Cavanaugh found excuses to linger so long beside the
table that the noisiest guy started giving him the go-away-you-fairy-or-
I'll-smash-your-face look. Fortunately, before this could happen, the two
silent men ordered more beer. Both had Texas accents.

The two men playing pool were talkative enough, but neither one
was the voice on Melanie's tapes.

Discouraged, Cavanaugh left the Bull Shift for his car. The humid
night settled around him like damp, itchy wool. So far he'd tried thirty-
four bars, an average of six-point-eight per night, rounded off. One more
bar would bring it to a clean seven.

By the car's dome light, he consulted his list. Next was the Alligator,
farther from Fort Detrick than most, but maybe the drive would clear
his head. Better switch to club soda, except that these bars weren't the
kind of place where you could order club soda and not be noticed.

Cavanaugh hadn't even reached a bar stool when he heard him.

Not looking around, Cavanaugh sat at the nearest table. He ordered
a vodka and tonic, then turned around to study the special sandwiches

listed on a blackboard. The voice on Melanie's tape sat with three other men. They all had a buzz on, but they weren't drunk. Cavanaugh turned back and sipped his drink.

". . . so then Rollins says . . ."

"Are you ready to order?" a waitress asked Cavanaugh.

"No . . . yes . . . a, uh, a roast-beef sandwich, please."

". . . don't even know how to . . ."

"Would you like horseradish on that? Or mustard?"

"No."

". . . but not before Mitchell gets to them first, see. So then Rollins . . ."

"How about lettuce and tomato?"

"No!" Cavanaugh said, before she could absorb more sound waves with mayonnaise, ketchup, or hot sauce. She strode away, looking hurt.

". . . that'll teach 'em not to screw up like that again!" All four men roared with laughter. Cavanaugh waited, but another man picked up the conversation, talking about a hot night with his new girlfriend. Cavanaugh went to the men's room, closed a stall door, and activated the wire under his shirt.

When he returned, he took the chair closest to his mark. The talk had turned to the NBA. Cavanaugh's man championed Larry Byrd over Michael Jordan. Nothing said was explicitly racist, but it didn't need to be. Cavanaugh recorded until the tape ran out. By then he had at least partial names for everybody: "Mike Goodman." "Tom Somebody." "Somebody Romellio." Melanie's baiter was "Ed Lewis."

Cavanaugh allowed himself to finish his vodka and tonic.

Back at his motel, he sealed the tape into a sturdy mailer and addressed it to Dr. Jonathan Pritchard at the Psycholinguistics Center of Syracuse University. Next he wrote a letter, addressed to Felders's residence, explaining what he'd found and asking Felders to check FBI records, plus his clandestine CIA sources, for "Ed Lewis." Also "Mike Goodman" or "Somebody Romellio." Cavanaugh didn't know whether Felders would do this, but if he had to place a substantial bet, he'd guess yes. Before anything else, Felders was a good cop. He might not like the odor surrounding a genuine lead, but once he smelled it, he'd follow through.

Cavanaugh lay back on his lumpy motel bed, staring into the unair-conditioned insect-humming darkness. He felt very, very good.

❖   ❖   ❖

The next day he ate a huge breakfast, signed the lease on an apartment in Leonardtown, arranged to have his furniture brought there from storage, had his car inspected, and generally acted like a man who knew what he was doing.

But how much did he really know? That question needed concentrated thought. Cavanaugh sat on the bed in his soon-to-be-vacated motel room. At his feet Abigail chewed happily on a strip of molding she'd torn off the dresser. Housekeeping never had materialized. The room was a mess, although he had swept up all the nonuseful bugs and thrown them into the Dumpster. This act was witnessed by the motel clerk, who merely shrugged. Cavanaugh wondered what else that particular Dumpster had held over the years.

Not his problem. His problem was malaria reading. Think it through.

Evidence so far: Ed Lewis, with some undefined connection to Fort Detrick and/or the CIA, had made numerous hate calls to Melanie.

Possible reason, judging by some of the content: To persuade her to return to Atlanta, which would remove a skilled and experienced expert from the malaria team. Alternate possible reason: The guy just liked making hate calls to attractive black women.

Evidence so far: *Somebody* had deliberately engineered the malaria reading parasite. Even the CDC and the FBI had finally agreed on that. Reason: Unknown.

Possible reason: To kill off as many blacks as this particular genetic feat would accomplish. Alternate possible reason: To test the parasite for possible use elsewhere. Alternate possible reason: The parasite had been inadvertently created in the lab and had inadvertently escaped. (Melanie had said that "inadvertently" creating a complex genetic mutation this complex, where three separate genes that worked together were the only ones altered, was impossible. Cavanaugh wasn't so sure. He wasn't a scientist, but he wasn't a militant either. Let the possibility stand.)

Evidence so far: Whoever had created malaria reading, it wasn't Michael Sean Donohue. The grand jury had found that every item seized in Donohue's apartment was "normal" to a microbiologist, even a dismissed microbiologist working on his own. That included the cage of live *Anopheles*. Donohue was merely professionally interested in the epidemic and so was examining the microbiology involved. Defense had apparently produced a dozen other respected microbiologists to say they were doing the same thing.

Of course, grand jury proceedings were supposed to be secret, but reporters had literally camped on the courthouse steps and investigated, interviewed, and ingratiated themselves with every single person who went in and out. No secrets were left, including the fact that sixteen witnesses had testified that Seton's "informant," Curtis P. McGraw, was a liar and a cheat and ate babies for breakfast. Or whatever else it had taken to discredit his affidavit saying he been confided in by the defendant. Seton, in the view of the FBI, had been misled by an artful con man. Seton, in Cavanaugh's view, had collaborated in a very public false report.

Why would Seton do that? Seton wouldn't, not just before his retirement. Not unless he'd been forced to agree to a false report. Forced how, why, and by whom? Unknown at this time. But the point was that the informant report, like the search warrant based on it, were both padded shamelessly. Which, in turn, led to the real point: Michael Sean Donohue didn't do it. Period. Even though the Bureau had spent an awful lot of time and trouble trying to prove he had.

Why? Unknown. Possible reason: The FBI had genuinely believed Donohue was guilty. Alternate possible reason: The FBI had believed it until a certain point in time, and then belief at the top had weakened; but by that time the Bureau was into Donohue so deeply and publicly, and under such pressure to arrest *somebody,* that they had gone ahead. It had happened before. It would happen again.

Evidence so far: A lot of people had been removed, one way or another, from this case. Moreover, they had all been removed in the same short time span, as July turned into August. Cavanaugh himself suspended for a trivial offense. Melanie sent away for a "rest." Farlow promoted to Geneva, three and a half thousand miles away. Dunbar promoted to Budapest, roughly ditto.

Possible reason: Coincidence. People got suspended or promoted all the time. Alternate possible reason: Somebody very powerfully placed had been conducting a cover-up. This person, or agency, had brought into the conspiracy everyone who had to be told: Farlow and Dunbar, for two, and bought them off. No, that wasn't right: Dunbar was a man of rigid honesty, and from what Cavanaugh had seen and heard, so was Farlow. So if they had agreed to a cover-up, and to be removed far from the place it was going on, they must have some other motivation.

What?

Who wanted something covered up, and what was that something? And how had a cover-up become necessary in the first place?

The cheap motel mattress sagged so much under Cavanaugh's weight that now his back ached. He moved from the bed to the chair, which turned out to be not much of an improvement. Abigail moved with him. He went on thinking.

Okay, take a stab at putting it all together. Pick from all the possibles, combine them at will, and see what kind of scenario you get.

Start with facts: Fort Detrick had once been the authorized center for army development of biological warfare weapons. The program had been located at Detrick since Franklin Delano Roosevelt inaugurated bioweapon research in 1942. Somehow the CIA had ended up with jurisdiction over bioweapons. In 1975, CIA director William Colby testified before Congress that all bioweapons had *not* all been destroyed when they were supposed to be, even though the president and the secretary of state had both issued directives to destroy them all—oops, Congress, sorry about that. Instead, the CIA had maintained stocks of selected bioweapons, some at the fort itself, some with private pharmaceutical companies that Fort Detrick had worked with extensively. Only a few—a very few—people had known this. The list did not include the president, the secretary of state, the attorney general, or the director of the FBI. Colby had been ordered to dump whatever bioweapons remained and to stop developing new ones.

These were facts. Facts a few decades old, yes, but still facts. Did anyone believe the CIA had complied with the second desist order when it had ignored the first? Or that the CIA was now perfectly open and honest with the president—especially a Democrat president?

Cavanaugh did not believe these things.

Okay, now build on the facts. Possible scenario: Fort Detrick was still experimenting with secret bioweapons and still restricting this knowledge to a handful of outsiders, probably CIA. Top elected and appointed officials, maybe including all of USAMRIID, did not necessarily know this. Secret research had developed malaria reading for use in, say, Africa, and had tested it in southern Maryland. . . .

Cavanaugh's mind stopped. He didn't believe it. Yes, they might well be constructing bioweapons at Fort Detrick in the name of national security. But sub-Sahara Africa—mostly poor, mostly disorganized, mostly struggling—was simply not a threat to the United States. Or to anyone else in the world of smart missiles and satellite surveillance. For the United States, bioweapons against Africa just didn't make national security sense, not even as a deterrent. And testing them on its own citizens—no. He just didn't believe his government had, or would, do that. Yes, there were racist individuals who would do that—millions of them, maybe—but the CIA had nothing to gain and too much to lose by coming to public light in such a way. No, that wasn't what had happened. Back up and start over.

So say that Fort Detrick *was* developing the stuff, for unknown reasons, and it had escaped inadvertently somewhere near Newburg, Maryland. Fort Detrick, or one of its tenant organizations, knew it. They'd tried to stop the epidemic before it became public. They'd tried using elephant mosquitoes, *T. rutilus,* ordered off the usual bookkeeping from Fielding's in Baltimore. That was "Project Birthday." The elephant mosquito larvae were supposed to eat the *Anopheles* larvae and wipe out the parasite vector. But it hadn't worked. *Anopheles* had flourished anyway, and the *Plasmodium reading* parasite had spread, and the epidemic had swung into full force. Meanwhile, Senator Malcolm Peter Reading had died, thrusting the whole problem into public light. Fort Detrick was in trouble.

So then they'd tried an alternate plan: the old hide-in-plain-sight. They'd let the CDC call in USAMRIID, and as a patriotic duty, the U.S. Army had cooperated in wiping out the malaria that the CIA had created. Did USAMRIID know that the rescuer and the villain were both housed in Fort Detrick, side by side? Maybe not. USAMRIID, like other military operations, worked on a need-to-know basis. Colonels Colborne and Sanchez did not need to know where a biological threat originated in order to fight it. Possibly both officers had driven in and out of Fort Detrick every day, not knowing that one of its windowless, triply secure facilities housed the actual enemy.

Cavanaugh shifted in his uncomfortable chair. Until Abigail barked, he didn't even hear the knock on the door.

So USAMRIID and the CDC, trying to keep turf wars to a minimum, had cleaned up the medical mess. But there were still problems for the CIA: the CDC on-site team and the FBI.

The CDC team knew too much about the manufactured nature of this disease, and at least some team members were all-holy-hell bent on finding out who had done the genetic engineering. The scientific community was a close one, and geniuses in it, as everywhere else, were rare. There was a chance the CDC could trace the biological trail back to Fort Detrick.

Meanwhile, the FBI was in hot pursuit, getting hotter as the press dumped fuel on the very public blaze. No one in the FBI knew about the bioweapons at the fort, but the FBI was damn good once it focused its full, all-resources-available attention. It was focusing now. There was a good chance the FBI might focus and focus and focus until they caught sight of the CIA. That, too, had happened before.

So the CIA had made a decision.

More knocks on the door, more barking from Abigail. "Mister? You in there?" called a female voice.

"No," Cavanaugh called back.

Say that at that point the CIA, backed into a corner, decided to cut off both investigations at the source. They brought in the head of the CDC and the director of the FBI and told them what had happened (whatever it was). They explained that national security was at stake, that national security demanded public secrecy. National security, they said. National security, NATIONAL SECURITY, **NATIONAL SECURITY.** Director Broylin believed in the importance of national security; you weren't picked to head the FBI otherwise. Cavanaugh didn't know about the head of the CDC, a Dr. Saul Wentzel, but he did know the scientist had once been in the military. A soldier.

"Open up, Mister! I know you're in there!" A female voice.

"Go away. I'm busy."

What next? Broylin and Wentzel had called in Farlow and Dunbar, who were leading the actual investigations. And told both of them why the investigations had to be stopped. Neither man had liked it—witness Dunbar's uneasiness the day of Michael Donohue's arrest, which he had known was a charade to pacify press and public. That's why the arrest warrant had not evoked national security. That would mean express authorization by the attorney general, who didn't know what the CIA was doing. And Dunbar had quieted his conscience—mostly—by telling himself that Donohue would be released by a grand jury anyway. There just wasn't enough evidence.

Then both Dunbar and Farlow had been promoted to Europe, where their uneasiness would not be connected to this case.

A key turned in Cavanaugh's lock.

He sprang up and flung open the door. A massive woman in a dirty apron stood beside a cart with cleaning supplies. "Housekeeping, Mister."

"*Now?* You haven't come all week!"

"I got sick," she said flatly. "I'm back now."

"Well, you're too late. I'm checking out." He closed the door, put on the chain, and returned to his chair.

Dunbar and Farlow safely removed to another continent. And the two most unruly team members, himself and Melanie, likewise removed: Cavanaugh for a minor transgression; Melanie for caring so much, and so aggressively, that she lost self-control. The cover-up leaders must have been ecstatic when she'd slugged that cruel punk in Burger King. Before that, some renegade CIA member had tried to scare her off by using the vicious Ed Lewis, of the dirty-tricks section (or whatever they called it) to make hate calls. They thought the calls would make her leave town. They didn't know Melanie Anderson.

And that was it. All the evidence explained, the scenario complete. Except for two crucial details: *Why* was malaria reading created? *How* did it get loose? Without those answers, all Cavanaugh had was a lot of fancy conjecture.

After all, there were other possible scenarios. Here was one: The epidemic had been created not by the CIA but by a foreign or domestic terrorist group, one with both money and malice. They didn't need a logical reason because even at the best of times these groups weren't very logical. They loosed the disease in southern Maryland, which was 25 percent black and poor enough that the malaria might get firmly established before it was really noticed. Poor blacks dying is not news. But a U.S. senator at an outdoor family party happened to get it. You can't plan everything. The CDC and the army stopped the epidemic, the FBI made an honest mistake in arresting Donohue, and Farlow and Dunbar were promoted because they were valuable men. Dunbar was uneasy because his wife was having an affair, or his kid was on drugs, or he had hemorrhoids. Ed Lewis had seen Melanie on TV, saw that she was a babe, and jerked off to making kinky tapes that, in his mind, degraded her. Cavanaugh was removed because he'd violated a legitimate rule, and Melanie was ordered to take a vacation because she clearly needed a vacation. And he, Cavanaugh, was an overly imaginative ass.

He needed proof. Of anything at all.

He picked up the phone. It had gone dead. He unlocked his door to head for the pay phone in the motel office, but the cleaning woman still stood blocking his path, smoking a cigarette, as immobile as a rooted thorny tree.

She said, "Check-out time's in twenty-two minutes."

"Right," Cavanaugh said. *Now* she had become time conscious. Well, the office pay phone was too public anyway. So was his—or any—cell phone. Cavanaugh went back into his room and threw his increasingly disorganized belongings into his always disorganized car. Abigail squeezed on top of a pile of blankets, shirts, and a VCR. Cavanaugh left The Pines to find a working, private, noncleaning-woman-haunted phone.

Officer Tess Muratore, please."

"Who do I say is calling?" The Maryland State Police dispatcher sounded bored. But apparently Tess was physically present, a break Cavanaugh hadn't expected. He'd expected to leave a request for her to call him back, which she might not have done if she didn't remember who he was. They'd only met at a few parties.

"My name is Robert Cavanaugh."

After a few moments, which Cavanaugh spent reading the unoriginal graffiti in the phone booth, Tess spoke. "Yeah?"

"Tess, this is Robert Cavanaugh. Judy's friend."

"Not from what I hear."

She did remember him. What had Judy told her?

"I'm with the FBI, and—"

"Not at the moment, you're not."

"You probably read in the *Post* that I'm on temporary suspension. It's minor. What isn't minor is malaria reading, and I'm trying to—"

"I'm not interested in talking to you," Tess said. "Bye."

"Wait! It's important. Just meet me somewhere for five minutes, Tess. It's about malaria reading. I really do have something!"

"Not if you had the Hope diamond." She hung up.

Not a successful call.

Cavanaugh fished out another quarter and called Felders. Maybe Felders had found out something about the connection between Ed Lewis and Fort Detrick.

"This is the Felders residence. We'll be away from the Washington area until August 23. You can leave a message here with or for Tom, the housesitter."

Cavanaugh hung up. Felders didn't want anyone to know his house was empty. There was no "Tom." And there was no way to reach Felders until he returned from vacation.

Not a successful call.

"The Victorian Roses Bed and Breakfast. May I help you?"

"Melanie Anderson, please. She should have checked back in this morning."

"I'm sorry, Dr. Anderson is scheduled to return to us today, but she hasn't arrived yet."

"Thanks. I'll try again later."

Not a successful call.

"AT&T, Customer Service." A female voice, lilting and perky. "May I help you?"

"Yes. This is Robert Cavanaugh. I'm calling to see if phone service has been turned on yet in my new apartment in Leonardtown, Maryland. The landlord was going to let your people in. My customer number is 4678K."

"Let me look. Are you Mr. Cavanaugh?"

"Yes."

"Robert Cavanaugh?"

"Yes!"

"There's been a slight delay. The installation crew will reach your area next Tuesday."

"Next *Tuesday?* You promised me it would be this week!"

"I'm sorry, sir, there have been unavoidable delays. Can I help you with anything else?"

"You can get me my phone!"

"We're working on it, sir. Thank you for calling AT&T."

He had his mobile phone, of course, but anybody with simple equipment could listen in on it.

The universe was not cooperating.

✿   ✿   ✿

And then what did he say?" Judy said.

"I already told you twice," Tess answered.

"Tell me again."

Tess rolled her eyes. The two women, Tess still in uniform, sat in Judy's new living room, which she had declared to represent a brand-new start to her life. The apartment was as minimal and hard-edged as she could make it, while retaining most of her old furniture. The chintz sofa had been recovered in sleek white parachute nylon, accented with red Mylar throw pillows. The sofa shared an area rug in shades of red with two white, steel-framed director's chairs. Judy's old coffee table held two wineglasses, a gleaming bowl of red flowers, and an abstract white stone sculpture. The only other furnishings were plain white curtains, a poster of Edvard Munch's *The Scream,* and an enormous red-leaved plant in what appeared to be the chassis of a miniature UFO.

Tess said, "What I like about this apartment is that it's so . . . airy."

"Tess, forget the apartment. Tell me again what Robert said."

"He said he 'really had something' about malaria reading. He said he wanted to meet with me for five minutes. He didn't think I'd remember him. He described himself as 'Judy's friend.' Jude, I don't like how much you're investing yourself in this totally dumb conversation. The man's a jerk. Forget him."

Judy said nothing.

"Only you can't, can you? Judy?"

"No," Judy said, very low. "It seems I can't."

"But you're trying, right? You keep busy? You date other men? You see your girlfriends?"

"In the last two weeks I've had three dates with three different men. I also had two lunches with friends, two movies out, and dinner with my old college roommate. I wrote seventeen thousand words of science copy, some of it quite good, and mended clothes ripped four years ago. I also joined a gym, signed up to tutor inner-city kids on Wednesday afternoons in September, and started two avocado plants and a lemon tree from seed. Tess, don't twist around so on that sofa!"

"It's too slippery," Tess complained. "I liked the old upholstering better."

Both women fell silent, contemplating Judy's sofa.

Finally, Tess said slowly, "You know what it is. By our age, most people are married, or they've decided they don't want to be. If you're a single woman and you want a serious relationship, you're like someone walking through a potato field in November. You search over the potatoes that the harvest missed, but they're mostly shriveled or wormy. So you wait in the middle of the empty field for some other woman to decide she doesn't want the potato she picked after all and to throw it back. You're just waiting for that, which is humiliating. And meanwhile, you're developing a vitamin-C deficiency and getting scurvy."

Judy just looked at her.

"Okay, you don't like that theory. Here's another. Women still don't have equal say in this fucking world. We're not the choosers; we have to wait to be chosen. We're like merchandise on a shelf—say, glassware. And some are cheap plates and some are Wedgewood and some are chipped or whatever. And some—like you and me—are high-quality, oven-tempered, hand-painted casseroles. But hand-painted earthenware is a minority taste. It doesn't appeal to everyone. It also needs the right handling and other care. So the chipped plates get taken and the flashy wineglasses. Rich guys buy the Wedgewood. And the hand-painted earthenware just sits there."

"Let me get this straight," Judy said. "You're saying we're *casseroles with scurvy?*"

Tess considered. "Yes."

"Well, I'm not! And neither are you! We're not begging for anybody else's potato or sitting on a merchandise shelf. Tess, you don't really believe all that."

"Sometimes I do."

"Well, don't. I'll bet nobody else wearing that uniform has ever come up with such pathetic theories."

"Don't bet on it."

Judy laughed, then stared deeply into her empty wineglass. "Tess, I want you to see Robert."

"Oh, Jude, it won't help you with him. He—"

"I don't expect it to help me. You don't even have to mention me. In fact, I prefer you don't. But Robert's a good agent, even if he knows subzero about women. If he says he's got something important on malaria reading, he does. If he says he needs some input from you, he does. See him."

"You really want me to?"

"Yes."

"Okay," Tess said, reaching for the wine bottle. "But I won't like it. He treated you really badly, Judy."

"He's still a good FBI agent."

"And that matters to you. Still."

"Yes," Judy said. "So agree to see him, Tess."

"All right," Tess said. "I will."

By Saturday, Melanie still hadn't returned to Washington.

Where the hell *was* she, Cavanaugh worried. From a pay phone he called his FBI voice mail, the CDC, her mother's house in Mississippi, Melanie's apartment in Atlanta, and the airline she'd been booked on, to see if there'd been an accident. There hadn't. Nobody had seen Melanie. Mississippi informed him that she was in Atlanta, and Atlanta informed him she had gone home to Mississippi.

Where was she? And doing what?

The FBI voice mail, to his great surprise, did have a message from Tess Muratore. He met her at a coffee shop near D.C., after spending his second night in a sleeping bag on the floor of his bare apartment. It was the first time he'd seen Tess in uniform. She looked much different than the attractive, midthirties party goer in bright dresses.

"Weekend shift?" he asked pleasantly, as he sat down opposite her.

"Look, Robert, I'm not here to make small talk. I'm only here because Judy asked me to, and only on business."

"Judy asked you to?" His breath tangled around his tonsils.

Tess scowled. "I'm not going to talk about Judy. Tell me what you want, or I'm out of here."

"Okay." He settled firmly in the booth, still surprised that the mention of Judy had affected him so strongly. "I've gone on investigating malaria reading. I think I've got something, but—"

"You 'think'? On the phone you were sure."

"—but I need some help. I need to know if there were any vehicle accidents near Newburg reported to the state or local police during the week that the CDC has established as the first seeding of the area with altered *Anoph*——"

"Shit, Cavanaugh, every reporter in the city has gone over and over the vehicular accident records," Tess said, with disgust. "They're open to the public. You mean the FBI doesn't know that?"

"Of course the FBI knows that." Cavanaugh kept a tight rein on his irritation. "We've checked out every police report within twenty-five miles. What I'm talking about is a vehicular accident that didn't make it into the record."

"If a cop shows up at the scene, a report is filed."

"Not if it's a military vehicle carrying top-secret classification."

For the first time, Tess's expression changed from contempt to something else. Cavanaugh didn't know what it was, but it was definitely something else. She said, "A military vehicle? What type?"

"Unknown."

"Regulation or unmarked?"

"Unknown."

"From where?"

"Fort Detrick."

"Registered to whom?"

"Could be anyone, but it would finally belong to the CIA."

"Going where?"

"Unknown."

Lines rucked Tess's forehead. "Could happen. But if there was no report filed, there's no report for me to find."

"I know. But you can find out who in the state troopers or county sheriff or local police was on duty those nights—"

"For an entire week? Everybody was on duty."

"All right. Narrow it to May 2 or 3. The CDC says those are the most likely seeding dates, judging from the resulting epidemiological curves. Once you find out who was on duty, you can discreetly talk to them, see if anything happened."

"Don't tell me to be 'discreet,' Cavanaugh. I don't need tutoring from you. And why should anyone at the scene of a military vehicle accident talk to me? I don't have jurisdiction, and I don't know the locals. And in case you never noticed, a lot of southern law-enforcement types don't like the whole idea of women troopers on principle—let alone ones who poke into their jurisdiction. And even if I found the right officer, he or she might have put together the malaria connection by now and be too scared to talk. Or maybe just be uninterested in talking to an FBI agent who arrested the wrong perp."

Cavanaugh said, "I know it's a long shot. I'm just trying every lead I can, looking for the one that will crack it. *You* know how that is, Tess."

Her face said she did, although she resented his assumption of colleagueship. Cavanaugh held his breath.

Finally, she said, "I do have a second cousin in the Charles County Sheriff's Office . . ."

"*Yes.* Please. That's one reason I asked you. Cops always seem to be related to other cops. I appreciate your help a lot. And, Tess, while you're here . . . how is Judy?"

Tess stood. She tossed fifty cents on the table, even though they hadn't ordered yet.

"She's doing terrifically. Dating a lot, very busy. If I get anything, I'll call you. If you don't hear from me, assume I came up with zip."

"But about Judy—"

Tess didn't even look back as she strode out the door.

"Doing terrifically . . . Dating a lot . . . Very busy . . ."

Well, that was good, wasn't it? It sounded as if Judy was happy. Cavanaugh wanted her to be happy. She deserved to be happy. Even if he felt like—

"You ready to order?" the waiter asked him.

Cavanaugh raised his head. "No," he said. "It's way too late."

S E V E N T E E N

Within the next five or ten years, it would probably be
possible to make a new infective organism which could
differ in certain important aspects from any known
disease-causing organism.
  —Charles Poor, Acting Assistant Secretary of the Army
   for Research and Development, testifying before a
  subcommittee of the Committee on Appropriations,
     House of Representatives, 1969

Melanie spent only seventeen minutes in the Baltimore-Washington
airport. Running as fast as she dared with over a hundred insects sewn
into her dress, she reached the gate barely in time to make her connecting flight to Atlanta. She'd booked the connection from midair, 35,000
feet above the ocean, on her way back from Kinshasa.

In Atlanta she took a cab directly to the CDC. It was Friday evening;
practically no one was there except security staff and, waiting for her impatiently in a level-one lab, Joe Krovetz. That call, too, she'd made from
the plane, saying as little as she could. Plane phones were not secure.

Melanie knew she was not a lab specialist. She could, of course, use
the standard techniques, including the scanning tunneling microscope,
to identify a microbe. But she could not identify minute changes in
minute structures on minute parasites. Nor could she isolate genetic

251

changes in DNA. That was very specialized microbiology, and Melanie had been trained as a physician, a general practitioner. At the CDC, she'd functioned as a top field investigator, not a research specialist. She needed someone who could examine at the subcellular level the specimens she'd brought back from Congo. Someone trained, careful, and good.

Gary Pershing would have been her first choice. He was among the best in the world at extracting, sorting, and analyzing DNA. But Pershing had never really liked Melanie or her wilder ideas. Was that because of her personality, because she was female, or because she was black? Also, despite his great talent, Pershing was basically a politician. He might very well be hoping to move up into Farlow's vacated position. If so, he wouldn't want to rock too many orthodox political boats.

That left Krovetz. He was young, but his training was recent, thorough, and in the right area. And no ideas were too wild for Joe Krovetz.

He was waiting for her in the lab. He'd started a beard, probably in an attempt to look older. It made him look like an underage Hollywood-style thug.

"Mel, you look like shit. When did you last sleep?"

"Doesn't matter. I have samples we have to analyze, Joe. Right now. All weekend."

"Samples? From where?"

"Africa. Kisangani Zone, Congo."

Krovetz's eyes brightened. "Tell me."

She did, as she wriggled out of her loaded dress. Even though she'd finished the long explanations standing in sandals and a black slip, Krovetz didn't ogle her. He listened intently, but his eyes and fingers were already busy cutting open the tiny pouches in the dress and carefully extracting the precious samples.

When she'd explained everything, and had handed him her genealogy charts from Yamdongi, Melanie left Krovetz working at the lab bench. She covered a cold lab table with a blanket from the supply closet and lay down. Within thirty seconds she was, finally, asleep.

Felders didn't call Cavanaugh, didn't mail him, didn't leave a message with his landlord. Instead, Felders showed up.

Cavanaugh had been unpacking his possessions, which had finally arrived by truck from storage, in his Leonardtown apartment. This was a problem because there were more possessions than there was apartment. He'd already stuffed his allotted four-by-six basement storage cubicle so full that he'd had to ram his shoulder into the door to get it closed. He'd stored his grandmother's dishes, which were too fragile to use and too family to discard, on the top shelf of the bathroom closet. In the tiny kitchen, frying pans, pot holders, and wineglasses surged over the minuscule countertop and frothed over onto the floor. Abigail, worn out from tearing apart a twenty-pound bag of dog food, slept on Cavanaugh's winter parka. When the doorbell rang, Cavanaugh felt relieved.

"Marty! I thought you were still on vacation."

"I'm back."

"Well, come on in."

Felders prowled around the living room, stepping over spilled dog kibble. "Love what you've done with the place."

"The apartment doesn't like me."

"Already? Add it to the growing list. Isn't your suspension pretty much over?"

"No," Cavanaugh said. Felders would remember to the day how long the suspension lasted. Something was up.

"Listen," Felders said, which meant the real conversation was ready to start. Also, the more important the topic, the more peripatetic he always became, and now he paced from window to bookcase to galley kitchen, crunching kibble underneath. "Listen, Bob—three things."

"Shoot."

"When Dunbar leaves for Budapest, I'm heading the Baltimore Field Office."

Cavanaugh felt his smile almost break his jaw. Once again he'd report to Felders. Felders was the best agent Cavanaugh knew. Felders would drive the field office until it ran like a Corvette. Felders would get him out of southern Maryland. Felders would—

"You're not supposed to know this second thing," Felders said. "Hell, I'm not supposed to know it either. But the OPR has finished its report on your case and—"

"Finished?" Cavanaugh said. "That's impossible." It had only been three weeks. The OPR never finished in three weeks. There had to be interviews, follow-throughs, a preliminary report from the field to Head-quarters, more follow-up, a final report written by the OPR investigators themselves . . . Three weeks was impossible. Not unless somebody very near the top was pushing very hard . . .

Felders said bluntly, "Loss-of-effectiveness transfer, to be im-plemented immediately. To the Resident Agency Singleton, North Dakota."

Cavanaugh sank onto a chair. *Singleton, North Dakota.* J. Edgar Hoover used to banish agents to Butte, Montana, but this was much worse. At least Butte was a city. Singleton was a pockmark on the prairie.

"Third thing," Felders said—he didn't believe in sympathy—"about Ed Lewis. He's not at Fort Detrick; he's an equipment maintenance me-chanic at a place that makes cardboard boxes. But he lives in Frederick, as close to the fort as a civilian can get. Was rejected for army service at eighteen due to severe lordosis. Born in Georgia, engineering degree from Georgia Tech. Until two years ago worked in Bangor, Maine, as a plant engineer for a textile factory. Not married, lives alone, spends a lot of time with Goodman or Romellio at bars or sports events."

"The profile that Pritchard drew," Cavanaugh said. *Singleton, North Dakota.*

"Your other two guys, Mike Goodman and Jack Romellio, do work at Detrick all right. Fort logs show them signing in and out daily. Goodman and Romellio are on the CIA payroll. Low level. They won't know any-thing about anything. But the Payroll Division is interesting: 'Special Projects.' I couldn't get any more on that. Heavily classified, and the CIA doesn't much like sharing even unclassified knowledge with us."

An old story. But Felders's ferret expression said there was more. Cavanaugh waited, watching his almost-again-boss grind dog food into powder on Cavanaugh's new carpet. Felders jingled the change in his pocket as he paced, harmony to restless melody.

"It gets better, Bob. Goodman and Romellio are clean, of course, but Lewis has a police record. He left Bangor because he was fired as plant engineer for harassing an employee. A black woman."

"Well, well," Cavanaugh said, although he knew it came out a little hollow. *Singleton, North Dakota.*

"Lewis has been arrested once, for stuffing hate propaganda into mailboxes. Suspended sentence. But the interesting thing is that he refused to say, even under oath, where the mail originated. For that he got an additional three months for contempt."

"You're not suggesting—"

"Of course not, Bob, stay real. The CIA's on our side, remember? The hate mail was from a white supremacist group. What's interesting is that Lewis served his whole sentence without spilling any beans, to anybody. A close-mouthed kind of guy, Lewis. Loyal in his own peculiar way, racist, underemployed, loves the paramilitary. A perfect guy for a dirty-tricks section to use on outside jobs. Cash under the table, no paper trail to the fort, no random gossip."

"All conjecture," Cavanaugh said.

Felders shot him an amused look. "Of course it's all conjecture. Do you think they're going to send me a notarized affidavit that Fort Detrick hired Ed Lewis to scare off Melanie Anderson? Bob, Bob, Bob. I thought I'd taught you that cases got built brick by intermittently conjectural brick. And don't look so gloomy. You're not going to Singleton, North Dakota."

"I'm not?"

"Not if you can turn conjecture into fact. You've got one more week."

"Very funny."

"Not really." Abruptly, Felders stopped pacing and jingling. "Your career rides on this one; we both know that. But also a whole lot more. For the first time I think you've got something, although I still don't know what. But there are just too goddamn many coincidences here."

Cavanaugh stood. "Felders, I need you to—"

"You need me to get the Fort Detrick transport logs through eastern Charles County on the dates around the beginning of the epidemic. But I can't, Bob. Not without a subpoena, which I doubt I could obtain. And even if I could, it would alert the CIA that we're looking; and even real coincidences would be buried deeper than the Mariana Trench. I was hoping you had some sort of unofficial bread-crumb trail."

Cavanaugh said slowly. "I might."

Felders's bright eyes turned brighter. "Aha. And from the look on your face, is this a bread crumb with lipstick?"

"Two bread crumbs with lipsticks."

"Two? You never learn, do you? Well, follow your bread-crumb trails before the end of next week. And remember what happened to Hansel."

"Gretel saved him from the witch's oven."

"Just barely," Felders said. "And not before he got his balls singed. Be careful, Bob. And be quick." Felders left.

Be quick. Great. But how does one be quick with no phone calls from either Melanie or Tess? Until both women reported back to him, there was nothing Cavanaugh could do.

Melanie woke stretched out on the metal lab table, still in her slip. All her bones ached; she was too old to be sleeping on lab tables. At the other end of the room Krovetz worked quietly. Light streamed in the window.

"What . . . what time is it?" She struggled to sit up. Her joints groaned.

Joe said, "Noon. Melanie, come look—"

"*Noon?* On *Saturday?* Good Lord, I slept fourteen hours! Have you worked straight through?"

"Pretty much. Come look at this, Mel."

With difficulty she slid off the table, keeping the blanket wrapped around her. Not that Krovetz would notice, or care if he did. The tone in his voice said something else gripped his mind, and Melanie felt an answering surge of adrenaline. Joe held out magnified microscope pictures.

"Look, Mel. These are dead red blood cells from your dead mosquitoes and larva. The cells have been colonized by *Falciparum reading,* all right. Only the cells with Hb S."

"So it *was* malaria reading in Yamdongi."

"Of course it was. You already knew that. But look at *this* data."

More papers. Melanie studied them, blinking in the light from the window, her blanket slipping off one shoulder.

"Joe, I'm not up on this end of things, but this seems to say—"

"That this batch of *Plasmodium reading* has all the same DNA alterations as our old friend, the parasite carried by *A. quadrimaculatus* in Maryland and Virginia. The altered surface peptides bind only to sickled cells. The knobs adhere preferentially to vascular endolethium of brain tissue. The protein expression drops nitric acid levels. It's the same genetically engineered mutant, all right, only this time in *A. gambiae.*

"But look here, Mel, at this picture. It's typical of the samples you brought home."

Melanie looked. The picture, like the others, was a magnified photo from the scanning tunneling microscope. It showed *P. reading* in the sporozoite stage, the way it lived in the salivary glands of anopholine mosquitoes. But instead of showing the familiar long, asexual threads, these sporozoites looked like they'd been through a violent war. Torn, burst fragments littered the slide. Those not torn apart were misshapen. Tiny specks dappled the background like spent shrapnel.

"What is—"

Joe thrust another picture at her. "Look at this version. I stained the sample."

As soon as she saw the second picture, with its various components stained in conventional colors, Melanie knew what she was looking at. "A virus! The parasite was killed by a virus!"

"Yep. In the asexual sporozoite stage, in the salivary glands of the mosquito. Apparently the virus didn't harm the mosquito at all, as far as I can see. Of course, all your samples are dead—"

"Carbon tetrachloride," Melanie said swiftly. "I gave the kids killing jars. Did you allow for that?"

"Of course I did. I worked all night, Mel, testing your mosquitoes for *Plasmodium reading* and then concentrating on the ones that carried it. I figured that since adult female *Anopheles* feed on blood, anything we're looking for that didn't kill the mosquito outright would probably show up in the mouth area. That way it starts in the mosquito and goes into the victim, or starts in the victim and goes into the mosquito, or— most likely—goes both ways after the first transmission.

"So far I've looked at eighty-six of your mosquitoes and tabulated them into three groups: those free of all *Plasmodium* parasites, those carrying the usual *Plasmodium falciparum,* and those carrying *Plasmodium reading.* Then I examined the last two groups. I looked not only for mangled *Plasmodium,* but also for fragments of RNA, protein markers— all the usual indicators of a viral presence. Next, I put some of the saliva through the centrifuge, just to be sure the parasites and the viruses did indeed separate out at different densities. And they did. Here's the tally."

He thrust a chart at her, hand drawn but very clear in Joe's block letters:

Saliva from Dead *Anopheles Gambiae,* Yamdongi Village,
Kisangant Zone, Congo (S = 86)

	A. Gambiae free of Plasmodium	A. Gambaie carrying P. Falciparum	A. Gambaie carrying P. Reading
Parasites intact in salivary glands	NA	26	4
Parasites destroyed in salivary glands, no virus fragments present	NA	0	0
Parasites destroyed in salivary glands, virus fragments present	NA	0	56

Melanie stared at the data for a long time.

There it was.

There it was. Proof that the epidemic of malaria reading in Yamdongi had not been stopped by normal mosquito-control methods. Nor by running its natural destructive course. Nor by Doctors Without Borders administering humanitarian aid. Proof that someone, or some group, had deliberately intervened with another genetically engineered organism, a virus that killed *Plasmodium reading* but not the mosquito carrying it. And it had worked. Somebody had come up with engineered biological control of malaria reading, and it had killed over 93 percent of the parasites. Furthermore, the cure had appeared within a few months of the disease, an impossibly short time to create a new organism on the DNA level if you were starting from scratch.

Therefore, whoever had created the disease had also created the virus that cured it, in advance.

She, Melanie, *was not crazy.* Malaria reading was a deliberate experiment in genocide. An experiment to see if black people could be killed at whim by releasing infected *Anopheles,* and then if black people could be saved by releasing the virus that killed the disease. The black victims, in the United States and in Congo, had been guinea pigs for a controlled experiment: guinea pigs for the disease; guinea pigs for the cure.

And if Robert Cavanaugh was right, the trail for this monstrous act led to Fort Detrick.

Blindly, she reached out and groped for Joe, and the next thing she knew, she lay numbly against his chest. Not sobbing, not crying, not moving. She felt paralyzed by the horror of what she'd just deduced, and she reached for the warmth of another human being—any human being—with no more volition than a frost-gripped plant trying to reach for sunlight.

"Joe . . ."

"I know," he said, patting her back. "I know," although of course he didn't. Not really. He wasn't at risk. He was white.

"Mel, listen to me. There's another piece here we haven't gotten yet. The virus in Congo moved from the vector to the victim, or vice-versa, and once the mosquito bit someone else, the mosquito was no longer a vector. The virus saw to that. The mosquito would give the virus to the human, of course, but let's presume that the virus is harmless to humans. That's logical. The next mosquito who stings that human will get the virus. But *only* if it stings a human who's already been stung once. That's not an efficient enough way to spread the virus to ninety-three percent of the parasites. No, there's got to be more here."

His logic calmed her a bit, focused her away from the horror and toward the logical problem.

"So listen to this," Joe went on. "I think the virus had to be put *first* into the human population of Yamdongi. But how? How do you infect an entire village with a blood-borne virus without attracting attention? You need a method that the villagers are already accepting without question."

"The vaccine," Melanie said slowly.

"The vaccine, yes. The vaccine serum must have carried not only whatever chloroquine derivative they're trying out now, but also the engineered virus. I'll bet that now everybody in Yamdongi carries the virus in their bloodstream. Sick people, healthy people, everybody. And I'll bet more: that the virus, when we take it apart, will carry a full battery of ways to elude the human immune system as long as possible, so it would stay in the villagers' bloodstream long enough to infect a lot of other villagers. God, I wish we had blood samples from Yamdongi! Do you know where the vaccine serum came from?"

"Brian Spencer said it was given to Doctors Without Borders by the World Health Organization."

"By WHO! Then it could have originated in any of the WHO signatory countries, and WHO must have records of—"

Behind them, the lab door opened. "Oh! Excuse me . . ." A hasty slam.

Melanie whirled around, too late to see who it had been. She'd still been leaning against Joe. Her blanket had slipped past her hips, exposing her in her black slip. Joe's arms had been around her. Both their hair mussed, hers from sleep and his from the lack of it . . .

"Who was it?"

Joe said, "Suzanne Dreyfuss. A lab tech."

"Oh, God. And us standing here like . . . like . . . Does she gossip?"

Joe shrugged. "They all gossip. Don't worry about it."

"'Don't worry about it?' Joe, do you have any idea at all how hard I've worked not to appear . . . shit, shit, shit!"

By Monday this Suzanne Whosit would have it all over the CDC. *And I walked right in on them Saturday afternoon in Lab 6 and she was wearing only a . . . SHIT.*

Joe stared at her, his downy brow wrinkled. "Calm down, Mel. It's no big deal."

He didn't get it. He never would. And, come to think of it, that was one of the reasons she'd always felt comfortable with Joe: he didn't "get" the usual social barriers and so walked right through them. It made things so much fairer. Melanie calmed down.

"What I want to know now," Joe said, "is the mechanism the virus uses to destroy *Plasmodium*. Maybe it jams the reproductive machinery or disrupts *Plasmodium*'s food-transport tubules. Stanford is producing some good work on that. Damn! We need live, infected *P. reading*, we need blood samples, we need—Mel? Are you listening?"

No. I'm pondering the virtues of insensitivity. "Yes. Just take me over the data one more time."

He did, and she stood there in her slip, nodding as Joe took her deeper into his data, losing herself in the terrible and fascinating knowledge unlocked from the dead mosquitoes of Yamdongi village, Kisangani Zone, Democratic Republic of the Congo.

INTERIM

The boy set the glass jar on the kitchen countertop. He rummaged in the cupboard, looking for peanut butter, jelly, and bread. When he found them, he began to make himself a sandwich, humming the tune from *Star Wars*. The jar buzzed.

"Hey, Amy-Balamy. How ya doing?"

Amy, not quite two, made no answer. She toddled to the table and reached for the jar with the interesting noise. The boy, his back to her, didn't notice.

"You want half a sandwich, Amy-Mamy? You want—oh, God, what you do? You little bitch! Oh, baby, don't cry, you done cut yo'self . . ."

He pulled the wailing baby back from the broken glass on the floor. Blood smeared her hand. Mosquitoes buzzed around the kitchen.

The boy forced himself to think. What did Mama do when somebody got cut? Wash it. Yeah, wash it. He picked up Amy, carried her into the bathroom, and balanced her between his body and the sink, bending his knees a little to take her weight. This close to her, he could smell that she'd shit in her diaper again. As soon as she saw the cool water run from the tap, she stopped crying and started to splash. The cut wasn't deep. The boy wrapped a clean sock around it and taped the sock to the baby's hand.

Now what? Clean up, yeah. And catch more bugs for his school project. But what else for Amy? What a pain in the ass she was. He scowled at his little sister, now sitting on the bathroom floor happily chewing on the sock.

The boy went very still. *That.*

Should he call Mama at work? No, the boss didn't never like it when he did that. Mama said. But he couldn't do nothing, this was serious.

He dialed 911.

"I got emergency! My sister—"

"What's your name, honey? Do you know your address?"

The white 'ho thought he was a little kid! Fuck her. The boy said, making his voice as deep as he could, "My baby sister got herself bit by a mosquito. Send a ambulance in case she done got this new malaria!"

The white voice changed. "She got bitten by a mosquito? Just now? Is she showing any allergic reactions? Trouble breathing, or anything like that?"

The boy peered into the bathroom. Amy was stirring the water in the toilet with her bandaged hand.

"No. She look okay."

"Then you have nothing to worry about, honey. Malaria reading has been over for several weeks. But if you give me your name and address, I'll—"

The boy slammed down the phone. He pulled Amy out of the toilet and smacked her, not hard. Now he would have to put a whole other sock on her hand, change her shitty diaper, clean up the broken glass, and collect a different batch of bugs. All before he dropped Amy off at the sitter on his way to school.

But he didn't got nothing to worry about. Nah. Nothing at all. The white lady done said so.

EIGHTEEN

As we seek to reach the issue of accountability in a secret agency, we are left repeatedly with a record that is utterly beyond understanding.
—Sen. Walter Mondale discussing the CIA,
Select Committee to Study Government Operations
with Respect to Intelligence Activities, 1975

Cavanaugh finally bullied the phone company into installing his phone on Saturday morning. When the telephone installers left, grumbling, he blanketed Maryland and D.C. with brief messages giving out his new number. Two hours later, the phone rang for the first time. When Cavanaugh heard Judy's voice, he both tensed and loosened. His neck tightened and his knees loosened, although it would have felt better the other way around.

"Judy?"

"Yes, it's me. I have a message for you, Robert."

A message? Her voice was cool but not cold. Professional. What did that mean? He sat down on his just-cleared-off living room chair. Moving boxes, unshelved books, and crumpled paper still littered the living room. Abigail rooted under his chair for spilled kibble.

"I'm listening, Judy." He tried to make his voice as warm as possible. Maybe hers would absorb some of the heat.

It didn't. "The message is from Tess's second cousin in the Charles

263

County Sheriff's Department. He tried to reach Tess but she's away for the weekend, so he called me. There's another deputy sheriff on his way to your new place right now. His name is Ray Keller."

"Right now," Cavanaugh repeated, to keep her talking. "Why right now?"

"Well, to me he sounded like one of the guys who stews and broods over a situation until he can't stand it anymore, and then, to relieve his mind, has to act *right now.* You know the type?"

"Sure," Cavanaugh said. "Wouldn't you say Karen Saunders was like that?" Maybe mentioning mutual friends would remind Judy of all the good times they'd had with their friends. The picnics, parties . . .

"Ray Keller says he really needs to talk to you, Robert. I hope it's useful information."

"I do, too. If you want, I could call you later to let you—" But she'd already hung up.

Cavanaugh threw the packing boxes and most of the crumpled paper out of the living room and into the bedroom and closed the door. Judy hadn't said where Keller was driving from or when he'd started. And come to think of it, how had Judy known the address of his new place to give Keller? She must be keeping herself aware of his moves. Maybe that meant she was also aware of—Abigail barked and Keller arrived.

He looked about twenty-five, and not as nervous or brooding as Judy had indicated, although there certainly was a controlled tension in his stance, in the cords of his neck, in the way he gripped his car keys. Blond crewcut, sunburned face, wary eyes. Cavanaugh could easily imagine Keller in the uniform of a deputy

"I'm Ray Keller. You Agent Robert Cavanaugh, FBI?"

"Yes. Come in."

"Can I see some ID, please?"

Cavanaugh suppressed a smile, revised his estimate of Keller's age a few years downward, and brought his credentials from a locked desk drawer. Abigail sniffed at Keller, who relaxed just enough to rub her ears.

"Okay," Keller said, handing back Cavanaugh's creds. "I work with Jack Cordaro, who's kin to Tess Muratore. I have something to tell you. Outside, in my car."

The kid was afraid the apartment was bugged. Cavanaugh doubted this, but he followed Ray Keller to his own car, a three-year-old Escort, much cleaner than Cavanaugh's vehicle. Before they got in, Keller patted him down for a wire. Cavanaugh permitted it.

He sat quietly beside Keller, giving the deputy the chance to tell it in his own way.

Finally Keller said, "I was in the military. Marines. Four years. I just got out seven months ago. We learned to respect the chain of command. We also learned to respect our country." Abruptly he looked away, frowning suspiciously through the side window at nothing in particular.

Now Cavanaugh had a handle on the situation. He said, almost casually, "And that's your dilemma now."

"Yeah."

Another long silence. Outside the car, two teenagers dawdled past, licking ice cream cones. A gaggle of tourists strolled toward the war monument on the grassy island in the middle of Leonardtown. A cat stalked by. Cavanaugh thought regretfully of New York City informants, who talked at New York City speed.

Finally, Ray Keller let go. "On May 2 of this year, at three twenty-seven in the morning, I witnessed a vehicular accident on Route Three-oh-one, Charles County, Maryland, while I was on duty. A four-door 1997 green Chevy Lumina hit a deer. I saw the entire accident. I was heading north on 301 and the Chevy was heading south. The deer, a full-grown buck, bolted from the woods and ran right in front of the Chevy. It hit him head-on. The deer was thrown onto the shoulder and the car swerved, did a one-eighty, bounced into and out of a ditch, and hit a tree with the rear half of the vehicle's right side. The right rear door and fender were smashed in. The rear windshield and taillights shattered. The rear seat dislocated and was driven upward at approximately a forty-five-degree angle, and that wrenched the trunk open."

Keller had been over and over it in his mind, Cavanaugh saw. This stilted wording was the report Keller hadn't written at the time the accident happened. Why not? He prompted, "Was anybody hurt?"

"Only bruises and minor cuts. The occupants consisted of two Caucasian males in their forties, in civilian clothes. After ascertaining that neither was hurt, I asked to see driver's license and registration for the vehicle. The driver then asked to speak to his companion alone. I refused to allow that until identification had been produced, at which point the two men exchanged glances and produced military credentials."

Suddenly Cavanaugh could see it: the deserted highway, bordered for long stretches by heavy woods close to the pavement. The only illumination the headlights of Keller's County Sheriff car. The oncoming high beams of cars traveling in the opposite direction, not slowing down just to see one more speeder caught in the predawn. The headlights would cast shifting shadows on the stern faces of the two men, on the much younger Keller in his almost-brand-new uniform, on the wrecked car half thrust into the shadowy woods, its trunk yawning wide. And on the warm night air, the smell of blood from the deer.

Keller continued, "Their ID said they were both colonels, stationed at Fort Detrick. They showed me official orders that said they were transporting Special Compartmented Information Materials to the Naval Surface Warfare Center at Dahlgren, Virginia. They said that in the interests of national security, I should not file an accident report about hitting the deer. They gave me a phone number to call on my cell phone to verify that."

Cavanaugh said swiftly, "Do you remember that number?"

"Yes, but it doesn't do any good. I know because I . . . I called it again. A month later, when all that malaria reading stuff hit the news. I just wanted to . . . The vehicular accident occurred in the township of Newburg, about half a mile from the Potomac River Bridge. On television they said the plague started in Newburg, so I thought . . . although I didn't see any mosquitoes fly out from the twisted boxes and stuff in the car trunk."

No, Cavanaugh thought, Keller wouldn't have seen any mosquitoes. They'd all have been gone by the time he parked his car, ran across the highway, and made sure the people inside the wrecked car were unhurt. The mosquitoes would have flown into the woods, dispersed in the dark to the undisturbed ravines and the scattered barns and the quiet pools of stagnant water thick with scum to nourish newly hatched larvae.

Keller said, "When the CDC and the Health Service people issued all those guidelines for not getting sick, and the army started the insect spraying, I called Fort Detrick. The switchboard told me that the two colonels weren't stationed there. They just didn't exist." Keller's voice changed. "They'd showed me fake IDs."

Cavanaugh said, still casually, "And you resented that."

"Yeah. I mean, I was a *Marine*. We know enough to comply with national security concerns, without being lied to. I didn't file any report.

And then after the plague got started, I wasn't sure that . . . I thought . . ."

Cavanaugh said, "You weren't sure what was the right thing to do."

"Yeah. And I wanted to do the right thing. I still want to."

"You are, Deputy Keller." Cavanaugh tried hard not to sound like a school principal. Judy had been right. This boy, no more than twenty-three or -four, was caught in a vise that had squeezed presidents and attorney generals. Proper legal procedures versus national security. No wonder Ray Keller had been feeling mangled for almost four months.

Keller stayed silent, looking away, so Cavanaugh tried to help. "You saw the FBI getting involved, and all the epidemic victims dying, and you didn't know if what you'd seen had any connection to the epicenter of the outbreak. You didn't think so, but when Tess's cousin started asking about unreported vehicle accidents during the first week of May, you suddenly weren't so sure."

"I was never sure," Keller said, surprising Cavanaugh with his vulnerable honesty. "But I told Jack no, and then thought about it for a week and then I called the number Jack was giving out. An answering-machine message said that anyone with information for Tess should call her friend Judy Kozinski. Who sent me to you."

"Which was the correct action. In fact, your information may be tremendously important to the FBI, which is also concerned with national security." Maybe that would make Keller feel slightly better. "I have some more questions, Ray. First, what were the aliases the two men gave you?"

"Col. Eugene Willis Thompson and Col. David Edward Broderick."

Neither name meant anything to Cavanaugh—not surprisingly, if they were indeed aliases. Questions jostled each other in his mind. He chose carefully among them, trying to get to the important ones first, before Officer Ray Keller lost his personal indignation, or decided his conscience was satisfied, or otherwise changed his mind about adding to Cavanaugh's case against the government of the United States.

He waited impatiently for Melanie to call, walking up and down his apartment, Abigail trailing at his heels. When he caught himself jingling his pocket change, he stopped instantly. Jesus, he was turning into Felders. He planted himself in a chair and tossed Abigail's tennis ball for her to fetch. Across the living room, through the archway to the kitchen, bounce off the wall above the countertop, roll back toward the living room until the dog snatched it up. When he broke a water glass on the kitchen counter, he stopped that.

The phone rang. Cavanaugh snatched it up. Somebody wanted to sell him life insurance.

By four o'clock in the afternoon, he was reduced to cleaning the apartment. By five, everything was unpacked and put away. By six, the moving boxes were torn down, bundled, and tied for recycling. By seven, Abigail had had a bath, which she hated. By seven-thirty, the bathroom sparkled. At 7:52, Melanie rushed through his door. She looked like she'd been through a tornado.

"Melanie! Why the hell didn't you call? I'd have picked you up at the airport!"

"I drove. Didn't want to stop to phone. Robert, we got it. We got it."

"Tell me."

"The vaccine that the Doctors Without Borders gave to everybody anywhere near Yamdongi was deliberately contaminated with virus. The virus attacks *P. reading*—and *only* the reading strain of *Plasmodium*. It kills—what's that smell? Like coconuts?"

"I gave the dog a bath. Go on."

"You bathed Abigail with coconut-perfumed shampoo?"

"It was all I had. It was Judy's. Go on!"

"The virus kills the sporozoites in the *Anopheles* salivary gland. Probably also in human blood, in the brief time before the sporozoites burrow into the liver. Any *Anopheles* that then bites a vaccinated human is made free of *P. reading*. That's why the epidemiological curve drops off so suddenly. In Congo, the epidemic was stopped by the virus in the vaccine. In Maryland, it was stopped by USAMRIID, using conventional procedures. Whoever created the epidemic didn't dare test the virus antidote in the U.S.A. Every infectious-disease facility in the world had people in southern Maryland taking field samples and analyzing blood. The virus would never have stayed secret."

Cavanaugh nodded slowly. "That fits . . . that fits."

"Fits what? Robert, have you got anything to eat? I don't think I've eaten since yesterday."

He didn't even hear her, thinking deeply. Melanie went to the kitchen, grimaced into the refrigerator, and hastily slapped together a cheese sandwich.

"I'm back. Fits *what?*"

He told her about the accident with the deer on Route 301 on May 2.

Melanie put down her sandwich, uneaten. "From Fort Detrick."

"Yes. Maybe. The names were aliases; that could be falsified as well. But it supports the theory that the epidemic wasn't supposed to happen here. The infected mosquitoes got loose *by accident*.

"And then the army, or the CIA, or whoever, couldn't risk using the virus antidote. They'd lost half their bioweapon; they didn't want to risk exposure of the other half. And the U.S. has the resources and manpower to contain malaria by conventional means, so they did that."

"But Africa doesn't have those resources," Melanie said. "So to fight against any black nation, you just vaccinate your own black troops and then let loose batches of malaria-reading-infected vectors. Within a few months at most, a substantial percentage of your black enemy has died of cerebral stroke."

"Yes," Cavanaugh said. He couldn't look at the pain on her face.

"And the world would probably never even know you violated the Geneva Convention. After all, in the middle of a war on a continent full of malaria anyway, who's going to do parasite-strain research on dying soldiers? Bury them and get on with the war."

Cavanaugh said nothing.

"And we *created* that. The United States. Created it and tested it in Yamdongi; and incidentally, if those 'coloreds' ever get too uppity again near home, well, nobody wants to think of that. The blacks are good citizens of course, but if those niggers do get out of line—we're ready for 'em all right."

"Stop that," Cavanaugh said. To his surprise, she did. Instead she looked directly at him and said tonelessly, "So what are we going to do? Do you have a plan?"

"Yes. No. I mean, it's not sturdy enough to call a plan." *The best-laid plans of bugs and men . . .* "But we're going to do it anyway."

"Tonight?" Same colorless tone.

"No. It has to be Monday morning, when people are back at work. I need your help, Melanie. You'll be taking risks with your career."

"Like I care anymore. Work for a government that can do *that*? I'll emigrate to Africa."

Cavanaugh couldn't tell if she meant it. Her voice was so expressionless. And her personality was so volatile. Militant, brilliant, paranoid, idealistic, emotional, angry as hell underneath. Not a person that you could count on to stay on your side through an entire strategy.

As if he had a choice.

He told her what he intended them to do on Monday morning.

He didn't sleep well Saturday and Sunday nights. Abigail snuffled and twitched on the floor beside his bed. It reminded him of Judy's soft snoring.

The dog opened one eye when Cavanaugh got up, cocked her ears when he pulled on jeans, and bounded into activity when it definitely began to look like walking might occur. Cavanaugh left her off her leash. If anybody was around at four in the morning to object, too bad for them. He and Abigail slipped past Melanie, lying on her stomach on Cavanaugh's sofa. Melanie snored, too, but it just wasn't the same.

He'd never seen Leonardtown at this hour. It was beautiful. Maybe it had always been beautiful, and he'd just disliked the place too much to notice. He still disliked it, but now, a few hours away from decisions that could blow apart his life plus a great many others,' Cavanaugh's sharpened senses took in the town as if he were seeing it for the first time.

The main street, Washington, was divided by oval, grassy islands and surrounded by stately buildings. In the fading starlight they looked like ghosts from the past, which they were. The courthouse, red brick and tall white columns, in the style of antebellum plantation homes. The ceremonial cannon, brought from England in 1634 for the "defense of Saint Mary's City." The original jail, now a tourist attraction, where once prisoners were held for execution for such offenses as "rifling a trunk of lace while the mistress of the house lay dead in childbirth." The bottom of Washington Street sloped steeply toward the Potomac, where once "His Majesty's ships of war" had dropped anchor. Yes, Leonardtown was beautiful, but it was the bellicose beauty of three-and-a-half centuries of conflict.

God, was he doing the right thing? *Was he?*

It was generally not a good idea, Cavanaugh thought, as he sat on a pristine white bench in the courthouse garden, to take on one's own government. One stood a good chance of losing, of course. The government held all the aces. But that wasn't the real danger as far as Cavanaugh was concerned. The real danger lay in discovering how that government had played its previous aces.

Cavanaugh knew he was an idealist. He'd seen that clearly as long ago as Quantico, during initial training. Cavanaugh had looked at his fellow trainees and realized that they wanted to become agents for various reasons. Carrera's family had been cops for three generations; the Bureau was the upscale version. Johnson had been in the air force; she liked risk and action. Williamson admitted he'd been influenced by movies about the Bureau. Moreno liked the government benefits and government pension.

Cavanaugh was different. English major, fugitive from the corporate world, lapsed Methodist, he actually believed in the law, in its necessity, its function, even its saving grace. Without law, Cavanaugh believed, humanity would otherwise turn not only "red in tooth and claw" but probably in brain as well. Law was humanity's last, best hope of checking its own natural savagery. Law might—and did, constantly—fail in specific application. But at heart American jurisprudence was sound, and it kept sound at heart the government for which it was the scaffolding. Specific corruption might grow, but law ensured that it could not grow very long or deep without eventually being exposed and condemned. That was why Cavanaugh had become an FBI agent—to do what had to be done to protect the concept of law.

He'd learned to be careful about whom he admitted this to.

But it was true. Cavanaugh loved being an FBI agent, and not for family tradition or movie glamour or risk or action or a good pension. He simply liked fighting on the side of law. He liked nailing the bad guys.

But what if the side of law was also the side of lawlessness? What if the government that, despite its frequent falls from grace, he still basically believed in, what if that government *was* the bad guy? Killing for experimental purposes, seeding American and African villages with bioweapons just to see what would happen, perverting the law as a matter of course to carry out and cover up its own murders? "Well, of course," many people would say (Cavanaugh's ex-wife among them), "what do you expect? Governments are like that, and American democracy is no different. Look at Watergate, for example."

But Watergate was not mass murder. In fact, Cavanaugh had always felt reassured by Watergate. Minor corruption, major condemnation. Malaria reading embodied just the opposite—if it had been deliberately conceived by, manufactured at, dispersed by, and exported by a group or groups at Fort Detrick. Major corruption, minor condemnation. By, among others, the FBI that Cavanaugh believed in.

The real danger of taking on the FBI was finding out how rotten its soul might be. And then deciding if you could still bear to be a part of it.

"Get thee glass eyes,/And, like a scurvy politician, seem/To see the things thou dost not." King Lear.

Was Cavanaugh seeing a thing that "dost not"? Or was he seeing, all too accurately, what was?

Abigail, tired of sniffing at flower beds and peeing on the sundial, nuzzled Cavanaugh's feet and whined. He stood and walked on. Maryland Historical Society, grocery store, pharmacy, barbershop, Betty's Custom Framing. The air smelled of honeysuckle. Sometimes it seemed to Cavanaugh that all of Maryland smelled of honeysuckle.

Maybe he should just let sleeping dogs lie. Sleeping jackals, sleeping vultures, sleeping carrion. What did it matter? In a hundred years they'd all be dead anyway. Him, Melanie, "Colonels Thompson and Broderick," Director Broylin, all the relatives of malaria reading victims. Dead and forgotten. And the world would roll on anyway. Who was Cavanaugh to presume to affect its course? Hubris, pure hubris.

Cavanaugh realized he must have been walking longer than he'd thought; the sky had lighted and the stars had disappeared. Abigail trotted toward the grassy island in the middle of the street, which held that mandatory southern town centerpiece, the Civil War monument. Cavanaugh followed.

But it wasn't a Civil War monument. It had been erected November 11, 1921, to Leonardtown soldiers killed in World War I. GLORIA PRO PATRIA MORI. Well, maybe in 1921 the phrase had been less hackneyed and more heartfelt. There were two separate lists of names.

COLORED

Raymond G. Biscoe Pvt., 16th Co., 154th Dep Brig. Died Camp Meade 10-7-18

Joseph H. Branson Pvt., Co. A, 333d Labor BN A.E.F. Died France 9-23-18

Thomas Briscoe Pvt. . . . .

Ten names, total.

WHITE. Seventeen names. All the "Colored," shunted off to their own list, had been privates. The "Whites" had ranged from private to first lieutenant. All were equally dead.

Cavanaugh hoped like hell that Melanie didn't wander down from his apartment and see this monument. He didn't want to listen to the explosion.

But the monument sealed his decision.

"Abigail! Come on, girl! Here, Abigail!"

The dog loped to him. Cavanaugh walked back to his apartment and into the day.

NINETEEN

It is the right of the American people to know what their
government has done—the bad as well as the good.
—Senator Frank Church, Select Committee
to Study Government Operations
with Respect to Intelligence Activities, 1975

Ready?" Cavanaugh asked Melanie. She'd showered, dressed in a conservative blue suit, and sat drinking her third cup of strong black coffee.

"Ready."

Cavanaugh turned up the phone volume so that, if he held it slightly
away from his ear, she could hear both sides of the conversation. He
punched in the first of the numbers on his list.

"Good morning, Federal Bureau of Investigation. Can I help you?"
Cavanaugh didn't recognize the mature female voice. Possibly it be-
longed to one of the Betty Bureaus who'd married themselves to the
FBI decades ago. In that case, he already knew the script.

"This is Agent Robert Cavanaugh. I'd like to speak to Director
Broylin."

"I'm sorry, he's in a meeting right now. Have you discussed your concern with your special agent in charge?" Meaning: *Why are you violating the chain of command?*

"That's not possible. I need to speak to Director Broylin."

"If you'd like to leave a message, I'll see that he gets it." Meaning: *At the bottom of a huge stack of irrelevancies. If you had anything interesting, it would come through your SAC, and Director Broylin is too busy for trifles.* Betty Bureaus were fiercely protective of their bosses. They had a bad time during administrations with accessible, open-door directors, but that didn't describe Broylin.

"I would like to leave a message, yes. Please tell Director Broylin that I have some important information about Project Birthday."

"I'll give him the message." Meaning: *You're bothering him about a birthday party?*

"He'll know what I mean. It's a top-clearance CIA project." Cavanaugh gave his phone number.

"I'll tell him." And now her voice said, *A nut in the ranks of agents?* If he'd been a common citizen reporting a stealth UFO landing on the White House roof, her tone would be more respectful. Prophet in his own country. But at least he'd upped the chances that she'd actually tell Broylin. Betty Bureaus were as protective of the FBI's reputation as of their bosses' time. Cavanaugh repeated his phone number.

Melanie poured herself yet more coffee. Usually Cavanaugh would drink anything with caffeine, but now he turned his eyes away from the stream of hot coffee cascading into Melanie's mug. His stomach roiled.

The director of the CIA and the commander of Fort Detrick were also in meetings. Their receptionists also took messages.

"Now we wait," Melanie said.

"Now we wait," Cavanaugh agreed. "And forgive me for asking, but why are you suddenly so calm and poised, when all through this you've been . . . been . . ."

"A raging lunatic," Melanie said calmly. "But that was when I thought nobody would do anything. Now somebody will have to." She took another quiet sip.

Cavanaugh wished his anxiety worked that way. Obviously it didn't. He circled the tiny room, pacing and jiggling, feeling like Felders.

Forty-three minutes later, the phone rang.

"Agent Cavanaugh, please."

"Speaking."

"This is Assistant Director Arnold Sutton. I understand you have a message for the director."

"Yes, sir. The message is that I must meet with him today. It's urgent."

"A meeting is not possible, Agent Cavanaugh. The director's calendar is completely full. And I think you already know that your request is in violation of proper Bureau procedure. Please tell me the nature of your concern."

"My concern is about Project Birthday. And I—"

"There is no such project in the FBI."

"Yes, sir, there is. I'm sorry, sir, but there is. It's top clearance."

"I repeat, Agent Cavanaugh, that I know of no such project within the FBI."

"No, sir, you don't. But the director does. And I have vital information about it."

"Vital information obtained how?" Sutton asked.

"I'll reveal that only to the director. But please tell him that I'm not the only one with this information, sir. Dr. Broylin needs to know that."

"Aren't you on OPR suspension, Agent Cavanaugh? For unauthorized disclosure?"

"Yes, sir. But the information I have for Dr. Broylin is independent of my status with the Bureau." Both true and not true. It was getting harder to tell the difference.

Sutton said, "You're out of line, Agent Cavanaugh. I'm taking due note of that fact. Please remain in your present location, keeping your present phone number free, until you hear from me again." The phone clicked sharply.

Melanie said, "What does that mean?"

"It means he was told to call me by Broylin. Otherwise, an assistant director who may or may not have heard of Project Birthday wouldn't call me directly. And he had my Bureau record right there in front of him. Broylin's taking me seriously."

"And the others? The CIA and Fort Detrick?"

"He'll check with them, or has checked with them, depending on who he needs to talk to and where in the country they are. But they'll stay in the background, let Broylin handle it. He's the one in hot water. I'm one of his."

"And now—"

"Now we wait."

"Okay," Melanie said, with her new unnerving serenity. "Want some coffee?"

Cavanaugh shuddered.

There were 642 books on his shelves, counting paperbacks. Two hundred ten medallions on the bathroom wallpaper. Six packages of food in his freezer. Four ants in his kitchen. Thirty-one dollars and forty-six cents in his wallet. Twelve stamps left on the roll. Melanie shifted to lemonade and spent most of her time in the bathroom. Serenity took odd forms.

The phone rang at 1:30 P.M.

"Agent Cavanaugh. This is Grace, Dr. Broylin's secretary. A car will pick you up in approximately twenty minutes. Please remain inside your apartment. Dr. Broylin will see you when you arrive in Washington."

"And my colleague. There will be two of us."

A sharp intake of breath. "The director is unaware of a second person."

"The second person is Dr. Melanie Anderson, Epidemic Intelligence Service, Centers for Disease Control. Background already on file. Please tell Dr. Broylin that Dr. Anderson is fully aware of everything I know."

"I'll inform Dr. Broylin," Grace said, not warmly.

Melanie said again, "Now we wait."

"Now we wait."

There were twenty-two CDs in Cavanaugh's collection. Seventy-three tapes. Immigration had occurred in the kitchen; the four ants were now nine.

Cavanaugh didn't know either of the agents in the Bucar. Probably they belonged to the director's security detail. Everybody exchanged credentials. Throughout this, Cavanaugh couldn't shake a feeling of unreality—weren't they all on the same side?

Were they?

The Hoover Building, possibly the ugliest official structure in D.C., didn't lessen the unreality. Watched by his escorts, Cavanaugh signed in. As a field agent, he no longer had a Headquarters pass, and he'd never had the electronic code for the director's suite. Melanie signed in with him and submitted to a weapons search without even a protest. Cavanaugh didn't know if that was a good or bad sign. Their escort took them up in the elevator to the director's suite and punched in an electronic code.

Peter Broylin sat behind his desk, facing him. Sixty-three years old, thin and fit and mostly bald, he followed a spate of younger, more liberal directors who all had, one way or another, been media disasters. Too concerned with the field at the expense of Headquarters, too concerned with Headquarters at the expense of the field, too flamboyant, too cautious, cheated the press, hogged the press, ran a sloppy ship, the ship engaged in piracy . . . Broylin had avoided most of this criticism by being honest, firm, and mostly invisible. He gave few speeches and fewer press conferences. Instead, he occupied himself with running the FBI through his chain-of-command, and running it well. Respected by both his agents and the general public, Broylin projected the personality of a stealth plane: powerful, finely tuned, and difficult to be sure of.

"Sit down, Agent Cavanaugh, Dr. Anderson."

They sat. The security detail, on cue, left the room. Cavanaugh knew they'd be watching, but not listening. Although that didn't mean that others might not be hearing whatever transpired here. The director's office included side doors, and Cavanaugh doubted that they all led to bathrooms.

"Thank you for seeing us, sir."

Broylin's much-praised efficiency included not wasting meeting time. "What do you want to tell me about a birthday project?" Cavanaugh heard the deliberate lack of quotes or capitals. Broylin was giving nothing away. Cavanaugh had about two minutes to establish his own credibility.

His throat suddenly went dry. Before he could swallow, Melanie said calmly, "We know that the Birthday Project is a bioweapons project funded by the CIA, created at Fort Detrick, and deliberately tested in Congo. And that some of the *Anopheles quadrimaculatus* genetically altered for the project escaped in a car accident on Route 301 near the Potomac River Bridge the night of May 2. Those infected *Anopheles* began the—"

"I addressed my question to Agent Cavanaugh, Dr. Anderson. We'll get to your information in due time."

"Fine," Melanie said, unruffled. But her eyes glittered.

Cavanaugh said, "Dr. Anderson is essentially right, sir. But I'd rather explain it by starting at the beginning of my personal involvement in this case, and following through. If you're not taping this conversation, I'd like to suggest that you do so."

"Go on," Broylin said expressionlessly.

As he told the story, step by step, Cavanaugh realized all over again how well all the pieces interlocked. The CIA car hitting the deer. The timing of the epidemic. The failed attempt to use elephant mosquitoes to unobtrusively end the plague. The targeting of Michael Sean Donohue, a credible decoy, to deflect public attention while USAMRIID and the CDC stopped malaria reading by conventional containment methods that aroused no suspicion. The uneasiness of Jerry Dunbar and Jim Farlow when they were told, as they had to have been, why certain facets of the investigation had to be kept secret. Both men's willingness to take promotions in other countries. The removal of Cavanaugh and Melanie, the two investigators too stubborn to quit and too low level to be brought into the cover-up. The hate calls to Melanie, indirectly traceable to Fort Detrick, to discourage her from staying in Maryland and expounding her genocide theories. The paper trail of unprecedented purchases of *Anopheles* to Fort Detrick. And, finally, the parallel epidemic in Africa, and the—

"I'll tell this part, Robert," Melanie said, and Cavanaugh found he was willing to let her. He wished he had a glass of water. Broylin had not changed expression. No skepticism, no disgust, no anger, no contradiction. He looked like a man hearing information he already knew.

It was real, then, as real as all the trash cynicism about government: the movies, the bad TV series, the routines of stand-up comics. The United States, which Cavanaugh had sworn to support and defend, had casually killed innocent people in order to test a weapon to kill more innocent people. *"The blood-dimmed tide is loosed, and everywhere/The ceremony of innocence is drowned . . ."*

". . . part that can't be explained away," Melanie was saying, "is the vector samples. The CDC now has samples of mosquitoes whose salivary glands show clearly what's been going on here. One set of genetically altered *Anopheles* to infect people—mostly blacks—with malaria reading. Another set of genetic alterations to vaccinate against the first. Human blood samples from Congo would confirm that to any lab in the world that cares to do so. The epidemiological curves are also hard data, Mr. Broylin. Not—what do you call it?—'circumstantial evidence.' Someone started that epidemic in Congo. Someone ended it. Both trails led to Fort Detrick. And if you think—"

"You have made some leaps to unwarranted conclusions, Dr. Anderson," Broylin said dryly. "As Agent Cavanaugh can—and should—have told you."

"Oh? Like what?" Melanie's eyes glittered again.

"Please wait here for a moment. Don't leave." Broylin stood and vanished behind one of the side doors.

They waited. For what? Cavanaugh didn't know. Maybe he'd never actually known anything anyway. About anything. Maybe everything he'd thought he'd known had been wrong, or incomplete, or falsified. Or maybe there wasn't anything really to know, to be sure of. *"Mere anarchy is loosed upon the world . . ."*

The side door reopened. Broylin came back in, alone. He resumed his position behind the desk.

"You present a very interesting problem, Agent Cavanaugh. So do you, Dr. Anderson. Who else have you told about your investigation and your conclusions?"

Melanie said quickly, "A few others. In writing. So if anything happens to us, those—"

"Who, Agent Cavanaugh?" Broylin said, as if Melanie hadn't spoken. The two men's eyes locked and held.

"No one, sir. We've told the whole story to no one. Although a few people know parts of it, such as Special Agent in Charge Martin Felders and CDC epidemiologist Dr. Joseph Krovetz."

"Goddamn it, Robert!" Melanie cried.

Broylin nodded slowly.

"I see," he said. "And I think you see, too."

"Yes," Cavanaugh said. "We're an interesting problem because you have so many choices about Melanie and me. You can keep us from going to the press, by threats or bribes or whatever. Or you can let us go and then do everything the Bureau is capable of to discredit what we say. Or you can try to convince us we're wrong about what we've uncovered. Or you can tell us the real truth, and risk everything on our voluntary silence."

Broylin said, without any flattery whatsoever, "I see we almost lost a good agent in Maryland when the OPR recommended transfer to North

Dakota. Tell me, Agent Cavanaugh, which of those choices am I going to make?"

Melanie said bitterly, "You're going to try to silence us," and finally Broylin turned his attention to her. "You mean, Dr. Anderson, that you think the FBI is going to kill you. Or arrange for a 'fatal accident.' Or immobilize you under Thorazine in some institution. Don't you?"

"Yes! I wouldn't put anything past a government that would do what you've already done!"

"And you, Agent Cavanaugh? Do you think that the FBI is going to assassinate you two?"

"No," Cavanaugh said slowly, "I don't."

"Then what?" Broylin sat back, waiting. Cavanaugh thought he'd never seen eyes so observant. Broylin, he remembered, had started out as a prosecuting attorney in white-collar crime, where instead of bodies stuffed in auto trunks, you got educated, smooth-talking men who gave themselves away in the details.

"No," Cavanaugh said. "You tell *me* 'then what.' Not the other way around."

"All right," Broylin said. He placed his hands flat on the desk in front of him. The fingers were long and thin. "I'm not going to threaten or bribe you—or Dr. Anderson. Implicit threats have already been tried, and neither of you gave up your investigation. Nor would you now, I think.

"Nor am I going to discredit you with the press. This isn't the Hoover FBI anymore. And the press isn't the respectful lackey it usually was in 1955 either. They'd jump all over this story, and you've uncovered enough truth that you'd stay credible anyway."

Melanie drew in a sharp, short breath.

"Nor am I going to attempt to convince you that what you've found is wrong, because it's not. As far as it goes, anyway."

Melanie said, "It's true. It's . . . true . . ." Cavanaugh glanced at her, but she'd caught herself before she reached either explosion or tears.

"I said, 'as far as it goes.' Which is not far enough. So of all your choices, Agent Cavanaugh, I'm going to tell you the truth. The rest of the truth."

Cavanaugh got out, "And then . . ."

"And then you two will be the ones with a choice to make." Broylin opened his desk drawer and drew out an unmarked green folder, but didn't hand it to Cavanaugh. "What I'm going to say, I have authorization to tell you. But only because the circumstances are so unusual."

Melanie demanded, "Authorization from whom?"

"Wait," Broylin said. "The facts first. Fact one: There are people, important people, who disagree violently with the decision to tell you what I'm going to tell you. Fact two: You would never be told this if you hadn't pushed the Bureau to this point. Fact three: What I am going to tell you could, conceivably, place you both in physical danger, although not from the FBI or the CIA. Shall I go on?"

"Yes!" Melanie said. "You're only trying to intimidate us!"

"No, I'm not. Those are facts. Here are more. The infected *Anopheles* mosquitoes that began the malaria reading epidemic were in fact en route from Fort Detrick to a location in Virginia when they were released by the car crash. However, they were not developed at Fort Detrick. They were there because a Counterintelligence team, a joint FBI/CIA effort, had captured the mosquitoes in an intelligence operation conducted against a foreign government that was working within the borders of the United States."

"Oh, right!" Melanie said. "What foreign government?"

For the first time, Cavanaugh saw a sign—a very little sign—of anger in Peter Broylin. The director's left hand tensed, and his wedding ring slid slightly along the tautened flesh of his ring finger. That was all.

"Please wait, Dr. Anderson. The *Anopheles* captured by the FBI and CIA were analyzed and, yes, bred at the army's Medical Research Institute at Fort Detrick. Access to the project was highly restricted, as you can imagine. But labs take up physical space, as you well know. Many people knew something was going on in those restricted labs, although they had no clear idea what. With any operation of any size, there are always fringe people who are not included but think they should be, and some of them make shrewd guesses. One of those people—we now know who—ran an unauthorized dirty-tricks cell of nonarmy personnel. One of those made the hate calls to you, Dr. Anderson, a fact that has only come to light in the last week."

Melanie said nothing, but her face told Cavanaugh she believed none of it.

Broylin continued. "At Fort Detrick, the Medical Research and Development Command used the captured and bred *Anopheles* to develop

a virus that would counter malaria reading. They couldn't, as you sur-
mised, use it in Maryland. Too many visiting scientists. The virus would
instantly become the public property of the international scientific community, and its value as a counterweapon would be gone. The CIA
reasoning, of course, was that if one nation could discover how to genetically alter malaria to fatally attack sickle-cell hemoglobin, so could other
nations. The United States needed to hold the vaccine as a secret counterweapon in case we ever needed it. USAMRIID knew nothing about
the vaccine. Colonel Colborne assured us that USAMRIID could stop
the epidemic in southern Maryland using well-applied vector-
destruction techniques, and the FBI-CIA Counterintelligence force let
them go ahead and do it."

Broylin looked directly at Melanie. She said, reluctantly, "They succeeded. But not all nations can afford 'well-applied vector-destruction
techniques.'"

"My point precisely. The vaccine should be saved for locales or conditions where vector destruction is impractical. Jungle terrain, impover-
ished nations, battlefield conditions. So we didn't use it in Maryland."

Melanie said, "But you did in Congo! You killed so you could test!"

"No, Dr. Anderson. *We* didn't."

Broylin finally pushed the green folder toward Cavanaugh. He
opened it. Copies of a half-dozen short CIA documents, each stamped
with highly restricted clearances, each paper slashed with blacked-out
words, sentences, phrases. Cavanaugh began to skim.

Broylin said, "We didn't start or end malaria reading in Congo, Dr.
Anderson. Someone did, yes, but it wasn't us. It was another nation."

"Bullshit! You said you captured the infected *Anopheles* from an enemy nation and you developed the vaccine at Fort Detrick—and that nobody else had it yet! It was your little secret!"

"That's true. We developed it, and we kept it from the scientific community for reasons I've explained. The 'enemy nation'—"

"Developed the same vaccine, just by sheer coincidence? I don't believe it, Broylin!"

"I was going to say, the 'enemy nation' is the error in your reasoning.
No enemy nation developed the vaccine. Nor do any know that the
United States has it."

"Then what the hell is going on?"

Broylin didn't answer. He looked at Cavanaugh, who had finished skimming the thin sheaf of documents. He wished he could have time to study them more closely, but he knew he wouldn't get the chance. He would never see these particular papers again.

He was surprised at the steadiness of his own voice. "The same nation both started and ended the epidemic in Congo, Melanie. And, yes, it was a test. They had the genetically altered mosquitoes because they had created them. And they had the vaccine because we gave it to them."

"*What?*" Melanie said.

Cavanaugh looked not at her, but at Broylin. "We gave the vaccine to them because they're not an enemy nation at all; they're one of our allies."

"Oh, my God," Melanie said. Broylin said nothing. He wasn't going to confirm or deny, Cavanaugh realized, at least not yet. Broylin was going to let Cavanaugh do what the FBI had hired him to do in the first place: put things together.

He put it together.

"The FBI does counterintelligence against foreign agents within our borders. That's why the Bureau was working with the CIA when the team busted the original lab that created malaria reading. The other country was creating it here rather than abroad because . . . because . . ."

Despite herself, Melanie came to his aid. "Because in the United States there's more equipment, more talent, everything much easier to hide. Scientific equipment can be openly ordered, with no comment, from thousands of different sources."

"Yes," Cavanaugh said. "And we caught one of our allies at it, right under our noses." God, the accusations and counteraccusations that must have gone on behind locked doors. Over secure hotlines. In diplomatic pouches. It must have been a zoo.

Cavanaugh continued. "So the United States appropriated the infected *Anopheles,* sent them to Fort Detrick, bred them to research and create a vaccine . . . Where were the mosquitoes going when that car hit a deer near the Potomac River Bridge?"

Broylin said, "I can't tell you that."

Pharmaceutical house, Cavanaugh guessed. Historically, Fort Detrick had contracted out some phases of its bioweapons work. Or maybe the mosquitoes had been going to another military installation. It didn't really matter. This particular batch of bugs never got there.

"Go on," Broylin said, and Cavanaugh did.

"Detrick created the vaccine. Just before or after malaria reading got loose. They couldn't use the vaccine here, but they didn't need to. However, the other nation knew the U.S. must be working on a counter-weapon. Nothing else is logical. The other nation wanted the counterweapon, whatever form it took. We didn't trust them—"

"Surprise, surprise," Melanie said bitterly.

"—so they forced our hand. They started a second malaria reading epidemic where the scientific community wouldn't really notice anything strange unless they were looking for it. In Congo. Where malaria reading could easily spread horrifically unless the United States supplied the only existing way to stop it. The vaccine."

"This is an ally?" Melanie demanded. "Who is it?"

Cavanaugh concluded simply, "So in order to stop the deaths in Africa, we gave our ally the vaccine. Because we had no choice. If we went in and administered it ourselves, it would have to be through the CDC, who'd certainly notice its effect on the epidemic curves. And who would then tear every atom of the vaccine apart. They'd want to use it everywhere in the world, blowing its use as a counterweapon. And the ally nation would end up with the vaccine anyway; they'd just analyze the villagers' blood samples. So we let our ally have it, and they administered it through Doctors Without Borders, who are too damn overworked to analyze anything."

"Who?" Melanie said. "It has to be one of the signatories of the World Health Organization, Brian Spencer got his meds from WHO. Israel? Germany? One of the South American nations? Malaria is endemic in South America!"

No, Cavanaugh thought. *Not South America. Not Israel, not Germany.*

"Who?"

"I can't tell you that," Broylin said. "Not now, not ever. Information here is given on a need-to-know basis. You know enough already to understand what happened, and why, and the position in which you've put the United States internationally."

Ireland, Cavanaugh thought.

Michael Sean Donohue had IRA connections, a fact that had never hit the press. They'd been too busy jumping on his part-black ancestry. The key was the level of evidence.

Melanie thought the FBI had enough hard evidence—"not just cir-cumstantial!" she'd cried—to convict in a court of law. But Melanie wasn't a lawyer. Neither was Cavanaugh, but like all agents, he'd picked up a fair amount of law. The U.S. government lacked the hard evidence to convict the terrorists. That meant this investigation was still going on, and it was probably a joint effort of the American and Irish governments, maybe even the Brits as well, against a common enemy within friendly borders.

It had been some radical branch of the Irish Republican Army that had created malaria reading. And it had been the Irish Republican Army that Broylin had meant when he'd said "*. . . could, conceivably, place you both in physical danger, although not from the FBI or the CIA.*"

The IRA, whose savage tactics—if not ultimate aims—were con-demned by even the Irish government. The IRA, who had always en-joyed rich backing among Irish-Americans. The IRA, who hadn't hesitated before this to kill off civilians in its quest to break Northern Ireland free of England. Who, of course, knew how fast the immigrant population of London was growing. Cavanaugh suddenly saw, as clearly as if it had been included in Broylin's green folder, his own initial read-ing about sickle-cell trait. From an on-line encyclopedia:

IN ANCIENT TIMES, VEDDOIDS CAME FROM THEIR HOME IN
INDIA ACROSS THE RED SEA LAND BRIDGE INTO AFRICA. WITH
THEM THEY CARRIED THE GENE THAT CODED FOR AN
ABNORMAL FORM OF HEMOGLOBIN: THE SICKLE-CELL GENE.
SICKLE-CELL TRAIT IS STILL VERY COMMON IN CERTAIN
SECTIONS OF INDIA. . . .

And in Indians who immigrated to London.

But, wait—wasn't London too cold to support malaria mosquitoes? Cavanaugh remembered more of his reading. London had been plagued with malaria every summer, right up until the midnineteenth century. The disease came in the spring on sailing ships, flourished all summer, and died off in winter, only to sail in again next spring. Oliver Cromwell had suffered from malaria all his life. And Oliver Cromwell's London wasn't the urban heat sink that the great city was today. Over one sum-mer, malaria reading could create enough death and panic in London to bring down the British government. Which was, in fact, what it had been created to do.

Malaria had not been created to destroy blacks, after all. It had only been tested on them, in order to force the United States to share the vaccine. And the test site was Congo only because in that vast rain forest of disease and poverty and isolation, more death would just blend right in. It was as cold-blooded an action as Cavanaugh and Melanie had feared all along. A monstrosity, an abomination.

But not by the United States.

All this tore through Cavanaugh's mind in an instant, almost before Broylin had finished his last sentence. Cavanaugh couldn't reply. He sat, mute and dazed by the gut-loosening shock of relief.

Melanie repeated, "*Who?* If you think we're going to buy your concoction without even being told who created the epidemic . . . Besides, all you've really given us is an alternate set of possible circumstances! You haven't given us any good reason to believe the alternate set is the truth."

"I've given you everything I can," Broylin said. "Except this. Watch."

He pressed a button. A very large projection suddenly appeared on a blank wall to their right. A world map, in colors that did not correspond to national boundaries.

Broylin, still seated behind his desk, said, "Light green indicates areas where virtually none of the population is positive for sickle-cell trait. Dark green indicates roughly three to ten susceptible individuals per hundred square miles. Blue, a concentration of susceptible individuals that could cause personal suffering but not political disruption. Red, a population in which an unchecked epidemic of malaria reading could cause considerable economic disruption, political consequences, and human suffering."

Cavanaugh stared at the projection. The FBI didn't do this kind of international forecasting. The map had CIA woven all through it. London was red.

Melanie shot back, "An epidemic wouldn't cause that much disruption if *we* stepped in with the vaccine for everybody."

Broylin said, "There are places on earth where that just isn't feasible."

Cavanaugh followed Melanie's gaze. She stared at Africa. Africa, where no vaccination program, no matter how well planned, had ever succeeded against the poverty, the tribal conflict, the shaman resistance, the rain forest and desert and isolation. Yamdongi had been only one small village, carefully targeted. In a city like Kinshasa, malaria reading would be more than politically devastating; it would be an unstoppable apocalypse.

Cavanaugh said carefully, "But there are places where it *is* feasible to efficiently administer vaccines. The United States, as we've already seen. Or London."

Broylin didn't react. "Yes. The largest risk, as Dr. Anderson well knows, is to Africa."

Melanie said, in a different voice, "Who created malaria reading, Dr. Broylin?"

"As I said before, I can't tell you that. But I can tell you this: The United States knows who it is, and so do at least two of our allies. We're working with them to trace the disease all the way back to, not only its creators, but to its funding on two continents. We need time to get them all, and enough evidence to convict under the laws of two different nations. It's an international effort being carried out by very high levels of the governments involved. And I'll promise you this, Dr. Anderson. If the investigation isn't finished one year from today, you will sit again in that same chair in this same room, and I'll personally tell you who created malaria reading. Until then, your government needs your silence."

Broylin turned to Cavanaugh. "You told me before, Agent Cavanaugh, that I had to make a choice about you and Dr. Anderson. Now it's you two who must make a choice: go to the press or stay silent. If you go to the press, two things happen. First, our investigation is compromised, perhaps fatally. Second, every nation in the world will know that malaria reading is a bioweapon and that a counterweapon exists. They'll start working on duplicating it immediately. That may force the original developers of the disease to use it *now* for their own political purposes, if they're going to use it all. Thousands could die. Or millions. Possibly tens of millions, if Africa is again the target."

Melanie cried, "But I don't even know if your story is true!"

Broylin said, "You know as much as I can tell you. You have to make your choice from that. *Both* of you, taking into account the needs and national security of your country."

That last, Cavanaugh realized, was intended for him, even though

Broylin continued to look at Melanie. So Broylin didn't have every angle covered after all. He'd misjudged Cavanaugh. He'd expected that patriotism would ensure Cavanaugh's silence, once Cavanaugh understood the danger to his country. Patriotism, loyalty, national security.

But Broylin was wrong. The Director belonged to another generation. He'd gone through Vietnam, Watergate, Nixon. Patriotism wasn't a given to that generation; you had to convince people of it, through logic and argument. Maybe even Melanie thought that way.

But Cavanaugh was thirty-two. The United States didn't have to earn his loyalty. He *wanted* to be loyal, to believe . . . in something. To hold Robert Cavanaugh, all the United States had to do was to convince him that his country was not a monster.

And it was not. The United States had not created malaria reading; it had only created the antidote. And it had released that antidote to save lives in Congo.

"Agent Cavanaugh?" Broylin said. He touched the button a second time and the map disappeared.

But . . . Broylin was an Irish name.

No. No. That level of paranoia wasn't justified, must not be allowed to exist. At least, not in him.

But . . . he had no hard evidence of an American/Irish/British investigation, except the CIA documents in the green folder, and those had so many key words blacked out that they could, just conceivably, apply to another situation entirely.

No. More paranoia.

But . . . another year would allow much more development and testing of the deadly parasite . . .

No. Everything Broylin *had* said fit with the information Cavanaugh and Melanie had uncovered. Broylin's explanation felt solid and true.

But . . . how had Michael Sean Donohue passed an FBI polygraph if Donohue had known about malaria reading?

For a second, the room spun and almost shattered.

No, it could be explained. Donohue had definite IRA ties, but that didn't mean he knew about every single campaign the IRA ran. The IRA, like the CIA, operated on a need-to-know basis. Donohue's concocted arrest could have been an FBI diversionary tactic, a plausible suspect brought into custody both to placate a panicking public and to mislead the IRA into thinking the FBI/CIA knew less than it actually did. If

Donohue had known nothing about malaria reading before the date of his polygraph, he would have tested clean.

Broylin still stared at him. Cavanaugh had to choose. On the basis of incomplete evidence, with reasonable doubt, without any guarantees about the future. He still had to choose.

Slowly he said, "You have my promise of total silence on everything connected in any way with malaria reading."

"Your country thanks you. Dr. Anderson?"

She still stared at the piece of wall where the map of Africa had been. Cavanaugh knew he would never tell her about Michael Sean Donohue's IRA connection. Her concern was all for Africa, which she still thought was the main target. It was only to protect Africa that she would agree to silence.

She said, "One year? In one year from today you'll either conclude your investigation or tell me who anyway?"

"One year," Broylin said.

"Then . . ." She swallowed, tried again. "Then, yes. I won't tell the press. Or anyone else."

"Thank you."

There was a long pause, thick with unspoken words, complex and twisting as DNA. Melanie finally broke the silence. "So now what? We're free to leave?"

"You were always free to leave, Dr. Anderson. You haven't been charged with anything, and this is not a police station."

Melanie snorted, and the strange, thick atmosphere dissolved. "Right. Do we sign anything first?"

She was a scientist, after all. As if any of this would ever be put in writing by the Bureau—or by the CIA or the White House, if they were involved, which Cavanaugh rather doubted. It wouldn't be the first time a president had been left out of a CIA loop.

"No signatures are necessary, Dr. Anderson. Agent Cavanaugh, your own car is in the employee's garage, brought here at my request."

And searched, no doubt. Bugged? Maybe. It didn't matter. He was due for a trade-in anyway. He took the gamble. "Am I going to need that car in Singleton, North Dakota?"

"No. You're being reassigned to the Baltimore Field Office."

Baltimore. Under Felders. It wasn't a bribe. Cavanaugh had already agreed to silence. A reward then. Or a sweetener, to remind him of how much he'd almost lost.

The center had held, but the edges were as frayed and soiled as ever.

"Well, then, let's go," Melanie said, not very graciously.

In the elevator her ungraciousness turned to pensiveness. But she waited until they were seated in Cavanaugh's car, pulling out of the parking garage, to say, "Robert."

"Yes?"

"That's the first meeting I ever saw you sit through without doodling."

It was true. Doodling hadn't even occurred to him.

She added, in another tone entirely, "How many lives did we save today?"

He glanced at her rigid face and said gently, "A lot, Melanie. A very lot."

"Is that true?"

"I believe it is, yes." *On the basis of incomplete evidence, with reasonable doubt, without any guarantees about the future.* He pulled onto Constitution Avenue.

"But do we believe it because it really is true, or because we so badly *want* to believe it?"

But he knew he couldn't answer that one, and he didn't even try.

T WENTY

The whole of science is nothing more than a refinement
of everyday thinking.
　　　　　—Albert Einstein, *Physics and Reality*, 1936

Melanie parked in her usual spot at the CDC. As soon as she left the
car, the Atlanta heat seeped into her nostrils, her clothing, the spaces between her hair shafts. God, it must be over ninety, and it was only eight-
thirty in the morning.

Inside, air-conditioned cold. The abrupt contrast made her sneeze.
Her office was in a basement, which, due to the eccentric building design that added levels by building them down the slope of a steep hill,
was well above ground level. This "basement," like every other floor of
the CDC, was jammed with freezers: old freezers, new freezers, upright
freezers, horizontal freezers, freezers that barely managed minus ten
Celsius, freezers superchilled by liquid nitrogen. All of the freezers held
biological samples, the frozen lifeblood of the CDC. They also all
hummed. Melanie squeezed around a Forma Scientific blocking a third
of the corridor and headed to the lounge for a cup of coffee.

As soon as she entered, the knot of people by the Mr. Coffee stopped
talking. One blushed. Another said, too heartily, "Hi, Melanie. How are
you?"

"Just fine," she said. What had they been discussing? Her slugging

292

that kid in the Virginia Burger King? Her getting sent home for a "vacation"? Her and Joe Krovetz caught in a clinch, she in a black slip?

She said, "So much gossip, so little time," got her coffee, and left.

"Hey, Mel, you see this?" Joe, her cogossipee, waited in her office, looking blessedly unaware that he should feel embarrassed. He thrust a newspaper at her. The article was on page one, even though it was clearly an editorial.

FUTURE PUBLIC DEFENDERS NOT TRADITIONAL
LAW ENFORCEMENT
FBI DOWN, CDC & USAMRIID RIDING HIGH

The past few months should make us all aware that something important has shifted in the political universe. Our major enemies may still be other people, but our major defenses are no longer traditional law-enforcement agencies. Now, the people who defend us best are those trained to detect and counter the highly sophisticated weapons of modern technological guerrilla warfare.

Cops are out. Scientists are in.

A wealth of evidence supports this startling statement. The Federal Bureau of Investigation mobilized all its vast resources to search for the people responsible for the recent malaria reading epidemic that caused the deaths of 1,012 citizens. The FBI came up empty. So did the police forces of two states. So did the unofficial investigators of the press, who occasionally in the past have dug up leads that have broken cases baffling official law enforcement. But not this time. Despite excellent work by such reporters as Libby Turner of the *Baltimore Sun*, the fourth estate didn't protect us from anything worse than having to wait for the six o'clock news to hear the latest death statistics.

Not so the Centers for Disease Control in Atlanta and the United States Army Medical Research Institute for Infectious Diseases at Fort Detrick, Maryland. Working alongside the United States Public Health Service, the CDC and USAMRIID protected us through excellent and immediate programs for blood testing, prophylactic medicine, and mosquito control. They solved their part of the mystery, through the CDC's brilliant field and lab work to identify the genetically altered parasites and their vector. And they taught us how to protect ourselves, through both organizations' clear, concise, and widely distributed guidelines. Together, USAMRIID and the CDC saved countless lives. Unlike the FBI.

This suggests that, in a future increasingly dominated by the biological breakthroughs, the real protectors of the American public will be not the gun-toting G-men, the Eliot Nesses of popular legend. Instead, quiet and bespectacled scientists will . . .

"Take it away," Melanie said. "God, the trash the papers get away with."

"Well, aren't you in a sweet mood," Joe said, without rancor. "I thought you'd be pleased. We come off pretty good."

"Yeah. So?" Melanie wished she could tell Joe the truth. Although she recognized that he didn't really need it. Joe'd been curious about who had engineered the parasite, but not as curious as he was to unravel the DNA manipulation that had gone into it. Without Melanie's prodding, he would drop the cause aspect, as he had almost done before she burst in on him fresh from Africa. Joe cared a lot more about how disease worked than about why. And now she couldn't tell him that *Plasmodium reading* was still out there. Someplace. At the whimsical disposal of someone. To, undoubtedly, be used sometime, on more innocent people.

"So nothing," Joe said, folding up his newspaper. "We have a meeting at ten. Did anybody tell you?"

"We returned exiles get told nothing. What kind of meeting?"

"With Farlow's replacement. Probably just a get-to-know-you gabfest."

"I can hardly wait."

"See you then," Joe said, out the door. "And, oh, Mel—don't drink that coffee. Your present mood will shatter the cup."

"Hahaha. You should have gone into show business."

"That's what my mother says, too."

And she, Melanie reflected, should have gone into plumbing. Something where you got to deal with hard, cold pipes that delivered water, instead of hard, cold people who delivered diseases in order to grab or keep power.

She closed her office door and put her head in her hands. *I can't do this. I can't putter around my office doing diddley, can't go to another pointless meeting, can't study malaria statistics knowing that each could be undiagnosed* P. *reading. I can't—*

If not this, then what? What can I—

Abruptly Joe was back, bursting in without so much as a knock. "Mel! Mel! The meeting's moved up!"

"And this causes your joyful rudeness, Dr. Krovetz?"

"Not that, you blockhead! Listen, there's dengue fever in Gabon!"

"Dengue fever?"

"Massive outbreak. Must have come in by ship or by infected carrier. And the first teams for dengue are already deployed in Manila and Brasilia. The head is asking for volunteers, preferably people with field experience in malaria."

Both mosquito-borne. Although malaria was *Anopheles* and dengue was carried by *Aëdes*. Still, Melanie could see where the experience might transfer. And Gabon. She spoke both Bantu and French, and she picked up local dialects fast. Dengue was a fascinating parasite, with multiple strains . . .

"Is it break-bone or hemorrhagic?" she demanded.

"Hemorraghic. Even some septic shock, sounds like."

"*Aëdes aegypti* or *Aëdes albopictus?*"

"Unknown. But from the disease's aggressiveness, I'd guess *albopictus.*"

The Asian tiger mosquito. That meant the parasites could be transferred to and from an array of other warm-blooded hosts, including rats. In 1981, dengue fever carried by *A. albopictus* brought down 10 percent of Havana.

Joe said, "I'm going to plead and grovel and reason and bluster and generally convince the head that I should go to Gabon. But *you* don't have to do all that. They asked for you specifically."

"For me? Who asked specifically?"

"I don't know. But you're on the dengue team, if you want it. You want it? Stupid question, look at you smiling again."

"I'm not smiling. I'm just wondering why all of a sudden I'm a favored daughter."

Joe looked at her keenly. "You sure you don't know? Anyway, since you have all this new-found weight, will you throw it around on my behalf?"

"Of course. You think I'd go to Gabon without you?"

"Then let's go tell the head how indispensible I am."

Melanie said suddenly, "We're ghouls, you know. As much as . . . as anyone else. We depend on disease."

"Yeah," Joe said. "I know. Come on!"

They walked as fast as possible to the new director's office, dodging freezers and colleagues, trying not to break into an unprofessional run.

Cavanaugh ripped open yet another cardboard box and pawed through it. Damn it, where *were* his ties? All right, Abigail had chewed up the blue one with red books on it, and he'd gotten mustard on the brown one. Mustard, the dry cleaner had informed him in a tone that said he should already know this, didn't come out. But that still left eight or nine ties somewhere. On this, his first day at the Baltimore Field Office, he wanted to wear a suit and nice tie.

Hopelessly he opened another suitcase and then another cardboard box. Everything had arrived in Baltimore from Leonardtown only yesterday. The suitcase held winter sweaters. The box held dish towels, a mismatched pair of sheets, candy-striped throw pillows he swore he'd never seen before, and his high-school yearbook. God, this was the worst move yet. Where were his ties? Where were his spaghetti kettle and his bathrobe? And whose throw pillows were these?

Giving up, he threaded his way among boxes, books, Styrofoam peanuts, and Abigail's chew toys to the front door. He would have liked to check his e-mail and make a cup of coffee to take with him, but the mouse had somehow become separated from his computer and as yet the refrigerator held no milk. In fact, the refrigerator wasn't turned on yet. Just as well. There were probably boxes in it, possibly containing somebody else's ties.

The one thing he could find—could always find because there was such an abundance of it—was a letter from Earl Lester. The boy wrote him three or four times a week, letters full of information about obscure insects. Obviously the kid had adopted Cavanaugh, who hadn't even known he was on the market. He answered Earl when he could, but Cavanaugh knew he was not a faithful correspondent. Still, he seemed to have acquired, somehow, some responsibility for Earl. Maybe the simplest thing to do would be to just drive down to Rivermount on Saturday and set the boy up with some kind of secondhand computer. Then they could do e-mail. And Earl could research bugs on-line, which would give him a lot less time in which to write Cavanaugh.

Of course, at the moment Cavanaugh couldn't even find all the components of his own computer, let alone set up somebody else with one. Not to mention finding his ties.

He fled to the orderly serenity of the Beltway at rush hour.

The size of the cream-colored brick building that housed the Baltimore Field Office delighted him. The throngs of agents in the hallways delighted him. The fact that none of them was Seton delighted him. He reached Felders's office.

"Well, well. Six minutes late on the first day. A new job and you couldn't wear a tie?"

"I tried a—never mind. Good to see you, Marty."

"We'll see. It's too bad you're late because you have a team meeting in fourteen minutes, which is barely time for you to do your paperwork, find your vehicle, and hear about the case."

"A case? I have a case?" Cavanaugh said. "What is it?"

"Big. Bank robbery in Baltimore last night, three million dollars. But that's not the juice. There are links to heists in other states, organized crime, maybe even the unions . . . Big. And hot."

"Very hot. Am I—"

"Hot stuff yourself? So it would seem. Here, Bob, I'm supposed to give you this."

He handed Cavanaugh a piece of paper. Thick, creamy paper with a decorative border and raised FBI seal. Even before he read it, Cavanaugh knew what it was: a special commendation for undercover FBI activity.

So that's the way it was going to be. Commendation. Big cases. And probably other sweeteners, direct and indirect, coming down discreetly from the top. Was Broylin rewarding Cavanaugh for his patriotic silence, or merely increasing the odds that it would be maintained?

No matter. That was how bureaucracies worked.

Felders sat on his desk, crossed his legs, and jiggled his left foot. "So—are you holding out on me, Bob? Did I call in all those markers over Fort Detrick for nothing—or not?"

Cavanaugh looked levelly at Felders. "Don't ask me, Marty."

"'Don't ask me.' All right. I won't. You hear about Seton?"

"What about Seton?"

Felders switched to jiggling his right foot. "Retiring early. Big party next week."

And that also, Cavanaugh realized, was how bureaucracies worked. Seton had undoubtedly been given a choice: Which do you want? An OPR investigation into this huge pile of falsified 302s you've submitted? Or allowing your name to be signed to a bogus report about an informant who's also having an investigation dropped if he signs the same bogus report? Seton had chosen the latter. Although, being Seton, the deception probably hadn't bothered him as long as nobody outside a handful of FBI agents knew the truth. Seton was retiring with a nice party and a full pension, his long record marred publicly only by one bad judgment about an informant. Could happen to anybody.

However, Cavanaugh knew, as Felders did not, that Seton's reprieve was only temporary. When the government finally went public with its full case against the IRA, the journalists would dig into every detail of everybody's actions, including Seton's. Then they'd flay him alive. Almost Cavanaugh could feel sorry for Seton. Almost.

Felders said, "Now your meeting is in nine minutes. Conference room."

"I'm on my way."

"And get your ass over to our house for dinner tonight."

Cavanaugh smiled. "Got it, Chief."

He found his cubicle, signed in his password on its computer, and checked it by calling up his e-mail. In two minutes he was back in Felder's office. "Marty? Could I take a rain check on dinner? In fact, could I leave right after the case meeting?"

"Leave? Why?"

Cavanaugh thought of saying, *I have to unpack; they're all these boxes and I can't even find my ties . . .* but a good look at Felders's face changed his mind. He and Felders had always been honest with each other. And Marty was—had been—could be again—his friend.

"It's Judy. Yesterday I sent her flowers and a letter, but she just sent me an e-mail, and . . ." Men didn't talk to each other like this, even men who were friends. Judy's e-mail had said, *Thanks for the roses. Don't call me.*

"Judy?" Felders said. "She fucking you over?"

"No. More my fault."

"I always thought she was too good for you."

"Yes," Cavanaugh said simply, and the two men stared at each other. Then Felders shrugged. "Go after her then. But after the meeting. You can work the weekend for the time you'll miss. And if you do get lucky, I don't want to hear about it."

Which meant, Cavanaugh knew, *Good luck.*

After the meeting he raced to Judy's new apartment. It was in an acceptable but not upscale part of D.C. She came to the door in shorts and T-shirt, her red hair frazzled from tugging on it, which meant she'd been writing. She went still.

"Robert."

"Judy. You look wonderful," he said, which was true. Thinner, more toned, glowing. What had she been doing to herself? Or someone to her? Behind her, the apartment looked different from Judy's other places, too. Stripped-down, minimalist. Not a knitted doohickey in sight.

"Thank you," Judy said. "I just sent you an e-mail asking you not to call me."

"I know. I got it. But I'm not calling; I'm here. Can I come in?"

"I don't think so. I'm on a deadline for a big science article."

"I won't stay long."

"You won't stay at all. We don't have anything to say to each other, Robert."

"Not true," Cavanaugh said. "*I* have something to say."

She studied him. "You look different, Robert. More . . . I don't know. Just different somehow."

"Good. Because what I have to say is different. Judy, will you marry me?"

She went white, then red. But the chromoscape lasted only a moment. Afterward she said calmly, "Don't you have to wear a tie to work anymore, Robert?"

"Yes. Will you marry me?"

"No."

Despite his shock—it had always been she who pushed, he who refused—Cavanaugh didn't gape at her. He shifted his weight, planting his shoes more firmly on her threshold. Still, his startlement must have showed; Judy smiled faintly.

"Surprised you, huh? I'm sorry, Robert. It's not that I don't . . . still . . ." Her voice broke and he took a hopeful step forward. But she held up a warning hand. "No, don't. You don't understand, Robert. I need to be able to trust my husband. Trust him not to disappear, not to be unfaithful, not to generally treat me like an albatross around his neck. I had all that before with Ben, and I don't want it again. You just aren't trustworthy. You appear, you disappear, you move back with your exwife, you reappear when you want to. No, *no*. I don't want that. I'm sorry."

She closed her apartment door.

Robert knocked on it again. Nothing happened. He said through the hollow-core metal door, "Judy, please open up. I have something else to say. Please open."

"No."

"Then I'll say it through the door." He stopped to think, to say it right. "I made a bad mistake, letting you go. I didn't want to have to . . ." What was the word those talk-show shrinks used on the radio? "Commit." He didn't want to use it; Judy deserved better than radio psychojargon. " . . . to choose. But I choose now." *On the basis of incomplete evidence, with reasonable doubt, without any guarantees about the future.* "I choose a life with you."

Some muffled words from beyond the door. Curses? Maybe, but maybe not.

"I want to marry you, Judy. Please open the door."

He waited. The door didn't open. But from behind it she said, clearly this time, "Oh, damn it, Robert . . ."

"Will you marry me?"

"No. I don't know. I can't believe you'd ask me *now*. No. Maybe."

Robert drew a long breath. From *maybe* it wasn't ever that far to *yes*. Not if you stuck with it.

"I'm leaving now, Judy. But I'll be back after work tonight. Okay?"

"What time?"

He calculated rapidly. "Six-thirty. Count on it, sweetheart."

No answer. But it was okay. She'd be here.

Cavanaugh drove back to the Federal Bureau of Investigation in Baltimore to get down to work.

EPILOGUE:
SIX MONTHS AFTER

Melanie walked wearily out of the makeshift Nigerian hospital, which was the usual polyester-tent-and-wood-hut misalliance, toward the river. It fell here abruptly into a waterfall. The air at the top was clean and sweet, with the fresh, living scent of water. Melanie drew in deep, great breaths and rubbed the back of her neck.

Lassa fever. And at the beginning of an epidemic this far from even a moderate-sized town, forget the protocols; everyone did whatever was necessary to fight the epidemic. She'd been moving patients all day.

A small Nigerian boy scampered toward her. "Miss! Miss!" he called, obviously glorying in his English, which had a strong British accent. "Some person rings you by this telephone!"

He actually held Dr. Duchamp's portable phone in his hand. Marveling that Duchamp would let it out of his sight—it was their only quick link with the rest of the world—Melanie took the phone from the interested boy.

"Hello?"

"Melanie? Robert Cavanaugh. Have you seen the *New York Times*?"

The New York Times. Here, on the far edge of nowhere, in the midst of an epidemic. Ah, Robert.

"They've broken it, Melanie. They've made the arrests on malaria reading. In Ireland."

"Ireland?"

"Yes. I couldn't tell you before, but Broylin . . ." The connection filled with static.

"Robert? *Robert?*"

No use. The connection didn't clear. Maybe the satellite was out of range. Was that how these phones worked? Maybe she'd heard wrong. Ireland? How could that be?

"Miss, miss, come, come! The mother of my mother!" Another child, looking anxious. Another victim.

Melanie pushed malaria reading to the back of her mind. She was burning to know what had happened. But Ireland was far away, and America even farther. Lassa fever was here and now.

She followed the child to the mother of his mother.